TRY TO SURVIVE

Casey Urban

eBook ISBN: 978-1-7331876-0-2

Print ISBN: 978-1-7331876-1-9

DEDICATION

For my family, who have always been my biggest supporters.

CHAPTER 1

Jenn

"Alright, listen up cadets," Sergeant Blue barks from the end of the hallway.

He wears his usual stern, displeased expression as he watches the last of the cadets of our platoon scramble at their doors for lineup. As he strides down the line, everyone's careful not to look directly at him, making sure to maintain their stares blankly ahead of them while straightening up to perfect their posture. Sgt. Blue is not someone you can risk slouching in front of. In his right hand, he wields his infamous sleek black baton that we are all too familiar with.

"Today is May 1st, which means your monthly Evaluation Day is here once again. You will compete against each other in combat and weaponry, but also in your knowledge of tactical and survival skills. As you know, this will determine your rank in this platoon, the importance of which I should not need to remind you."

I stand there in line listening with everyone else as Sgt. Blue hints yet again at the threat of expulsion that constantly looms over our heads. As our country's leading military academy for the past hundred years or so, the Bellator Army Academy (BAA) has strict oversight over our performance to ensure that the school maintains its status. In December, when the school year ends, the cadet with the lowest rank in each platoon is expelled. It's uncompromising and harsh, but it's necessary and we know that; the military can't risk slackers, but more importantly, the academy won't risk its stellar reputation.

So, what happens after expulsion? Under society's premise that workers should provide only for other contributing workers, 'Rejects' of vocational tracks are outcast by society to live on the streets and are denied the basic amenities that society produces. However, according to the government, expulsion of a Reject military student is considered a danger to society. Therefore, the BAA has independently pioneered its own "progressive" solution for its failed cadets. Unbeknownst to the outside world, those expelled from the BAA are sent off to a remote island. No one really knows what happens on the island, but the rumor is that if you can beat whatever challenge is waiting there and prove yourself a worthy soldier, Headmaster would readmit you back into the BAA. However, the program was instituted nearly 40 years ago during my parents' first year at the BAA, and as far as we know, no one has ever come back. Some think this system makes the threat of expulsion even more daunting. Still, others find the mystery preferable to the known harsh reality of living out your days as a Reject. I don't care to contemplate either option much.

"Competitions will begin promptly at 06:30 after PT and breakfast," Sgt. Blue announces, finally arriving at the other end of the hallway. He turns around sharply, and from my peripheral vision I can spot him glancing in my direction. "In the meantime, Cadet Bellator will assist in leading the morning run. True to her name, she has come in first rank consecutively since January. The rest of you could learn a lot from such an example."

I ensure to maintain my firm expression as I bask in my accomplishment and the envy of the other cadets. This is the reason Sgt. Blue's threats about expulsion have never induced fear in me. My ancestors founded this school and since then, generations of Bellators have passed through. I was meant to be more than a soldier; I was meant to be the best. It's in my blood and my rank as number one only makes it official.

At my command, my platoon sets off with me at the head of the two lines. I lead my platoon out of our barracks and into the

Company Area, a common area for all of the Level 2 cadets that is surrounded by the barracks. Almost 17 years old, I am in my last year in Level 2, one of the four Levels that we must pass through in our training at the BAA. Each Level lasts 3 years except for the 4 years of Level 1, which begins at age 10 upon our assignment to the military vocational track by the National Education System. At the end of Level 4, after you pass a final evaluation, you graduate and are fully integrated into the United States Army as a career soldier.

The two other Level 2 platoons, representing the two younger years of Level 2, begin emerging from their quarters as well in perfect formation, ready to start today's training. Reaching the door to the Company Area, I open it to exit onto the large expanse of fields and training grounds that cover the Level 2 campus.

The night's darkness still blankets the entire landscape, and a chilly breeze brushes over the area as we walk to the jogging path to begin our morning routine. It had rained the night before and the morning dew is still visible on the grass along with scattered puddles of mud that haven't had time to dry.

"Alright cadets, keep up," I command. A few of them roll their eyes. Others quickly look away from my stern glare.

I begin the routine, starting off our jog slowly before gradually increasing the speed as we run the course. Behind me, I hear the splashing of boots through the countless puddles as we trek across the fields, spraying up mud on the shins of those behind them. I make a sharp turn into the forest, bringing the group through the tricky terrain and steep hills.

"Is this too hard for you guys?" I yell back between breaths as I make another turn to lead the group up another hill. "I said keep up!"

I hear the others increase their pace, the heavy boots of the cadets creating an uneven thundering behind me. My platoon has been together since we entered this school. With our number now at 93 cadets, we've decreased over the years from the original 100. While I don't know most of their names, I've learned their skills and their limits—and how to challenge them. I know that a good soldier always knows how to size up their competition, and everyone is everyone's competition here. And what better way to show off one of my greatest assets— my speed— than to make everyone else feel slow? Satisfied with their heavy breathing and occasional grunts, I check back briefly again to gauge their condition. Perfect formation.

Ultimately, I make another sharp turn, leading the group out of the forest and back into the large field on campus. I gradually decrease our group's speed until we reach the main field where we started.

"Damn man…I don't…know how…you're not dying after that," Cadet Coleman mutters to Cadet Parks softly.

Cadet Xander Parks was the first to turn 17 years old this January, making him our oldest cadet. Built like an ox and standing at six feet tall, he is also the largest and strongest of our platoon. We've sparred off multiple times during the competitions, but my quicker speed has been the only way to beat his brute strength and keep him down in second place. While he's the biggest threat to my position, all I see is that he's the first of the losers below me. The King of Losers.

"Cadet Parks was merely competent," I say loudly, catching their attention. I try to disguise my pants as sighs. "Now, get back in formation. We still have the rest of PT to get through."

***

After PT and breakfast, we begin the competitions promptly at 06:30. With thick steel walls and an incredibly high ceiling, the competition room seems to extend forever and is set up with dozens of stations for evaluation. From the archery ranges, sparring rings, and shelves of weapons, to the survival simulation centers, we are tested on anything and everything. Evaluators stand attentive at the side of each competition, analyzing how well we've mastered certain skills. They each carry tablets to take down notes on our technique and performance.

Synthetic overhead lights bathe the entirety of the room, exposing us for complete scrutinization. Still, the lights don't give off enough heat to protect us from the blaring yet silent air conditioning that keeps the academy at an uncomfortably cold temperature. Event after event goes on as the hours pass with each cadet following his or her own assigned schedule.

As I wait in line for my turn in the combat ring, where a cadet brawls with another of similar rank, I spot Xander finishing up at the station next to me. His sword gleams a brilliant silver as he whips it around, slicing the heads off of countless practice mannequins. In order to develop the basic skills of combat, Levels 1 and 2 at the BAA focus on the martial arts and combat with rudimentary weapons. This is our last year before graduating onto the modern weapons and warfare training of Levels 3 and 4.

"Looks like I'm sparring you." The voice suddenly catches my attention, but yet, before I even turn to see Cadet Owen Coleman at my side, I can already smell the strong stench of body odor reeking from his body.

"Why would I compete with you?" I begin, turning back around to return my attention to the combat ring. "You're not even in the top three."

"I'm in 4th place," he states.

"And I'm number one. Do you see the discrepancy, or should I use my fingers?" I respond simply, still not bothering to look at him again.

"Well, I guess I'll see you in the ring," he says shrugging. He then reaches past me to point at a board above the combat ring where Sgt. Blue had reshuffled the sparring partners. "Rogers in third is signed up to challenge Parks for second rank, and Zhu in sixth is challenging for fifth. That leaves me without a partner, so Sergeant Blue signed me up to challenge you for first. He must think I have what it takes."

"Or he wants to break your ego. I hope you know what you're getting yourself into," I say firmly, but he raises an eyebrow in confusion, so I clarify. "A quick loss."

"Actually—"

"Actually what?" I challenge, annoyance breaking through my formal tone. He cowers a little under my scowl. "I'm going to be completely honest with you, ok?"

"From you, I wouldn't expect anything else."

"I've watched you spar against the other cadets. You punch in slow motion and your reflexes are non-existent," I remark harshly. "I'm only agreeing to this fight because it'll make the judges laugh."

"Someone's bound to beat you. They have in the past," he says half-heartedly.

"And now they don't," I reply, grinning and then turning back to the combat match. I scan the nearby evaluators to make sure our conversation is not drawing attention. Lifting my chin, I let my tone settle back into content formality. "What's the name of this school, again? Starts with a 'B'…what was it?"

"Bellator Army Academy," he says, clenching his jaw a little.

"Right," I say, dragging out the word. "Bellator is also *my* name. Don't forget that."

"You know, you talk really highly about your name," he says, raising both his eyebrows. There's something else in his expression—satisfaction. "I wouldn't rely on that too much."

"What are you talking about?" I ask confidently.

"I overheard some of the evaluators talking earlier," he says, and his eyebrow spikes up again. "Turns out your family name isn't in as good a place as we thought."

"I'm tired of this conversation, are you going to get to the point?" I ask, heaving an exaggerated sigh to feign boredom. Yet, I can't help but land my eyes on him again, waiting for the rest of what he has to say.

"Your parents were caught helping the rebellion," he says as my face begins to fall. "They're calling the Bellators traitors now."

"Very funny," I sneer. Still, Owen's words have already caught the attention of some of those around me in line, and I feel eyes begin to draw toward me.

"Fine, but when they rename the school, I'll still be here to say I told you so," he explains, and my jaw locks in a mixture of embarrassment and anger. "You might not be."

"You're very brave talking to me like that," I state, gritting my teeth together.

"Why? Are you part of the rebels too now?" he responds immediately, and I feel blood rise to my cheeks.

"Hey man, I think that's enough," Xander says roughly, suddenly appearing behind Owen. He places a hand on the boy's shoulder, moving him away from me.

"Suddenly, I'm looking forward to the sparring ring," I say, reinvigorating my confidence.

"An evaluator looked this way," Xander warns, placing a large hand on Owen's chest when he takes a step forward. "You may have already hurt your ranking. If you both keep running your mouths, Sergeant Blue may just punish the whole platoon."

"Cadet Bellator!" The bellowing call catches me off guard, and I jump slightly. Behind me stands one of Headmaster's burly personal agents. He wears a perfectly fitted and unwrinkled black suit to match the black dusting of hair on his head, his black shades, and earpiece—all the standard uniform of the cookie-cutter agents. "Headmaster would like to see you in his office."

I glance up at the ceiling, where cameras hang down, watching over the competitions. Steaming with anger, my eyes lower, landing on Owen with a look of pure loathing.

"Follow me, cadet," the man commands.

CHAPTER 2

Riley

After answering the last question on the tablet regarding poisonous berries, I glance up at the evaluator sitting opposite me as he examines my responses on his sleek tablet. His ID says his name is Mr. Eriksson— a surname of Scandinavian ancestry. Though with tanner skin and dark eyes, he likely has mixed ethnic roots. His typing is unbalanced as he types an evaluation. His right hand lags a little behind his left; he must've injured it recently. By the subtlety, I presume it's only a small ache or pulled muscle. Monthly instructor evaluations are coming up and so he may have overdone himself practicing. The dark bags under his eyes indicate he's stayed up all night probably worrying about his new injury—but that won't work to his advantage either. If he messes up just a little due to his twisted wrist, then he'll be penalized. After only a few seconds, he looks up at me.

"Well, Cadet Amore, it appears your results on your Survival Skills practical exam are satisfactory. You've got a very good eye and a sharp intellect. If you keep this up for the rest of your competitions today, then you should expect to increase your ranking," he says, motioning me to hand my seat over to the next person in line. "You are expected to spar off against Cadet Hart now in the hand-to-hand duel."

"Thank you." I nod firmly, clenching my jaw shut to hide the nerve-racking feeling building up in my stomach.

When I leave the room, I turn my attention over to the archery range, where critics flock around Cadet Jack Anderson as he finishes firing arrow after arrow into the center of several distant moving targets. I try to watch as many of the other cadets' competitions as possible. Though it's unlikely that I'll ever compete with most of them, my curiosity motivates my wandering eyes. In fact, it doesn't matter who or what is around me, I'm always curious to watch. Every person and every object has a story, and my eyes yearn to flip through the pages of each one. But with Jack, I can't help but let my gaze linger longer.

He's always strived to break the Level 2 archery record, set years ago by another competitor, and has been the only one since to come close. It's mainly for this reason why he's made it to 20th place rather than for his knowledge in close one-on-one combat—or for his knowledge in anything really.

"Cadet Anderson, I have to say we are delightfully impressed by your immense achievement," one of the critics says, checking his stats. "The board will be sure to take this astonishing illustration of your talent into deep consideration when calculating your rank."

"Cool," Jack says after a moment, and though a heavy blink breaks his blank stare, his eyes still appear distant and inattentive. "Sir."

As I walk over to the sparring ring, I watch the current battle between two cadets. With the critics examining every move, each player fights ruthlessly to increase their ranking. I'm ranked 72nd out of the 93 in the platoon, but I know the only thing keeping my rank afloat is my academic knowledge. My physical combat skills... aren't so great. Thin, weak, and unintimidating. Nobody takes me seriously in the sparring ring.

"Hey blondie."

I hear the familiar voice and all too eagerly spin around.

"Cadet Anderson," I greet, my lips curling into a smile that reaches my eyes as the tall boy steps over to me.

"Did you get a chance to see some of my shots?" he asks. Though he struggles slightly to catch his breath, he plays it off nonchalantly as he nods his head in the direction of the archery range.

"I may have caught the end of it," I nod, pursing my lips together to contain my grin. "I saw you nearly miss a shot."

"I guess I was just distracted by you acing your Survival Skills practical," he says with a smile. Not just *a* smile, it's *his* smile: full of cheerfulness and infallibly capable of brightening my day.

"Is that so? Even though I took it in a separate, sound-proof room?" I ask, letting a single eyebrow raise.

"I guess I don't even have to watch to already know the outcome," he says, flashing his smile again.

"Well it's the only thing I'll be acing today," I remark.

"Don't say that."

"C'mon, what's Evaluation Day without a little self-deprecation," I say again sarcastically, and he shakes his head.

"Hey, on the bright side, it's one of our last before graduation," Jack says. "And then we're onto Level 3 and all of the skills we just mastered become useless."

"Very uplifting," I say sarcastically.

"I mean we won't have to worry about our ranks getting us expelled. I never understood why the mandatory expulsions of the lowest rank stop after Level 2," he says.

"Probably because we'd start to run out of cadets," I say with a shrug. "They also probably figure that by Level 3, they've invested too much in someone to kick them out. From there on, it's just about making sure they keep following all the rules."

"All 7 million of them. I guess that never goes away," he states more seriously, taking a step closer to me— not too close. I interlock my hands behind my back.

"Never," I confirm. I quickly let my eyes glance around, scanning the faces of those nearby—especially the critics. "They've got eyes everywhere, you know. What they don't find, the cameras do."

"Not everything," he says casually through a sigh, looking down. He then flicks his eyes back up and I'm struck by their blue brilliance. His energetic smile slowly begins to reappear, forcing my lips to curl up as well.

From my peripheral view, I can see a nearby critic glance up in our direction. Nonetheless, Jack's eyes stay locked on mine, and I resist the extent of my smile for the sake of a guise of formality. Everything sucks here at the BAA...but not Jack.

"Well, I wish you luck in your competitions," I state again.

"You too," he says back simply, but the twinkle in his bright eyes brings a flush to my cheeks. It's a look that he's used constantly for me for the past few months. It's his only way to communicate that he cares about me...that he even loves me. I just know he does.

"Alright, next up is Cadet Amore and Cadet Hart in the sparring ring," a voice announces, catching my attention.

"Don't sweat it, you'll do great. Hart is no match for a girl like you," Jack says. Even though I know his words of encouragement aren't true, his charm convinces me otherwise. "I'm serious. You're like the smartest person in this school. You've got this in the bag."

He lets his large hand briefly drag across my smooth arm before turning and walking away. I let my eyes stay on him for a while longer as he parts. When I do finally manage to tear my stare away, I quickly scan the room until they land on the large raised platform where Cadet Hart and several evaluators stand, waiting for my arrival. I take in a deep breath, shivering slightly underneath the chill of the room, before starting off in their direction. I contemplate hiding in the bathroom until they forget about me and move on. Sometimes it would be just so much easier to be invisible.

"Cadet Amore?" one of the evaluators asks me as I step past the line of fellow cadets and onto the white platform of the sparring ring.

"Yes, sir," I squeak, and he takes note of my lack of confidence.

"Alright, the match will take up the common rules from your training," another supervisor begins to say, whilst typing away at his tablet intently. His voice is monotone, and he shifts his stance in attempt to relieve the pressure on the legs he's been standing on all day, scoring match after match after match.

As he continues to explain the standard instructions and rules, my focus shifts over to my opponent. Cadet Hart has always been one of the ugliest, largest cadets in the BAA that I had ever had to spar against. Though somehow only managing to receive the rank above mine, she stands at nearly six feet and scowls at me through her small, gray eyes. In all my times sparring with her, I've found that her weaknesses lie in her overconfidence, eagerness, and lack of sound strategy. She usually jumps in with limbs flying, and I do my best to let her tire herself out.

Her skin is pale and thin, allowing for blemishes and numerous blue veins to stand out. My eye catches the small mass of dried blood just sticking out from under her shirt sleeve—an indication of a wound. The placement of the gash has the potential to limit her range of motion in her left arm and thus could be exploited to my benefit. Even if I couldn't beat her strength, I could use her injury against her.

"Cadet Hart, are you ready?" the supervisor finally asks.

"Yes, sir," she responds gruffly, her voice a low growl and hungry as if she is planning to eat me.

"Cadet Amore, are you ready?"

My eyes flash quickly over Hart once more, making markers on her wound and certain pressure points around her neck. Her eyes continue to glower at me.

"Yes, sir."

"You may begin," he announces, and I feel my heart drop as countless sets of eyes focus in on the match.

"C'mon, Hart, you can take her," I hear someone call from the crowd, instigating a devilish smirk to curl on Hart's lips.

"Hope you won't miss your pretty little face too much after I rough it up a bit," she growls in a deep voice.

With a loud yell, she lunges at me, but with quick agility—and admitted fear—I jump aside and allow her to fly past. Then, acting quickly, I attempt an attack, striking my fist into a soft spot on her neck, followed by a chop at another spot with my other hand. My power is lacking, and the potentially debilitating attack seems to have no effect on her.

Before I can even react, she grabs my small arm with her meaty hand, pausing for a moment as I fruitlessly try to pull away. After getting satisfaction from my struggle, she grabs my shoulder with the other hand and, releasing a strong grunt, flips me over her head. There's a loud thud as I slam onto the hard floor. Achingly, I struggle to push myself up on sore arms. My eyes begin to focus again just as I am grabbed by the collar and raised up a little. Even through my haziness, my eyes scan over her body, and before she can throw down the heavy punch she'd been gathering, I strike out at the wound on the arm holding me. She yelps in pain, letting her grip on me loosen enough to allow me to wriggle out from her grasp.

Rage visible in her eyes, she begins throwing out a volley of heavy, eager punches in my direction. I take advantage of her slow strength, which is now weakened by her now open wound leaking blood down her arm, and I nimbly dodge each swing. If I could just get her arm one more time…

Her slower movements and increased breathing indicate fatigue, and I time the slowing rate of her energy. During her recovery time between attacks, I spin around and thrust a hard kick into her abdomen. She staggers back a little, grabbing my leg and suspending me in the air. Fearing the worst, I strike forward, chopping her arm in her weak spot again. She releases my leg, but before I can create a strong enough counter move, she charges at me again, grabbing both of my shoulders and throwing me to the floor. I skid across the smooth white surface; the only traction is caused by the dried blood spots of previous matches, and I slide all the way across the ring to collide with the metal gate. A buzzer goes off.

"Alright cadets, time for Round 1 is over," one of the critics suddenly announces in a mundane tone and I hear the excited chatter of the few next in line, eager for their turn.

As for the evaluators, one of them yawns and the others jot down a few notes on their tablets with expressionless faces.

"Let's try to make this next round more interesting."

Cadet Hart retreats to her starting position, eyeing me down as I rise to my feet. I walk back over hesitantly to face the much larger woman.

"Cadet Hart, are you ready?" one of them announces, resetting the timer. As I raise my hands back up into ready position, a wave of nausea suddenly rushes over me.

"Yes, sir."

"Cadet Amore, are you ready?" he asks again, his hand ready to start the timer. I blink a few times to clear my eyes, and my head starts to feel heavy. My arms droop downward, and I glance nervously around me to notice everyone's eyes staring me down. "Cadet Amore?"

My nausea worsening, I suddenly break from my stance, rush over to the opening in the gate, dash down the few steps, and run across the large training room. I hear the evaluator's stern voice call my name again, cursing my lack of discipline, but I disregard it and continue running. One hand covers my mouth and the other sways at my side as if trying to increase my speed. Shutting the door behind me, I fly down the hallway into the nearby bathroom to release the vomit that I know is coming.

CHAPTER 3

Jenn

The war was controversial from the start. Soldiers were sent without an end in sight. Many never returned. People forgot what they were fighting for. Resistance from disenfranchised soldiers started with propaganda and sabotages but eventually escalated to mutiny and organized rebellion. Yet, no matter how weak and fractured the military became, the war continued, only fueling the soldier rebellion even more. Instead, harsh punishments and propaganda started to be used to combat rebels. At the BAA, association with the rebels is considered unforgivable. I figured my parents would feel the same way...

I remember first finding out about their crimes only last week. Management of rebellious activities, distribution of rebel propaganda, sabotaging communication lines, and conspiracy for violence directed at the Capitol building. The Federal Justice Enforcement department was quick to lock them away for presumably death row. A week of interrogation followed for me. The FJE worked tirelessly to test me for any connection with their crimes and extract any information...a formality, really, since the close monitoring and physical isolation of cadets from society would've made it impossible. Most importantly, they wanted me to prove my commitment and loyalty to the BAA; they wanted me to prove I'm not my parents.

I hold my head high as I walk through the heavy double doors into Headmaster's office. The steel walls lack any windows and carry up to an unnecessarily high ceiling. Adding to the sense of ominous intimidation carefully implemented here, the massive office is empty of any furniture except for a single wide master desk and a padded leather chair. This lone furniture is planted on an elevated semicircle shaped platform that takes up a good third of the floor space. That's where Headmaster sits, towering over the rest of the room as if on a throne.

Differing from his agents, Headmaster dons an impeccable dark gray suit with a golden tie. He's bald from age and not a single stub of hair is visible on his wide square jaw. However, despite being close to 60 years old, he has managed to maintain a rather fit stature like the idealized sculpture of a military man.

My footsteps echo in the hollow room as I stride over to stand at the bottom of steps that lead up onto the raised platform. When I get there, I stiffly throw my hand up in a silent salute. The bleak room, particularly colder than the rest of the dreary BAA, sends an icy shiver down my spine. We wait in silence. I know he knows I'm here, but he doesn't acknowledge it; he just proceeds to continue writing whatever he was working on before my arrival.

I flinch when the door behind his desk opens, and a woman steps out to stand beside the desk. Nauseatingly pristine with hair styled perfectly in place and a dainty scarf around her neck, she is clearly out of place here. She holds a sleek tablet close to her side and a recording device in the opposite hand.

Headmaster's pen freezes and he slowly places it down. Then, I watch as he takes in a deep sigh, raising his head with his inhale. The expression he gives me displays annoyance. He nods slightly, allowing me to drop my salute.

"You're a competent soldier, Cadet Bellator," he says, and though he's too bothered to speak with much effort, his voice booms across the room, echoing between the walls. "This isn't a pleasant conversation for me to have with you."

"What are you talking about, sir?" I say, shifting in my stance.

"As you know, I have eyes and ears all over this complex in the form of cameras. I see and hear everything," he continues, his beady dark eyes staring directly back at me. "I think you know what I'm talking about."

"I presume you're referring to Cadet Coleman, sir," I say nonchalantly, tightening my lips. "He was just trying to psyche me out before our match. With your permission, I request to be excused as I have a match to win."

"No, cadet." As Headmaster folds his hands on his desk, I feel my heart fall through my stomach. Maintaining his gaze on me, he tilts his face slightly toward the other woman in the room. "Proceed, Mrs. Meyers."

"Hi, Cadet Bellator, my name is Mrs. Meyers, and I am with the Federal Justice Enforcement team working with the BAA on your case. I have been recording this entire conversation," says the woman at Headmaster's side, whose many plastic surgeries force her face into an airbrushed, expressionless stare. Almost robotic, she speaks as if the conversation had tripped her 'on' button. It didn't help that to my knowledge she hasn't yet blinked. "We want to thank you for your cooperation this past week in your questioning. We are happy to inform you that your investigation is officially closed."

"Thank you, ma'am. My loyalty lies with our government and always will," I assert, nodding. "I will ensure that my loyalty will remain evident throughout my—"

"Amongst the escalation of the rebellion, we have noticed rebel ideology spreading within the BAA itself, inspiring mutinous, violent acts of resistance against our staff," Headmaster states professionally, disregarding my words. "This dissension is primarily originating from students sympathizing with convicted family members."

"I'm not guilty of this, sir," I state. "I do not sympathize with my parents. And if I notice such tendencies in others, I—"

"I know," the woman says, her pristine red lips curling and pushing the makeup-covered skin of her cheeks into dimples. "But as you know, however, your parents, General Thomas Bellator and Colonel Mariana Bellator, have been involved in the treachery against the country for some time now and are thus partially responsible for the chaos, unrest, and rebellion against the caste system of our stratocracy. It is my duty to remind you that, ever since the military has rightfully ascended to govern the country years ago, an emphasis on discipline has been incorporated into the law. We cannot allow such dissention from our ranks, especially in our schools."

"The BAA has come to the decision that it is best to proactively eliminate threats in order to ensure the stability of our establishment," Headmaster announces.

"This is insane," I blurt out, briefly losing my composure. I glance back at the woman with the recorder. "Sir."

"Cadet Jennifer Bellator, you are expelled from the Bellator Army Academy, effective immediately," Headmaster states simply, clasping his hands together on the desk in front of him.

"Sir!" I exclaim, unable to hold my tongue back. The rage builds under my skin, and I clench my fists powerlessly. "I request a reconsideration, sir. I'm the highest rank of my platoon. I am a dedicated cadet of the BAA—"

"This is not up for discussion. With familial pressures in support of the rebellion, I am making the executive decision that you pose a risk to this school. Your rank and leadership only furthers this risk," he articulates, picking up his pen to fill out a paper on his desk.

"Thank you for your cooperation, Cadet Bellator," the woman says, and I cringe at her tone of satisfaction. The tips of her lips curl up, struggling to smile through her cemented skin.

"I'm a soldier, and my loyalty is to our country," I state sternly, my eyes trained on the recorder as she clicks it off.

"Of course you are," she says, giving me her small grin again that is confined greatly by the limits of her botox and reeking of forced sincerity. I furrow my eyebrows at her condescending tone. "I believe my work here is done. Ms. Bellator, it was a pleasure."

The click of her high heels resounds as she leaves through the back door behind Headmaster's desk. She only shoots Headmaster one final, quick glance of victory before disappearing. When the door closes, it leaves a loud echo to resound throughout the room. Headmaster takes in a deep breath and lets it out slowly, his eyes still fixed on me.

"I…" The words come out in a croak, as if my body refuses to speak despite my brain's command. Silence passes as my head spins, trying to grip onto my thoughts. "I did nothing wrong, sir."

"Your family is to be convicted of the highest crime in the country: treason," Headmaster murmurs absentmindedly as he shuffles through some more paperwork on his desk. My jaw stays firm in stoic expression, but I try to ignore the sudden heat that crawls across my skin and reaches my cheeks.

"My loyalty lies with the government, that's what I've always followed," I repeat.

"The BAA will not be taking that risk," he says again, letting his dark eyes rest on me for only a moment before returning to his paperwork.

"Aren't you concerned about the school's name, sir?" I ask quickly. "My ancestors built this school."

"We are enforcing this expulsion criteria for several students in strict opposition to the growing rebellion. At the BAA, we maintain our values regardless of individual circumstances in order to help the government crackdown on treason and promote stronger discipline in our gracious country," he says, a sly smile on his face as he returns his gaze to me. "If that requires removing the tarnished Bellator name from the school, then I look forward to leading the renaming commission."

"To re-name the school in your honor?" I ask, my voice nearly shaking. Though my intent is to sound firm, my words come out rushed and more like the plea that they are.

He finishes the form on his desk and places his pen down.

"Jennifer Bellator, you are officially expelled from Bellator's Army Academy and will be promptly sent to the Island tomorrow morning," he announces strictly, and a wave of horror washes over me as the reality hits.

"I still have a chance to redeem myself on the Island," I say quickly. "If I pass that, then I get re-enrolled."

"You won't come back," Headmaster says again, his low voice daunting.

Suddenly, the doors behind me swing open, catching my attention. In step five agents, each clad heavily in body gear and carrying assault rifles.

"Jennifer Bellator," Headmaster continues. "I have so graciously provided you with several guards to escort you back to the barracks, where you will stay until your departure tomorrow."

"I'm coming back from the Island," I state firmly as the officers flank me on either side. "I will."

CHAPTER 4

Riley

The toilet flushes as I leave the stall. I walk up to the sink and let the cool water wash over my hands before bringing it up to my face to wash out my mouth. Then I slip a small mint from my pocket and slide it into my mouth. I had swiped it from an instructor the other day. Looking up at my reflection in the mirror, I see a tear stain on my cheek and lazily wipe it clean.

I take in a deep breath and stay there for a moment, not wanting to face the humiliation of going back out there. As I stare at myself, my mind grapples with my own reality: I just darted away from an important match in front of all the examiners. My score won't recover from this. Somehow, I muster up whatever of my courage is left and quietly slide out of the bathroom.

"Cadet Amore," a man's voice suddenly says, startling me and making me raise my hanging head.

"Yes, sir," I answer, freezing as I see one of Headmaster's personal agents step forward toward me from across the hall. I give him a polite smile, which he outright ignores.

"Headmaster would like to speak with you," he demands, his face strict and unmoving.

I try to suppress the nerves curdling in my stomach as the agent motions down the hallway, and I hesitantly begin walking. He follows close behind as if to make sure that I don't try to make a run for it—something I was admittedly considering for the second time today.

The hall is exceptionally quiet and the only noise comes from the sound of our footsteps on the steel floor. The long walk down the winding hallway gives me time to dread over the worst possibility. I imagine myself being scolded by him as he looks down on me from his desk. I try desperately to come up with an excuse for why I had run out. Perhaps I heard someone yelling from the bathroom and went to save them. Or Cadet Hart put a bomb in the toilet, and I went to diffuse it. Maybe I have food poisoning.

I've been to Headmaster's office only once before when he informed me of my parents' deaths. I can still remember that day vividly as if it happened earlier today. He was my mother's childhood friend and ultimately became a longtime friend of my parents. When the National Educational System said I had 'prior exposure to the military path' and assigned me accordingly, Headmaster was one of their first calls. It was their personal connection to him that got me accepted into the BAA. Since their death, he hasn't even acknowledged me. On my graduation from Level 1, he refused to make eye contact with me while shaking my hand.

Finally, after the long trek to the top floor of the Level 2 complex, we reach Headmaster's office. I wrap my shaking fingers around the cool metal handles of the double doors, and they open slowly and simultaneously.

There he is: sitting in his throne at his desk. His beady eyes slowly raise until they land on me and I feel my heart, which had been audibly pounding in my ears the entire trip here, stop.

"Cadet Amore," he says, his intimidating voice thundering throughout the hollow steel room. "Come here."

"Sir," I mutter, stepping closer across the long room until I reach the bottom of the steps like a servant before a king. As per the rules, I salute.

"Well, it sure has been a while since I've seen you," he remarks, the crease between his eyes deep from constant frowning.

"Yes, sir," I reply timidly. "It's an honor—"

"I was there when you were born," he suddenly says, cutting me off. I continue to stare at him, trying to decipher the meaning in his words and what to expect next. "Your parents loved you so much."

I am caught off by his words, but I refuse to smile or let down my firm expression at his words of warmth. There's a hidden coldness beneath them.

"They were so hesitant to let you come to the BAA. They weren't sure if their darling little girl was suited to be a soldier, not that they had a choice," he continues, staring at me as if waiting for a reaction. I bite my lip. "When Dr. Andrews informed me that you were pregnant, I thought it must be a mistake. I thought your parents raised you right."

I feel a shiver run down my spine, and time freezes for a long moment as we remain motionless in absolute silence. I struggle to find the right words, but he has caught me speechless.

"Sir...I'm not sure I know what you are talking about—"

"Yes, you do, cadet," he snaps at me, and the blood pulses to my cheeks. He just stares at me with a disappointing look, and I lower my voice, humiliated.

"How did you find out, sir?"

"Your performance has been decreasing," he answers sternly. Headmaster isn't one to drone on about a topic; he doesn't have the time. His straightforward promptness cuts out much of the evidence supporting his accusation, but I know challenging it would be mute. "A 2-month pregnancy was confirmed on your mandatory annual checkup yesterday."

"I'm so sorry, sir," I say quietly, the guilt making my eyes well up with tears.

"You are scheduled with Dr. Hill for an abortion immediately," he continues stoically. "You were very aware of our policies when you violated them. Your punishment will be evaluated and implemented as such."

"What about the father, sir? He is not yet aware of the situation," I say, softly.

"Cadet Anderson was identified using genetic analysis of the embryo's DNA in your blood," Headmaster states, nodding. "Usually, he would also be subjected to the same punishment. However, due to unrelated circumstances, Cadet Anderson is already expelled."

"Expelled?" I exclaim, a little more forceful than I thought, and I catch myself. "Might I ask what for, sir?"

"There will be an announcement tomorrow when the cadets are sent to the Island," Headmaster says, tightening his lips into an unbudging line.

"The Island?" I ask after a pause, my voice shaking. "He'll die, though, sir."

"This is not a discussion, cadet, is that clear?" he demands. "Now, I believe you have an abortion appointment to attend."

"No," I mutter, barely letting the word slip through as a whisper.

"*Excuse* me, cadet?" he barks. When I don't answer, he slams his fist on the desk. "I asked you if my words were clear."

"I'm not having the abortion, sir," I say, letting my gaze drift up to him again.

"That is not an option, cadet," he replies, narrowing his gaze. "The BAA is for training the best of cadets, not for indulging in personal desires."

"I'll go to the Island, sir," I mutter, shaking my head in disbelief at my own words.

"I am your Headmaster, and you will respect my decisions as such," he growls, his deep voice thundering. "Now, leave me office at once, cadet, you are dismissed."

"I wish to keep my baby, sir," I repeat. "I understand the consequence. I am willing to face expulsion. I am not your best soldier, anyway."

"Is that so, Cadet Amore?" he says, his dark eyes still piercing into me. "You understand the ramifications of being sent to the Island?"

"I do, sir," I say as I look up at him, desperation glimmering in my glazed eyes.

"Very well. Since you are unwilling to comply with the abortion order, Cadet Riley Amore, you are expelled from the Bellator Army Academy, effective immediately," Headmaster declares, still without removing his stare. "You shall be sent off the Island tomorrow."

My lip begins to quiver, and I feel a terrified tear slide down my cheek.

"Your parents would be disappointed in you, Ms. Amore," he says stoically again, staring back at me with expressionless eyes.

"I'll alert the guards to bring you to your room, where you will stay until tomorrow morning. When they arrive, you'll be dismissed."

I hesitate for a moment, frozen with fear and denial, and I avert my eyes from him. Yet, shaking with fear and devastation, I'm unable to contain my tears any longer. I twist on my heels and part for the door, taking off running down the empty hallway, headed nowhere in particular. I hear him call out to me, but his voice is drowned out as I disappear in the building.

Suddenly, I am jolted to a stop as I slam into something…well, someone.

"Riley," Jack says softly, his hands on my shoulders to steady my anxious movements. "What's going on?"

"Shouldn't you be competing?" I ask, pulling away from him. I wipe my cheeks with my hands as my crying ceases.

"Headmaster wanted to see me," he responds. "Wait, what happened with you? Where did you come from?"

I squeeze my eyes shut, still turned away from him as I come to terms with the inevitability of my secret coming out. Glancing behind me to check for Headmaster's agents, I grab his arm and pull him around the corner of the hallway.

"Jack, I have to tell you something, quickly," I mutter, shaking my head in guilt. "I'm so sorry."

"Sorry for what? Talk to me," he says again, walking closer to me. He places his hand on my shoulder again in sympathy, but I shudder at his contact. "Love, please."

I'm caught speechless as I stare into his wide blue eyes that plead me with concern.

"Jack, I'm pregnant," I say hesitantly. At first, he doesn't react, at least not visibly. I see him take in a deep breath and hold it. "For two months now. Headmaster just found out."

"You're pregnant," he repeats, furrowing his eyebrows as his brain continues to process the news. Overcome with emotion, I can't respond. "Is Headmaster making you get rid of it?"

"No," I say, my eyebrows tilted upwards. Suddenly, my heart beat begins to race, and he looks away, still processing the news. He doesn't see how my eyes widened in fear or how the red rushed to my pale cheeks. "I have to keep it...I'm expelled."

"Come here," he says, shaking his head before pulling me into a hug. I let out a sob as I lean into him, burying my head in his shoulder, and he pulls me tighter.

"I think you're expelled too, but I don't know what for," I mutter, and I feel him rub my back. "He's sending us to the Island tomorrow."

"It's ok," he murmurs, letting his mouth lean on the top of my head. His words come out forced as if he knows that's what he's supposed to say when someone is upset. Neither of us believes it is ok.

"No one's ever come back…" I begin to say.

"Hey, it's ok, it's ok," he murmurs again unconvincingly, holding me a little tighter.

Suddenly, I hear footsteps coming down a nearby hallway. Before they can turn the corner into our hallway, I quickly separate from Jack and take a step back.

"There they are," one of Headmaster's agents says as he turns the corner, standing only a few feet away from us. Accompanying him are several heavily armed guards. "Cadet Anderson, you're supposed to be seeing Headmaster. He is waiting."

"Are the escorts necessary, sir?" Jack asks as the group approaches us.

"They're Cadet Amore's escorts," the man clarifies, his face hardened into a scowl.

Humbled, I look away, wiping my cheeks with the palm of my hand. The group is upon us now and the bodyguards begin to circle me. Instinctively, I begin to step back to maintain personal space.

"Wait, Riley," Jack says, grabbing my wrist before I am closed off. He pulls me toward him and wraps his other hand around my back. He then swiftly leans me back, swooping down to lock his lips with my own. With my eyes wide in shock and my arms hanging out uselessly, I hear the agent exclaim in disapproval.

"Cadet Anderson!" he yells, and two of my bodyguards spring into action, separating us.

I try to catch glimpses of Jack through the wall of men forming around me. I find him doing the same, but the agent grabs him forcefully by the arm and swings his baton straight into Jack's gut. "Headmaster will be hearing about this."

"What's he going to do, expel me?" I hear Jack quip through his staggered breathing as the agent forces him to stand back up.

Before he parts back down the hall, I catch his smirk. I feel my own expression soften into a slight smile, and I adjust my position to keep my gaze on him as he continues to walk away.

I suddenly become aware of the coldness in the building as Jack leaves, my skin feeling stripped of the comforting warmth that his hands provided. In its place, only the harsh cold air conditioning remains—a coldness I am convinced is maintained by Headmaster to freeze the hearts of his soldiers.

CHAPTER 5

Jenn

It's nighttime now, and I fold my uniform on the table beside my bed just as I do every night. It begins to dawn on me that tonight is the last night that I sleep here. I glance out of the small square window beside me, blocked off with thick glass and several steel bars. The sky outside is a thick blanket of darkness with the new moon tonight. The artificial chill of the air conditioning rushing in from the vent above me simulates the icy lips of the breeze outside.

Suddenly there's a knock at my door. I already know who it is. To ensure that I don't escape, my escorts have stood guard outside my door. They keep routinely checking in on me ever since they brought me back to my room.

"Yes, yes, believe it or not, I haven't vanished into thin air yet. I'm still here," I say upon opening the door to face the multitude of armed servicemen standing just beyond the door frame. They all give me the same expressionless face.

"You are wanted at Headmaster's office," one of them says.

"What for?" I ask, but they do not respond. Instead, they part a little to make way for me out into the hallway.

They surround me as we walk, and I stare at the smooth steel tiles beneath my feet and watch it turn to textured cement as we step outside. I fantasize about escaping the barricade around me and rushing off into the forest I know lies to my left. I'm powerful, but I knew I would never stand a chance against the armed guards despite how much I'd like to pretend I would. Even if I did evade their grasps and guns long enough to slide into the forest, I wouldn't make it past the impenetrable wall that surrounds the massive complex.

I watch the ground change from cement to steel again. Finally, after taking an elevator, we walk a familiar path to the office I had been escorted out of just earlier today. When my guards part, I see that Headmaster still sits upon his throne, looking down at his royal guards and the exiled peasant.

"What's this about, sir?" I ask after he dismisses my salute.

"You have a phone call," he replies sternly. I raise an eyebrow, and he motions to the single telephone placed at the forefront of his desk. "I wouldn't keep them waiting."

I hesitate a moment in a standoff of sorts between the two of us, not even breaking eye contact with a blink. Slowly, I step up to the desk and grab the landline phone.

I know who it is before I even speak.

"Jennifer." The responding voice is powerful even through the phone. Deep, articulate, and forceful, the voice of my father instantly fills me with an intimidation that outperforms even Headmaster.

"Where are you?" is all I can think to say.

"On Death Row," he says simply.

Suddenly, I feel my mouth dry.

"I talked to Headmaster today," I start, speaking in a firm voice. "They ended my investigation."

"They did, didn't they," he states through his teeth.

"You're fighting for the resistance," I say.

"Proudly," he says, and the calmness of his voice sends a chill down my spine. "But they didn't need more than a suspicion to put me on Death Row."

"You betrayed us—our name—and everything the Bellators stand for, everything you ever taught me," I say. "You betrayed the army."

"You know nothing," he jeers, his voice coming in sharp through the phone and making me jump. "I'll always fight for the army. For our self-respect. For our lives to be taken into account."

"You're going to die," I say tentatively.

"With purpose. For the future. You have no idea what's going on outside the walls of the BAA," he responds in a low voice.

"I don't understand," I begin to say, furrowing my eyebrows.

"You wouldn't," he states in disgust. I can almost picture him running his hand over his face to calm his irritability. His tone is demeaning like an impatient general half-listening to the petty request of a private.

The memory of my father is burned into my mind. In my head, he's always scolding me. Cold, brash, and distant, his voice bellows into my ears as he drills the words 'discipline' and 'respect' into my head. He hits me harder, daring me to flinch, as he threatens that I need to learn to be tougher and stronger. Always tougher and stronger. With unwavering loyalty to fuel motivation for my future fights. The government needs the best soldiers, and the Bellators are meant to be the best soldiers. He tells me it's on me to uphold that. Yet, now tainting my memories, I hear the echoes of when his treasonous crimes were read aloud to me.

"You're wrong," I say suddenly, inciting not only surprise in him but in myself as well. I try to compose myself. "You turned your back on everything. I'm a true soldier, and I stand by the government and the BAA."

"You're a child," my dad says, disregarding my statement. His voice is monotone yet vindictive.

I open my mouth to speak but I can't. I've always been the only one that could incite rage in him, and he's always been the one that could make me feel so defenseless.

"I'll be executed tomorrow," he says in response. "I wanted to say goodbye. I already said goodbye to your mother. Her date is the following day. I presume she will be making her last call tomorrow."

"Mom's calling tomorrow?" I ask quickly, letting my panic bleed into my tone. "No, no, she has to call today."

My words are followed by silence, having fallen on unreceptive ears. My eyes fall as my jaw locks with firmness.

"I'm expelled," I say, partially hoping that my mom would somehow hear. If only she knew. "They're sending me to the Island in the morning."

"Is that so?" he asks, and I search for emotion in his stern voice. "I assume that students have returned since my time there."

"No…no one's ever returned," I say, squeezing my eyes shut.

"You're still a Bellator," he states sternly. There's a change in his tone. Behind the disconnected, gruff tone, it's earnest and genuine.

"I am," I restate.

"Be a Bellator on that island then," he says. I press the phone hard into my ear to ensure that I'm capturing every word. I yearn for the sound of a sniffle, or at least a sigh. "It's a shame you won't hear from your mother."

"Dad, I…I love you," I squeak. "I love you both."

More silence. Yet, I wait. I've been waiting for 16 years. I need him to say it back. For all the pain he caused me, I need to know that he feels more than resentment toward me.

"Your mother loves you," he says at last. "Fight on that island, Jennifer. Don't disappoint me."

The line goes blank, and I slowly lower the phone. I have to take in a deep breath to hold myself together. I could already taste the blood from the tongue clenched between my teeth. The crowd of heavily armed goons that surround me again suddenly provide a sense of relief. At least this way, I am forced to be hidden from the world.

CHAPTER 6

Riley

The sun isn't even over the horizon yet when I am woken up by a pair of Headmaster's agents barging into my room. They toss me a uniform consisting of cargo pants, a simple black sweatshirt, and Level 2's signature lime-green tee-shirt with a golden number 2 on it.

After changing, I am escorted out of my room. Down the hall, I can see Jenn, Xander, and Jack being escorted out as well, each also wearing the same uniform. Even on her expulsion day, Jenn still stands with perfect posture and her chin high. With the muscular build of her short stocky figure and her hair, dark and sleek, still pulled back tight into a bun, she still looks like a proper cadet. Yet, still, there's something behind the tightness of her face and stiffness of her jaw. Slightly puffy exhaustion circles round out under her eyes, which threaten to close under heavy eyelids.

We are brought across the campus in silence. At last, doors open up into one large room with a high, dome-shaped ceiling. However, despite the large space, the only thing in the room is a table with four backpacks on it along with a rack of weapons on either side. Standing menacingly behind the table is a group of Headmasters' armor-glad agents. Our footsteps echo off the empty walls as we stride across the long room.

"Welcome to the preparation room," one of the men announces proudly as we begin to near him. "The backpacks have food, water, and medical supplies. Pick one weapon each."

Jenn grabs the nearest backpack and easily slips it on before quickly moving on to the left rack of weapons. Her eyes scan the contents, glancing over to the right rack briefly. Finally, she spots it: her axe. Made of steel as light as wood, the handheld double-sided axe has edges sharp enough to easily slice through bone. It's become such a staple of hers that the others in Level 2 dubbed it 'the Bellator axe.'

I hesitantly peer into the backpack closest to me and find it filled with simple medical supplies. Taking just a few seconds to rummage through it, I take note of the materials inside: bandages, painkillers, ointment, a tourniquet, and a syringe. Jack opens one as well, and I glance over to watch him ruffle through its contents. When he notices me, he holds it out to me, showing me the varied array of nonperishable foods.

Jack chooses his longbow next. Gleaming silver with a black handle, it stands out from the other standard black BAA bows. It had been made special for him last year by the school as a prize for scoring highest in an archery competition. The matching arrows are silver as well and end with a fletch made of white feathers streaked with bright green. Everyone thinks he picked the green color to correspond with Level 2's signature green color, but he told me he picked it to match my eyes. Beside him, Xander is sifting through an array of long swords.

I spot an array of gleaming knives, each set in a pocket in the belt. I slide one out and hold it in my hand, weaving it between my fingers with ease. The heavy blade shimmers with silver light. They're meant to be thrown but are also useful in close combat. While Jenn and Xander must remain in a limited distance from their competitor and Jack must be far, the wielder of the throwing knives can be either. While the others may lose their weapon, throwing knives come in multiples. I don't know what the terrain is where we are going, but I do know that the portability of the knives will be an advantage as well. I'll prepare for anything.

I lift the belt and wrap it around my waist. Suddenly, the agent by my side stops me, taking the weapon in his own hands along with my backpack. I glance around at the others and see the agents doing the same to them—probably for caution in case we rebel.

"Your transportation is waiting outside," the main agent says at last.

I feel a guard nudge my back from behind me as we are led around the table to the opposite side of the room. The wall on this side is entirely composed of a large steel garage door that slowly begins to pull up with a resounding rumbling noise. Sunlight bleeds through in greater amounts, and when my eyes acclimate, I see the stretch of a wooden dock hovering above the gleaming ocean.

Is this it? I keep waiting for the agents to provide us with armor vests or at least padding of some sort, but they don't. *We have absolutely no protection,* I reiterate to myself, taking a deep breath. *Maybe we don't need it. Maybe the island won't be so bad.*

The sun beats heavily down on us, and as we make our way over the wooden boards on the wharf, my stomach twists in knots. There it is: the simple, nondescript wooden sail ship that will bring us to Expulsion Island. It's tethered to posts on the dock, letting it float in place in the water, and a single wooden ramp connects its deck to the dock. The boat's sails stand with defeated strength on the flat deck like an old man who has seen much better days. Remnants of pale green stain the faded Level 2 flags, and the fabric flutters weakly as the wind brushes past it. I avert my eyes, trying to keep from vomiting from anxiety.

Suddenly, one of the agents beside me nudges me slightly, and I glance over at her. She looks blankly straight ahead, walking as uptight and in formation as the other agents around us. Then, I notice the edge of a ziplock bag sticking out of the sleeve of her blazer. Her hand extends slightly toward me. Our shoulders already nearly touching, I extend my arm toward her as well. My finger brushes up against the cold plastic of the bag and I pinch it with my index finger and thumb, pulling it quickly into my grasp. Letting the sleeve of my sweatshirt conceal my hand, I move the bag between my fingers, feeling the contents.

"Pills," she mutters, remaining indifferent, still staring ahead, as if she hadn't said anything.

"For what?" I ask again, but then we halt to a stop, and my eyes shoot forward again. Waiting beside the ramp leading to the boat are two more of Headmaster's agents.

"Riley Amore, Jack Anderson, Jennifer Bellator, Alexander Parks," one of the two agents says. "The ride should take about a week depending on the weather. Over there is your captain, Billy."

I glance up at the elderly captain sitting on a wooden pedestal that juts out of the deck at the head of the boat. He hunches over a steering wheel that he firmly grips onto. His starving figure wears a gray shirt and matching pants, each tattered with rips that reveal a box-like device strapped around his midsection. Billy cranes his neck around, peering through a few straggling strands of long hair to glance at the boat's occupiers. Scars, new and old, run in all directions across his face, and I can tell that behind his ripped-up lips, he is missing a significant number of teeth as well.

"And now a message from your Headmaster: Farewell," the agent continues.

Without any more to say, we start forward again toward the docked boat. It's a rather small boat with a completely flat deck and there's a latch built into the floor on one side, presumably leading down into a small cabin.

"Brown pill for abortion," the agent beside me suddenly says as we begin walking again, catching me off guard. Her mouth barely moving at all, her voice comes out low and barely audible, and I have to strain my ears to hear her over the noise of our footsteps. "No matter when."

"Pardon me?" I ask, shocked.

"Others are nutrition pills," she mumbles, explaining. As we walk up the small ramp onto the wooden boat, the deck creaks loudly under our weight. "One every few days for seven months."

"Why are you doing this?" I ask under my breath as we all regroup on the deck of the boat. The agents around us each hand us our chosen weapons and dress us in our backpacks.

"Because you're not supposed to survive this," she mutters again in my ear as she slips on my backpack from behind. "The backpacks, the weapons, it's all for show."

"What's there?" I mutter back, barely able to speak.

"Something you could've never trained for," she whispers, strapping my belt of knives around my waist. "Find Bella. Make sure she's alright."

"What's your name?" I ask in a small voice as the agents finish up their work and the sails are hoisted up.

"Dana," she whispers back, glancing cautiously toward the others. "Look after Bella for me."

I spot Jack as they attach his quiver to his back. He steals a glance at me, his eyebrows upturned and his lips pursed. Suddenly, I notice the agent beside him pull out a syringe. Before I can call out, however, I feel a needle be inserted into my skin as well, and I choke on my breath. Black spots cloud my vision, and I feel myself losing my balance. Jack's image fades from my view as someone helps me to the floor. As my vision gets darker, Dana's face appears above me against a blue sky backdrop.

"I believe in you," she says, her voice muffled, getting quieter by the second.

CHAPTER 7

Jenn

I awake to the sudden sound of a blood-curdling scream.

Springing up, I take in my surroundings. Maybe only 10x10 feet, the four of us are all in the small wooden cabin of the boat. A ladder leans up against one of the walls, leading up to a latch in the ceiling. Against an adjacent wall is a simple bed, consisting of an unstable rusty metal frame—one of the legs is shorter than the others to make it wobble, supporting a small rough mattress with a poorly woven blanket. There are two small windows: across the bed and across the ladder, allowing the intense sunlight to swarm the humid cabin.

"Aghhh!" the gruesome scream resounds again from the deck above us.

Jack's eyes dart over to the ladder, and he scrambles to his feet, reaching for his bow as he goes over to it.

"Jack!" Riley calls out in a hushed voice, her voice groggy as she wakes up. "Get back down here."

"Are you an idiot? What are you doing?" I retort.

"Don't you hear the yelling? We have to help," he replies hurriedly. By the time he reaches the top of the ladder, the yelling suddenly stops, and he freezes.

I blink my eyes a few times before rising to my feet as well, and I see Xander do the same. A thick layer of dust and dirt covers nearly everything, including the floor where I had just been lying. Dried mud fills the corners of the room and the wood splinters off the walls and floor. The whole place reeks of sweat and the mold that climbs onto the sides of the ladder and in between the cracks in the wooden floor. On one side of the floor, the wooden boards splinter up as the jagged end of a rock pierces through.

"The boat's not moving," Riley says, looking over to the window.

Ignoring the blinding sunlight, I peer out. Directly outside our boat, sunlight reflects off a bed of varying sized boulders, glazed by the ocean that gently brushes against their sides. Though beautiful, I know their rigid, sharp edges threaten our boat. This bed of rocks, only about the length of our ship, acts as the transition from water to land along the entire shore. The rocks gradually fade in numbers and size as the terrain shifts to a long shore of golden sand. The thickness of this sandy shore is about three times the boat's length before it transitions into a large forest of dark trees.

"We're here," I say before turning around back to the others.

"We should go up," Jack says, his ear now pressed firmly against the latch in the ceiling.

"What do you think happened?" Xander asks.

"The captain of the ship?" Riley speculates, looking over to Jack for confirmation.

"It's stuck," Jack says, attempting to push open the sealed latch.

"I'll get it," Xander offers, waiting for Jack to climb down before climbing up.

"Yay, King Loser, our hero," I murmur sarcastically under my breath.

"I'm just trying to help," Xander responds, yanking on the handle of the latch. "You don't have to be so vile about it."

"Vile is my middle name," I remark to which Riley just rolls her eyes. "You got something to say to me, Barbie?"

"Got it," Xander says proudly after ramming into the latch, making it fly open and causing dust to spray everywhere as well.

"They gave us a lock and key," Riley says, picking up the two items from on top of the mattress and inspecting them. "It's for the latch."

Xander climbs out of the cabin first. After waiting for his signal, we all follow suit.

A fresh blast of that sickening ocean air sweeps across my face as I emerge from the cabin. Having come up last, I have to push past the others in order to see what they are staring at. Like a leather grip, a thick shear of skin wraps tightly around a section of the ship's steering wheel on both sides where one would usually place their hands. The skin is coated with dark blood, which smears on the wood of the wheel as well and drips slowly onto the floor beneath it. Billy, the captain, is gone.

"What the hell?" I mutter, staring at the horrific image.

"His hands must have been glued to the wheel or something," Xander explains, his stare following the dripping blood that slides off the skin before joining the small crimson pool spreading on the deck. "It must've ripped off when he ran away."

"But why would he do that?" Riley stutters.

"I don't know," Xander murmurs. "Looking for food maybe? If his hands were glued to the wheel, he wouldn't have been able to eat."

"He would've starved to death if he had no food during the trip. They strapped a device on his abdomen to give him enough nutrients to get him through," Riley explains quietly, her eyes still staring in shock at the scene before us.

"Then why didn't we waste away?" Jack asks hesitantly, and I catch him trying to discreetly feel his stomach for any attached device.

"Encepalomortcet," Riley infers again, and Xander raises an eyebrow. "Freezes our biological clock. If that's what they injected us with, our bodies are exactly how we were when we stepped onto the boat at the BAA, physically."

Jack's jaw hangs open slightly as he stares at the deck before him, stupefied, while Xander just slowly nods.

"I would say something must've scared him off," I say, reverting the topic back to Billy.

"Like an animal?" Jack asks.

"Or a person," I suggest.

"Who even is he?" Riley asks, her eyes still trained on the wheel. "Where'd Headmaster get him?"

"Most likely an outcast. You become a nobody if you flunk out of your career sector. Headmaster takes advantage of that," I answer. Though her question wasn't explicitly directed at anyone, I could tell she was expecting an answer from me. I remember my dad telling me this information when I was younger to emphasize why I had to work hard. "He recruits them as free ship captains while helping to clean up our streets of Rejects. They're supposed to end up dying."

"Oh my god," Riley mutters.

"What? Were you hoping to hear about Billy's high-grade salary and his life in a luxury suite with a family of five?" I remark sarcastically.

"Where do you think he went?" Xander asks as he stares at the dense forest before us.

"That way," Riley says, pointing over to the opening in the forest where a bloody handprint marks a tree trunk. Her voice shakes slightly with concern, and I give her a look of disgust for not remaining strong in a tough situation. "My bag's filled with medical supplies. We could still catch up to him."

"Yeah, he obviously needs help. I think we should go after him. He couldn't have gone too far," Jack pitches in. Riley's gaze lingers on him for a little as he speaks.

"You guys know what this is, right?" I say, stepping in front of the others, who all give me questioning stares. "This could be the test. We need our captain back so that we can sail the hell off this island and back to the BAA."

"I don't know, I think we should think about this for a second," Xander chimes in. "We don't know what's out there. Let's just talk about this as a team—"

"There's no time for that. And just so we're clear: this isn't a team," I say, spreading out my hands as if laying out a map. "*I'm* the highest ranked soldier here, and so I make the calls here. Clear?"

Without even waiting for an answer, I begin walking toward the edge of the deck, trying to suppress my nerves. Folded neatly beside the ledge is a rope ladder made misshapen slabs of wood roughly strung together on either side. The apparatus hardly seems structurally sound, but it'll do. I climb down and land squarely on the soft sand below with the forest looming before me in my sights. Whatever had spooked Billy lies within those trees, but unlike him, this is what we were trained for: to be brave and face challenges head on. I need to follow through on that training, especially in my enrollment at the BAA depends on it.

"I'll get my backpack," Riley says as she quickly scurries from the deck. As I begin to trek across the sand, I hear footsteps behind me as the others gain up enough courage to follow my lead. I silently sigh with relief.

"You sure you know what you're doing?" I hear Xander ask, having jogged up to join my side.

"Maybe I'll finally find a worthy opponent to take me on. It'd be refreshing to have a real challenge for once," I boast confidently.

"The sooner we get this done with, the better," he says.

"Why are we talking?" I demand. "We're not friends, you know that, right?"

"Anyone ever tell you you're a great conversationalist?" he remarks.

"Fine, which of *your* relatives got you expelled?" I ask, rolling my eyes.

"Both of my parents worked with yours in the resistance," Xander says. My lips tighten reflexively, but I keep my gaze trained ahead, careful not to look at him. Beneath us, the ground fades from sand to grass as we enter the forest. "My dad's military, but my mom worked for the administration of the BAA. They're both executed by now. It makes you think, doesn't it? Why are our own military personnel helping the rebels?"

"No, as a matter of fact, it doesn't make me think anything," I say, still avoiding looking at him to feign disinterest. "I don't care what my parents did in their spare time. All my life, I've known the BAA and the military as somewhere I belong. Headmaster took that from me. My anger resides with Headmaster and Headmaster only."

"It's still so messed up, though," he says, following right behind me. "He's washing his hands of us like we're tainted. Making an example of us to the other Level 2 students to scare them into submission. It's the same thing they're doing with the executions of our parents."

"It's more than that with my expulsion," I continue. "He's taking advantage of my parents' mishap to get rid of the Bellators and re-name the school after himself. If I'm still there, he can't justify it, so he's going to say I was a threat too."

"That's a big assumption, you know," he says, and when I look over at him, I see his eyebrows furrowed in doubt.

"Well, I'm right," I retort quickly, narrowing my eyes. "But it doesn't matter. I'll be back at the BAA before he even has time to order a new sign for the school."

"Did you get a phone call with your parents?" he asks casually, and I feel a shiver run through me.

"No," I state. "Even if I did, my dad and I would have nothing to say to each other."

"They give them calls before their execution—"

"What are you doing?" I blurt out, stopping in my tracks and spinning to face him.

"What do you mean?" he asks, his eyes wide with surprise.

"Are you expecting me to start crying or something? Talk about my feelings?" I snap. "Just because I'm here, doesn't mean I'm not still the same cadet here as I was back at the BAA. This is all temporary until we get back to the BAA and I get my spot back. We have a mission in front of us. For right now, I'm focused on this mission and just this mission. You should do the same."

"My bad, 'Sergeant'," he mocks slowly. "But you do know the only other option for you to talk to is tweedle-dee and tweedle-dumb behind us."

"Don't remind me," I murmur and turn back around to continue walking. "Even back at the BAA, they both walk around with these wide eyes. It's like she's perpetually terrified of her surroundings and his brain is too small to even process his."

"You don't have to always do everything by yourself, you know," he says again calmly. "I know that if it was me it would be nice to see that someone has my back."

"I hate teamwork. If there's something that needs to be done, I can do it myself," I grumble through gritted teeth, unlatching my axe from my side to slash away a low hanging branch. "I don't give a crap about people, and you guys aren't special."

"I don't buy that," he objects, and I stop again when he appears by my side. "You can't hate everyone."

"Well, you're wrong," I comment bitterly. "I'm my father's daughter. I was born without a heart."

"We'll see," he says again with a small shrug as he moves around me to continue forward. My eyes follow him for a moment as he continues up through the trees before I start walking again. Behind me, Riley's and Jack's footsteps become audible.

***

With a swift swing of my axe, I slash away another group of underbrush hanging from a tree. We've been navigating the forest for what Riley has counted to be exactly thirty-two minutes following traces of blood on the trees that we assume belonged to Billy.

The forest is quiet; much quieter than I would've expected. Not an animal can be heard and even the buzzing of flies is inaudible — although the bug bites still scatter over my skin. I hear my stomach growl, breaking the silence of the forest, but I purposely slash away another bout of overgrowth to cover the noise.

"Hold up, guys," Jack suddenly calls out to us, and Xander and I instantly whip our heads back to him. Sitting on a large fallen tree trunk is Riley, who is holding her head in her hands while Jack stands over her.

"Quit with the drama act, you just got more sleep this past week on the boat than we all did in the last year; you have nothing to complain about," I scold with my arms crossed.

"I'm just a bit nauseous, Jenn," she says in an exhausted voice.

"You think a leisurely walk through the forest before breakfast is hard? We do worse each morning at the BAA," I say impatiently.

"I don't think a break would hurt anyone. Besides, the heat here is unbearable," Jack says, sitting down beside Riley.

"Oh, you two are such babies," I mock again in a disgusted tone. "While you stay here and feel sorry for yourselves, I'm actually going to go do what we're supposed to do. Figures I'm the only one taking this thing seriously."

I turn back around and push past Xander to continue trekking through the overgrowth. Suddenly, a sharp scream resounds through the forest, sending a shiver down my spine. I take one quick look back at Xander before taking off in the direction of the noise. Leaves and branches smack my face as I run past them, keeping my mind focused on the source of the consistent screaming.

One second I'm bursting through the trees, and the next I'm stumbling on the grassy floor as a blood curdling shriek pierces my eardrums. I see our one and only captain on the floor and realize that I must've collided with him in my haste. His face is sallow, an ill-looking yellowish color with blue pulsing veins clearly visible under his thin skin. His strained eyes bulge out of his head with such intensity, it hurts just to look at it. I watch as his exhausted figure crawls across the grass to crumple lazily against a nearby tree and hold both of his bloody hands up for protection.

"Oh god, you're more pathetic in person," I remark, standing up. Riley scurries past me and over to him, with Jack carrying her backpack and quickly following behind.

"It's alright, we're here to help you and get you back to the boat," she mutters reassuringly, crouched down beside him as Jack opens the medical backpack for bandages.

"Go, leave," Billy moans, frantically glancing around at the trees. His voice is as broken as is his appearance, and it squeals with the vitality of someone without a will to live. "This isn't a test, you're not meant to go back. You have to leave before they get you."

"Who is 'they'?" I demand. "What are you talking about?"

"Behind you!" the old man shrieks, his eyes full of fear. Instinctively, I spin around just in time to grab the two raised arms coming at me.

As I resist my attacker, I reopen my eyes to see the man whose snapping jaw is only inches from my nose. The skin on his face is a decaying gray color and rotted and thinned to the point that I could see each individual vein in his strained face. A potent, toxic stench emits from his mouth, instigating my gag reflex. The lips that were expected to surround the mouth had been either torn or rotted away and now fully expose his yellowed teeth which chomp at me feverishly. His eyes are fully widened, staring at me in surprise yet still distant as though he wasn't even looking at me at all. It's as if he had no consciousness of what he's doing.

Just as my arms are beginning to weaken against his strength, the crazed man collapses to his knees. Jack's arrow pierces his thigh, and taking advantage of my attacker's position, I thrust out a powerful kick to his jaw. This sends him flying backwards onto his back, but yet he instantly picks himself off the floor unhindered. His eyes lock on me again.

Xander appears behind him, unsheathing his long sword. He holds back the man's arms to restrain him and places his blade against his neck, waiting for him to stop resisting. It's then that I notice my attacker's shirt: green with the BAA insignia detailed under the number '2' on his left pec.

The man doesn't stop struggling, and his chaotic movements weaken Xander's hold on him. In his struggle, the man recklessly jerks his body to get away and, in doing so, slices his neck across Xander's thick blade. Jets of blood spray out of the man's neck, collapsing onto his shirt and hiding its BAA indicators under a crimson sheath. Yet, unimpeded by the significant amount of blood pouring out by the gallons, he continues to wriggle free of Xander's grasp and stumbles forward to me again.

As he gets near, I swing around, sending my foot flying again straight into his forehead and knocking him back down on his back. My adrenaline pumping through my veins, I know this is my moment. It's a sickening thought, but I don't have the chance to think about it. I twirl my lightweight axe once in my hand before swinging it back down into my attacker's chest. His rib cage caves in under the powerful weapon and I feel my blade puncture his internal organs. Satisfied, and horrified, with my work, I rip my axe from his body and spray blood and pieces of tissue through the air.

We all stand around the disfigured beast, inspecting its mutilated body. Then, collectively stopping all of our hearts, the man stirs again. His eyes flick open and his jaw snaps desperately at the air as he tries to get back up.

Jack slips another arrow from his quiver, notching it quickly into his bow before pulling the string back, aiming it, and then letting it fly into the beast's face. Everyone stands in shock and fear at the creature that now lay still in the dirt, a long arrow protruding from its forehead. A trail of blood slides down his face in a jagged river as it bumps into the creases and wrinkles of his leathery skin.

"Guys we should get going," I warn, eyeing more moving figures in between the trees. Beside me, Jack hesitantly retrieves his arrows from the creature's body. "I'll lead us back. Behind me, Jack. Xander, you and Riley help Billy."

"I'll run first and clear the path. I'm strongest, they'll face me first," Xander says hurriedly, already jogging away. "We go this way."

"Xander!" I scold, astonished at his rejection of my plan. "Get back here and go with the plan!"

"I want to stay with Riley," Jack contests, dragging my attention as Xander heads into the tree and begins clearing the overgrowth with his sword.

"No, and keep an arrow in that bow at all times," I command, gesturing a chopping motion to direct him to follow after Xander.

"C'mon!" I yell back to Riley, who struggles to pull the older man.

Grudgingly, I fall back to drape Billy's other arm over my shoulder. As we dart through the forest, shadows flash between the trees as more threats close in on us.

"Where are they coming from?" Jack yells out, glancing frantically around us. Just as one of the cannibals comes out of the forest, Jack instinctively pulls back his bow, letting an arrow fly into its shoulder. The man, wearing a dirt-stained orange jumpsuit, stumbles back from the force but recovers quickly in his pursuit of us.

"We just have to push just a little harder, Billy. We'll get there in no time. You're safe," Riley encourages as we help Billy walk. I mentally urge him to keep moving and rush faster forward; I can now just barely see Xander ahead of us.

Devoid of any energy, Billy collapses to the ground, pulling down Riley with him. She struggles to help him up and the moaning of the approaching beasts increases.

"Come on, we don't have time for this," I say impatiently while trying to hide the fear in my voice. I roughly yank Billy back to his feet, and Riley scrambles to her feet as well to resume her position.

"Billy, you can do this," Riley says again, draping his arm over her shoulder. I look around for Jack and Xander but all I find is a thick wall of the underbrush of the forest, painted with the shadows of the approaching monsters and flashes of their orange jumpsuits.

"We have to go," I repeat as the haunting sound of moaning resounds from the forest. "Riley, you carry him on your own."

"Oh god," Riley says under her breath in a panic, eyeing the shadows in the trees.

Suddenly one comes out of the forest, invoking a gasp from Riley. He's smaller than the other ones we saw—actually he's smaller than me. I hesitate, examining his younger build as he limps toward me with hungry eyes and a snapping jaw. I wait for him to come closer before kicking him back easily. He stumbles back, and I follow up with sweeping his legs from beneath him, letting him crumble to the floor. He doesn't wear an orange jumpsuit like the others, and underneath the faded red staining on his shirt, I can make out the number '1' on his left pec.

"Follow the broken overgrowth!" Riley calls out through heavy breaths from behind me. Up ahead, I spot broken branches and torn leaves: that's the way.

We try to run as fast as we can through the dense forest. I try to lead the way, but Riley ends up calling out the directions, easily spotting any signs of Xander and Jack's path. When it's not clear, I use my axe to swiftly slash away any stray low hanging branches blocking our path. The stench of the beach grows stronger with each step we take. Even Billy has acquired a newfound strength and runs with Riley.

It all happens so fast. As Riley and Billy round a tree, a child is already emerging from the overgrowth beside them. With rotted skin and a grisly appearance, the child wears the same dark, blank expression as the others. I assume it must have been a girl by the long strands of muddy hair draped over her face. It doesn't matter.

She reaches out and is able to snag ahold of Billy's free hand. Billy's body is jerked back by the forceful grab, causing Riley, with one arm around his waist, to stumble mid-step as well. Not even given time to react, they both watch with frozen horror as the child, latching on with a cannibalistic hunger, immediately pulls Billy's wrist toward her mouth. Copious amounts of blood cascades quickly off his skin as she sinks her teeth deep.

Riley releases an extended, utterly horrified scream as the child then tears off the mouthful of flesh. Major blood vessels and strips of skin stretch away from the rest of Billy's arm as the child wrangles with her bite from the heavily vascularized area. She cranes her neck sharply, ripping off the bite successfully while spraying drops of blood across both Billy's and Riley's faces. Unable to fully comprehend the situation, my eyes shift into overdrive, rapidly switching focus between the murderer and the victim.

Blood spurts and pours from the broken arteries and the old man he shrieks while watching. Riley tries to pull Billy as she lurches desperately away from the feasting cannibal, but the child maintains her hold on her precious meal. In an act of impassioned defense, she lashes out with a high kick at the grisly attacker, striking her straight in the face and knocking her to the ground. Losing consciousness, Billy is also losing his stance. He lays his head on Riley's shoulder, but she fumbles to hold his weight.

"Riley!" I call out, running over to help carry Billy.

Before I can grab him though, yet another cannibal appears, sinking its teeth directly into Billy's exposed neck. With ravenous hunger, the cannibal rips a large chunk of flesh out, and jets of blood gush from the hole made. In addition to soaking the old man's own chest, the crimson blood sprays out and all over Riley who, still screaming, finally releases Billy and collapses backwards.

I manage to wrap my arms around Riley from behind, frantically yanking her to her feet as more brutes wander closer yearning for their own taste of Billy's blood.

Together, Riley and I run from the scene, only looking back once to see Billy disappear in the growing crowd.

The sight of so much blood makes my stomach churn. I've never been afraid of blood; in fact, I've actually longed for the day when I'd be on the battlefield and see the blood pouring from my enemies. Though this is nothing like my fantasies: this is a real life.

We burst out onto the sand and sprint across the shore to the boat where Xander and Jack both have been anxiously awaiting our arrival. Upon seeing us, Jack drops his aimed bow and instantly runs forward to catch Riley in his arms in an embrace.

"You're okay. You're okay…" he comforts her, hugging her tightly in his arms and smoothing her hair.

I look back up at Xander who is already staring back at me. He doesn't bother asking where Billy is. He knows, and he knows we could be next.

CHAPTER 8

Riley

"Jack, lock the door," Jenn commands as we scramble into the cabin below the deck. Her voice is stern and cold, and I find myself fearing it somewhat like I fear the voice of Sgt. Blue.

"How?" he asks quickly, walking down the ladder behind me.

"I'll do it," Xander offers, moving around Jack and climbing back up the small ladder to secure the lock on the latch. "How far were they when you got away? Are they still coming?"

"I don't know. There's no telling what they'll do," Jenn murmurs, frantically checking the window.

The images of Billy being devoured back in the forest burn into my memory, and when I look up at Jenn, I can see it's the same for her too. She hovers at the window, and I watch her shoulders heave up and down slowly. Her eyes stop darting between the trees and settle into a glossy stare. After another few moments, she tears herself away from the window.

"You *left* us," she scolds, though the hidden emotion beneath her stern voice unsheathes itself for just a moment to allow a squeak to slide into her words. Her attention is trained on Xander. "You didn't listen to my order, I was supposed to lead at the front of the group, but you ran ahead and then you *left* us!"

"We ran straight into a pack of them, I was leading them away-"

"You stick to your job! We were carrying an *injured* man!" Jenn exclaims again, her rage accentuated into a frenzy. I cower under her shouts and instinctively dart to the window to check the treeline again.

"I was leading them away, and I called for Jack to help me, and it *worked,*" Xander continues earnestly. "We were heading into a dangerous situation straight into a crowd. We would've been surrounded. Jack and I did the best we could, but by then, we lost our way and decided the shore was the safest direction to go to meet with you."

"And you left us defenseless. You disobeyed me, and then you abandoned us," Jenn spits. "That's not a team."

"Oh now you're all about teamwork?" Xander remarks, throwing up his hands mockingly.

"I'm about doing what we came here to do, and staying alive while doing it!" Jenn yells. When she hesitates in her next words, I can see her lip quivering just slightly. She heaves another breath. Pushing out her jaw, she pushes rage into her words. "And now a man is dead because of you. Our ship captain, nonetheless."

"I'm so sorry, Riley, we really tried," Jack suddenly says from my side. The blood staining my clothes had rubbed off a little on Jack as well so that we're both smeared in Billy's blood. I don't respond.

"I'm sorry," Xander says, turning his head toward the ground.

"You better be," Jenn sneers at both of them. "Next time…listen to my direction when I give it. We're not here to play."

"What even are they?" Xander asks, pivoting the conversation.

"Bunch of cannibalistic natives," Jack mutters, his quiet voice still humbled.

"Most were wearing orange jumpsuits," Xander adds. "Probably some sort of former prisoner colony."

"Not all of them," I say, my voice almost inaudible. "Some were wearing BAA clothing."

"What?" Jack says, having been the only one attentive enough to hear me.

"They were wearing our clothes. Different levels. It's just…" I say hesitantly, now under the stare of everyone. "Remember George Tursin?"

"What?" Jenn says as she contorts her face in confusion and irritation.

"He was in our platoon. He got expelled at the end of last year for being the lowest rank, right?" Xander explains for me, and I nod.

"I saw him," I say eerily. "When we were patching up Billy."

"The one that attacked me?" Jenn asks, her expression still unchanged. "No way."

"You saw him; he was still wearing his Level 2 shirt. It was him…but different. He changed," I continue. "I think it's something on the island that is making them act like this."

"Like what?" Xander asks, intrigued.

"I don't know," I say under my breath. "A disease? A parasite? Maybe one that impacts the brain? He used to be one of us and now all he wanted to do was kill us…bite us. Just like everyone else we saw in the woods. That little girl with Billy…"

"Like rabies," Xander adds. "Makes the infected person aggressive."

"But in this case, it makes them also cannibalistic," Jenn states.

"We killed George," Jack says under his breath, stealing a glance at Xander and Jenn before letting his eyes rest on a spot on the wooden floor, seemingly mesmerized.

"No, we didn't," Xander says, less reassuringly and more matter-of-fact as he tries to make sense of things. "He was already far gone with whatever sickness was eating his brain. It wasn't him as we knew him."

"What's happening?" Jack shakes his head, still taking everything in. I wonder if his heart is racing almost as fast as mine. "And his skin…it's like he was rotting away."

"The person inside him was dead," Jenn says.

"I agree," I say, and Jenn locks eyes with me. "You could see it in their eyes. They're not conscious of what they're doing. Like a machine."

"A machine that tries to eat us?" Jack suggests, frightened by the thought. "How is that possible?"

"Stop asking so many questions, Peabrain. You think we know the answer?" Jenn snaps, making Jack jolt.

"How can you be sure it was even really George?" Xander asks, horrified as well.

"I…I guess I'm not," I admit.

"It doesn't matter if it was him or not," Jenn states. "The fact is that these people were wearing BAA outfits and acting rabid. That's all we know and all we need to know."

"And that it's possibly contagious," I interject. "Everyone seems to have it here so we need to be…"

Suddenly, I feel the warm touch of skin graze across my hand: Jack's hand. Hesitant at first, and without daring to look up at me, he slides his hand in mine so that our fingers are intertwined. It's an unknown touch. The rough skin of his fingertips that brush against my hand could've belonged to anyone, even a stranger's, and I wouldn't have been able to tell; but, it's his. His gentle caress is a feeling that engrains from the muscle memory of my skin to the deepest parts of my brain. Frozen with uncertainty, it takes me a moment before my fingers gradually curl into his so that we entwine more. Even then, he won't look at me. With my heart racing, I think back to when he kissed me in the middle of the BAA hallway.

***

We don't move from the lower deck for the rest of the day, fearful of those undead creatures returning. We figure that the boat is the only place we knew was safe for sure and that it would act as a hiding spot should the creatures come back.

"Where are they?" Jenn mutters under her breath, finally tearing herself away from the window. She's been standing beside it, keeping a constant vigil on the treeline. Outside, the sun is now beginning to set, casting a deep orange light across the beach and decreasing our visibility of what lies between the trees.

"They must be at a different part of the beach," Xander grumbles. He slouches on the ground, leaned up against the wall across from the ladder with his arms outstretched across his bent knees. "While we holed up in here, we could've been gone by now, gotten a head start to the other side of the island,"

"There is no head start," I respond, my head shaking autonomously. Like a video, Billy's death plays over on repeat in my mind: the blood, the screams, but most importantly, the eerie silence as we left him behind. My lip quivers in horror as I continue. "They can be anywhere, everywhere. We happened to be in their way."

"Plus, we don't want to be on any other side of the island," Jenn states. "We need this boat to get out of here."

"How? Do you know how to sail this boat back? 'Cause I certainly don't," Jack mutters. It's more than frustration, though. With feelings of sadness and fear mixed in, it's hard to decipher exactly how to feel. He sits beside me on the bottom bunk of the bed, and my eyes linger on him as he talks. Ever since our hands separated, I've been yearning for his touch again.

"Well, you don't know how to do anything," she immediately snaps back. "It's bad enough that I'm the only skilled one on this ship. Am I really the only one who can put effort in? I'm starting to think that none of you even want to go back to the BAA."

"Our ship captain just *died*," Jack exclaims, raising his voice a little in exasperation.

"Jack's right. And our boat is probably damaged from the landing across the rocks," Xander reasons. Devoid of energy, he talks slowly and lets his head nod with his words. "You see the boat they gave us. This isn't a military boat; it's scraps thrown together for a one-way trip."

"First of all, Jack is a dimwit. Second, I'm sorry, I may be mistaken, but didn't we just come from a military academy? I didn't realize that cadets would give up so easily in the face of misfortune," Jenn remarks, crossing her arms. In the dim light that breaks through the glass of the window, her tanned skin is highlighted, illuminating her the most among the group. "I'm *serious*, people. Sure, we're expelled. We all have treasonous relatives that got us into this mess. But we're still capable cadets, so stop acting like dead weight."

"Jenn, there's no need to be—" Xander begins, but his voice drags too slowly, and Jenn doesn't let him finish.

"No, Xander, when the going gets hard, you have to go harder," she immediately barks.

"Trust me, I want to get off this island just as much as you do," I add from where I sit cross-legged at the edge of the bottom bunk. "We just need a moment to just take in everything that's been happening."

"Can it, Barbie," Jenn commands sharply.

"I actually have a question," I say hesitantly again, trying to ignore Jenn's disapproving glare. "Let's just say we do figure out how to get this boat into the water, what do we do then? How do we navigate back home?"

"We'll figure out a way," Jenn says, throwing her hands up in an exaggerated shrug.

A silence follows. Xander slouches further down the wall, keeping one leg bent up and the other flat.

"Alright," Jenn says, dragging out the word. "I'm going to give this ship a quick checkup to see what we're dealing with. Barbie, come with me. We'll be right back."

"Ok," I mutter. As I separate from Jack, I already start to feel devoid of the comfort his presence gives me. At this moment, there's nothing I would rather want than to snuggle up with him and rest for the day. I suspect Jenn just wants me as a reference if she doesn't know what she's looking at. Besides, if I don't go, we'd never hear the end of it.

Together, Jenn and I travel to the back of the boat. The sun is finally setting, casting a dim but beautifully colored light across the water and coating everything in an orange and pink hue. Still, the calming incandescence of the sun doesn't make the sight of the wrecked boat less disheartening. Wood splinters and fragments scattered across the sharp rocks, which have completely torn through the bottom of the boat.

"Damn," Jenn remarks as we stare at the shredded boat. "Unfixable, right?"

"I think so," I agree, glancing into the water where more of the wreckage hides. "The boat won't sail with the bottom filling up with water. The water will seep through the breaks in the lower deck and the boat will sink..."

"Damn…" she repeats.

"We watched someone die." I don't know why I said it. Maybe because I haven't been able to truly think of much else besides it. Maybe I just wanted her to agree with me and verify that it wasn't just in my head.

Slowly, she rises to her feet, holding her hands up in defense. "If you need a pep talk, you talk to your boyfriend, not me."

"You were there," I say again, watching her. "You saw the same thing I did. Those things tore him apart and…ate him. How can you be so put together after something like that?"

"Because if you haven't already noticed on so many, many, occasions, Riley, me and you are completely two different kinds of people," she replies with a shrug.

"You can't tell me it wasn't…terrible," I say, unsure of an adjective that could pinpoint the horror.

"It was…gruesome," she admits, her eyes wandering down a little. She then takes in a deep breath and collects herself. "But you know what? Maybe it's better for him this way. He was suffering while he was living. Maybe those things did the poor man a favor."

"A favor!" I shout in disbelief. "Geez, what is wrong with you?"

"What?"

"You can't honestly think his death was a favor," I say, dumbfounded while staring at her wide-eyed. I can feel my energy spike in my tired body.

"I *think* that if I was constantly in his state then yes, maybe it is a blessing in disguise," she says again sternly.

"Just…stop," I say, holding up a hand and closing my eyes. I feel vomit building up in my throat, but I force myself to swallow it. "Just stop talking."

"What? The man was crazy. Completely mental. He was glued to the boat. He was beaten up. He was suffering. What's the point of living at that point?" she argues pompously, defensive at my disagreement.

"You are sick, you know that?" I say, shaking my head in disgust.

"No, I'm not. Why do you care so much anyway?" Her voice is especially vile as she taunts. I sense a curiosity in her insistence in this conversation, as if she's arguing just to argue and wants to push me to see what happens. "He wasn't anything to you. Even if he lived, he would just be a burden to us."

Unable to hold my vomit back anymore, I turn to the side and throw up onto the sand. Jenn looks on with disdain.

"You have got to man up, Riley," Jenn scorns, folding her arms. Still leaning over, I glare at her. "Did you learn nothing at the

BAA? We're trained for this. Prepared for situations like this. We're supposed to be able to handle death."

Without the burning sun above, the heat of the island has begun to withdraw as well, and a cool breeze sweeps across the shore from the ocean. Stranded on this island with my hands on my knees and the taste of bile on my tongue, I've never felt weaker. I've never felt more alone as Jenn berates me, unaware I'm in my third month of pregnancy.

"I *know* what we learned at the BAA," I say, forcing my voice through my tired lips. I push myself up again.

She looks like a stranger to me. Back at the BAA, we used to get training scenarios like this to test how we would react. She'd always be serious and disconnected emotionally, like a robot going through the motions. I always figured it would be different when it became real. I was wrong. She's still just as cold and disconnected.

"But how?" I finally continue. "How can you just…be so ok?"

"Because I'm a soldier," she says matter-of-factly. "If you want to survive, Riley, if you want to be a soldier…you're going to have to get stronger. Being weak isn't going to get you anywhere. Especially not here."

"There's a difference between being weak and being human, Jenn," I say through gritted teeth.

"Is there?" she asks before turning around and walking away.

"Soldiers are human, Jenn," I call out, but she isn't listening. I wait a moment before following her to the deck.

At the wheel, Xander and Jack are examining the skin still attached to the wood. Jack glances over, but I head straight for the cabin, hanging my head low so as to not attract attention.

"How's the back?" I hear Xander ask Jenn.

"Trashed…all of it. We can't fix it," she replies, putting her hands on her hips.

"What happened with her?" He asks, lowering his voice to almost a whisper.

"She's just being dramatic about Billy's death," Jenn replies, just as quiet.

I quickly open the latch and slip into the lower deck, closing the door behind me to shut their voices out. I drag my body over to the lower bunk again and let myself curl up lazily on the stiff mattress. It doesn't provide much comfort but at least it gives me a place to lay my head.

Looking over to the window across the room, I stare at the horizon. The red sun has now nearly completely disappeared behind the edge of the sea and left little orange fire to blend into the dark sky above it. The water sparkles with radiant colors as it reflects the sky. The wind seeps through the cracks in the walls and bites at my skin, forcing me to feel the sharp chill of the night.

It won't always be like this, I think silently to myself. *We'll make a home. And then, people will come back for us and whisk us away on another ship. We'll sail and never stop sailing until we've reached a kinder place. They'll come.*

"When you walk do you start with your left or your right foot?" Jack asks suddenly, taking me by surprise as he descends the ladder into the lower deck.

"I...don't know," I answer, furrowing my eyebrows.

"I wonder if people are right foot or left foot dominant," he continues, striding over to me.

"What are you doing down here?" I ask plainly, and then turn over in the bed to face the wall instead.

"Well, I started off just walking across the deck to see which foot I led with..." Jack begins and then stops, confused as usual. "What's wrong?"

"I don't know," I mumble as he sits on the edge of the bed inches from my back. I feel my heart stop for a beat, and I have to remind myself to finish my thought. "I just…I know he wasn't much but…Billy…"

"It was pretty traumatic for you," he says, and a silence follows. Just as I'm closing my eyes, he speaks again. "Can I hold you?"

"Yes," I say softly, trying to hide the shaking in my voice. I hear him shift on the bed beside me until I feel his arm drape across my waist. "You know I'm always here for you, right? If you need me. Or even if you don't need me."

"It wasn't just traumatic, Jack," I say again, my voice almost a whisper.

My words hang in the air for a while and the silence begins burning. My cheeks beat bright red as I struggle to contain all the emotion that's been building up within me. Anguish, fear…rage.

Combined, they build up a pressure inside my chest that makes me want to explode for a release. The pressure rises to my throat. Suddenly, I pull away from Jack's hold, sitting up on the edge of the bed, and he does the same.

"Can I…tell you things," I ask hesitantly, feeling the vomit leave my throat. I only steal a quick glance over at him when he doesn't respond right away. "Is that ok?"

"Ok," he says, not quite grasping my words.

"I remember when my parents told me that I got into the BAA," I mutter. "I had no say in applying, of course, but I knew of the accomplishments they made in the military, and I was so proud to become like them."

"You *are* like them, Riley," he offers as reassurance.

"I'm not. My parents knew Headmaster; that's what got me enrolled in the BAA. I don't even think I passed the BAA entrance exam," I say, letting out a pained laugh. I take a breath before continuing, letting my voice descend again into a serious tone as I speak the thoughts that I've never shared with anyone before. "When their airplane was shot down, I was 10 and stranded in a life that I realized I didn't want to be a part of and didn't fit in with."

"Riley…"

"I really wanted to save Billy. I *really* wanted to. It wasn't his fault he's here. He was just like us. He did nothing wrong." My eyes begin to glisten with tears, and I choke on my words. "I thought that maybe if we helped him then *maybe* things wouldn't be that bad. And *maybe* it was justified why I became a cadet and that it wasn't just all a big mistake. But this island…I'm not cut out for it. I never was. I'm never going to be the soldier my parents were."

"Come here," he says, leaning down to pull me into a hug. Embraced by his warm body, I slouch into him, hypnotized by the feeling of protection and safety. "You are cut out for this."

"I don't want to be," I say again, and my welling tears finally spill over into a soft sob.

"I know," he says quietly as I cry into his shoulder.

"I'm so sorry," I say, retracting from him. "You don't want to hear my complaining."

"What are you saying? Of course I do," he objects quickly. He takes a moment before continuing. "My uncles were executed for working with the rebellion."

"I'm so sorry," I say, taken aback by the sudden confession.

"My relation to them is what I was expelled for," he explains. "If you're being so open with me, I want to be open with you. We don't really have anyone else right now."

"Thank you," I say, offering a small smile. "I'm sorry to hear about what happened to your uncles. It must've been hard for you."

"Maybe it was for a reason," he replies. "I mean I wouldn't have wanted you to be alone out here. You shouldn't have to go through anything alone anymore."

"Why?" I ask, daring to look at him through low eyes.

"Because," he starts, but stops midway, dumbfounded with his mouth slightly ajar. It's as if lost for the words to describe something he sees as so obvious. "I'm the father of our child."

"Is that all?" I ask again but regretting it instantly. I should've just accepted his answer. It was sweet and now I'm pushing things. Yet, a part of me is glad I said it. I want to hear it; I need to know, and I need to hear it right now.

He looks at me for a moment— this time, lost for all words. He knows what I'm saying, but he doesn't know how to say it because we never have— to each other or anyone in our lives. My heart is racing as I wait anxiously for his response, and I wonder if he can hear it as it flutters. Finally, he responds.

"No," he says quietly— quiet enough to mask the slight quiver in his voice. His blue eyes are trained on mine with unwavering and earnest eye-contact, and his eyebrows are slightly raised. I wonder if he's self-conscious of his heartbeat, too. "I'm here for you. Baby or not."

Somehow, in my darkest time, he made me smile. Seeing this, a small comforting smile blooms on his lips as well. I bring my hand up to caress his cheek before pulling him into a long, meaningful kiss.

***

The next day is spent mostly doing nothing. We're not sure what's safe to do.

There's a loud crash as Jack smashes the window in the lower deck with Jenn's axe. Instantly, fresh air smelling of seawater pours into the cabin, replacing the humid heat.

"Ah, much better," he says with a huge smile, clearly just as exhilarated by the idea of smashing something as he was by the fresh air. "It's so muggy in this cabin."

"Be careful, there's glass everywhere," I point out from my spot at the base of the ladder.

Using one of my knives, I cut off the pant legs to my jeans, turning them into shorts. After slipping them back on, I shove the pant legs into my backpack and turn to the bucket on the floor before me. I splash some of the water in my face and then take a rag to wipe it dry. The water mats down the free strands of hair that border my face, having fallen out of the loosened ponytail that flops against my neck.

"You can't tell me it doesn't feel better in here now," Jack says, breaking off any glass shards still attached to the window frame as crisp fresh air rushes in. When he turns around to look at me, I see that his hair is matted with sweat and his shirt dampened around the collar. "It's a beautiful night out. Hey, come here."

"There's glass everywhere—"

"Well, don't step on it then. C'mon," he quips lightheartedly, and I grudgingly walk over. He wraps his arms around me in a hug from behind and holds us in place to face the window, looking out into the night.

"It's pretty," I say quietly, leaning my head back against him. Still, as I take in the view, I find myself scanning for the sight of a boat on the horizon. There's nothing but the vastness of the sea.

"You're pretty. And look, Mars is out. The big one right there," he says.

"That's the moon, you dufus," I respond, rolling my eyes jokingly.

"Let's pretend it's not," he says again and though I can't see him, I know he's flashing a goofy smile. I shake my head, shutting my eyes as I chuckle.

"Just…be careful of the glass," I say as I separate from him again, careful not to crunch on top of it myself.

I squat down and begin gathering up the largest shards of broken glass before standing back up to assemble them in a pile in the corner. Suddenly, I'm knocked off my feet but instead of falling back, I'm swooped up in Jack's arms bridal-style. I wrap my arms around his neck as he spins, swinging me around with him. Finally, after dancing around the room, he slows to a stop, placing me on the bed and leaning in so that our noses barely touch. With one hand around his neck, I bring up the other one to place on his chest and feel his heart beating like mine.

"What was that?" I ask through my laughter.

"I just really like seeing you smile," he says.

"Well, it worked," I joke, smiling brightly.

He hasn't taken his eyes off of me, and his lips still curve into his silly grin. He suddenly shoots forward and places a quick kiss on my lips.

My breathing nearly stops, and for a moment, I have the urge to cautiously look around for Headmaster's agents.

"No guards to catch us," I say, raising my eyebrows in excitement.

"A silver lining," he says.

"I agree," I whisper, my smile still beaming. *This*, I remind myself silently, *this is the paradise you chose. No regrets.*

I reach out and caress his cheek. His jaw is rough with the ends of and I run my fingers over it. His hair is also starting to grow out from his once shaved head and prolonged exposure to the sun has started to turn it a lighter brown.

"Stop touching my beard," he teases, whisking his head to the side, and I shut my eyes in a laugh. When I open them again, he's frozen in place with his head still turned to the side.

"Jack?" I ask hesitantly, sitting up as my grin fades like the color from his face. "What's…"

My words trail off when I follow his gaze out the window in the cabin that peers out onto the sand beside the boat. It takes me a moment to decipher the image but then I see it. In the darkness of the night, the moon casts dim light upon an enormous herd of black figures walking along the shore toward us, rapidly approaching.

"Stay here." Jack is already off me and starting toward the ladder.

"Where are you going?"

"Jenn and Xander are still outside. I have to warn them."

"I'm coming with you," I say, standing up and going over to where he begins to climb the ladder.

"No, Riley, you have to stay here. Hide, I'll be right back," he insists, placing a hand on my shoulder earnestly before scrambling out onto the deck.

I immediately duck down, my eyes darting around the room, searching for a safe space. I crawl over to the window that looks out to the sea and stick my head out. On the other side of the boat opposite of the herd, I spot Xander and Jenn strolling along the shore. They've strayed farther than I thought, nearly the same distance away as the approaching horde. Jack runs to them and his silhouette shrinks and becomes less visible against the dark sky and darker sand with each step he takes. The only light comes from the moon, but its slight luminescence dwindles on Jack's body until he is just a small smudge of darkness in my vision. After a brief moment, I see his smudge, along with Jenn and Xander, flee into the water to hide within the rocks abutting the shore. I am alone.

I retreat back to the floor, fear pulsing throughout my veins. I feel my heart throb faster and shivers run up my arms as if the temperature had suddenly plummeted. Huddled on the floor, I can still see out the window to watch as hundreds, thousands— hundreds of thousands— of bodies wash across the sandy shore like molasses spreading out across a surface. Their horde covers the beach as far as I could see. Frozen in fear, I watch helplessly as they all walk across the sand like a constant machine, all searching for food.

I crawl underneath the bottom bunk, squeezing into the tight fit. From my spot, with the weight of the beds above me grinding my spine, I'm hidden from anyone— or anything, rather— that peers through the window.

I shut my eyes and, as the hour goes by, I listen to the hungry growls and sloppy footsteps outside as they continuously wander on through the sand, surrounding the boat. My breathing is ragged, and I try to control it to prevent the sound from potentially alerting anyone to my position. In an attempt to distance myself from my situation, I retreat to the place in my mind where I've always found solace and begin to mentally run over lines of prayers.

Bodies clumsily crash into the wooden sides of the boat as if trying to mimic the rhythmic waves of the sea beside us. Unlike the water, however, their thuds against the walls of the boat are uneven and rough.

At last, they begin to cease. Clutching my hands together, I begin to recite a prayer of thanks when suddenly a sound on the upper deck grabs my full attention. I hold my breath as I hear the creaking of wood and the squish of wet shoes sloshing against the floor. Its uneven, rough pattern matches the footsteps of the cannibals walking across the shore. I squeeze my eyes shut, wishing to be invisible. That's when I hear it step on the latch. The lock jingles and its metal knocks against the ladder.

The lock: it's open. My eyes shoot open and the being standing on top of the latch stops moving. The latch finally quiets, until the cannibal begins to move again, and it rattles again. There's a loud crash as they collapse onto the door, attracted by the sound. The force whisks the lock into its jingling dance again, letting it tease its fate several times before finally slipping from the latch on the door. Its drop feels like a bomb, and noise explodes as it clatters against the steps of the ladder before smacking against the wooden floor.

I know I only have moments before whoever is above me gets through. I try my best to squeeze out quickly from my place underneath the bed. Somewhat surprisingly, in trying to get to the intriguing sound below them, the cannibal hits on the door instead of opening it. Behind the sound of the banging, I hear a grunt of determination mixed with the building rage of frustration. The deep groggy voice leads me to believe I'm about to face a male.

As I scramble over to the ladder, he slams down hard on the door and it pops up briefly. Fear striking through my heart, I am clambering up the steps at this point. However, when I reach out to grab at the latch, the beast hits the door again and it catches on his foot, allowing space for him to fit his arm through. I slam the door down on his wrist, but he continues to push his arm through further. Slowly, his skin, squeezed between the deck floor and the latch door, peels back until he manages to reach nearly his entire forearm through the hole.

His peeled arm erratically, flinging the blood that's dripping from it. His possessed arm finally clenches my shoulder, and I feel my whole body crumble with fear and repulsion under the brutal grasp of his blood-seeking fingers. Blood splattered on my cheek, I swing my face away, gasping, when I feel my foot slip from my foothold on the ladder. Before I can fix my stance, I am thrusted backward, plummeting back to the wooden floor.

I feel my heartbeat pulsing blood all the way to my pounding head as I try to regain control of my spinning sight. Shapes begin to distinguish themselves again and I make out the image of the man at the top of the ladder. Propping myself up on my elbows, I barely have enough time to crawl backwards and out of the way before he crashes through the open door after me and tumbles down the ladder. He falls on his forearm, which splits in two. The bones pierce straight through his thin skin and his wrist and hand dangle uselessly. Still, blank eyes stare at me with a sociopathic frenzy. He reaches out, grabbing my ankle with his one good hand. Unlike the rabid cadets that had killed Billy, this man dons an orange jumpsuit and could blend in with most of his horde.

Kicking desperately and functioning purely off adrenaline, I reach back and grab the first thing my hand touches—the blanket on the bed. I rip the wool blanket off and throw a punch as hard as I can straight at my attacker's mouth just as it is about to wrap its jaw around my calf. My punch knocks in some of its teeth, but my fist is completely wrapped in the blanket so I remain unscathed. I shove the blanket into the beast's mouth in a panic, removing my hand, and it bites down as hard as it can on the rough cloth. My eyes dart around my surroundings again, absorbing every detail and looking for something easily accessible. I spot my belt of knives in the corner and instantly throw my body in its direction. With my reach limited by the beast's hold on my ankle, my fingertips are just able to reach the hilt of one of the knives and I hastily wiggle the blade out of its sheath. I feel the beast's grip tighten and the blanket fall loose from its mouth onto my foot. Just then, I shoot back up, sucking in a breath of air as I jam my knife straight into the eye of the monster. Blood sprays out as I force through the resistance of his brain.

He immediately stops moving, lying motionless on the floor before me. I am just as frozen as I stare upon the corpse of a man I killed.

At last, I slowly peel his dead fingers off of me and scramble to my feet. My hands shaking, I mindlessly pick up the lock on the floor and close the latch permanently; however, the silence of the night already tells me the majority, if not all, of the horde has already passed by. Exhaling a long breath, I stare down at the mess of blood under me.

Perched up on the ladder, I resume my frozen stance, subconsciously pressing my back up against the latch as if someone were trying to force their way in. Suddenly I hear footsteps above me and jolt alert. There's a soft knocking on the latch.

"Riley." It's Jack's voice.

A sense of relief overcomes me and I rip off the lock and swing open the latch before he could even repeat my name. I shoot out of the hole and leap into his awaiting arms. He staggers back a little but catches himself and wraps his strong arms around my back to pull me in closer. He's soaking wet, hiding the tears that I let fall freely into him.

"It's alright. It's ok," he whispers as he rubs his hand on my back.

CHAPTER 9

Jenn

Weeks fly by. It's been nearly a month and a half since the herd first swept the beach—Riley's been tallying the days on the floor. Since then, the herd sweeps by every few days, always from the same direction. We cower in the corners of the cabin for safety each time. We tried to create a raft out of the broken wood pieces on the boat so that we could sail out into the ocean, but nothing we threw together could get past the high waves offshore and we gave up after four tries. Our food supply has long since run dry as well. We had started spearing fish from the ocean, but other than a few small fish and oysters, it's been unsuccessful. Today, it was decided that we try the forest again.

We had started our hunting trip during sunrise, and in the hour or so since, I still haven't heard a single bird chirp or a single squirrel chatter. Silence. It's as if the trees themselves were afraid of the monsters that I know lurk between them.

We decide to space ourselves out a little to appear as less of a visible crowd to potential prey, minimize aggregate noise, and cover more ground. Jack is distanced just out of sight to my right while Riley is far to my left, though she occasionally strolls closer to remain within a more comfortable distance. With her throwing knives and his bow, they are our designated hunters, Xander and I walk together in the space between the two. Our main purpose is to hold any of the game and to be on standby in case we encounter any more of those eerie cannibals.

"Thanks for helping me out the first time we were in the forest. When that thing attacked me," I mumble to Xander in an uninterested tone. When I don't hear a response, I glance up to see him looking at me, his lips not so much smiling as his eyes were. "You and Jack came through for me. I realized I never thanked you."

"Jack was the hero there. He got it off of you," Xander says, shrugging it off.

"I'll have to thank him later," I say again, nodding.

"You sound surprised that he saved your life?"

"I just wouldn't have expected he would," I respond.

"Believe it or not, there are actually kind people in this world," he says with a quiet chuckle.

"Rarely, especially people from the BAA," I quip, careful to keep my voice down as I peruse the forest trees.

"You sure about that?" he replies, but I don't respond. He phrases the question to incite doubt with my opinion, but I know what he wants to say: *it's not them, it's you.* "Then consider me a better person than most of the BAA."

"Yeah, well, I'm not," I say with a shrug. "So, don't expect another 'thank you.'"

"To be honest, I wasn't even expecting the first one," he says, smiling. "Whenever someone tries talking to you, they usually end up regretting it. Or on the floor. I'm feeling pretty grateful right about now."

"What can I say? If you get too close to the snake, it bites," I gloat.

"Yes, ma'am," he replies, faking seriousness. "You know if you were larger and uglier, you'd be pretty intimidating. You would have made a great drill sergeant."

"*Would have?*," I repeat. "*Will* make a great drill sergeant. Future tense. If I choose to pursue that. My future's not over just because of this hiccup."

"Future tense," he repeats, catching my attention. "If there's one person that I know will make it off this island and make something of themselves, it's you."

I let out a small breath as a chuckle and turn my gaze to look between the trees. Just then, I hear a soft thud coming through the trees from my right.

"I'll go see what it is," I say to Xander before heading off, scanning the forest for glimpses of Riley's blond hair.

I find her crouched down beside an area of heavy overgrowth. Approaching, what first hits me is the heavy stench emitting from the area. Gag-inducing and putrid, a waft of the dense smell sticks to the back of my throat, burning. Only then, after covering my hands over my mouth, do I notice the severely decayed body of a girl in the overgrowth. Her small body is missing most of its skin and fleshy tissue, having lost it to time, allowing her bones to protrude prominently from underneath her clothing—an orange jumpsuit similar to the majority of the people in the herd on the shore.

"Saw the…shoe sticking out here," Riley chokes from her crouched position, hands cupping her mouth and nose, too petrified with utter disgust to move. Sticking lamely out of the woman's foot is one of Riley's silver throwing knives. "Thought it could've been…an animal or something."

Finally, unable to handle the stench, she gets up off the ground and staggers a good distance away before stopping and leaning over on her knees.

"Get a grip," I sneer, holding my breath as I pull the blade out of the corpse's shoe. Though the gruesome body appears aged by months of lifeless decay, there's a rather clean looking mark on the woman's forehead: an unmistakable stab wound. Something that clean, along with the surrounding undried blood, would hint that it happened not too long ago. She must've been taken down by someone. But…who?

"Jenn!" I hear Xander's voice in the distance. It hadn't occurred to me how far I've traveled from them.

I'm about to call back out to him when the breath is knocked from my lungs. Something wraps around my neck and I can't breathe. Something covers my mouth and I realize it's a hand. I try to move and break free but I can't; my restrainer is too strong. My eyes start to blur, the sight of the woman on the floor fading out of focus and the distant voice of Xander tuning out.

"Xander help!" It's Riley's scream.

I hear the whip of a knife fly past my ear and land with a hard thud into a nearby tree. My attacker is noticeably caught off guard by the way his grip on me loosens slightly and my vision shakes as he moves, dragging me along with him. I hear him struggle with someone with his other arm—probably Riley who I assume has tried to take some of my attacker's focus.

I bite down hard on what must be a finger, and I taste the salty blood ooze out. My kidnapper, a confirmed male, screams out in pain in a husky voice. The instant his grip loosens, I duck under and slide out. Though gasping for air, I spin back around, my heel flying into his chest. I attempt to do another flying kick but he grabs my foot mid-air, flipping it and causing me to fall down in the grass head first.

"Jenn!" Xander yells again as he bolts into view and lunges into the man behind me.

I turn and see them wrestling. By the looks of it, the man is a lot bigger than Xander and a lot more nimble and lively than the cannibals we've encountered. I charge into the brawl just to receive a heavy blow to the stomach that knocks me straight down. I clutch my stomach, doubled over in pain. The man is on top of Xander now, pressing a stick horizontally on his throat.

Suddenly an arrow shoots into the calf of the man and he screams, releasing his hold on Xander and falling back. Jack runs over, hooking his arms under the guy's shoulders, restraining him as Xander recovers, holding his throat. The stranger smashes Jack back against a tree and then turns around and delivers a blow to his face, blood splattering out onto the tree behind him.

I hear Xander audibly unsheathe his sword and I unclip my axe, but the man has already changed his attack. He drops Jack and swiftly yanks Riley in front of him. In an instant—almost too instinctively—he has his long dagger in his hand and pressed up against her throat.

"Let her go," I demand immediately, stepping closer, and from the corner of my eye, I see Jack scramble to his feet.

CHAPTER 10

Riley

The blade is cold against my flushed skin. It's only when you're on the receiving end of the blade do you truly notice how cold it is and how daunting that cold feeling can bc. It's the feeling of metal sharpened to the point where it has the capacity to slice through skin, through muscle, through blood vessels, and end everything. He wouldn't know it but he would end two lives with one kill.

My eyes flutter open and shut in waves as I try to control my heavy breathing, since every exhale pushes me ever so slightly into the blade at my neck. My eyes are wet and slick and through the flutters of my eyelashes, I see Jack not too far from me. He tries to aim an arrow steadily, but I notice the unusual sway in his bow from his shaking arms. He's never done that before. Would he be willing to kill him like this? Is that what we do now?

"Why'd you attack us?" Jenn demands.

"Did you see the size of that deer? Stuff like that is hard to come by. Taking down a few kids would be a lot easier than finding that again," he replies with a shrug. His voice is low and husky, dragging like the growl of a wild cat during a hunt.

Jenn looks over at Jack in confusion.

"I had been tracking the deer for a while but finally got the chance to shoot it at about the time you left," Jack explains quickly, only taking his eyes off me briefly to glance at Jenn.

"Take me to it," the man demands.

"Why would we do that?" Jack spits out at him. He's lowered his voice in an attempt to cover the waver in his voice. His aimed bow wavers more now as well, as fatigue begins to settle in from holding the string back.

"You caught a deer I want. I caught a girl you want. Would you like to make a trade?" the man behind the knife spits right back at him, giving his blade a little jiggle to emphasize his hold on my life.

"If we give you the deer, you'll let her go and you'll leave us alone," Xander states, laying out the terms of the deal.

"And if you don't…" the man growls, grazing his knife across my skin again.

"You die," Jack finishes, narrowing his eyes. I can't help but flush. It's sort of romantic to see him like this, no?

"I doubt it." The man's gruff voice brushes past close to my ear as he leans in teasingly. "But she will."

Jenn and Xander exchange shifty looks. But the decision is already made because there never really was one. By now, I'm sure they've all noticed the small gun hanging in a holster at the man's waist. Jack drops his aim.

***

Jack leads us to where he shot the deer, having left it in its place after hearing commotion coming from me and Jenn. I'm still hostage to the burly man, and we walk in the back of the group. He still wraps his arm around my shoulders, keeping the knife at my throat. He places his other hand against his thigh as he limps from the wound in his ankle. I wonder if Jack regrets not making the injury worse. He looks over his shoulder every now and then to make sure I'm alright. Worry streaks his face each time.

Finally, we make it. Lying dead beside a tree is the deer with an arrow sticking firmly out of its neck. There is a second arrow not far from it, coming in at a different angle, indicating that Jack must have shot it a second time while the deer was already staggering to the floor.

"There," Jack announces, defeated. "It's yours. Now let her go."

"Throw down your weapons."

"This wasn't part of the deal," Xander objects immediately.

"I'm making it part of the deal," the man barks back. "You still want the girl? Throw 'em down. Can't have you trying anything."

There's a long pause. Hard stares. Uneasy glances. I begin to wonder if they are contemplating if I'm worth it. I tell myself they're not, though.

Jack throws his bow down first, letting it clatter to the floor in front of him. Xander and Jenn follow suit and throw their weapons on the floor as well.

"Now step back," the man commands again, and they oblige. "More. More. Now turn around."

"No," Jenn states, her notoriously cold stare making the blade seem warm. "Let her go first. We did our part, you do yours."

"I'll do you one better." The blade at my neck suddenly clatters to the ground beside Jenn's axe, and there's a sudden release of pressure as he lets me free from his grasp. "Keep your deer."

A mixture of skepticism and utter confusion paints each of my friends' faces. Hesitantly, I step away from him and the others come to meet me. When Jack and I reunite, he pulls me in close to him.

This is the first time I actually get to have a clear look at my captor's gruff face. His chin, strong and firm, is coated with a thick black beard. Dirt covers his sunburnt and peeling cheeks and blends in with a few scars that run in all directions. His beady eyes narrow themselves into a permanent dark glare filled with intense seriousness and deep-rooted anger. His sharp eyes bounce off the others before landing on me, the intimidation making me shrink back. His eyebrows are thick and low and his unkempt mess of dark curls hangs above them. He wears the maroon Level 4 shirt, but the color is all but faded and the sleeves roughly torn off. With a young face, he appears to be in his early 20s. Yet, his build, though muscular, takes on a rugged form distinct from the sharply defined muscles of a BAA soldier. Rather than being built through PT, he's been hardened, strengthened, and yet worn down by the daily toils of the island. He's not new here.

When Xander takes another step forward, the man immediately straightens up, puffing up his chest as a gorilla would do to assert dominance.

"What's the catch?" Xander asks.

"None, keep it," the man says again. "I got a camp. Other survivors. Welcome you to join."

"I didn't realize there were other survivors here," I say, a sense of hope suddenly stirring within me.

"There aren't a lot," the man says again. "Mostly just undeads around here."

"Undeads? Is that what you call them?" Jack asks, still not trusting him.

"Pretty much sums them up, don't you think? Dead people come back to life as undead monsters. We call them what they are," he quips.

"Come back to life?" Jenn asks. Unwilling to drop her wary guard, her expression is straight-faced, but her tone conveys the condescending skepticism when asking a conspiracy theorist about their ideas.

"Yeah, come back to life," the man repeats firmly at Jenn as if daring her to call him crazy. "They were once people and now they're…well, they're 'undeads'."

"We think they have some sort of parasite or disease that's making them act like this," Xander suggests. "We're pretty sure it's contagious."

"Well, you got that last part right," the man scoffs. "But you clearly haven't seen the reanimations yet? Must be new around here?"

"He's toying with us," Jenn says.

"Wish I was," the man retorts simply. Curiously, I lift my gaze back up to him and my heightened eyes catch the slight sorrow in his. "Did the undeads bite any one of you?"

"No," Xander announces, glancing around at the rest of our shaking heads. "Who are you?"

"Who wants to know?" he replies nastily, his rough voice coming out as more of a grunt.

"You have a camp?" Jenn asks with suspicion, bringing the conversation back to his words earlier.

"Yeah," he answers. "We could use some new additions. Where were you guys camped up?"

"You still trying to rob us?" Jack asks, wary and hopelessly confused.

"If I wanted to rob you, I'd have slit your throat the moment you shot the deer," the man scoffs.

"I'd have heard you sneaking up on me," Jack contests.

"You didn't," the man says again, an eyebrow raised. "Been following you the past half hour."

"So why did you attack us then? Why pull this stunt?" Jenn inquires, except this time with interest rather than aggression.

"It was a test," I bud in when the man doesn't answer, and he looks over at me with surprise. "Your hold on me was too loose. You were controlling me, not restraining me. The blade was held too loosely too. You placed the middle part over my skin to emphasize its presence on my neck whereas if you really had the intention of killing me, you would have placed the end near the hilt on my skin so that your slice would drag more blade. You threatened us with your knife when you had a gun on your hip; if you were willing to take us out, you would've been better prepared with a weapon that outmatches all of ours. But, instead you used a knife, which gave the illusion that they could've fought you off the deer with me as the only casualty."

"You knew?" the man questions, his eyes narrowed.

"Not for certain," I correct, shaking my head, but that doesn't stop his smirk.

"Why didn't you say anything?" Jenn barks out accusingly, her temper triggered again and her arms folded. I see she's already retrieved her axe and attached it to her waist. "You just played along?"

"Not really. I could've been wrong. And if I wasn't, then there must've been a reason for what he was doing," I explain.

"You really do catch everything," Xander mutters, his eyebrows furrowed.

"I wanted to see how you'd respond," the man says, talking to the group, but his eyes are still on me. "Tested you in a fight first, which wasn't impressive by the way. Then your values. What meant more to you: your team or your food?"

"We pass?" Xander asks.

"Barely." His tone is sharp and rigid, but I can see the tips of his playful lips trying to resist a smirk. He knows he got us all scrambled and skeptical and he's enjoying the chaos he caused.

"We're camped on the shore on our boat," Xander finally says after a long pause, referring to the man's question from before.

"Your boat survived the rocks?" he asks, letting his shock overpower his intimidating facade momentarily.

It's now that I realize that his eyes haven't been still this whole time. He bounces them around between us and the surrounding trees, and I can tell his hearing does the same. I attribute it to acquired island-bred instincts, keeping him on his toes at all times and ready for any surprises. That's something the BAA can't teach you.

"I mean it's still trashed, but we made it to shore," Xander explains.

"Which direction did you come from?" the man asks suddenly, his face drawn in confusion.

"That way I think?" I respond, pointing through the trees. Jenn scowls at me for giving away information.

"The southern end of the island? Huh," he remarks and the rest of us exchange glances.

"What are you saying?" Jack asks.

"Most boats come from the east side. The shore there is littered with thousands of sharp rocks—and I'm not talking about the ones on the sand. Out a few hundred yards or so is a long stretch of rocks," he explains. He hides the pain in his left ankle from where he had been shot by Jack, and he leans on his right leg. "The boats always sink, and then the cadets have no choice but to swim to the island. We call it the Graveyard of Ships, and it's Headmaster's way of ensuring we can't get back."

"Yeah, well, our boat is no use anyway," Jack comments. "We just use it as a hut."

"The shore is the worst place to be. You must've run into the herd, right?" he asks.

"The herd?" Jenn asks.

"There's a herd of undeads that circles this island along the shore. Get in their way, they'll tear you to shreds," he explains.

"We saw them," I say timidly, trying hard to prevent the images of the experience from flooding back. I feel the heat of the others' stares. "It comes by a little over every 3 days."

"And you guys stayed? Damn, are you stupid?" the man asks rhetorically. His eyes shift behind us again, and I begin to sense that a part of it is because he's not really interested in conversing any longer. He's mission-focused and his sights are set on his next moves.

"Where's your camp?" Jenn demands. It's striking to compare her refined aggression to the man's looser, more animal-like presence. She retains the perfect posture of a BAA soldier, contrasting with the way he slouches his hulking shoulders like he's ready to spring.

"Further into the forest, near the center of the island," he answers to which she just slowly nods her head.

"You haven't even told us your name yet," I say, making the man turn to look at me.

"Blake," he responds in a gruff voice after a moment of hesitation.

"Riley," I reply politely with a small smile. He eyes me curiously.

"You have a gun," Jenn interjects, finally comfortable with the man enough to explore her curiosity of the small handgun at Blake's waist. "Rumors at the BAA say they stopped giving these out to those expelled from Level 3 and 4."

"They did," Blake grunts, pulling it out for us all to see. "'Cause it made things easier for us out here."

Guns are highly publicized as the essential weapon of an advanced soldier, and Headmaster's agents walk around with them all the time. However, training doesn't start until Level 3— next year if we hadn't been expelled.

"Let me see it," Jenn demands, stifling her yearning interest in the weapon.

"You're funny," Blake responds after taking a second to look her up and down.

A noise ticks off my ear, and my eyes shoot up to where a lone undead hobbles through the trees, getting gradually closer. This one's a boy. With so much blood tainting its body and tattered clothes, the color of his shirt was indistinguishable, but a worn number is still marked on his chest: Level 1. He's missing a significant amount of facial features, but his height hints at his young age. He could've been sent here after his first or second year. He notices us and hisses, opening his mouth to allow a grizzled tongue to flick at us.

"We should go," Jack says, noticing the undead when he hears me gasp.

"You should put it down," Blake says. "Put him out of his misery."

"We don't kill if we don't have to," Jack states.

"They're already dead," Blake reiterates.

"I got him," Xander says confidently, walking over to the beast with his sword gripped firmly in his hand.

As Xander nears the walking corpse, it becomes excited, raising its decayed and gruesome looking face and hobbling faster. The sight of it tripping over its own feet without taking its hungry eyes off of us is sickening. These people truly are gone.

Xander waits until it's in reaching distance and then stabs it straight through the abdomen. Unhindered by the wound, the undead pushes forward, dragging its body further down the blade and Xander struggles to rip out his sword against the pace of the advancing undead. However, stepping back, he manages to pull it out and slices upward, slitting the undead's throat. A cascade of blood is immediately released from between the ends of the slice in the undead's leathery skin, and jets of blood shoot onto his shirt. Like before, this still doesn't stop the beast. Xander has just enough time to bring the hilt of his sword back down to smash on the top of the man's skull, knocking it to the ground.

"Geez Xander, he said put him down, not brutalize him," Jenn remarks.

"I tried!" Xander exclaims as the undead squirms at his feet.

"How does it do that?" I ask, and though I grimace as I speak, my words are driven by curiosity.

"They're not like us. They may not be smart, but the head's the only thing that matters," Blake grunts, putting his bag back on and beginning to walk away. I watch as Xander gets down on his knees, holding the undead to the floor, before sliding his blade into the back of its skull.

"Where are you going?" Jack asks, making the older man slowly come to a stop and turn around.

"As much fun as chatting has been, I've got a camp to get back to," he says casually. "Don't forget to dress the deer. You stole that food away from me, I'll kill you if you waste it."

"What good would dressing it up do?" Jack asks, raising his palm in confusion. He turns to me to determine if his confusion is justified, and I chuckle.

"He's a keeper," Blake remarks sarcastically to me, winking once. He turns away again to keep walking, but calls back out to us.

Xander watches Blake disappear through the trees before moving his attention to Jenn.

"He's got others," he states blatantly, biting his lip.

"We don't need them," Jenn says. "I'm not going to go deeper into the forest when our goal is to get off this island. I say we go back and build another raft."

"Every time we build one it just sinks the moment we put it into the water or it's torn up by the rocks," Xander says. "We're soldiers, not engineers."

"How can you be contemplating this?" I speak up. "A camp is just about what we need. They could help us out a lot."

"How can we trust him?" she says again, shutting me up. "We don't know him. We don't know where he's taking us. He could be planning something."

"We have to give him a shot. Give the camp a shot," Xander defends again, glancing back into the trees. Blake's already disappearing through and I can barely still see him through all the vegetation. "Look, we have to decide quickly."

"I say we go," I say, finalizing my opinion. "What chance do we have out here?"

"A good one," Jenn counters. "The reason they made a camp is so that they could learn to survive on this island. I want to get off it. Besides, we're assuming that he's even telling the truth."

"True, I mean he didn't take the deer…what if he's a cannibal," Jack says under his breath, widening his eyes. Jenn furrows her eyebrows, but I shrug.

"Could happen, I guess," I mutter, letting my voice trail away under the judgmental stare from Jenn.

"Our other option is to just wait on the shore for the herd to come by again," Xander says. "We'd miss out on a chance of finding a reliable food source. It's decided…we're going."

Jenn contemplates his words carefully for a moment.

"Fine," she says finally, and I release the breath I'd been holding. "We'll give it a shot. But stop acting like you're some leader of this group."

Xander just ignores her. "Hey Blake!" he calls out, rushing after the man.

"Jenn, wait," I call out just as Jenn's about to run after him. I reach out to grab her shoulder. "I know you're not one for working with even more people—"

"What's your point?" she says, blinking impatiently, and I let go of her arm.

"Please just…try to give this place a shot, really," I say.

"If things go wrong, you're on your own," she mutters threateningly before turning back around and heading off. "I'm not sticking around for a shit show."

CHAPTER 11

Jenn

Blake helps us field dress the deer. We all had known the procedure from our survivalist skills training—except for Jack, who had not only questioned the ration behind putting clothes on a dead animal, but also inquired about where we would acquire such clothes. We all take turns in pairs to carry the small deer as Blake leads us through the dense forest along a trail he seems to have memorized.

"So where exactly are we going?" Jack asks cautiously, rubbing his arm against his side. I notice a deep red rash on his right arm with the small lump of an insect bite in the center of the patch. Beside him, Riley unabashedly looks around us. Her head swings about like a child in a candy store, letting her large eyes scan the terrain.

"Does it matter?" Blake spits back. "It's safer than where you sorry pricks camped out at the shore. Lucky to be alive."

"These undeads..." Riley begins, practicing the term. "Most of them wear orange jumpsuits."

"And I've since trained to shoot at anything orange," Blake quips back.

"They're prisoners?" she asks.

"They are," he responds again, relishing in her discomfort. "Dumped on the island in bulk a few times a year by a heavily armored ship on the west shore. They're already undead when they pour out onto the island."

"You've seen it? Have you tried boarding this ship?" I call out, still skeptical of any story this man says.

"I've seen people try," he heaves in a chuckle. "But even if you can get past the waves of undeads wandering out of the lower deck, the upper deck guards will blow you to pieces."

"How many survivors do you have?" Xander asks, carrying the front of the deer opposite where I carry the end. "At your camp, I mean. You said you have a camp?"

"Yeah," Blake mumbles gruffly. "I did."

"Do you have a name for this camp? Like how people name forts or institutions," Jack asks, absentmindedly.

"Tell me how many other camps you found so far," Blake growls through gritted teeth. "I promise you won't get mixed up."

"So how many people are there at this camp?" Xander asks again.

"What's with all the questions, huh?" Blake barks back. "I don't even have to take you four with me. Shut the hell up already and keep your eyes peeled for undeads."

We continue the trip in silence, and the hours drag on. At one point, we have to stop to rest, and Blake shares the fruit that he'd been holding onto in his backpack. It's cooler in the woods as opposed to the humid heat of the beach, and as the sun sets and the light ceases to bleed through the canopy, the chill of the approaching night begins to settle in. It's almost refreshing. Finally, we stop our trek.

Before us is not a clearing in the woods as I expected the camp to be, but instead a wall of densely packed pine trees. Their height, about 2 stories, falls short of the high canopy of the surrounding trees. Between the individual pine trees, a diverse selection of overgrown vegetation and bushes thrive like the moss that spews through cracks in pavement.

"Give it." Blake motions for my axe.

"No," I sneer.

"Then no camp," he challenges, crossing his arms. "Easy as that."

"Is this another test?" I scowl.

"No," he states, frowning. Reluctantly, I hand over the weapon.

"You got anything else on you?" he asks us as he grabs Xander's sword from his hands.

"Don't trust me?" I ask sarcastically, holding up my hands. "I thought we were becoming friends."

Blake collects Jack and Riley's weapons before turning his attention toward the impenetrable wall of greenery before us. After a few seconds, he moves aside one of the branches on a tree, bringing along with it a large group of the overgrowth. He starts to step inside this hole, holding the branch out for us like one would with a door.

"What'cha waiting for?" he asks, a sly smirk on his face.

"What the hell is this?" I blurt out, looking at the entrance.

"We call it the hedge," Blake explains. "The ones that built this camp made a fence to keep the undeads out. Over time, planted some trees, some bushes…the rest is history. It makes us less conspicuous to undeads passing by."

I finally push past a hesitating Xander and step into the hole after Blake. Pine needles scratch my face and twigs crunch underneath my feet on the dirt floor as I move through the pathway. The path is rather congested, with branches and leaves coming in from all sides, and includes two turns.

Blake steps out first and I follow directly behind, only to receive a blow to the mouth from a branch snapping back. I pull the pointy branch from my face and step out, glaring at Blake.

"Who are they?" I hear a voice and immediately turn toward the origin of the noise. It's a woman. She stands tall and holds her height with pride: her spine is stiff and straight, and her shoulders are pulled back to puff out her chest. Still, despite the radiance of confidence emanating from her stance, her face is worn with crease lines drawn in the skin in her forehead above her relaxed eyebrows. She dons a navy-blue Level 3 shirt, but the maturity in her features hints at an older age. On either side of her stand two others: a boy holding a gleaming sword and a girl with a sickle.

I step to the side to allow room for the others to come out of the hedge, but the movement triggers her and she instantly raises the handgun she's been gripping in her right hand.

"Found them by the shore," Blake says, making his way toward the group. He then points at me. "They got a deer, though."

"You check them?" the woman asks, refusing to lower her aim.

"No one's bit. They got some supplies, weapons. They're capable of holding their own and contributing. They're good, Becky," he mutters, while leaning over to her. "Thought we'd need some members like them with everything that's been going on recently."

"Good," she says rather quietly to Blake, eyeing us suspiciously. She then shakes her head and bites her lip. Her hair is dark and sleek like mine, but she wears it cropped short so that it barely reaches as she pushes it behind her ear. "Andrew's not going to like this."

"Oh, *hell* no!" The exclamation comes from a large man with dark skin that storms over toward us. The timing seems to emphasize what the woman said. "Again? What's with you and scraping up all the dirt and bringing it here?"

"You say that every goddamn time. What are you saying we do? Leave 'em out there?" Blake replies, defensively.

"That's exactly what I'm saying," the man says again. Built from his training at the BAA, he has a towering figure that stands over the rest of the campers. Jack is the only other person that may stand taller, but his thin body and delicate face defeats any intimidation that could be interpreted from his height alone.

"They're already here," the woman speaks up again cautiously. "Why don't we speak with them and just give them a chance, alright? You never give anyone a chance, Andrew."

"You're right. I don't. Not when you let in every damn stray that this piece of crap picks up," Andrew shouts, motioning toward Blake.

"What'd you call me?" Blake shoots a deadly glare at Andrew.

"A single-minded piece of shit," Andrew provokes.

"You better watch your mouth, sunshine," Blake warns, pulling his fingers into a tight fist.

"Save it for later," the woman commands and then turns wearily back to me, and I can't tell if she's expecting me to step in to defend our right to be here.

"We'll contribute what we can," Xander offers immediately. "We brought a deer. I'm sure we could help find another. We're good fighters too."

"What are your names?" Becky asks.

"Jenn Bellator," I say, lifting my chin. "Yes, as in Bellator's Army Academy."

"Damn, and yet you're still here with the rest of us," Andrew comments.

"I'm Xander," Xander introduces himself. "Just…Xander. And this is Jack and Riley."

"Give them a chance," the woman repeats to Andrew.

"If it wasn't for that undead attack last month, we'd be way overcrowded, starving," Andrew remarks, his tone more spiteful than rational.

"Don't say that," Becky scolds. "That was devastating, and we lost our friends."

"Oh, sure, now you care? Didn't seem that way when you were darting away from the scene, leaving them to die," Andrew sneers and Becky pursues her lips in restrained anger. "Were they your friends back then?."

"If we want to protect ourselves from undead attacks, we need the manpower," Becky argues, ignoring his sharp words.

"We need to protect our own. And we do that by keeping the camp's food for the camp's members," Andrew says again. "I don't care about your savior mentality. We barely have enough to sustain ourselves and you want to keep adding *more* to our group?"

I catch Riley looking around again. Her deep green eyes retain their natural doe-eyed expression as they dart around the new campers and the campground behind them. Her gaze seemingly paints the scene like a paintbrush stroking back and forth, and I wonder what she sees and what she notices. I turn my attention back to the campers, narrowing my eyes.

"What do you mean by 'undead attacks'?" I ask.

"Pipe down, princess," Andrew says quickly, dismissing my existence.

"It was just a question," I affirm.

"Yeah, well, you don't get to ask questions, princess. We don't even know if you get to stay," Andrew barks this time.

"Alright, call me princess one more time and you'll be picking your teeth off the floor," I snap back instinctively.

"Wow, big threats for a little girl," he mocks, narrowing his eyes at me, and I silently breathe in as his hulking figure takes a step closer to me. "Save it for your Level 2 playground. This isn't the BAA anymore, sit down."

As he nears me, I feel his towering shadow cast over me. But as his darkness covers my body, my vision darkens as well.

"There are no rules here and you're just another piece of crap Blake picked off the shore," he continues. "I'm serious when I say I can bash in your skull."

His words echo in my head like he's repeating them endlessly. The image of him darkens again in my vision and this time, I feel the air thicken around me. Something triggers inside me: it's familiar, yet foreign. It's a feeling of pure intimidation and predation that I didn't know I could feel from anyone else besides my dad.

"Hey, don't talk to her like that," Xander says suddenly, raising his voice and stepping closer.

"You think you can tell me what to do?" Andrew scowls at Xander.

"You think you can threaten my friend?" Xander counters, standing taller and puffing out his large chest a little.

"Xander, it's ok, I got this," I insist quietly, feeling my head and vision begin to clear.

"No, I think I want to hear what else this guy has to say," Andrew says. "Unless he needs his girlfriend to stand up for him."

"I'm not his girlfriend, moron," I protest.

"Oh, ok, so then you won't mind if I mess up his face a little," Andrew teases, a smirk on his face.

"Alright, I think we all need to calm down," Becky commands, raising her authoritative voice.

No one speaks as Xander and Andrew stare at each other, waiting for the other to make a move.

"Andrew, back off," Becky commands.

"Since when can you tell me what to do?" he sneers, stealing a glance in her direction.

Blake steps up behind her, scowling at Andrew. Andrew hovers for a bit, before abruptly striding off. As he leaves, his shadow releases from me and the clouding darkness lightens up completely.

"So," Becky begins, breaking the silence. "I'm Becky, by the way. The four of you all came together?"

"Yeah," I say. She had to have known that we were able to grasp her name by now through the conversations; still, she made it a point to introduce herself on her terms. I respect it.

"Where you guys coming from?"

"Back at the shore. We set up at our boat," I say, to which she raises her eyebrows. "Yeah, our boat survived the rocks, somehow."

"The shore's not safe, you know that right?" she says, and I can't help but feel like she's testing me, making sure we're not complete idiots.

"Yeah, the herd doesn't make the best company," I bluff, keeping my guard up. "We were planning on moving into the forest after we scouted it a little more."

"Sorry about Andrew," she says after releasing a deep breath. She places her hands on her hips and takes a moment to look at each one of us, vaguely resembling a more benevolent version of a sergeant readying themself before announcing the morning's tasks.

"It's fine." I shrug. "There are scarier things than one angry man."

"Hey, don't forget that one angry man was behind all of us," she says, gesticulating around her, and I assume she's referring to Headmaster's involvement in the creation of our island punishment. Above her lighthearted smirk, her unwavering eyes aren't smiling. After a moment, even her small half-smile fades, and she claps her hands once. "Anyway, you already met Blake. This over here is Bella and Noah."

Becky points to the two teens that were standing behind her. Noah, though clearly younger, stands tall and lanky beside the girl named Bella, though they both wear Level 2 shirts. I strain my memory to recognize their faces, but I don't.

"Oh, your bruise," Becky says to Xander while examining the swollen eye he had earned during his struggle with Blake. He tries to wave her off, but she persists. "Go with Bella, she'll help you get the swelling down, so you'll actually be able to see out of your eye. She's the medic around here. The rest of you can come with me, I'll show you around."

CHAPTER 12

Riley

A large clearing in the dense forest, the camp is completely fenced in along its perimeter by the thick hedge. We had entered through the east entrance, of three entrances total, on the long end of the rectangular camp. Immediately upon walking in, on the left is a pyramidal pile of cut down logs presumably for storage. On the right is a large wooden platform, known as the east post. These wooden structures, one beside each entrance, are constructed along the hedge to look over to the other side. Each one consists of several vertical logs holding up a fenced in wooden platform. Becky said they were the posts they use to keep watch for threats.

As Becky shows us around the camp, I pay close attention, scanning the details of the area and taking an inventory of their resources. The terrain of the land isn't entirely flat, but rather the camp seems to be built on the uneven side of a hill, allowing for a gradual decline. A stream cuts through the camp, parallel with the long edges of the camp's rectangle, and sections off nearly a third of the total area. The hilly terrain causes the water to run quick and trickle over a small waterfall. Clay buckets and empty water containers are stationed near this waterfall in order to utilize the fresh water source. A few meters south of this station is a small bridge, constructed of several logs strapped together with vines, used to cross the water.

Further downstream, the stream bisects. The larger of the two daughter streams turns at an angle and exits under the hedge at the southwest corner of the camp. This is the main continuation of the water flow that will continue down the island, carrying clean water to nourish the wildlife.

The smaller stream, though smaller, still carries a rather quick flow and bisects again. A portion of it angles east and flows into a small pool before exiting out of the camp on the south end. Next to this pool are piles of clothes, weapons, and other tools: the cleaning station. The other portion of the stream exits after passing through a small wooded area of the camp, where it flows into another pool for use as a bathing area. The south entrance and south post are stationed near the end portions of these streams to scan for any blockages or animals attempting to drink the dirtier water. Due to the decline of the terrain allowing for the angled flow of water toward the southwest, the south post has an added ability to partially keep watch on threats from the west.

Taking advantage of the soil in the region, much of the camp is used for agriculture. The west fields consist of the entire west ground sectioned off by the stream. The east fields, on the other side of the stream, take up the northern third of the remaining campground. A thin path slices through the east fields, leading to the north entrance and the north post beside it. In order to avoid the risk of groundwater contamination, no agriculture takes place around the bathing and cleaning areas.

"What's over there?" I ask, pointing toward another small wooded area in the southeast corner of camp.

"That's our version of the bathroom, also known as our compost station," Becky explains, watching me to see if I understand. "There's a container for number 1 and a container for number 2."

"What happens to the… excrement?" Jack clarifies, grimacing while carefully choosing his words.

"We do what we have to," Becky says with a sigh. "We turn it into fertilizer for the fields. We need our crops to grow and the climate here isn't always favorable. The urine we use for detergents for cleaning clothes and tools."

"Smart," I remark, nodding in approval. Though she doesn't explain the details of the composting methodology, if it has worked for the campers thus far, I assume it must be safe.

"The one caveat is if you're sick," Becky adds quickly, holding up a finger. "Downstream of the bathing region, right before the stream exits the camp, there's a separate area to do your business. That way we don't risk contaminating our compost."

The rest of the eastern portion of the camp consists of a large clearing. Becky leads us to the center of the clearing where a total of 21 tents are set up in a circle around a dining area consisting of five logs positioned around an extinguished bonfire. Some of the tents are creatively made from animal skins and furs sewn together and held up by vines strung to bones. However, the majority were made out of the fabric of old clothing, predominantly our black sweatshirts from what I could tell.

"This is where we eat and sleep," she says, indicating the area. "There are sixteen of us and since the twins share one, there are…eight empty tents. That's more than enough."

She clasps her hands together at the end and forces a smile.

"You guys did this all yourself?" Jenn asks.

"There were others," she says, taking in a deep breath, surveying the arrangement of tents, and nodding aimlessly a couple times. Through her upbeat tone, I see a sadness diminishing the optimistic attitude she struggles to put up. Her eyes drag from tent to tent, the stories of each one replaying in her head. Names and faces of the prior campers rest on the tip of her tongue, haunting her to remember them by way of the hollowness of their prior beds. It's why her smile never reaches her eyes. "Many others."

"I'm sorry," I say politely.

"How long have you been here?" Becky asks, eager to change the subject. She raises her eyebrows above her tired eyes.

"Long enough to see what those things out there are capable of," Jenn responds vaguely, and I silently scoff at her feigned wisdom.

"Who'd you lose?" Becky asks, searching Jenn's stoic expression.

"The captain on our ship," she answers slowly, seemingly unsure of whether to fake grief or remain hardened. Her resulting tone of voice ends up coming across as if bragging about a scar. “Saw him torn to bits not just a few feet from me.”

“I’m sorry to hear that,” Becky says, furrowing her eyebrows.

“We’ve been on the island for about a month and a half I’d say,” I add, answering Becky’s original question to which she nods. Unlike the others, I have only been astutely keeping track of the days to keep tabs on my pregnancy.

“Not many make it that long all still together,” she comments.

“I just don’t even understand what’s happening,” Jack says bluntly. “How do you know the undeads are…dead? And why are they that way?”

“Well, to answer your second question, no one really knows. What we do know is that it’s not an accident,” she says. “The undeads are prisoners sent here by the hundreds. They wear those orange jumpsuits, which is honestly pretty helpful in distinguishing them in the forest. Whatever you do, don’t wear orange or else we will probably accidentally kill you.”

“What about the undeads wearing BAA clothing?” I inquire, studying her for answers.

“With the undeads, it’s not just their violence that presents a danger: they carry this infection in their bite. Even just one bite will kill you...then you come back,” she explains darkly, glancing between the three of us. “It will spread like a wildfire throughout your body. If you’re not already dead, you’ll get hit with a fever. You get weak and frail. The infection eats at you, burning you from the inside out. Your body essentially shuts down. We’ve had people suffer for days, three or four at most, and you just can’t do anything about it. You end up dying. Sometimes, we shot those that got sick just to put them out of their misery. If you’re shot in the head or your brain is destroyed in some way, you get to skip the next step.”

“Coming back?” I ask to which she nods slowly.

“You come back,” she repeats. Her words are cold, almost frightful. She shakes her head and looks at the floor. “It happens all the time. We’ve had so many funerals.”

“And you’re saying that anyone who gets infected, dies and is…resurrected somehow?” Xander confirms slowly.

"We don't know how, but yes," Becky says. "You can get torn to shreds, but as long as their infection gets into you and your brain is unharmed, you will come back in whatever mangled form you died in. They're mindless, uncoordinated, rotting versions of their old selves that just want to feed on others. Nearly indestructible too. Nothing you do to injure it will cause it pain or slow it down. The *only* way to put them down for good is by destroying the brain."

I imagine Billy walking amongst the herd now, half devoured. A pinch of nausea haunts my stomach as I think about his fate and how it could befall any one of us. Back at the boat, when the herd came…they were all victims too.

"Have you had any deaths recently?" Jenn asks.

"Unfortunately, yes," she continues hesitantly. "Just last month, I went out with three others on a typical hunting trip. The herd usually stays on the shore, but they can gather in large groups in the forest too. I was the only survivor."

"That's…" I begin to say, caught speechless. My eyes catch Blake strolling on the opposite side of camp.

"Crazy," Becky finishes my statement for me, watching Blake as well. "Blake was supposed to come with us, but we made him stay back to work on something else. Nothing was his fault, but I can see guilt in his eyes."

"He just wishes he could've helped," I state, to which Becky nods slowly again.

"He's been through a lot. He's…seen the most, lost the most, endured the most," she explains wearily. As she often does, she takes in another long sigh before continuing. "But he still goes out hunting—he's the only one who still will willingly. He's the only one who still gathers newcomers, even though the shore is a day's trip away."

"How long has he been here?" Jenn asks, furrowing her eyebrows as she stares at Becky.

"He's been here the longest out of all of us. Ten years," she says, raising her eyebrows at Jenn.

"Ten?" Jenn repeats, aghast.

"And he came from Level 4?" I ask, recalling his maroon shirt.

"Not even close," she says, much to my surprise. "Fourth year of Level 1. He was only 14. Almost everything he's learned, he's learned from here. He's even mastered the gun without the BAA's fancy instructors. "

"He was lowest rank?" I guess.

"I don't know," she replies, pouting her mouth with admitted uncertainty. Though, the way she tightens her lips into a straight line afterwards tells a different story. "That topic is a little taboo here, anyway. Everyone has their own story, but we're all here one way or another, so that's all that matters."

"Oh, sorry," I say.

"No worries," she responds, waving me off.

"How long have *you* been here?" Jenn asks this time.

"Five years," she says, letting her gaze rest across the camp. She blinks a few times slowly as she nods her head. "Came here from my last year of Level 3. I was 19. You never realize how young you were until you're older."

"Any words of guidance for us newbies?" Jack asks.

"Oof, tall order to sum up the island like that." She breathes out a small laugh, loosening up with Jack's lighthearted tone. "Do what you need to. Try to survive…the best you can anyway."

I could tell her answer wasn't what Jack was hoping for, given by the way he bites the inside of his cheek. I don't like her answer either, personally. Though, we shouldn't be surprised. There's no ultimate hack to surviving; there's just attempts and failures.

"Anyway, you're here for a tour," Becky says, forcing her weak smile. "C'mon, let me show you our storage cabins."

"Oh, watch your step, love," Jack says, touching my arm, and I step over the exposed root from a nearby stump.

"Huh, 'love'. That's not a nickname you hear much of," Becky comments. "I like it."

"Yeah, her last name's Amore, which means love in Italian. The nickname just made itself," Jack responds, shrugging.

"That's very sweet," Becky says again.

"Yeah, and all she calls me is 'doofus,'" Jack says, exaggerating an outraged tone.

"Oh, shut up," I remark with a chuckle and he flashes me a wide smile.

We are walking away from the tents and toward east field, which is blooming with crops, when Becky suddenly spots a pair of campers strolling along the grass.

"Hey Lie, Vincent! What are you doing?" Becky calls out to them. "You're supposed to be keeping watch."

The woman looks at Becky with a disgusted, ugly expression as she passes us, blatantly ignoring the question. Her eyes lay claim to an Asian descent and her hair, pin straight and black like her irises, runs long past her hips and flows behind her like a cape when she walks. Small in stature, her size appears dwarfed compared to the tall, muscular man that strides beside her.

"Lie, I asked you to do something. We all have jobs around this camp, you know that," Becky says authoritatively, clearly annoyed. "North post, especially, to look out for anything contaminating our water upstream."

"I'm taking a bathroom break if you must know. Noah's covering for me," Lie says, finally stopping to face Becky. The words leave her mouth with a bitter taste to them.

"That's impossible, Noah was just with me," Becky says, clenching her jaw.

"Oh well. Then I guess he's not." Lie shrugs, then twists her lips into a malicious smirk before taking off again.

"And what about you, Vincent? You were supposed to be on south post," Becky says, turning to the man beside Lie.

"Place got me burning up," Vincent remarks, his sloppy words bellowing. He doesn't stop walking, but turns and lifts his arm, where boils blister among his sunburn.

"And if an animal drinks our downstream water when no one's looking, then what? We get spoiled meat," Becky scolds.

"Hey." The voice startles me, and I spin around only to realize that the greeting wasn't meant for me. Standing beside Jenn is a new man. He has a very defined and wide jaw line and very dark eyes. Dark brown to match his eyes, the waves of his hair are messily grown out from the military buzz cut and is styled to the side to droop down beside his left eye. His sleeves are rolled up to the shoulder to expose his large biceps that shimmer with sweat droplets.

"You always sneak up on people like that?" she quips sharply, locking her jaw.

"I like the shock factor," he says simply. "Name's Anthony."

"Jenn." She holds out her hand and he shakes it, smiling politely.

"Did Jenn just make a friend?" Jack mutters softly, tilting his head down and away to make sure I am the only one hearing.

"Ant!" A girl calls out as she runs to Anthony's side. Long reddish-blond curls fall down in tangles level with her armpits. The bottom of her shirt is tied up over the collar to cool off in the heat, revealing her slim body.

"Who's this?" she asks, smiling brightly as she interlocks her arm with Anthony's and laces her fingers between his.

"These are the new kids Blake brought in," Anthony introduces. "Jenn, this is—"

"Kris," the girl says, pulling Anthony closer to her.

"Nice to meet you," Jenn states.

"I'm Jack." Simultaneously all three of them look over at Jack, who smiles brightly.

"I'm Riley," I say, admittedly more meekly than Jack did, yet still sharing his smile.

"Pleasure," Kris says briefly.

"Well if you need anything, we're always here," Anthony offers before the pair walks off. I watch them leave hand-in-hand.

"We're cuter." Jack's soft breath brushes past my ear, and I purse together my grinning lips to prevent from laughing. I nudge him softly with my elbow. Still, the light, energetic feeling I feel in my chest when he says those two words is how I know they're true.

Becky leads us over to the east field. Two children play in the midst of the pasture—most likely taking a break from whatever job they were assigned. One a boy and the other a girl, but I could tell that they were twins by their matching wild brown curls and deeply stained freckles. They wear identical yellow Level 1 shirts.

An automatic grin spreads delicately across my face as I watch them. Yet, in the back of my mind, I can't shake the image of the young girl that first bit Billy. I don't remember moving it, but my hand had placed itself over my growing abdomen.

"No one knows," Becky says, answering my question before I could ask it. "Not even they were given a reason why they were sent here. Can you believe it? I suspect it was because of overcrowding."

"When did they get here?" Jack asks.

"Late January. Only a couple weeks after the school year started." She stops herself to bite her bottom lip as she watches the children with a vacant expression. "They're only 10 years old."

"Blake found them?" I ask.

"Sure did," she answers.

"How?" I pry, coaxing her into sharing more of the information that I can see her holding back.

"Well, first, Blake found Noah a couple weeks after he arrived this past December. He had been separated from the others he was with and so, Blake and Phil went back to search. Found the twins curled up somewhere in the forest."

"Oh, man," Jack remarks.

"Yeah, they would've likely died out there. It's just one of those things of good timing, you know?" she says, letting out another sigh. "They had no clue what was going on. Now it's up to us to take care of them. They're like our children now, you know?"

Just then, the kids spot Becky and begin racing over.

"Are you new here? What's your name?" the little girl asks me enthusiastically. Her thick curls flow just past her shoulders and her huge animated eyes stare straight up at me. My wide grin returns.

"I'm Riley," I say, exaggerating my voice in a happier tone. "And what's your name?"

"I'm Ana," she announces in a proud voice, and then motions to her brother. "This is Charlie, my brother."

"Hi," Charlie says, playing with the bottom of his shirt. "Nice to meet you."

"Hey Becky, me and Charlie were wondering when our parents could come visit us?" Ana asks, stealing a shifty glance at her brother before setting her stare up at Becky.

"Visit?" Jenn suddenly asks, looking at Becky as well with a raised eyebrow.

"Hey, why don't you guys go run off and play for a while and I'll catch up with you later," Becky offers, and the two kids agree and run off again.

"What did you tell them?" Jenn persists, folding her arms.

"They're little kids. I can't tell them that they were supposed to die," she says, the inner corners of her eyebrows turning up.

"You want me to?" Jenn offers. "You can't just keep giving them false hope."

"It's not that they know nothing. They just think it's temporary. They just still think it's a test and that they'll be back soon," she explains. "They just arrived a few months ago. I'll tell them eventually."

"You know what, I'm going to go check up on Xander," Jenn says abruptly. "I'll catch you later.

CHAPTER 13

Jenn

Near the cleaning station is the infirmary tent. At least triple the size of the other tents, the infirmary tent is covered with the gruesome indicators of its purpose, namely the blood stains on the sheets. On the inside, the perimeter is lined with medical supplies organized on sheets of cloth, old backpacks, or woven baskets. Unfamiliar plants and ground up powders seem to make up most of the supplies. Clearly not supplied from the BAA, these herbs must be a product of the nature around us on the island. Xander is sitting on the ground alone; against his eye, he holds a small woven sack.

"Hey," Xander says casually as I walk through the curtain of the tent.

"Hey...how are you holding up in here?" I say, scrunching up my nose in disgust as I look at the blood stains. I can't even imagine what had gone on in here in the past.

"Starving. But the tent's not bad," he says shifting in the soft dirt. "They smooth the dirt so it's easier to sleep in. Much better than the mattress from the boat."

"What are you holding?" I ask, sitting down next to him, and he removes the dampened sack from his face. The blood has all been cleaned away, but the skin around his eye is still deeply pigmented and swells his eye nearly shut. The shimmer of a layer of moisture glistens off the affected area.

"It's filled with some sort of herb," he says, briefly examining it in his hands before returning it to his face. "We dipped it in some water. Bella said the swelling should go down soon as long as I just keep holding it like this and keeping the pack damp."

"Where is she now?" I ask.

"She told me she'd be right back. She's looking for some sort of rope that I could use to make this into an eyepatch," he explains with a smirk. "How's the camp? Bella gave me sort of a rundown on the layout and stuff. Everyone good?"

"I don't know." I ponder the question. "It's a big assumption just from a couple of hours. The camp looks secure but the people in it…a little less certain. I think we came at a bad time."

"What are you saying?" he says, not understanding.

"I think we should consider going back to the boat," I state, much to Xander's surprise. "I think we're better off avoiding any issues with the people here."

"Are you kidding?" he says, raising his eyebrows.

"No. Also, settling down here is just going to slow our progress of getting out of here," I state strictly, keeping my unwavering gaze with his single uncovered eye, black like the night.

"Not if they help us," he counters again, breaking eye contact to switch the damp pack around. "It's got walls, weapons, other people…"

"Have you seen these 'other people'? They're at each other's *throats—"*

"They've been through a lot—"

"They're a time bomb. And I don't think we should be here when it goes off," I affirm. A few drops of water fall from Xander's pack into the dusty ground, creating miniature dark, wet circles. "Me, you, Riley, and Jack are a unit now. We came together and we've been surviving together just fine."

"We're certainly not better off on our own," he says, letting his voice gradually become louder. "We were barely making it before."

"We have the deer. We can find more. We can look for fish. I think with good rationing we can hold out until we can figure out how to get off of this island—"

"Without a boat, there is no leaving. Not for a while. We're stranded here for the time being." He pauses for a moment and lets out a harsh scoff before immediately letting his expression fall again with a mixture of gloom and frustration. "We're not supposed to get off this island. Headmaster sent us here to die. We're stranded here, and we don't even know where 'here' is. We have to make the best of what we have. And if they know how to do that, then they're the ones who we should be looking to. Because otherwise we won't survive another month."

"We shouldn't settle for this camp," I counter sternly, though by stopping there, it comes out weaker than I intend.

"This is the best we have. You don't have to reinvent the wheel every time you need to ride a bike, Jenn," he continues, his jaw locking tightly. He takes a breath to collect himself before continuing and runs his hand across half of his weary face. With eyebrows drawn together in earnestness, he leans closer. "There's nothing to prove anymore. This isn't a test that you have to ace. This is survival; this is real."

"I'm not trying to prove anything," I state, glowering at him.

"You always say that Bellators—" he begins to say.

"My family name has nothing to do with this—"

"You're good enough, Jenn," he pleads, raising his voice to prevent my interruption. "But you have to see the same in other people. It's not just me, you, Riley, and Jack that are a unit. Everyone that got expelled is a unit. We're all in the same situation. We all have to work together to survive this island. And then…maybe all work to get off of it."

A silence hangs heavily over the tent when he finishes, and I'm caught at a loss for words.

"Oh, hi." A voice emerges from the tent's entrance before I can say anything. Bella standing there looking at us. "Am I interrupting something?"

"No…I was just leaving," I say with a moment of hesitation, still shaken by his words. Tearing my gaze away from Xander, I force myself to my feet off the dirt floor and make my way past Bella. Still, I can't help but echo his words in my head.

***

The sun is just beginning to set and the day's activities start coming to an end. The sky is still blue but the sun wanes by the second. Unlike at the beach, the sunset isn't visible behind the trees surrounding the camp. It'll get darker quicker out here in the forest. I'm alone sitting on the outskirts of the camp near the south exit. It would only take me a few minutes to be out of this camp. I could be gone from here forever before anyone could even realize my absence. It would be dangerous out on my own, but I could avoid whatever dangers this group awaits for me here instead.

"Hey," Becky says walking up to me, instantly ruining my fantasy of a discrete and clean escape.

"Hey," I say back, not looking up from my position in the grass.

"How's his eye?" she asks as she seats herself beside me.

"I think he'll make it," I reply caustically. The bitter taste from my argument with Xander infuses my words with a sharp sarcasm, but Becky smiles.

"You know, it's funny, the undead make you think about humanity differently," she says, turning to look across the camp where a few people can be seen going about their activities. "The undead just walk around aimlessly until they find their next meal. They're violent, but they don't know that; they don't know anything. But humans also destroy. Even if we know it will put us in danger. It doesn't make theoretical sense, but it happens. We can't seem to make a perfect thing."

"Skip the riddles, what are you telling me?" I ask plainly.

"I know what you think of us here. Bella overheard you and Xander," she mutters.

"Did I hurt your feelings?"

"I've tried my best to do what's right for all of us here and keep this place together. But you're right. This place—this group—we're struggling to stay together." Her words take me by surprise, and I can tell she senses this by my initial silence.

"Why are you telling me this?" I ask after a moment, furrowing my eyebrows at her. I watch as her stare drops, and she roughly pushes her thick hair from her face.

"Because civilization will never be perfect," she continues. After a second, she lets out a heavy sigh. "But we try. That's why the camp was made: for life. Civilization. We build tents and relationships and heal each other when hurt. We learn and try to make sense of the world and the undeads. We want safety, but we want more than that. We want a life with others, and we will always want to make the most of it. It's not perfect, but we try. Try with us."

"You think I should stay," I state blatantly.

"I think you should stay," she repeats, meeting my gaze. Worry lines make deep creases in her skin, attesting to the scars of the island's tragedies aging her body before time can.

"It's a matter of what I need rather than a matter of choice," I say again, eyeing her carefully.

"This group isn't the greatest, I know. I'll admit we're splitting at the seams," she whispers, and there's a gloom behind her eyes. "But as someone that's been here a long time, I can tell you this camp is better than anything you'll find outside."

"You don't know what I can do on my own," I challenge. "You expect that I'd die without you guys?"

"I can't not," she replies weakly. "I watched the undeads take three of our own last month. All I do is think about how that could be any of us. Sometimes I even think it should've been me instead. But that's the stuff that happens outside these walls. Don't risk that for yourself. We're all in this together."

"I'll have to think about it," I say.

"Alright," she mutters under her breath. After a moment of silence, she stands up. "I'm going to go work on dinner."

"Do you need help?" I offer, and she just shrugs. "What are you making?"

"Your deer."

We walk back to the campfire where there is already a girl kneeling by the flame, cutting what appears to be tomatoes on a piece of driftwood. I sit down beside her as Becky leaves to go gather more vegetables.

"'Sup," the girl says after giving me a double-take. "You the new girl?"

"That's me," I say back. The girl is short, like myself, and looks rather close in age as well. However, she wears the shirt of a Level 1 cadet. Contrasting her manly, rough features, her thin and rather frail figure reminds me of that of a child's.

"Name's Corinne," she says, shoving her stringy dark hair out of her face and behind her ear.

"Jenn," I respond. "You're…Level 1?"

"I *was*," she responds. "Was on my second year 'til I finally got the boot...or, actually, the *boat*."

"You're 12?"

"At least 13 by now," she clarifies. "Well, actually, probably more like 14. What month was it when you left the BAA?"

"May."

"Yeah, I'm a February baby. I was my platoon's expulsion two years ago. So, I guess I'm 14," she says. "Not that it matters anymore, really."

"What got you sent here?"

"I guess myself," she responds with a shrug. "I took the whole thing as a joke, really, and ended up as the lowest rank."

"Took what as a joke?"

"The BAA. All the lessons, training, the competitions," she explains, and I listen intently. "I just hate the way our society is structured, you know? I don't want to sit in line and get molded into another brainwashed, cookie cutter soldier. I figured that if I got expelled, I'd be happier begging on the streets or living on Expulsion Island because at least I'd still have my goddam free will."

"So, you let yourself fall to lowest rank?" I say again, clarifying.

"I figured I might as well. I wanted out and someone's gotta get expelled at the end of the year," she says casually as if we're talking about what outfit she had picked out for the day. "It was gonna be this guy Bharat Kaur. I'd see him crying like a wimp about it. Now he gets to stay. Wasn't gonna let the system ruin another person's life, you know?"

"Do you regret it?" I ask hesitantly, attempting to withhold my judgment from piercing my expression. She remains quiet, her eyes trained on the mutilated vegetables in front of her.

"He wouldn't have survived a day out here. I mean, as long as I don't die, then it's still worth it. I made it this far, gotta keep it going, you know?" she jokes, but it's weak, I can tell. Abruptly, she roughly brushes the back of her hand across her prominent hook-like nose before perking up her energy. "You gonna help us cook?"

"Yup," I say, and she hands me a shallot and a knife. Her hands are grimy and leave behind a small residue on the outer skin of the vegetable. I grimace but choose to bite my tongue and discreetly rub off the dirt. "Looks like you guys have a nice food system going on here."

"You mean the crops? Yeah, we're totally living the life here," she says sarcastically, nudging the small basket of vegetables by her side with her elbow.

"I meant, considering the conditions," I specify.

"Yeah, I gotcha, I was kidding around," she says bluntly, looking back down to continue chopping a tomato. "Our choices are rather limited though, which sucks, but it sure is better than nothing. Hey, you don't happen to still have any nonperishables from the 'Care Bag' that you were sent here with, do you?"

"No, why?"

"Ah, that's ok, it was a long shot. Usually by the time people join our camp their food bag is already empty. Otherwise, it's nice to shake up our food selection," Corinne explains.

I just nod and then turn back to my shallot lying sluggishly on the piece of driftwood. I hesitantly grip the knife in my hand, examining the onion-like bulb to decide how to begin.

"Yeah, I knew it. Here gimme that," Corinne says, taking both the shallot and the knife away from me. "You gotta take the first layer off. You're not trying to kill it, you just wanna slice it."

She demonstrates by gingerly slicing the shallot into thin slivers. Then she turns the slices on the side and cuts it again and repeats the process, efficiently dicing the shallot.

"I got it," I say, not willing to admit my ignorance. I immediately take a cucumber from the bucket, mimicking what she had just demonstrated.

"Yeah, but you don't want to dice a cucumber." She chuckles awkwardly at my incompetence. "Just slice that one into, like, slices…you know, like, how cucumbers normally are prepared."

We continue to make whatever we're making, slicing and dicing a variety of vegetables one after another. Using cucumbers, zucchinis, tomatoes, shallots, and other vegetables, we start organizing a salad of leafy greens.

"So, want to give me the rundown of the other campers?" I probe.

"Well, let's see. Becky's our camp-mom. Blake, you've obviously have already met," she explains, looking off into her thoughts. "Bella's the camp doctor, and Noah's training to help her out. Then there's the twins, our camp cuties. Let's see...there's also Anthony, Kris, Phil, Dwayne, Kyle..."

"And Andrew," I say before she can.

"Yeah, I heard he confronted you guys at the entrance," she explains, nodding her head to the side. I look over in that direction and spot Andrew lounging in the shade of the trees at the end of the camp's stream. Two people approach him, and I recognize them as the two that Becky had scolded earlier in the day when she found they had left their posts. "That uptight girl over there is Lie and the big guy next to her is Vincent. They all stick together like glue."

"I can see that," I mumble as I watch them briefly. My eyes are drawn to a thin red-haired boy that sits beside Andrew. "Who is the other kid?"

"Patrick," she responds simply. "He follows the three of them like a lost dog, doing whatever they tell him to do. It's kinda pathetic."

"I would think there would be more than just 16 people in the camp considering how many kids are sent here," I say.

"Yeah, well, we can't help everyone that's expelled. Most die within the first month they come here," she explains, looking down. "Anyone that's here had to have been recruited by Blake or someone while out in the forest roaming. And even when they come to the camp…I mean no one is ever really safe as long as there are undeads on the island."

I glance back over to watch Andrew's group. He jumps up and grabs a hold of a low branch, before proceeding to lift his large body up in a pull-up. His dark muscles gleam with sweat, and when he lets go of the branch, Patrick is near at his side offering him a dark green canteen of water. Andrew roughly takes the water from the small man before unnecessarily shoving him backward, nearly knocking him off his feet.

"Do they always keep to themselves?" I ask, weighing a large potato in my hand.

"Always, and they rarely do any of the work," Corinne remarks, putting a little more power into cutting her own potato.

"Well, maybe that has to change," I suggest.

"What are you gonna do? Beat them up?" She chuckles.

"I'll have you know that I am rank one at the BAA," I respond, squinting my eyes at her exaggerated tone and lifting my chin a little as I speak.

"You mean, you *were* rank one. And besides, it doesn't matter," she says again, raising her eyebrows and giving me a funny smile. "Skill on *this* island doesn't rely on checking off narrow criteria in highly controlled conditions. Andrew could dust you off with a little salt and you could pass for a French fry to him."

"I'm not rank one because I checked off a few boxes. I'm a Bellator, fighting is in my blood," I boast. "Everyone at the BAA knows it."

"Well, you're not at the BAA anymore," Corinne says again, stopping her work to focus on me. "I'm going to be real with you because I actually think you seem pretty cool. No one *here* is scared of you. You're just the new kid in the group and everyone is watching you. Actually, after dinner tonight, I am 93% sure that the rest of the campers will quiz me about what we're talking about right now. Andrew's tough. And not like 'Level 2 tough'. He came from Level 4…four years ago. No one can stand up to him like that and win. And if you do try, you're lucky if you only leave with a broken bone and a bruised ego."

"I think you underestimate me," I state, rolling my eyes briefly.

"Just don't say I didn't warn you," she just says, returning to the food.

I look over my shoulder towards the sound of footsteps and see Becky joining us with two pails of water. She hangs one up above the fire, letting it warm up, before joining us.

"Blake's skinning the deer for the stew. Did you do that?" she asks as she sits down beside me, pointing at the cut-up vegetables.

"Oh yeah, it was all me," I boast sarcastically.

"Oh sure. I've just been sitting here looking pretty," Corinne jokes, finishing off some more sweet potatoes. I force a little laugh. "So, Jenn. Besides your status, what do you miss most about life before the island?"

"Corinne," Becky scorns the young girl.

"It's fine," I insist, smiling at Becky for her concern, then turn back to Corinne. In truth, I yearn to say 'security.' The security of having my life *set* had given me purpose. I knew what I was going to do in the morning, I knew what I was going to do at night, and I knew what I was going to do the rest of my life. Now, every day is a new horror, and my future is as obscured as the depths of the ocean lapping the shore of this wretched island. "Probably my bed. It's been a while since I've had a good night's sleep."

"I'd rather have no bed than go back to the BAA," Corinne remarks. "I really hated that place. Society, too. I mean, who turns prisoners into undeads and then uses them to murder cadets? Never gonna go back even if they drive a boat all the way out here to get me."

"Drive a boat?" Becky questions her choice of words teasingly.

"*Sail* a boat? Whatever the word is." She smiles, nudging me in the arm. I flinch a little when she touches me. Back at the BAA, I would've broken that arm.

"I miss the showers," Becky says, still staring down at the vegetable she's cutting. "Damn, what I would do for a nice, warm shower."

"That's fair," Corinne says in agreement.

"You finished making dinner yet?" Andrew suddenly blurts out as he appears in front of us. Flanking him are Vincent and Patrick.

"No," Becky replies.

"Maybe you should do more cooking and less giggling. This isn't girltime. I'm hungry," he barks out at us, grabbing a handful of the chopped vegetables and spilling some in the dirt. "Tell Blake to find some more goddamn meat around here, too."

"He's doing the best he can; we all are," Becky says. "You're just going to have to wait with everyone else until dinner is ready."

"Your 'best' is slow," he mocks, turning back around. "I'd go out myself and teach Blake how to make a goddamn hunt, but I wonder if I'll mysteriously end up dead like the three last month."

Something triggers inside me. It's his tone, his threat of violence, his rage. Within me, an anger of my own boils, familiar yet always repressed.

"I'm sure you have something better to do than throw food on the floor like a toddler," I sneer. I see Becky shoot me an icy glare while Corinne tries to smother a smirk.

"I'd watch that little mouth of yours," he barks back at me. "You're not even a part of this camp."

"And yet I can still tell how much of an asshole you are," I say. "You want to pick up those vegetables you spilled?"

"You want to come over and say that to my face, princess?" he threatens, his eyes narrowed at me.

"Yeah, I think I will," I respond without thinking and I rise to my feet. Beside me, Becky rises up too, watching me cautiously. "That way I can show you exactly who you're calling a princess."

"Who do you think you are?" Andrew jeers.

"I just don't give a crap about you and your greater-than-God ego," I say. "You think you can just push me around? I'd love to see how tough you look when I get over there and shove my foot so far up your—"

"Ha!" he exclaims before his voice falls into a low growl. "You're funny."

"Actually, how about you join us in making dinner?" I offer, my anger fueling my demeaning sarcasm. "It's a learning process, but I think even your brain can pick up on the steps. I'd be careful of the boiling water, though. It's really hot and god forbid you end up breaking a sweat."

He walks up to me, steaming with anger as he towers above me. His shadow creeps over me and, like before, the dark clouds in my vision reappear. I feel my heart rate shoot up until it's pounding in my ears. The air is thick. I tilt my chin up defiantly, cursing my shorter stature. I would do anything to just be able to look him in the eyes without feeling small.

With both hands, he pushes into my chest and I stumble back under his force. Instinctively, my first strikes out like a viper, smashing into his nose before instantly recoiling back close to me. His head is thrown back, and he blinks in utter surprise. After recovering, he brings up one hand to feel the blood now trickling down from his nose.

He winds back and throws out a punch of his own, but I easily evade it with a sidestep. I attempt to snap his arm with an attack targeted at the back of his outstretched elbow. When I try, though, my arm reverberates in pain as if striking a steel pole and I retreat, clutching my arm. He swings at me again with his fist, which collides straight into my face. Blood flies as my head is tossed backwards and I fall, landing in the pile of strewn about vegetables.

My hearing muffled and my vision blurred, I see Corinne fall to my side to help me up, but Andrew uses one of his meaty hands to shove her away. In my daze, he nears me and roughly grabs the shirt of my collar, lifting up my bloody face.

"Stop it Andrew," Becky orders, raising her voice. "What the hell?"

"Relax girls, I'm just bonding with the new kid," he says calmly, admiring my weakened position on the ground. "Every dog needs training."

"You crazy bastard!" Corinne screams out at him, and immediately, he releases me to lash out at her. He punches her across the face, and her small body falls backwards into Becky, who sloppily catches her.

I attempt to steady myself, but he grabs me again, clenching my collar. I reclaim my vision just in time to see his fist accelerating straight at me. I am narrowly able to evade it, throwing my body to the side and out of his grip.

Now on the floor, I try to take him down by sweeping my legs into his, but his stance is too strong to be knocked down. With one arm, he lifts me back up and flings me through the air. My view blurs as I'm thrown into one of the nearby tents and the back of my neck slams against one of the poles that holds it up.

As I begin recovering, he struts over to me, yanking me back to my feet. I attempt to throw a defensive punch, but my weak attempt fails as he easily grabs it, twists my arm, and then proceeds to throw me to the ground again. Dirt sprays around me from the grass when I hit the ground.

"Enough!" someone yells, yanking Andrew back. I catch just enough of a glimpse of the man to know that I don't recognize him.

Then, Xander appears by my side as well and extends a hand out to me, but I refuse it. When I look back up, I am just able to catch Andrew's smirk before he turns and strides away.

"You throw like a girl," I grumble, but he ignores me.

***

"Well, it's not broken, which is good," Bella says as she inspects my nose.

"Can't say the same about my ego," I say sarcastically.

"So…what was that about anyway?" she asks, dipping a rag into a bucket of water and then raising it up to wipe some dirt from my forehead.

"I don't know," I respond. "I just didn't like the way Andrew treats everyone like they're inferior. I wanted to put an end to it."

"And how'd that turn out?" she asks with an eyebrow raised.

"Humiliating," I say softly. "Did you see it?"

"Not really. I heard the commotion and came at the end," she says, continuing to clean the dirt off my face. "How's your arm?"

"I'm fine," I insist. "Why does everyone just let Andrew get away with this shit?"

"Because what is there to do? Everything's become a free-for-all, nowadays" she responds. "We used to have a leader. Everything and everyone worked like a machine."

"Who was your old leader?" I inquire.

"Evan. He never claimed the title, but everyone knew he was in charge," she explains. "The others would always say how he got them through some tough times. He died last month on that one hunting trip. Becky tell you about that?"

"Yeah, she said three people died," I say.

"Yeah, it was the worst tragedy we've had in a long while," Bella says, slowly nodding. "Becky's been trying her hardest to run things around here and keep everyone together. Andrew…well, he's got other plans. Everyone's sort of picked a side."

"Yeah, I can tell," I mumble, nodding. "What do they disagree on?"

"What don't they?" Bella says sarcastically, though I sense the truth behind it. "Becky always wants to save everyone and bring in newcomers; Andrew thinks newcomers are a burden and just extra mouths to feed. Andrew wants to militarize the camp. He wants to build walls lining the hedge, set up better fences, and then begin hunting down undeads around our perimeter; Becky says it's a waste of resources and too risky. She mainly just wants to continue how we've been, and focus on expanding more farming projects."

"Damn," I mutter. "They can't compromise?"

"Well..." Bella says slowly, contemplating whether to continue. "Andrew sort of blames Becky for the deaths of the three. He claims she left them to save herself. He thinks she's a 'usurper' and distrusts every *single* thing she does...*and* everyone who listens to her."

"Do you think it's true?" I ask. " That she left them?"

"I don't think it's fair to make assumptions about whatever happened that day," she replies neutrally. "No soldier leaves their team behind to die. Becky says that they died right in front of her. Andrew's accusations just put salt in the wound. Besides, Becky's the only one actually trying to maintain order here ever since. Things have to get done and it doesn't help when no one's doing their jobs."

"I'm guessing you're on Becky's 'side', then?" I ask, raising an eyebrow.

"I'm on whatever side will bring us back to normal and will keep this team together. We're all in this together, and I hate when people can't see that. The only enemies should be Headmaster and those undeads out there. Any violence around here is just...friendly fire," she says, shaking her head, and I listen intently. Her words mimic Xander's.

"The BAA taught us so much about competition," I mutter softly, staring blankly at the dirt. "But an army runs on cooperation. That's sort of what Xander was just telling me earlier."

"Exactly. I just hope that things don't get too violent, though it's probably inevitable. It always is, right? I just have a feeling something bad is going to happen. Tensions are too high around here. No one's getting along," she continues. She watches me carefully, her golden-brown eyes just a shade lighter than her hair. "You thinking of staying?"

"Yes," I respond after a long moment of silence.

"Why?" she asks, a confused expression on her face. "After everything I just said? This island…it really changes a person. I'm not saying that I want you to leave. I'm just saying that you should get out while you can— for your own good."

"No," I start to say slowly, still staring at the floor. "We should be all in this together, just like you said. A soldier doesn't walk away from comrades."

CHAPTER 14

Riley

Beyond the top of my tent, the darkness blackens the sky and even the stars have gone to bed, snuggled up in the clouds. Unlike the daytime when the sun scorches the earth in blaring heat, the night brings a biting chill that clings to my skin. I wriggle underneath my blanket, trying to cuddle against Jack's warm body. He's fast asleep, but my eyes are glued open and my ears are keenly listening to the outside. With each gust of wind and rustle of trees, I wince. It's been three hours and 39 minutes of this— according to my counting. Almost every night has been like this. All I see when I close my eyes are the undeads. The ones eating Billy, the ones swarming the boat…the one in the boat. I just lie there and pray for daylight to come. Three hours and 40 minutes now.

There had been so much blood, covering nearly the entire floor of the small cabin. I never want to go back down there. The images of the incident on the boat replays through my brain and I can feel my heart begin beating faster. The fear I felt during that moment comes back, and I flinch as I remember its grisly looking face and its mouth hanging open. It was going to eat me. It wanted to.

I sit up, breathing hard as the images of blood and death burn through my mind. I could've died like Billy—torn apart, flesh from bone, limb from limb. My baby would have died too while inside me.

"No!" I cry out before I could cover my mouth as tears begin to swarm my eyes. Jack immediately rises, sitting straight up, glancing around the tent anxiously before turning to wrap his arms around me. Three hours and 41 minutes.

"Riley," he says, squeezing me tight as I sob into his shirt. He slowly rubs my back with his hand.

"I just…," I try to say before letting out another sob, my chest starting to hurt from the force of my crying.

"Love, it's ok," he says reassuringly, squeezing me tighter. He pulls back a little, quickly glancing behind him at the small crack in the tent's opening before tilting his head down so that we're face to face. "You're ok."

"I'm s-so…sorry," I manage to say in between breaths as I slow my crying. "I didn't mean to scare you."

"It's fine," he says. "You didn't scare me. Is it Billy? Or…?"

"Both," I say quietly, looking down, wiping my cheek as my breathing finally slows down. "It's everything."

"It's ok," he insists again, rubbing my shoulder as he attempts to grab eye contact again. "I'm here. No one's going to get you. I promise."

"I know, I'm just…" I attempt to say, struggling to explain the battles I go through in my mind. "I'm scared."

"I know," he says. "Me too."

I wipe my cheek again as I feel a final tear drip from my eye. I pull my arms off Jack, crossing my legs in a pretzel style and hunching over lazily. Still facing me, he keeps a hand on my shoulder as his concerned eyes study me.

"I should've been there for you back there with what happened in the boat," he mutters. "You were in danger and I should've done something. I should've been there. I should've…"

"Jack, it's not your fault," I say, looking up at him.

"No, it is," he says, raising his voice a little, pulling his hand off of me and using it to hold his hanging head. Kicking himself, he suddenly stands up and explodes out of the tent.

"Jack," I call out, caught off guard by his outburst. I follow him outside and see him strolling away from the tents. He stops and runs his hands through his hair.

"I should've seen the herd sooner," he mutters. "I should've…ran back to the boat or brought you with me. Or at least locked the door from the deck side."

"Jack…" I say softly as he paces a little.

"No, I'm serious," he exclaims again. "Everyone was right. I'm an idiot."

"Jack, nothing with the herd was your fault."

"You were alone. That was my fault," he says again, his voice quieter now. "I'm supposed to protect you and our child always. How can I do that when I'm just so frickin' stupid?"

"You're not stupid, Jack," I say.

He's still facing away from me and I come up from behind him, placing both of my hands on either of his elbows and gently nuzzling my head against his back.

"You calm me down each night when I wake up screaming," I say, my voice just louder than a whisper. "That means something to me. You can make me smile even when I don't want to…even when you don't mean to. You *are* here for me. I wouldn't change anything about you."

He turns around and I slip both of my hands into his.

"I just feel bad," he mutters, and he lets his humble gaze drift from our locked hands to my abdomen. "I mean, I did this to you. Headmaster expelled you for the pregnancy I gave you. You shouldn't even be here."

"Jack..." I begin to say. I hold my breath for a moment, then let it go as I prepare to say what I'm about to. I can't bear to look at him. "He told me to terminate the pregnancy. I chose to keep it."

"You did *what*?" he exclaims loudly before slamming his hand over his mouth in regret. He proceeds in a hurried, but quieted tone. "Riley, what are you talking about?"

"He said I could only stay if I got rid of my baby, but then I found out that he was already going to expel you and..." I continue, shaking my head. "I thought the unknown with you and this baby was better than the misery at the BAA."

"Riley, people die here!" Jack screams through his whisper.

"You would've died here," I say quickly. "Your child would be dead anyway. This gives us a chance!"

"Riley, you're *insane*," he says, releasing my hand only to pinch the bridge of his nose.

"Our child has a chance, now," I insist again. "Whatever happens, we'll be parents."

"You could've had a *life*, Riley," he says again earnestly. "You shouldn't be here running for your life from the undead and scavenging for food."

"I didn't know it would be this bad," I say meekly, releasing my other hand from his.

"I mean...me neither, but still," he says, then heaves a sigh as he rolls his eyes. "I knew it wouldn't be *great* here. This isn't a place I would *choose* to go."

"I didn't want to let you go. I thought we had something so special at the BAA…" I continue, suddenly feeling water well in my eyes.

"You did?" he asks, his voice small and humble. As soon as the words leave his lips, a jolt sends through my chest, both calming and yet panicked as the reality sets in. The world around me feels physically heavier and even my shoulders slouch under the burden of the moment. I feel the world around me change as I'm confronted with a possibility I had never considered…the possibility that I was wrong about us.

"Maybe I'm the stupid one, after all," I say through my lost breath, my voice carried by the wind.

"Just...crazy," he corrects. "I'm still the stupid one. That's us, Crazy and Stupid."

"Did you not feel the same about me, Jack?" I ask tentatively.

"I do," he says, his humor dissipating as he states the words with seriousness.

I study his face for a moment before responding. Long lashes flutter around his bright eyes, and the moonlight complements his beautiful features all the way down to his smooth lips. Suddenly, I feel a lump form in my throat, and I have to muster up my courage to speak again.

"I love you," I squeak, saying the phrase to him for the first time.

"Riley," he begins to say, lost for words as he looks into my eyes.

"You don't have to say it," I say, smiling before reaching my arm up to touch his cheek. I stand up on my tiptoes and pull him down into a long kiss.

"I love you, too," he gently whispers as we separate. Exhaustion hangs heavily on his eyelids and he presses his eyes closed for another long moment before he lazily opens them again. "And I promise that I will do *everything* in my power to protect you and our baby. We can do this."

My gaze remains fixed on him for another long moment as I absorb his words.

"No regrets," I say, the words nearly inaudible through my barely parted lips. But the words weren't meant for him anyway. They were for me: a satisfied reassurance. We can do this.

As Jack and I climb back into our tent, my mind goes back to that night that the herd had attacked us.

Jack, Jenn, and Xander all eventually passed out due to exhaustion. Everyone except me. Being careful not to wake Jack beside me, I slip out from under his arm and crawl out of the bed. I hadn't cared before or even noticed, but the blood on my shirt had hardened, making the now red fabric stiff. I gingerly unlock the latch and climb out onto the deck. The frosty gust of wind blows swiftly across my skin and I shiver, glancing around the beach to make sure that it's clear. I follow muddy footprints down from the deck to the sand. The rocky golden sand is laden with indentations from feet, and dead leaves and twigs are strewn everywhere. Entire patches of sand are clumped together with mud. I follow the boat around to the back where the large rocks gradually replace the sand and lead to the ocean. I step carefully from one rock to another, so as not to slip on moss or step in the icy water. Finding a large, rather flat rock, I stop to perch myself down on it, looking down at the reflection of the silver moon in the still water.

I strip from my shirt and dip it into the water. Blood melts off the cloth and flows like smoke through the water, curling in tendrils and turning the water a sickening shade of crimson. I squeeze the color out of my shirt and the water falls back into the ocean. The moonlight reflecting off the shimmering water makes the rust color seem brighter. I lay the now damp shirt on a nearby rock to dry and bring my hands to rest on my stomach. I'm on my third month of pregnancy.

I fought for my life today. I survived. We survived. That must mean something.

I reach into my pocket and pull out the bag of pills Dana had given me and I stare at its contents. Then, I open the bag and pick out the large brown oval termination pill, enclosing it tightly in my palm.

I chose this path with Jack. Now I will survive it. And I will survive living the life I've yearned for. My baby will make it.

Standing up, I take a deep breath before I pull my arm back and chuck the single pill as far as I can. It falls through the air like the heavy raindrop of a summer shower, disappearing into the glistening water along with my easy way out. Overhead, the full moon continues to shine brightly, painting a beautiful sheen over the glossy dark water, which extends endlessly into the distance. I breathe, satisfied with my decision. There's no going back now. I'm keeping my baby.

CHAPTER 15

Jenn

Early morning sunlight pours through the tent like a sieve, and I have to block my eyes with my hands. I sit up from the dirt, the soil crumbling off my shirt. A nagging reminder of my tussle with Andrew, an ache spikes through the nape of my neck, and I am forced to freeze to stretch it out. I force my eyes open through the heavy fatigue that sits on them. As I leave the tent, I am temporarily blinded by the overwhelming sunlight before my eyes are able to adjust.

"Morning," Xander says casually, suddenly appearing by my side.

"What's that smell?" I ask bluntly. Everyone crowds around the central campfire where a billow of smoke spreads into the blue sky above us. Sure enough, hanging above the fire is a group of dead squirrels.

"Blake caught them this morning," he replies.

"Damn..." I murmur, admiring the sight of the cooked meat. I nearly forget to exhale in between my continuous inhales of the smell. Using the back of my hand, I wipe off the sweat already beginning to accumulate in a sheen over my skin. "You know, I could've sworn it was the smell of my burning flesh. The sun never really takes a day off here."

"You could always cut your pants into shorts," he suggests, referencing how some of the campers around us have done so.

"And expose *more* surface area for mosquitos and sun poisoning?" I retort a little more aggressively than intended, and then follow it up with an exaggerated eye-roll.

"Suit yourself," he says with a shrug. "So…I know you don't want to stay, but I was talking to Riley and Jack last night and they really want to stay as well. I don't think we should split up. So, I was thinking maybe we should all sit down and discuss it and come to final decision for what's best for all of us—"

"Xander, I want to stay."

"You do?" he asks, letting his mouth hang open for a moment. "What changed your mind?

"You were right," I confess, offering a small smirk. "We're all in the same boat here. Soldiers stick together. It's our best chance at surviving."

He gives me a long and hard stare for quite some time before continuing. "You sure about this?"

"One hundred percent," I state. "C'mon, King Loser, lighten up, isn't this what you wanted?"

"I really think it's for the best," Xander replies after rolling his eyes at my comment. "I guess I'll go tell Riley and Jack."

"Okay, who wants breakfast?" I hear a man call out to the rest of the camp from where he's roasting the squirrels. It's the man that had restrained Andrew yesterday when we were fighting. I assume the boy's name is Phil as Corinne mentioned the name before, but I hadn't met him yet. He's tall and very well built with long blond hair pushed back over his head and behind his ears. From his neck dangles a small handmade wooden cross. "We got squirrels, salad…yep, that's pretty much it."

The camp gathers around the fire as Phil rations the cooked meat. Our plates are made of a slab of wood covered in tight vines that strap leaves against the wood. Phil hands me a tiny chunk of meat and Corinne places some lettuce leaves and small tomatoes on my plate.

Taking a quick glance around, I spot Becky sitting down on one of the logs with the twins. They are eagerly chatting with her, displaying only the energy a child could have in a mundane conversation. With all the rumors about her and the recent deaths, she hasn't earned my trust. And while I despise Andrew's leadership, I am not pledging to follow Becky either. I don't know what happened during that fateful hunting trip, but if suspicion has raised enough to help fracture the camp, then it's not miniscule. She talks a lot about building a community, but does she actually hold loyalty to its members?

"How did you guys get so many weapons?" I ask her as I get closer to her, instantly grabbing her attention.

"Oh, hi Jenn, good morning," she says, surprised. She motions beside her. "This seat's open."

"Oh, I just wanted to ask about the weapons," I say quickly.

"C'mon," she says, displaying a soft smile. She doesn't continue until I begrudgingly sit down on the open spot. "As for the weapons, it's like I said, we had a lot of funerals. Whenever we can, we retrieve their weapons and the supplies they carry. Other times, we scavenge the bodies of the undead. It's what keeps us going. But ever since Headmaster stopped giving out guns to the Level 3 and 4 castoffs, we've been pretty low on ammo."

I turn back to the lump of squirrel meat on my plate. Compared to the rations we were living on back at the boat, this is a luxury. I dig my knife into the meat and greedily eat the food.

"You should try eating slower," Becky advises. "Savor the meal. There's not enough for seconds."

She points to the fire and all the meat is gone, having been devoured by the large camp. I try eating slower, letting my tongue soak up the fatty taste of the meat.

"How was your sleep?" Becky asks me, and I ignore her briefly to finish the chewy bite.

"Definitely comfier than whatever mattress they gave us on the boat," I say.

"That's not saying much," she jokes.

"True," I say before shoving the last bite of squirrel into my mouth.

"Just wait until you make an imprint in the dirt and then the floor really becomes a bed," she says, and I smile back. "It's the best."

"Alright, listen up!" Blake announces, gathering everyone's attention. "Becky and I went over the assignments for today. Phil, you said you would go hunting with me today and I'm holding you to it."

"I never said that," Phil responds in a-matter-of-fact tone, yet says nothing further. Arguing with Blake is fruitless.

"Riley, Jack, you come with us too. You guys know how to use range weapons, so you might as well use them for the camp," he continues. "Lie, east post. Vincent, north post. *Try* to remain at your posts this time; you guys have the easy jobs. Bella, south post. Kris, Noah, and Andrew, you're on west field. Coco, take Jenn to east field. Look over the crops. And by that, I mean tend to them, don't just watch them."

"Don't call me Coco," Corinne comments, exaggerating a shiver of disgust, but Blake's already moved on.

"Patrick, it's your turn for compost duty," Blake says, pausing with a smirk as he relishes in the assignment of the unfortunate job. From beside me, Becky nods attentively, and I can nearly make out the motion of her mouthing along to his words. "Rack up some dried leaves to add to the poop compost. Then, transfer the pee over to the cleaning station. If you still got time after that, dilute the pee and start cleaning the dishes and clothes piling up over there."

"Can't wait," Patrick mutters.

"You…" Blake says, pointing at Xander.

"Name's Xander," Xander interrupts, raising his hand meekly.

"Don't care," Blake continues swiftly. "You and Becky can help out Tony, Dwayne, and Kyle— or, as I like to call them, the Three Muska-dimwits— with the fruit trees."

"Don't call me Tony," Anthony states, and Corinne chuckles.

"The name 'Anthony' is too long. You don't need all those syllables," Blake responds, shrugging. "Gotta condense."

"Fruit trees?" Lie asks.

"We were planning on replanting more of the local fruit trees like peaches and pomegranates right outside the hedge so they're easier to get," Anthony informs her. He is standing, arms folded, next to a seated Kris.

"Before you do that, though, do a full perimeter check on the fence. The *entire* fence," Andrew orders at Anthony, who doesn't even look at him. ""'Patch up any breaks."

"Of course, Andrew," Becky says. "That's why we decided to make their group a little bigger. Extra protection just in case."

"Bare minimum," he mumbles.

"But…Blake, I wasn't supposed be on that today," Becky continues, turning her attention over. "I was taking the twins fishing today."

"Our safety depends more on a perimeter check than fishing," Andrew retorts.

"Do we really trust her around undead yet though?" Lie mumbles, and I hear Becky take in a sharp breath of air.

"Becky, come with us today," Anthony states firmly, locking eyes with her. "We could use your help. I'm sure we'll feel safer with you around too. It'll probably be fine anyway, there was nothing on our perimeter check yesterday."

After a moment of consideration, Becky nods and then turns to the twins beside her. "Sorry kiddos, I have to call a rain-check on fishing today."

"But that's what you said last time," Ana complains, glancing at her brother for a moment. "C'mon, please. We really want to go."

"I'm sorry guys, I really am," Becky says with a heavy sigh. "But I can't today."

"I wouldn't mind showing them to the lake for an hour or so," Patrick pipes up, his squeaking voice commanding the stares of the whole group. "My duties won't take all day, so I'll have some extra time anyway."

"What if she takes us?" Ana suddenly offers, pointing one of her soft fingers in my direction.

"What?" I respond automatically, my eyes strained open in surprise.

"I mean…you should get acquainted with the lake at some point anyway. Would you mind?" Becky says quietly, looking at me.

I open my mouth to shut her down instantly, and my eyes migrate over to Ana, at first with the purpose of beaming a scolding glare at her for putting me in this position. However, I choke on my breath, speechless at the sight of her large eyes staring hopefully into mine.

"I…" I mutter, mesmerized by the young girl's youthful stare. Caught with uncertainty, I take in a deep breath. "Sure, I guess, why not? I'm sure the crops can watch themselves."

"You sure?" she verifies, drawing my gaze over to her.

"Yeah, I can figure it out," I say.

"Thank you so much," Becky says gratefully, a relieved smile breaking out on her lips. "Patrick, if you do finish a bit early, you can help Corinne finish up the crops in the east field."

"Yay!" Ana shouts out suddenly, and I restrain my smirk.

"The lake is just down the way over there. Maybe a mile or two—not far. It's within the hunting safe zone, so it's closed off with fences and you won't have to deal with the undeads," Becky explains as the campers around us begin to disperse. She points to two log cabins on the southern edge of east field and tents. "The fishing materials are over there where we keep the rest of our storage items. It would be on the left one; that one's dedicated for food."

"When should we go?" I ask, finishing my meal and handing my plate to Patrick as he comes around to collect them.

"Whenever you're ready," she says with a shrug. "I'm about to head off now. You might want to too, while the fish are still hungry."

"Jenn!" Xander calls me just then. I look back once at Becky and smile before she gets up and leaves. Behind her, Ana and Charlie smile at me anxiously.

"Can we go?" Charlie asks, grinning ear to ear.

"Yeah, I just have to talk to Xander first," I say. "Can you guys get the fishing stuff?"

"What fishing stuff?"

"You know, the poles, the buckets, the bait," I list, looking over my shoulder at Xander as he walks over.

"What's bait?" Ana asks, looking at her brother. Both of them wear the same puzzled look and turn back to me in unison.

"It's what the fish eat," I tell them, unsure of my own words and clearly not fixing the perplexed looks they give me. "It should look like a worm? I don't know, go ask Becky."

"Ewwww they eat worms?" Ana exclaims, scrunching up her face in disgust and causing me to chuckle a little.

"Ooh, can I touch the worms?" Charlie asks. Unlike his sister, his eyes are widened and filled with excitement.

"Yes, yes *you* can," Ana emphasizes, still disgusted at the thought.

"Okay," I say, biting my lip for a second as I watch them. "You guys do that. I'll meet you back here when you're ready,"

"Will do," Charlie says. The young boy smiles proudly, and the two scurry off. Xander appears at my side.

"What?" I demand, furrowing my eyebrow when I notice his wide grin.

"It's just—"

"What?" I repeat again, defensively.

"You're good to them," he says simply.

"I've hardly talked to them," I protest.

"And yet, they asked you to take them fishing," he continues, and I furrow my eyebrows.

"Their other option was Patrick. They were desperate," I say. "They don't even know me. And frankly, they shouldn't trust strangers so much. It's just not safe."

"They like you, just take it," he says again, grinning again through his shrug. "Maybe they'll get you to admit you're not as cold-hearted as you think."

"Your hopes are too high. I hate kids. They're just grimy undisciplined bundles of chaos."

"Hey, Jenn." I hear Jack from behind me, and I quickly turn around to see both him and Riley striding by.

"Did Xander tell you…?" I start to ask.

"He did," Riley says. The edge of her mouth curls into a teasing smile. "I think it'll be good for us. It's a good thing we ran into Blake in the forest."

"I heard my name and I shouldn't," Blake grumbles, startling Riley as he walks by. "Not unless one of you is dying or something."

"We're going to teach him how to hunt," Riley says giddily to me, and Jack scoffs. Her golden hair sways behind her as she flips her head between Blake and me.

"We going or what? I ain't got all day," Blake calls out again, now standing by the hedge entrance. Riley's eyes, light green like the beachgrass by the shore, drift by mine one more time before she and Jack head off.

"I should probably go too. I have to find the other guys or else I'll get left behind," Xander says. "When are you coming back?"

"Probably by sunset," I guess. "How 'bout you?"

"Probably the same," he says as he begins walking backwards. "I'll see you then. And take care of those kids today!"

I just smile in return and watch him leave. The camp site emptied pretty quickly with everyone going their separate ways. With the dry sun still beating down on my skin, I almost mistake the lingering smell of squirrel meat for my sizzling skin.

Patrick is hunched by his tent alone, and I catch him staring at me with his small beady eyes. I shift unevenly on my feet. The sun shoots into my eyes and I look away, but after recuperating, I steal a glimpse back at him to see him unchanged.

"What are you looking at?" I call out.

"You." His voice is eerily plain.

"Yeah, well quit it, your beady stare is weirding me out," I remark.

"Take care of those twins today," he mutters, mimicking Xander's last words. A small smirk rises from his lips like a venomous snake.

"I plan on it," I say firmly, the annoyance creeping into my voice. "Look, it's too early in the morning for whatever you're doing. I'm not trying to start something."

"Andrew's nose says otherwise." As soon as he says those words, he turns red and his façade breaks. "Well, like, you know, when you hit him yesterday. I meant to say you picked a fight."

"And since you're his personal assistant, you're saying I picked a fight with you too?" I clarify, raising an eyebrow in amusement.

"I'm just letting you know that you're on his bad side," he says, at last standing up as he starts to depart. "And that's not a good place to be."

"I'm a Bellator, hun," I say, walking over to meet him. "*My* bad side is what you should be concerned with."

He grumbles something inaudibly as he continues to walk off.

"Freak," I mumble to myself.

CHAPTER 16

Riley

Species and species of flora thrive along the bases of the thick trees this deep in the island's forest. I examine them, trying to identify them the best I can and taking a mental inventory of the presence and abundance of any known herbs and edible plants. Blake's been leading the way on the hunt all day. Though it seems like we've been wandering aimlessly for the past few hours, every now and then I see my mental landmarks in the forest surrounding us.

We had split up into groups of two: Jack is shadowing Phil while I follow Blake. We're still in shouting distance, however, for safety reasons. Jack brought his bow, while I was given a bow from the camp's storage. Still, I opted to bring my throwing knives as well. Blake carries two sacks on his back, but all we've caught so far are a couple rabbits, a squirrel, and an opossum. We'd happened upon a rabbit den, but Blake advised to leave it alone to allow them to grow. He explained that sometimes they'll even capture and breed animals so that they keep the populations resilient to the risk of over-hunting.

My brain absorbs details of the forest as the remnants of the setting sun creep through the gaps of the trees to paint slivers of greenery in golden light. We've been out all day.

"We should get back before dark," I say, but he ignores me. "Blake?"

"You think this is my first time out?" he comments sharply. Without looking back at me, he throws his arm out to the side, pointing off through the trees. "You see the tree with the slashes in it? We're nearing the safety fence. We'll be back to camp before sundown."

The safety fence surrounds the camp. Made of wood and bone, it marks the territory of our hunting grounds for small animals. The few larger animals that still exist on the island are beyond the fence…along with the undeads. Blake says the safe zone was set up for 'wimps'. We left the safe zone a while ago.

Just then, Blake crouches down and slides his empty bag from his shoulder. As I approach him, I look over his shoulder to see skeletal remains half-hidden under dirt and the tattered fabric of an orange jumpsuit.

"Was that an undead?" I ask, watching intently as he inspects the corpse before carefully picking out bones and shoving them into his bag.

"Was it the orange that gave it away? You're a fast learner," he quips sarcastically, and I purse my lips in frustration.

"And you're taking it?" I ask instead.

"Good material," he answers simply. "Fences, fishhooks, blade sharpeners, any tools we need. If you need to make something, bone is always a good option."

"So, the undeads still decay?" I continue, now staring at the skull at the top of the skeleton. It's not entirely decayed, but the skin covering it has thinned and grayed, clinging to the bone along with mosses and molds from the earth around it.

"Yup," he answers. "They wander around until their bodies fall to pieces."

"Incredible," I murmur. As he stands back up, I take notice of his gun at his hip. "Would I be able to see your gun? I've never held one before."

Blake takes a heavy sigh before silently handing over the weapon.

"Well, don't do *that*," Blake retorts, smirking a little as I curiously peer into the barrel. He lowers it away from me before slipping it out of my hands. "Ok, you're done."

"It's an incredible device, really," I say. "Incredibly deadly too. Must be convenient to have it out here, though."

"You talk a lot," he mutters, beginning to walk away."

"I've actually never gotten that before."

"Everyone probably just tunes you out instead."

My eyes wander past Blake and the dead body of the undead into the overgrowth surrounding us. Spotting a small bright blue spark of color in the greenery, I step past Blake to make my way over. As expected, hidden beneath the shrubs at the base of a thick tree trunk, a grouping of mushrooms pierce up from the dirt.

"These are edible and extremely high in protein," I explain aloud to Blake as I begin to collect them from the dirt. "They were always my favorite because their color is just so beautiful. Like a glimpse of the sky growing from the ground."

They're also the color of Jack's eyes.

When I turn back to Blake, he glances up briefly at me before turning his attention to the mushrooms in my hands. After a moment of thought, he silently throws me one of his satchels.

"So, you're sticking around camp, eh?" Blake says as he stands back up again and throws the bag of bones back over his shoulder.

"Yeah. We were all already on board; we just needed Jenn to agree too," I say, handing him back his other bag.

"What made her come through?"

"She didn't tell me," I explain. "I bet it was Andrew. She sees a monster in him."

"He doesn't scare her?"

"Probably does," I say, recalling the way her demeanor collapsed when he first approached her. "But that never stops her."

"Really?"

"She's stubborn… and crazy," I say, widening my eyes a bit at the word.

"Tough one, huh?" Blake smirks, glancing back at me.

"She is," I say, then smile.

As my eyes peruse the area, they're immediately drawn to a daunting image not far from us. Between the trees, with the sun sparkling from behind, a dark figure appears to levitate halfway through the air, hanging heavily from its own weight subjected to the pull of gravity—a body.

"What is that?" I ask, my voice low. I already know the answer.

Drawing his eyes expectantly over to the hanging body, Blake nods in assurance. "Means we're on the right path."

"What happened to him?"

"Some people just aren't cut out for these types of situations," he answers indifferently. "That's the easy way out—the weak way. I ain't got any sympathy left for people like that."

"You don't know what he went through—"

"Hell, we've all been through hell. Means nothing," he sneers, and I purse my lips.

"Well, why didn't you help him?" I ask, still unable to look away. "Why didn't your camp let him in?"

"The way to keep a camp safe is to keep it secret. Never met him," Blake explains, as the dark image begins to disappear in the layers of trees between us. "So close to camp too. Funny how help could be so close yet too late."

"It's not funny," I say so softly that he can't hear. I crane my neck as we walk away, trying to catch a final glimpse of the disappearing sight. Even after the body is completely out of sight, my eyes still linger, mesmerized and shaken by the memory of the slight swing in the wind.

Just then, my ears pick up on an almost muted, far-off and high-pitched screech. I am almost going to pass it off as a bird, but Blake stops. It's not a bird; it's the blood-curtailing scream of a person.

"Cut right through here," Blake says just then, and I begin to feel my heart beat faster, the blood churning in my veins. He's starting to jog a little, sidestepping really, as he hastily gives me directions. "Run straight. It's a shortcut."

"Blake," I stammer through my speechlessness as I scurry to keep up with him.

"You'll see the fence, hop it. Get back to camp, tell everyone to stay inside."

"Where are you going?" I ask quickly. I reach for the bow draped over my body, but in my haste, I fumble the weapon and it slips through my shaking hands. Drawn by the sound of the weapon that now lies in the dirt at my feet, he gives me a double take.

"Phil! Jack! Back to camp, now!" Blake suddenly calls out, his rough voice resounding, but I already see them running toward us.

"Head to the fruit trees, make sure the others are alright, then bring 'em all back to camp," Blake orders Phil as he approaches. Phil doesn't even slow down as he passes us, flying through the trees. In a moment, he's disappeared to follow Blake's command. "Jack, follow Riley straight back to camp."

"Where did the scream come from?" I ask Blake, trying to squeeze in my question before he departs.

"The lake!" he calls back before he, too, disappears into the forest ahead of me.

Silence dawns on the forest once again, and the only sounds seem to come from my heaving breaths.

"That's where Jenn is with the kids," Jack mutters from beside me. I feel his stare on me, but my eyes are unmoved from the spot where Blake left us. I drop to the floor and will my trembling hands to clasp the wooden bow.

"C'mon," I say through panicked breaths and look up at Jack earnestly. In one move, I throw the bow across my body again.

We're dashing back to camp now; I'm attempting to lead the way, and Jack trails just behind me. My blond hair slips gradually from my ponytail each time I whip my head around in my constant, impatient search for the "safe zone" fence. I try to steady my mind to search for the mental landmarks I made on the trees, but my eyes are more distracted looking for something else. Every now and then, I hear the moans and groans of the undeads as we fly by. Most of them are rather distant, but their voices echo in my brain behind the thundering of my anxious heart.

I spot the orange clothing of an undead in the trees before us and make a sharp turn to evade it. My head still turned to watch the undead fade from sight, I look back ahead just in time to catch sight of another snarling undead waiting in front of me.

With a gasp, I thrust myself to the side and the undead's outstretched arms just brush my shoulder. My foot loses balance on the uneven ground, and I tumble down the small hill. At the bottom, another undead snarls at me, but I quickly regain my stance to face it. From above, at the top of the hill, an arrow flies down to my rescue. It smacks into the side of the undead's head, whipping it sharply to the side before the undead crashes to the ground. Jack appears swiftly after, retrieving his arrow.

I unsheathe one of the daggers from my belt, weighing it in my hand as I watch another undead stumble towards us, with its mouth wide open for full view of its rotted teeth. The sickly pallor in its skin appears grayed as though every other color had been slowly stripped away with time. Full pieces of the dead flesh peel and hang off of its face, too weak and decayed to hold onto the surrounding tissue.

With a quick flick of my wrist, I release the knife, and the undead's head is thrown back with the slick hilt of the slim blade protruding from its forehead. Frozen for a second, it takes a moment before finally collapsing. I breathe out a deep sigh, touching the back of my hand to my forehead. I feel Jack's hand on my shoulder as my body relaxes in a weakened hunch.

"One less walking around," he mutters, noticing my apprehension. He's right.

Just a little braver, I tell myself. *Be just a little braver.* I let my eyes linger on the defeated body for a moment longer before we head off.

As we continue running, my eyes pick up on a glimpse of the low wooden fence up ahead. Before the fence, however, stand a small gathering of four more undeads.

From beside me, Jack strings two arrows and releases them simultaneously to impale two of the waiting undeads. I attempt to do the same, slowing down my jogging to focus; with a strike from each of my hands, I hurl two knives toward the group. One of the undeads falls to the floor from a fatal blow, but the other knife jams into the shoulder of a second one.

I hold my breath as I charge toward the last remaining undead, invigorated by the promising sight of our escape just yards away. I pull out yet another dagger, and when I reach the undead, I dodge its outstretched grasping hands to grab it by the shoulder. Fighting to hold it back, I wind my arm back and thrust my knife forward, straight into the beast's eye. It goes limp in my grasp, and I let it fall to the floor. Jack rushes past me to retrieve his arrows from his two slain undeads, which had been standing closer to the fence than mine were.

Just then, I am yanked back from a hand on my shoulder, and when I turn around, I come face to face with more undeads. I scream frantically as a beast tries pulling one of my arms up to its mouth. I feel another grab from behind me, and I cry louder, pleading for my life. Suddenly, I feel like I am back in the deck of the boat on the shore, panicking about all the ways I could be mutilated right now and how these could be the last few moments of my life.

A gust of air passes by me and the undead behind me drops, and the hot, wet air that it had been emitting on my neck disappears. Still holding my dagger, I raise it up and jab it into the skull of my attacker. When I whip the blade out, blood sprays out in a stream after it and the undead drops to the floor, letting its grip on my arm fall loose enough for me to shake it off.

I let my eyes linger on the bodies as I stand there, frozen and covered in the blood of others but none of my own. My heart still screams in my head, urging me to escape across the fence with Jack. And after a final deep breath, I do.

CHAPTER 17

Jenn

"Alright, if you feel something tug on the line, let me know," I say. In the midst of the grand lake, our small canoe floats and each of us feed our lines into the water. The rudimentary fishing poles are constructed out of long bones strapped together. A rope strings along the pole and ends in a curved needle fashioned from bone as well. "You're fishing for food, so we have to make this count."

"Got it." Ana nods as I help her lower her line. "Just as long as I don't have to actually touch the live bait."

"C'mon, that's the fun part!" Charlie shouts from beside her on the boat.

"How are you doing, Charlie?" I ask entertainingly, watching as he struggles with the live worms. One by one, the slimy pink insects drop from his hands and squirm desperately along the floor.

"Good," he just says as he picks another worm from the bucket. In an attempt to attach it to the hook, he cuts a fatal wound along its body and the suffering creature falls from his hands. "I think I got this thing figured out."

"Hey, look at what you're dropping," I exclaim, moving on the opposite side of Ana so that I sit between the two. "That's good bait."

"Sorry." He hands his reel to me and bends down to gather the freed bugs. "I got it."

"It's fine," I say, impaling a fresh worm on the hook for him. "Here."

"Thanks," he says, and I help him lower his line into the water as well. "I'm so gonna get a bite before Ana."

"Yeah, fat chance," she shouts over to him, smiling slyly to herself.

"Well, if it's competition you're talking about," I amuse, pointing two thumbs at myself, "my bets are on myself."

"Well, then it's a contest." Ana smiles broadly, holding out a hand toward me and I shake it.

The air is definitely cooler on the lake than at the camp and a slight breeze caresses my skin as it passes. The sun shines bright overheard and, without the trees blocking it, the sun's warm rays embrace us. I ready my own line, dipping it into the water, and close my eyes to enjoy the serenity of the soothing waves rocking the boat.

"How did you learn how to fish?" Ana asks.

"Never did," I say, smiling to myself as I sort through my memories. "But when I was younger, my nanny enjoyed it so sometimes she'd drag me to the lake near our house. I'd just chill with her on the boat. I thought she was the coolest for it."

"Were you close with your parents?" Ana asks innocently, her large eyes staring out into the water.

"No," I mutter, turning my eyes down to the water below as well. "Not really."

"Our parents are nannies," Ana continues on.

"Yup," Charlie says. "They would look after other kids during the day while our nanny watched us and then they'd come back at nighttime."

"I can't wait for visiting day when we get to see our parents again," Ana states, and I bite my lip silently. "Why are we on this island, anyway?"

"What do you mean?" I ask cautiously.

"Patrick said it's because the Headmaster at our school didn't want us around," she says. Though the words come out in a matter-of-fact tone, she steals a quick glance at me, urging me to challenge her.

"Patrick's just upset that nobody wants *him* around," I state.

"It's not true, is it?" Charlie asks from behind me, daring to say what Anna won't.

"Well," I say slowly, lost for words as I glance at the kids' inquisitive faces. "It's complicated."

"Why are we not wanted?" Charlie narrows his eyes at me. "Do you know?"

"You want to know? You deserve to," I start off firmly, cursing Becky for not taking the role upon herself to inform these kids. I take a breath and gather myself. "We're the misfits of the BAA; people who don't fit into Headmaster's slim ideals for a soldier. Whether that's because we were the lowest of our ranks or because we did something he didn't like. The reasons don't matter at this point. He wants us to be cookie-cutter soldiers and we're not. And now we're here."

"I didn't do anything, I promise!" Anna exclaims out immediately. "Maybe he sent us here by mistake."

"I don't know," I respond just as quickly, biting my tongue to stop myself from saying 'and I don't care.' I came here to fish, not to explain the dynamics of a corrupt institution. I turn my attention back to the water and impatiently swirl my line in hopes of attracting a curious fish.

"But why would he send us here with the undeads? Does he know that it's dangerous?" Charlie asks, earnestly.

Lacking the right words, I don't answer at first. But I know that I can't lie.

"I think so," I say finally with a sigh, and the twins exchange glances.

"Does he want us dead?" Charlie persists, his voice softened, and I purse my lips in frustration at this conversation.

"Look, I don't know, ok," I snap sharply. "The undeads want you dead. And since both you and the undeads are stuck on this island, that's the important part to remember. Got it?"

"Will they eat us?" Ana asks from my left. She bites her lip only to let it slip through her teeth's grasp, sniffling as her voice trembles in fear. As I watch her, my stern demeanor slips and I open my mouth, speechless once again. At my silent reaction, her face finally scrunches up and her tears glisten as they slide down her cheek.

"This conversation is over. Come here," I assert abruptly, wrapping my arms around the two of them to pull them close.

"I don't want to die," Anna mutters again into my arm.

"Wipe those tears. You don't need them," I demand, dragging my finger across her damp cheek. "You'll be ok. I promise."

***

"I can't believe I lost," Charlie grumbles as we each count the amount of fish we each caught. "Not fair."

"Yeah, I'm impressed," I say, turning to Ana. "How'd you get so many?"

"I guess I'm a natural," she boasts, holding up her hands in a shrug. She had beaten me with catching a total of four fish to my three. Charlie had lost with only catching one.

"Natural idiot," mumbles Charlie, and he smirks at his own comment.

"I beat *you,* didn't I?" Ana attempts to lift her bucket but gives up after struggling with the weight. Charlie rolls his eyes, and Ana revels in his defeat. "You're just a sore loser."

By now, the sun was starting to set, letting orange light bleed across the glistening lake. Everyone would probably be heading back to camp right about now.

"It doesn't really matter who won, as long as we got the fish, right? Regardless, we'll all be eating good tonight," I say, patting Charlie on the back. "We should get going though."

While I grab the fishing poles and my bucket, the twins pick up their own buckets with some difficulty, especially Ana who still struggles with the extra fish.

"Here, give me that." I let out a chuckle as I take Ana's bucket into my own hand. Out of the corner of my eye, I notice a lone bucket that we'd left in the sand by the canoe. "Ana, can you grab the bait bucket instead?"

"Sure," she says as she smoothes out the indentations on her palm made from the handles of her bucket. "Be right back."

We'd docked the canoe in a small cove off the lake. On the three sides of the cove bounded by land, the forest huddles close to the water, leaving only a thin strip of sand on the U-shaped land before it fades quickly into the grass. Fauna from the overgrowth of the trees hang over the shallow water, admiring its own green reflection in the soft, shimmering waves.

Between the fray of branches between us, I catch a view of Anna. Her bouncing curls sway as she darts off out of the forest and as she passes over the sand, her small feet kick up a golden spray behind her. I smile as she hesitates at the shoreline, admiring the scene of the setting sun. Her dark silhouette is outlined like a halo by the orange sun, giving her an angelic aura.

"I can carry Ana's bucket," Charlie offers, reaching out his hand toward the bucket in my grip.

"Not so fast, little man. We have to bring these all the way back to camp, and I can't have you wear out your muscles," I protest.

"I don't wanna just carry one fish, though. That's so lame," he says again, swinging his bucket gently.

"Why is that lame? Maybe the fish were too intimidated by you to get close. I don't know how fish think," I offer, raising an eyebrow and he chuckles. "Why don't we exchange buckets when we get close to camp, and we'll just tell everyone you carried it the whole time?"

"Deal!"

I roll my eyes at the silly conversation and bring my focus back to Ana. Just then, I'm struck at the sight of another figure on the shoreline. Approaching from the side of the cove, the figure of a man peels himself from the concealment of the overgrowth and hobbles across the sand.

"Ana!" I scream. The curls of her hair fly as she whisks her head around to face me. Instantly, I'm rushing forward at full speed toward her.

By the time she first hears the low murmur of the undead's dreary moan, it's already upon her. Shrieking, she begins to dart back up the shore, her feet dredging through the sand as she runs, but the undead reaches out, clipping her arm. She staggers forward, and the undead continues to pursue her, fumbling in his grasp on her arm. Finally, she collapses under the weight of the undead as it pushes itself onto her.

Through the stray branches from the trees between us, I am given a clear view of Ana on the ground, the undead now gripping her leg. Her shriek carries across the shore as the undead wraps its yellowed teeth around her calf. Blood spills over its lips as it clamps down on her skin. Greedily, it pulls out a bloody chunk of flesh and strings of skin and tissue stretch out from its origin before finally tearing. The blood bubbles and squirts out of Ana's leg, overfilling the hole created by the bite and dripping onto the sand. The undead is almost too busy chewing to notice her small foot slip from its grasp, and she lurches forward, clawing her way desperately through the sand.

Tears stream down her face as she cries, and for a moment—just a moment—our eyes lock. I'm still running and getting closer, but I feel the world slow down as the undead grabs Ana from behind and sinks its teeth deep into her neck.

"Ahhhhhhh!" Ana screams as dark crimson blood cascades down her neck and shoulder. The scream shatters my ears and the world becomes a huge blur in my raging eyes.

My shoes hit the sand as I burst from the forest. The undead rips off the large chunk from her neck and stares disgustingly up at me. It's mocking me, rubbing it in my face that I've failed. A long stream of blood squirts out from her severed arteries and crashes down on her shirt like a wave against the sand. The gushing flow of blood doesn't cease, falling quickly from the large hole in her neck.

Rage swells up in me as I reach for the axe at my belt. When I finally approach the two of them, I slice my axe right through the beast's face. The top half of its skull is flung from the rest of the body from the force of my attack, and its dead body drops with it.

"Ana! Ana!" Charlie yells in a panicked voice as he runs to her side where she had collapsed in the sand. Blood continues to pulse out of her neck and stain the sand around her. He hovers over her and cradles her face in his hands, horror-stricken as he watches his sister fade. He turns to me, yelling. "*Do something!*"

I drop my axe and run to the other side of Ana's body. A large chunk of muscle and skin in her neck is missing, exposing the ends of several severed blood vessels leaking her bright blood. I press down on the exposed wound, applying pressure in an attempt to slow blood loss. Blood slides in between my fingers and floods over my hands. I move my hands around, trying to find the arteries to clamp with my fingers but they are lost in all of the blood.

Her eyes jump between our faces rapidly and she struggles to talk, but her mind can't even process what's happening and her mouth can't form words. Yet, she's pleading to not let her die. Still,

I watch as her eyes slowly drift off until they become blank and she stares with an empty gaze straight ahead.

"Ana!" Charlie cries again in anguish as he stares at his twin's lifeless body. "Ana, please! Ana!"

"No!" I scream out as I apply even more pressure on her wound. "No, damnit! No!"

Finally, the bleeding begins to cease. For a while, I remain frozen, my hands still pressed firmly onto her weak neck. My heart continues to pound in my ears along with the dreary melody of Charlie's aching sobs. Then, sluggishly, my gaze becomes hazy as it moves slowly up her pale skin to admire her delicate features. Shaking my head, I lift my hands in horror and stare at the deep red color coating the skin of my hands and forearms. My head spins with unused adrenaline, and I can now feel how fast my breathing had become. Blood stains the sand all around us, running rivers in the ground's grooves and spreading further along the shore. I try to force myself to stand up, but my legs won't budge. I try to force myself to move at all, but I can't.

***

The night quickly settles in after Ana's death. The air is cool and even the moon is out in a cloudless sky, casting its light across the water of the lake. Time goes by slowly, each second dragging longer than the last.

"How much longer?" I ask Blake softly. He had arrived shortly after Ana's death. Apparently, there was a group of a few other undeads within the lake safe zone that he bumped into on his way to us. Ana's murderer must've gotten separated from the pack.

Phil and some of the others arrived a little while after Blake, but Blake sent them back to carry the news to the rest of the camp. He wanted to shoot Ana before she could turn, but Charlie refused to leave his sister's side. He screamed and cursed at us for trying to remove him, but it was only after Charlie demanded that we would have to shoot him too that we finally gave in. Blake and I now sit on the sand not far from where the child still hovers over his sister's body, grieving.

"Usually it takes a couple hours," Blake whispers to me. "Kids usually take only an hour for the virus to take hold."

"How long has it been?" I ask, my exhaustion preventing all but the minimal flutter of the lips to let the words escape.

"An hour," he grumbles, and I catch my breath, stealing a glance at him. He's holding his gun. "We should've handled it before she could turn."

Ana's face is pale, and the blood has dried around her neck and chest, dressing her skin in a maroon crust. The moon pours light across her hollow cheeks and glistens across her pale skin, painting her in a new sorrowful brightness. As I look at her lifeless body, I try to remember her bustling energy just hours before.

Then, something catches my eye—a twitch so slight that it's hard to even distinguish. It occurs in Ana's hand and then another appears in her shoulder.

"I'm so sorry Ana," Charlie whispers to his sister as he smooths her blood splattered hair. I see another twitch in Ana's hand. This one's bigger, nearly lifting her hand off the ground. Her shoulders readjust again and her head tics. "I'll go back home. I'll tell mom and dad."

"Charlie, come here," I order, but he ignores me. I stride across the sand and squat beside him. "Charlie, it's time. You have to go now."

Just then, I hear the deep heaving of Ana's breathing. Charlie still stares at her, watching her mouth shudder to confirm that's where the sound is coming from. Sorrow pours from his eyes in the form of a tear.

"I love you," Charlie croaks and he tightens his grip on his sister as if to prevent her from leaving.

We both watch silently as Ana opens up her eyes again, and for a moment—just a moment—she almost looks like Ana again. I try to pull him back from her, but he doesn't budge. I know I should, but I don't fight it; I'm too mesmerized by the resurrection of the young girl lying right before me. I gasp in a long breath of the cool air as I watch her distant, gray eyes wander over to her brother. I hear a low moan escape her lips as she attempts to raise herself off the ground.

"Ana?" Charlie whispers, choking on his sob. But this is not Ana. This time, grabbing both of his arms, I yank him from her, lifting him from the ground. She reaches for him, but I swing his body away and place him on his feet beside me.

Suddenly, a shot fires, and Ana's head is jerked to the side as the bullet tears through her brain. She falls back down into the red sand, motionless, allowing a fresh puddle of blood to form around her again. Charlie erupts in a scream, and I drop to my knees to hold him, allowing him to wet my shoulder with his sweet tears. His body is warm, and I relish in the comfort of having him still here with me. Though I shield his eyes with my body, my own gaze is glued to the crumpled body of the little girl. Her contorted head now stares blankly again out across the water from below the weeping bullet hole that burst from her mutilated forehead.

CHAPTER 18

Riley

After Phil brought the news of the tragedy that happened at the lake, a gloom had settled over the camp. It's quieter than I've even seen it. I keep a keen ear for crying but can't make it out. Abandoning their duties, everyone mainly keeps to their tents. Others group together in secluded areas to help each other in the grieving. As a newcomer, I'm not invited. All I know is to not impede, and so Jack and I keep to ourselves in our tent.

No one knows exactly what happened at the lake, and the uncertainty is maddening. Though, Xander had told Jack and I earlier that during their perimeter check, a part of the fence was found broken. No undeads were seen, and they patched up the fence without issue.

As I get water from the stream, I spot two of the campers, Dwayne and Kris reclining in the west field. Straining to hear over the sound of the rushing water, I make out snippets of their conversation: they're accusations about Jenn being involved in Ana's death.

"She was the only one there with them," Dwayne says at one point.

"I wonder if she tried to kill Charlie too," Kris poses.

Hours pass, letting the deep night settle in. Becky is seated on the grass not far from the tents, facing the east entrance of the camp. Anthony and Corinne sit on either side of her, and Bella and Noah lounge nearby on the grass.

"They still haven't come back yet?" I ask Phil, who sits on one of the logs around the campfire in the center of the circle of tents. He shakes his head solemnly. Like the others, his eyes are trained on the entrance in anticipation.

"Unfortunately not," he mutters. He places a hand against his wearied face, deep in thought for a moment before turning back to me. "You know, at the BAA, I always found Level 1 to be the harshest of the Levels. It uses force and threats to break down the child and rebuild them into a perfectly disciplined, mindless soldier. But this...to send a child here...is a different type of cruel. She was just a little kid."

Just then, he shoots up from his seat, his tall stature standing above me as he continues to stare into the distance. I noticed it too: the hedge had stirred, and the rest of the camp immediately reacted, stirring with it. Everyone is on their feet. Becky clutches her hands together while Corinne clings to her side, as if physical pressure could calm the storm of emotions inside Becky. The slight rustling sound of the leaves holds the entire camp hostage in silence.

After several more seconds of rustling, a body finally emerges, stepping out onto the green turf of the camp: Jenn. Her body is meek with exhaustion and her usually impeccable posture has finally broken. Brown hair, disheveled and sloppily pushed behind her ears, hangs loose to fall just past her shoulders. Her skin, though deeply tanned from genetics and the sun alike, seems to have lost the vitality it once held and seems paler. The most striking feature, however, is the deep red that coats the front of her body in a thick crust. Painting her hands and forearms, the blood also stains in splatters on the once bright green shirt that dons her torso. If I hadn't known better, one could even mistake her for one of the undeads.

"Jenn?" I call out softly, my gentle voice ringing through the thick silence. Her eyes, circled by deep purple, slowly rise up to meet me. She's there, yet, I see that a part of her isn't.

"Riley," she mutters through her breath, and I can see the sigh of relief that follows at the sight of a familiar face. After what she just experienced, that familiarity is undoubtedly comforting.

Suddenly, the sound of more rustling comes from the hedge and we all watch as Blake steps out next. His large figure contrasts with Jenn, who slowly moves out of his way. His eyes are down in sorrowful agony, and his body hangs in grief like Jenn's. But no one's looking at him. Cradled delicately in his arms lies Ana.

My heart falls as we all take in her lifeless form. Her head hangs limp and her pale lips are slightly parted as if trying to breathe again. Blake's arms are much too big for the small body he carries in them, and he all but conceals her entire form except for the glimpses we see of her head and the shoes that stick out the other side. As he readjusts his hold on her, I catch sight of the maroon painting her white skin in deep contrast along the entire circumference of her neck.

I hear a desolate cry as Becky runs over. No one stops her. At Blake's side follows a solemn Charlie, smeared and covered in his sister's blood.

***

The camp's graveyard is secluded from the rest of the main camp in a separate enclosure. About two miles further into the forest, it consists of a vast expanse of land with its own, though thinner, protective hedges. The entire area is filled with imperfect rows and rows of hundreds of lumps in the dirt that mark the graves of past campers. Walking amongst the seemingly endless graves, it's easy to get overwhelmed with the stench of upheaved dirt and death filling the air.

"Without headstones, how can you know who's who?" Jack had whispered to Phil as we walked.

"If they're important enough to you, you can't forget," Phil had answered.

Solemn, we all stand in a semi-circle around Ana's grave. The same silence hangs in air as when they had walked into camp. Our fear, hopelessness, and anger speak the words that no one says. I barely knew Ana, or frankly anyone at this camp, but everyone understands the weight of death. At this moment, we are all united as one, grieving over the loss of a little innocent girl.

Most of the blood was washed off Ana's sallow skin. With the wound cleaned now, I can distinguish the anatomically detrimental effect the bite had on this little girl. Her neck was thin and so the undead's jaws had easily clamped around and tore off the entire right side of the neck nearly down to the clavicle. With all of that damage, she must have bled out in less than thirty seconds. I shake my head somberly, biting my bottom lip only to release it immediately again.

Is this what I have to look forward to for my baby? I think to myself. *Is my future child destined to go through the same torturous pain of having their neck ripped out? Are we all just destined to die like this on this island?*

"The undeads murdered a child," Andrew announces suddenly, his voice strong with frustration. "Within our safe zone. This is exactly the type of thing I've been saying would happen."

"Andrew, not now," Blake growls.

"Starting today, we need to begin work on stronger fences," Andrew continues, louder. "Reinforce our walls. We begin clearing undeads from the forest, widening a radius gradually until—"

"Andrew, shut up!" Blake barks this time, overtaking Andrew's voice. "This isn't the place or time."

The group descends into a deep silence again, letting the strain of his words hang in our ears for a bit.

"I hate this place," Becky says suddenly, sharply piercing the quiet morning air. She shakes her head as she stares at Ana's still body in her grave. "This graveyard, I hate it. We come here when we're at our worst: when we lose someone. Ana should have never been sent to this island. Her death is one that makes you feel just…lost. One moment you're with someone, and then you realize that it was the last moment. In some ways I felt like Ana was my own daughter. I'll think about my last moment with her for the rest of my life. Wondering about what her last thoughts about you were. Or in general. Wondering what I would say or do differently if I knew that it was the last…"

She stops when her voice cracks and she has to clear her throat. She tries to compose herself, but her voice chokes again, and she pauses, holding her jaw clenched as still as stone.

I catch Jenn from across the circle just in time to see a tear slide down her cheek. I wonder if it's the first or just the tip of her emotional iceberg. By the time you see the smoke of a fire, the flames have already caused irreversible and extensive destruction.

"We have to try to stay strong through this," I hear Blake say, drawing everyone's attention. Once we lock eyes, he takes in a deep breath, and I pretend I don't see the gloss in his eyes too. "Unfortunately, what's done is done. Nothing we can do about it. We have to learn to live with it. That's just what we gotta do."

CHAPTER 19

Jenn

"Jenn?" Xander's voice comes from outside my tent. When I don't answer, he comes inside.

"What do you want?" I mumble, avoiding eye contact. I'd been staying in my tent for hours after the funeral, unable to muster the energy to leave.

"How are you holding up?" Xander asks softly. I don't respond. Instead, I just stare in the opposite direction as him.

"I'm not in the mood to talk," I say, but I hear his footsteps as he approaches me. "Can you please just go? I just want to be alone."

"Jenn…about Ana…"

"Can you just leave me alone?" I snap. It hasn't been just him that I've shooed away since Ana's death. Riley and Jack each made their attempts, earnest to mourn with me and learn my side of what happened at the lake. But it's been Xander's persistence that really ticks me off.

"It's not your fault, Jenn. I know that. We all do," Xander says.

"Oh please, you must've been hearing the whispers too," I say, pushing out the tired words through my exhaustion. "I wouldn't be surprised if people start saying I bit her myself."

"Ignore them, they're assholes."

"If you want to comfort someone, talk to Becky," I say roughly, twisting my finger into the dirt in front of me. "She won't even let me speak to her."

"I'll see Becky later. But I'm talking to you *now*," he emphasizes. "You can't blame yourself for these things, Jenn. This is all on Headmaster. *He's* the real killer, and you can't let him manipulate you into thinking you are. You had no control over what happened to Ana—"

"Stop *saying* that," I snap again, and he pulls away slowly, caught off guard. "Ana's dead. This is the second time I watched someone get killed right in front of me. And it's the second time I did nothing to stop it."

"There was nothing you could've done—"

"No, I—" I interrupt him, holding up a hand to silence him. My lip begins to quiver, and I take in a deep breath to steady myself. "I can hurt people. I hurt people at the BAA all the time. I'm good at it. If I can do that, why can't I even protect someone like Ana?"

"Jenn…Blake said they found that part of the safe zone fence had collapsed. He said it's an accident that happens every now and then when the undeads put a lot of pressure on it. There was nothing you could have done," he says.

"There was *one* undead, Xander! *One!*" I shake my head, letting it fall limply into my hands. I feel tears begin to fall down my cheeks and past my shaking lips.

"This isn't your fault," he affirms.

"It feels like it is," I attempt to mutter through my panting. He wraps his arm around me and pulls me in close. "A Bellator isn't supposed to fail, and yet, that's all I've been doing."

"You're not defined by your name—"

"Clearly," I scoff forcefully, shoving his arm off of me. "I shouldn't have been left alone with the twins; this never would've happened."

"Jenn?" Charlie's voice suddenly reaches us from where he stands at the entrance of the tent.

"Charlie?" I ask, immediately looking up at him and wiping my tear stained cheeks with my hand. "What are you doing?"

"I want to visit Ana's…I want to visit Ana," he says, trying to talk firmly. "Patrick said I should ask you to come with us."

"Us?" I ask.

"Yeah, Patrick and Vincent are gonna take me there," he responds. "Patrick said you should come too, just for safety."

"I'll come too, then," Xander speaks up.

"It's alright," I say, but he just shakes his head.

"I'll come," he insists again.

"Can we go now?" Charlie asks. "We should go before it gets too late."

"The sun's already setting," I contest. "It would be safer tomorrow."

"It can't wait. I didn't get time alone with her at the funeral," he persists. "It won't take long. I'm going with Patrick and Vincent anyway, I just wanted to see if you want to come too."

"I do," I say after a moment. I push myself off the floor and walk out of the tent with Xander following close behind.

"—and that's where this bad boy came from," Anthony finishes his story to Corinne, showing her the large scar running up the entire length of his left arm as they walk past our tent. "I'm telling you, do not mess with someone with a Morningstar. I still took him down though."

"Yo, that's wild," Corinne remarks, sauntering alongside him. "Man, did you get along with *anyone* at the BAA?"

"No, ma'am, I did not, and I did not want to. The only thing worse than all the rich-ass snobs in the platoons was the staff. Couldn't stand anyone on that campus," Anthony recounts with irritation.

"Is that what got you expelled?" Xander asks as we walk behind them.

The question innocently stems from curiosity, but it makes Anthony stop dead in his tracks. He doesn't even turn around; he just turns his head partially with his brow lowered over his pinpoint eyes, now narrowed into slits. After a few seconds, he resumes walking before him and Corinne separate to duck into their respective tents.

Patrick sits on one of the logs near the campfire. When he spots me, he nudges Vincent beside him.

"Ready to go?" I ask, tightening my lips in restrained impatience.

"Yeah," he responds, nodding and rising to his feet. He picks up a sheathed sword from the floor and straps it to his waist. My gaze travels over to Vincent's belt of weapons, consisting of a dagger on both hips in addition to a gun. The weapons seem dwarfed in comparison to his large build.

"I just need to get my axe," I say.

"Oh, I didn't know you wanted to bring it. I told Bella to clean it along with some of the other dirty weapons," Patrick informs me, and I furrow my eyebrows.

"Ask me first before you take my weapon," I say sternly, keeping my stare on him unwavering. His expression contorts with a raised eyebrow and suppressed smirk.

"Here," Corinne announces loudly as she emerges from her tent nearby. In a few strides, she reaches me at the campfire and hands over a small dagger. "I always keep some on me. You can take this one."

"You have any spares? I'm going with Jenn," Xander asks.

"Alright," Corinne says, reaching under her shirt and pulling another knife from the belt of her pants. "As long as I get them both back."

"Giving up your spares? Risky move," Vincent comments, flicking his eyebrows up in exaggerated concern.

"Yeah, well, I tend to feel safer when you leave camp," she remarks back.

"Thanks Corinne, this'll be all I need," I say before flashing Patrick and Vincent another glare.

"Why are so many of you going?" Corinne asks. "You really think it's that bad out there?"

"I was wondering the same thing too, why *are* so many of us going?" I ask, directing my question at Patrick and Vincent.

"You don't have to come," Patrick says, contorting his face again.

"Wait, you guys are going back to the graveyard?" Noah asks, suddenly emerging from his tent as well. "You think I could come?"

"What? Noah, I—"

"My friend is buried there," he continues, his eyes large and pleading. "We came here together. I try to visit his grave often, but I hate going alone. Mind if I tag along?"

"Jenn," Xander whispers to me, tilting his head sympathetically toward the kid.

"Fine, I guess you could tag long," I say hesitantly. "The more the merrier, right? We'll eat dinner when we return."

I head over to the exit where Charlie is already waiting. With each step I take, I feel the air around me growing colder as I get farther from the comforting heat of the campfire, and the biting chill of the night lingers by my side.

***

"I got the right," I whisper to Xander so softly that I'm not sure if he even heard me clearly. He and I are waiting in the nearby brush in the forest as two lone orange-clad undeads roam by. We are at the border of the graveyard, the entrance only a few yards away. He nods, and I step silently out of the overgrowth. When I'm close enough, I grab one of the undeads by its stringy hair and pull its head back to bury my knife into where the skull meets the spine. Blood squirts out onto my hands before the limp body collapses to my feet. My knife slides out, leaving me standing there with a clump of thin, dead hair in my hand.

The other undead turns around after hearing the commotion, and Xander leaps forward, grabbing its shoulder and stabbing his blade straight through the beast's eye. When he rips the knife out, the undead drops to the ground, blood oozing out from its punctured eye.

"Right here," Noah says as he leads us to the entrance in the hedge. I glance around the premises once more before stepping through the opening, which is simply just an opening in the thin hedge rather than a pathway like at the camp.

Compared to the forest, where the night's mist is caught in the canopy, a heavy fog now covers the graveyard. The wide expanse of land allows the air to settle and the hedge hugs it in, accumulating the fog into a thick cloud. I strain my eyes to see.

"Which way?" I ask Noah as I strain my eyes to try to make out the mounds of dirt up ahead.

"Straight ahead until you see the place with the fresher flowers," he says quietly. His straight black hair falls messily onto his face, and the paleness of his skin contrasts with the darkness of his hair. "I'll meet you back at the entrance in a little bit. I'm going to go visit my friend."

"Were you two close?" I ask him as Xander and the others make their way through the hedge.

"Well, it's one of the guys I was on the boat with when I came here," he responds, picking at his fingernails as he talks. "We were expelled together last year, but we eventually got separated on the island. A search party from the camp found his body and took it back to camp to bury. I figured it would be nice to visit again. No one should be forgotten, you know?"

"Alright, but only for a little bit. We should try to be back to camp as soon as we can," I say, and he nods.

"Hey," he says suddenly, grabbing my wrist gently. I see him hold out the handle of his gun, offering it to me out of view from Patrick and Vincent, who are arguing with Xander over which way to go. Noah's touch is cold, and his cautious eyes look at me from underneath his bangs. "I don't trust them. I never did."

"Thanks," I say but shake my head. "You keep it. I'll be fine."

"You sure?" he says, this time letting go of my arm. "If you need help, just call. I know Xander could probably do much more than me in a fight, but I want to help if I can. Everyone looks at me like I'm a weak link because I was expelled for being lowest rank...but I'm not weak. Especially with this gun."

"If I need help, I'll give you a holler," I agree, and he gives me a small nod before leaving.

"Guys, Noah said it was this way," I call over to the others. Charlie walks hesitantly up to me, glancing around the misty graveyard. I hold out my hand for him, and he grabs it. "Stay close to me, Charlie."

We find Ana's grave on the top of a grass-covered hill. On one side, the incline of the hill is steep before evening out into a plateau that melds with the rest of the graveyard's plain. The grave is distinct by its freshness, the many new footsteps that cover it, and as Noah had mentioned, the brightly colored flowers decorating the lump of dirt. That's what has become of her: a lump of dirt.

Suddenly, a gunshot explodes behind me, shattering the silence, and I throw myself on Charlie to knock us both to the floor.

"What the hell?" I exclaim, looking up behind me.

"My bad," Vincent calls back, though I can't see him through the mist. "I thought I saw an undead."

"Next time give a warning or something!" I yell, picking myself and Charlie off the floor. Patrick emerges from the fog and smiles when he sees us. Calm and at ease, he doesn't look shaken by the abrupt gunshot at all.

"Alright, just…go ahead," I urge Charlie, trying to withhold my haste to get this over with and leave this eerie place. He steps forward and kneels down next to his sister. I walk away, maintaining a distance far enough away to give them space, while also keeping an eye on him.

I shiver in the cold night and turn around slightly to see Patrick nearly ten feet behind me. Further back, I spot Vincent now crossing his arms, his silhouette shrouded by the fog.

"Where's Xander?" I ask.

"Watching the entrance," Patrick says back. "Making sure the undeads don't get in."

"The fog here can hide a lot, you know," Vincent calls out. "Can't risk letting something sneak up behind you."

"Why don't you check up on him, Vincent?" Patrick suggests, and Vincent's silhouette fades like dissipating smoke.

I grip my knife tighter as the cold begins to swarm me, and I shiver again. As I stare over at Ana's grave, I am forced to remember the image of the undead wrapped around her leg. The scene plays over and over in my head, I can't escape the sight of the undead biting a chunk from her neck. Her scream echoes in my ears.

After a few more minutes, I approach Charlie again, who plays with the petals of one of the yellow flowers laying on the dirt.

"Hey, are you cold?" I ask quietly, kneeling down by him. When he doesn't reply, I instinctively take my sweatshirt off and drape it around his shoulders. "Better?"

Kris had taken his shirt to wash, and so now the one he wears drapes over his small body like a dress. Its disproportionate size emphasizes his small body swallowed in the fabric. He nods silently to my words, still refusing to move his gaze from Ana's grave.

"You'll get through this," I say, rubbing his back. "We all will."

"I j-just…" he stutters, his voice full of despair, "I just thought there'd be more time."

"It always seems that way," I say, looking down.

"Jenn!" Charlie screams abruptly and I'm pulled out of my thoughts. His gaze is above my head, and instinctively, I thrust both mine and Charlie's bodies to the side, rolling out of the way of the heavy blade that swings beside us, leaving a small slice on my upper arm.

I'm yanked back by my ponytail and separated from Charlie. In the blur, I see a swinging blade coming toward my face and swiftly spin out of my attacker's grasp to dodge it, swiping my leg across my attacker's knees. In the same movement, I throw a punch into his face as he falls. I reach for my knife and pull it out from my belt as Patrick staggers back to his feet. I charge toward him, and as he swings his broadsword, I duck under it and lodge my elbow into his gut before following up with an uppercut that knocks his head back.

He swings the blade at me again, but I dodge, pushing his arms in the direction of the swing to throw off his balance. With a quick thrust up toward his face, I draw a red gash across his cheek with my knife, and then reverse the movement to slam my elbow hard against his temple. He staggers under the blow but recovers faster than I expect. When I move against him again, he dodges and counters.

I dodge his sword swing after swing and take advantage of a small break in his movements to deliver a high kick to his jaw. I come down with my knife on his shoulder, but he blocks my attack with his arm, leaving my knife hovering an inch above his skin. Suddenly, I feel a blow from the hilt of his sword as it smashes against the side of my head, and I fall to the floor, a trickle of blood sliding down my face. My knife skids across the dirt.

I leap off the floor and throw myself at him. His sword slips from his grasp and he wraps his arms around me, bringing me down with him. We both tumble down the deep slope of the hill before slamming into a tree that rests on the flat land at the bottom of the incline. I quickly rise to my feet, yank Patrick off the floor by the collar, and throw him up against the tree.

I wind up to deliver a punch, but he takes advantage of the time and my lack of a good grip. He pushes me off of him and throws his fist straight into my nose. I retreat a little, my vision blurry. He grabs onto me and throws me up against the tree. I try to shove him off, but he just wraps his large hands my throat, cutting off my breathing.

"You're dead," he taunts, a wicked smile blooming on his lips.

Unable to free myself from his hold, I quit trying to rip his hands from my neck and instead wrap my hands around his forearms, digging my nails into his skin so hard I draw blood. With black spots appearing in my vision, I thrust my thumbs into his eyes and push. He cries out in pain, loosening his grip on my neck. Gasping for air, I thrust my elbow into his neck, and he retreats away from me a little. He waits a moment before attempting to take me down with another punch, but I am able to dodge him, throw a high kick into the side of his head, and then push him up against the tree trunk once again.

"You're the reason Ana's dead, aren't you?" I yell. "You let the undeads into the lake safe zone. That's why you wanted to take the twins fishing. You're trying to kill Charlie, too?"

"It was to make a point about safety," he begins, speaking through deep breaths. He shuts his eyes momentarily to clear his vision. Just then, his face contorts in a smug smile and he blasts out a forced, almost crazed laugh. "But this…is for you."

Before he even finishes the words, in my peripheral vision, I see the glint of a blade flash. Off reflex, I throw myself back just as his hidden blade swings at me. The tip just barely grazes the edge of my neck, but I don't have enough time to even check if any blood was drawn. He swings wildly again, and this time, I dodge with more intent and reset my stance a few feet away.

"Everyone's a goner!" Patrick cries out loud, his voice manic yet prideful.

Just then, a series of shots catches both of our attention. With the heavy fog nearly occluding their figures from my vision, I spot Vincent and Noah in the distance. Vincent throws his shoulder into Noah's side, knocking the smaller boy to the floor. Blood squirts from the younger boy's nose as Vincent punches him repeatedly in the face. Noah throws his hands up to Vincent's face, but Vincent throws them off. With lighting speed, he whips out a blade from his belt and slams it down into Noah's chest.

"No!" I scream out.

Patrick charges at me, and I leap into the air, launching myself to deliver a double kick at his chest and push off into a backflip. His head crashes hard against the tree trunk, and I spin around again to swipe my foot sideways across his face to knock him to the floor. His knife flies from his hand, and in the darkness, I can't tell where it scatters. He initially tries to get back on his feet, but in a swift move, I stomp onto his neck and force him onto the ground again. Now on top of him, I connect my fist with his jaw multiple times until he's gargling blood.

Suddenly Vincent rams me from behind, and I am launched a few feet through the air. I quickly scramble from the dirt, recovering to face him. As he begins to raise his gun at me, I thrust out a kick toward it and it flings from his grasp. I launch another high kick to his face, but he grabs my ankle and flips me over, throwing me to the floor. I hear the sharp slice of a blade being unsheathed, and I somersault forward to reassemble on my feet.

Vincent charges at me again with another fury of punches and swings, one of which connects with my face and knocks me to the floor. But without giving me a chance to recover, he grabs my shoulder and yanks me back to my feet. He wields a dagger in his hand, and I know my life could end swiftly in his hands if I don't find an advantage. My heart beats out of my chest, yelling at me to protect it and to keep living. Driven either by my desperation or my fear of the lack of structure in this fight, I pivot my tactic, much to both of our surprise.

With an animal-like ferocity, I wrap my legs around his waist and begin grabbing handfuls of his spiky black hair. Just as he's about to throw himself to the ground so that I am crushed under his weight, I lunge forward and sink my teeth into his neck. He screams out in pain as I feel the warm blood ooze into my mouth. Infuriated, Vincent throws me off of him, and I land on the ground, looking up to see him clutching his bloodied neck.

He hollers out in pain, and I raise my hand up to my mouth to feel the streams of blood pouring from it.

Xander appears at last, grabbing Vincent's shoulders and yanking him away from me. He spins the stunned man around and whips his head to the side with a heavy fist to the face. Vincent counters quickly, blocking Xander's next punch. In their struggle, Xander tackles him to the floor, restraining him under his weight. Blood pours from Vincent's lip with each punch Xander delivers to his face. However, when Vincent manages to block one of the punches again, he counters and smashes his fist against Xander's eye, leaving him dazed for a moment.

"Xander, Vincent's gun!" I yell out, taking notice of the dropped gun. Xander scrambles off of Vincent, reaching for the gun, but Vincent grabs him by the collar and pulls him back. As he is yanked back, Xander leaps over at him, swinging down on Vincent with a punch that smashes into the top of Vincent's head and pushes him to the floor. Vincent swings back with a knife that nearly glides across Xander's chest. Xander falls backwards again, and Vincent climbs on top of him this time, grasping his knife tightly.

"Vinc—" Xander attempts to yell but before he can even finish the name, Vincent thrusts his knife downward into Xander's leg. In the same moment, a gunshot goes off. Vincent's head is tossed back, and a stream of blood explodes up through the air before crashing back down into the dirt. His body, tense and vehemently fighting just moments ago, becomes instantly limp and collapses down onto Xander, who still holds the gun in paralyzing shock.

I rush over to him. After dragging Vincent's body off of his, I drop to my knees beside him. He instantly tries to sit up, but winces.

"Don't move," I say as I lower him back to the ground. Blood rapidly dampens his pants around where he's been stabbed.

"I'm fine," he stutters, leaning back on his elbows. His jaw is clenched tightly, and he blinks rapidly as he looks on at the hilt of the dagger protruding from his pants. Working automatically, I strip Vincent's limp body of his sweatshirt and use it to apply pressure to Xander's leg.

I hear a noise from behind me and turn my head to see Patrick on his feet again. He stares on in horror at Vincent's dead body and picks up his dropped dagger, grasping it tightly in his hand. His gaze, crossed with rage and fear alike, slowly drifts to me.

Suddenly, another shot rings out and blood flies out from Patrick's back, splattering dark crimson onto the tree. Patrick freezes for a moment before falling to his knees. With a trembling hand, he touches his pulsating abdomen and examines the blood staining it. I look over to where the shot had come from and my heart sinks.

"Charlie."

The young boy stands nearly 20 feet away. Below Charlie's frozen open arms, Noah's gun lays at his feet. Patrick sits himself up against the tree, wrapping his arms around his abdomen as he clutches to his life. He struggles to regain his breath.

"Charlie," I say again softly, climbing back to my feet and starting toward him. He just ignores me and gathers the gun in his hands again. He walks toward Patrick.

Patrick eyes rise to meet the boy's, and I see his bloody lips curl into a sinister smile through his jagged breaths. A second shot rings out. At the close range, the back of Patrick's head explodes in a fray of gore, coating the tree bark behind him and the dirt around it. His body, lifeless, collapses at last. As the ring of the shot fades, the cemetery settles into a gloomy silence.

I haven't moved. I'm not sure if I've breathed. When Charlie turns back to face me, I'm not even sure if my heart continues to beat. Fog and darkness shield his expression from me, but he stands still. The night has only gotten colder, yet he doesn't tremble. I feel my hands rising up in defeat.

"Just like Ana," Charlie says quietly, and I feel my expression soften in despair for the child as I remember the sight of the bullet tearing through Ana's head. He drops the gun to land at his feet, and I lower my hands.

Just then, another shot rings through the air. Unlike the deafening blasts of the shots that killed Vincent and Patrick, this one is quiet and far away. Muffled by the expanse of the forest, the shot must've come from camp. Patrick's warning echoes in my head and I freeze, doubting the shot's existence in the first place. I must be imagining it.

Charlie had discarded the sweatshirt I lent him, letting it fall at the bottom of the hill nearby. Using Xander's knife, I slice fabric from the sweatshirt. It's not until now that I realize how much I'm shaking; I have to grab my wrist to stop the rapid movement. I fold up the cloth and firmly tie it around Xander's leg, where the blood still oozes out from around the blade. It's then that another shot goes off. Similar to the first, it must be coming from the camp.

I quickly gather up a few thick sticks in my vicinity, bundling them together before wrapping the ends of the tied fabric around it. I turn the sticks in the knot, tightening the tourniquet. As I tighten it, he flinches.

"Loosen it a little," he demands.

"It's too risky," I argue. "Depending on what the blade hit, if I loosen it, you could bleed out."

"If you tighten it, I could end up losing my leg," he says, looking at me gravely. "I'm keeping my leg. Loosen the damn thing."

I loosen it slightly and when I'm done, I look back at Charlie. He's hunching over Patrick's dead body.

Vincent's still body lies not even a few feet from me, lying on his back with his head tilted on its side. The whites of his wide eyes glisten in the moonlight, which casts an eerie shadow over his face. His throat is mangled from the bullet that tore through it, and his open neck feeds the thick pool of blood that appears black in the darkness.

"I killed him," Xander says in a low voice, attempting to sit up.

"It wasn't your fault," I immediately reply, placing a hand on his chest and another on the adjacent shoulder to gently push him back down, which he strongly resists.

"No, it was. He stabbed my leg; he didn't intend to kill me."

"He stabbed you where he was able to in the moment. He would've killed you if he—"

"But now he's dead. And it's because of me—"

"It was your reflex—"

"But look at him, Jenn. Look at what I did to him," Xander says again, unable to tear his eyes away from Vincent's dead body.

"No, don't look at him," I say again. My hand still on his chest, I feel his heartbeat beginning to increase and his eyes, glazed over, dart frantically all over Vincent's body. "You can think later. But, for now, it doesn't matter. Don't look at him, okay?"

His eyes dart back over to me, and I slowly lie him down on his back.

"I'm going to go see where Noah is. I'll be right back," I whisper calmly to Xander, and he nods in understanding.

Hesitantly, I turn back to Vincent, specifically for the rather large dagger still attached to his hip. I reach over, sliding the weapon off of his cold body before standing back up and dashing up the hill, following the trail Patrick and I made during the struggle.

"Noah!" I shout almost immediately when I see his hobbling silhouette coming closer. He collapses.

"Noah," I dart forward toward him and lean over his body. With the knife still protruding from his outer shoulder, his face is paler than usual and his eyes blink rapidly.

"I'm fine," Noah clears his throat as he clutches his shoulder. I help him stand back up and he shakes his head to clear his vision.

"C'mon Noah, stay with me."

Just then, I hear hurried footsteps from the entrance of the graveyard: heavy footsteps, the clanking of a gun slamming against a hip, long strides.

"Over here!" I yell out waving my arms. I don't know who to trust right now, but I know it's worth the risk. "Over here!"

To my relief, Blake emerges from the fog and hurries to my side. Beside him, Phil runs up holding a roll of bandages and a handgun.

"It was Patrick and Vincent, they attacked us," I say as Phil inspects the stab wound.

"Where are they now?" Phil immediately asks.

"They're dead," I say without even thinking, and Phil pauses momentarily. His face is pulled into a wearied expression, and his lips are drawn into a thin line.

"Heard the gunshots coming from this way. Never just normal stuff with you. I was gonna come alone but Lie insisted that I bring Phil with me," Blake says through his rough voice. "We gotta get back to camp quickly, though, I'm sure you heard the gunshots now happening over there."

"Lie told you to bring Phil?" I ask, my suspicions rising. "They're trying to get us away from camp. Who's left at camp? Riley? Becky? Bella? We have to get back there."

"You think Lie is planning something?" he asks.

"Her, Andrew, Patrick, and Vincent," I correct. "Patrick and Vincent brought us out here to kill us. They let the undeads into the lake that killed Ana. And now Lie and Andrew just lured you guys away. They can't take us all on at once, so they're going to try to take us out separately."

"Who else is here? What other injuries?" Phil asks.

"Charlie and I are uninjured. Xander got stabbed in the leg, but it's not as critical as Noah," I say, wiping the blood from my hands on my clothes.

"Stay with Xander, Noah, and Charlie here. Phil and I will head back over," Blake says to me quickly before turning his attention back to Phil.

"No, I'm going back with you," I say. "And we're taking Noah back. He'll die if we leave him here, he needs medical attention immediately once we gain control over the camp again. Phil should stay here and protect Xander and Charlie against any undead that were attracted by the gunfire."

"Alright," Blake says. "Jenn, you're with me."

"Can you help him walk?" Phil asks as he drapes Noah's arm around Blake's shoulders.

"What can't I do?" Blake smirks.

"Take care of Xander," I say abruptly to Phil, and he gives me a double take. "He keeps trying to loosen the bandage on his leg. If he does, he'll lose more blood so make sure you keep it tight. And he'll want to walk on his own. He's got a big ego, just ignore it. Let him lean on you; he'll definitely need help walking."

"He'll be fine," he says, spreading his lips in a small but warming smile. "Stay safe, guys. I mean it. Protect yourselves."

Phil instantly slides the gun out of its holster, handing it over to me. It's heavier than I thought it would be. I'm not used to the feeling and weight of the weapon, but I manage to fit it into my palm. With that, Blake, Noah, and I head off.

Needles and twigs scrape my face as I rush through the hedge's exit and out into the forest. However, as soon as I emerge on the other side, I start to hear the low moaning of an approaching group of undeads. Peering through leaves of overgrowth, I spot the group of three reeking undeads headed toward the graveyard.

Reaching at my belt, I slide out my knife and approach the trio. I jog a little up to the first and slam my elbow into the beast's face. The undead falls onto its back, and I stab down to bury my knife in its skull. When the next nears, I grab it by the neck and stab into the side of its head. The limp body leans its weight on me, smearing blood on my shirt as I struggle to free my blade. Buying time, I lash out with my foot at the third undead to hinder its advance. As I recover, the dead body falls from my arms and my knife slides out in my hand.

Evading my attacker's flailing arms, I grab its jaw from underneath, pulling its face up, and exposing its throat. I twist the blade in my hand a little before thrusting it through the underside of the undead's chin up to the brain. Blood sprays onto my shirt when I yank the weapon out.

With Blake and Noah following close behind me, we manage to reach the camp without any further altercations with the undead.

"They're expecting us to come through the north entrance 'cause it's closest to the graveyard. I'm going to go through the eastern entrance," Blake explains as we near the hidden passageway of the eastern entrance. At last, he stops to peel Noah off of him. "Noah, hide in the trees over there. Jenn, you stay with him."

"No, I'm coming," I contest as he disappears through the tunnel, resulting in silence as a response.

"Go," Noah says weakly from behind me and then clears his throat. "He can't do it alone. They need you. I'll be fine."

I nod at him and follow behind Blake. Behind me, I hear Noah pushing his way past the trees to find a safe spot.

CHAPTER 20

Riley

"Alright everyone, c'mon!" I hear Kris's calling from outside the tent.

"Ready to eat?" Jack asks me. With a rag in one hand and a pale of water beside him, he cleans his bow, wiping up and down along its length. Scattered around in front of us are his array of arrows, drying after undergoing their own deep cleanse. He steals a glance up at me for a second when I don't respond, but then rapidly returns to his work.

"You've cleaned that like three times. I don't think it gets any whiter," I tease.

"Twice! And sorry for trying to be hygienic," he quips and I roll my eyes. "All I know is that if I take care of it, then it'll take care of me."

"Well, right now, I think it's the cleanest part about you," I joke again. This seems to have gotten his attention and he swings his head around to me, mocking offense.

"Wow, look who's talking?" he scoffs, and my mouth shoots open in an exaggerated gasp. "We have the same resources, hunny. If I stink, you stink too."

"Rude!" I exclaim, propping myself up onto my elbows from my lying down position. "Well, maybe if you stopped using the water for your bow, we could clean ourselves instead."

"Fine, when I'm done with this, I'll fill it up again and shower," he concedes, defeated. Then, a quick smirk flashes across his face. "You going to help me?"

"Very funny," I mutter through my chuckle, shaking my head.

"C'mon, let's go. I'm starving," Jack says before standing up. He peers out of the tent opening. "Hey, where'd Jenn and Xander go?"

"I don't know, did they leave?" I ask, taking my hair out of my ponytail and shaking it out a little. I attempt to get up as well but fall back on my butt, holding the slight bulge in my stomach.

"You need help?" Jack asks, noticing my struggle.

"No, I'm just lazy. I don't want to move," I say, stretching. Ever since we arrived at the camp, we've mainly kept to ourselves. But since Ana's death, I can't help but feel like we've been ostracized and unwanted more than ever. No one trusts the new kids, especially when people are suspicious of Jenn's involvement. All in all, just leaving the tent makes me nauseous with dread.

He holds his hand out to me, and I grab it only to yank him down to me. He nearly falls onto me, and I let out a laugh as we lay back down in the dirt.

"Can't we just stay here?" I plead quietly. He pushes a strand of hair behind my ear, leaning in close to plant a kiss on my lips. "We could just stay in this tent and forget the world outside. Ignore all the death and dreadful things with me for a bit."

"And ignore all of the food until we starve to death?" he poses.

"It'll be worth it," I tease.

"Have I ever told you how much I love you?" he asks.

"Tell me again," I say, smiling brightly.

"Eh, well, you're alright," he says, leaning his face so close to mine that his words brush against my lips.

"Oh, am I?"

"Yeah, I think I'll keep you around," he says, and his nose brushes mine.

"Come here," I say while laughing, pulling him into another kiss. When we separate, I'm still smiling.

"Riley, Jack! It's dinner!" Kris's voice rings out again.

"C'mon, let's not make her wait," Jack says, pulling me up with him.

As we walk out of the tent, I feel the desolation of the camp's reality settle onto me again like a weighted blanket threatening to smother me. I grip Jack's hand tiger as we make our way over to the campfire where everyone is already gathered, lined up to get their food. Before us, the huge fire flickers in the moonlight, bathing me in heat as I get closer.

"Hey sweet cheeks," Andrew says, and before I can even look over at him, I feel him smack my butt, making me jolt in surprise. "What are you doing tonight?"

"What the hell?" Jack exclaims as Andrew nonchalantly walks by, winking at me.

"You got something to say to me?" Andrew taunts, turning to look at Jack.

"Yeah, keep your hands off her," Jack barks back, squeezing my hand a little.

"Why don't you make me," Andrew scoffs. He takes a step forward and pushes Jack lightly.

"Maybe I will," Jack says, releasing my hand and pushing Andrew back a little.

"Jack, it's ok," I mutter, my cheeks flushing red when I notice others glancing over.

"It's not ok. This guy's being a jerk and it's unnecessary," Jack insists, scowling at Andrew.

"Try *spelling* 'unnecessary', dimwit," Andrew mocks.

"Don't answer that," I immediately tell Jack, linking my arm around his and laying my other hand on his shoulder. "Let's sit down."

"Yeah, why don't you walk away," Andrew says, chuckling a little. "But don't be surprised if your little girlfriend leaves you for being such a coward. Ain't that right, baby? This is what a real man looks like."

Suddenly, Jack strikes out, knocking a punch straight into Andrew's mouth. The large man's head is thrown backwards and when he recovers, he's bleeding from his lip. He winds back and takes a heavy swing at Jack, who quickly dodges it before throwing another punch at Andrew's face.

"Alright, calm down," Blake says, grabbing Andrew from behind, struggling to restrain him from retaliating.

"Let's sit down," I repeat to Jack, grabbing hold of both of his hands.

"That was a bad move, beanpole," Andrew threatens, finally calming down after Phil joins Blake in restraining him.

***

Everyone eats their dinner slowly and in utter silence. Jack slides some of the meat from his plate onto mine. I look up at him and smile, silently thanking him, to which he just shrugs.

Then, there's a gunshot in the distance. Though it's just loud enough for us to hear, all of our heads perk up, letting the fire's flickering light illuminate our faces.

"A gunshot," Becky states stiffly, standing up. "Charlie… he's still at the graveyard."

"Do you think something's up?" Phil asks, looking over at Blake.

"They wouldn't risk shooting a gun if there wasn't," Blake grumbles in response, stuffing whatever was left on his plate into his mouth.

"I agree," Lie chimes in. "It doesn't look good."

"I'll go and see if they're alright," Blake announces, getting up while swallowing down the last of his food.

"Only you?" Lie asks, raising an eyebrow.

"Jenn, Xander, Noah, Patrick, and Vincent all are already there and armed with weapons. How much danger could there possibly be?" Blake says, narrowing his eyes at Lie.

"Great, Jenn and Xander, no wonder there's trouble. Leave it to the newbies of the camp. That worked out just awesomely for Ana," Kris sneers, and Blake's glare shifts to her. "What? Am I wrong to care about Charlie's safety?"

"Kris is right. These are lives at stake here," Kyle agrees, to which Becky's face goes pale.

"Phil and I will go see what's going on," Blake says. Still, with a tense jaw and accusing eyes, he shoots Lie a glare again.

"I'm coming too," Becky affirms, furrowing her eyebrows in confusion at her exclusion.

"No, Becky, I think it's better if you stay here," Blake insists. "It's alright; we'll make sure Charlie gets here safely. It's probably nothing too bad anyway. Patrick just probably freaked out over a band of undeads."

Becky looks at Blake with a worried expression as he runs back to his tent to grab a weapon.

"No, I really should go too," Becky says again, jogging over to her tent.

"Becky, it's alright. You stay here," Phil says calmly, stopping her and resting a hand on her shoulder. I see Blake lean over and whisper something to Bella, after which she instantly jumps to her feet and ducks into her tent. "As Blake said, everything's probably fine. We'll bring Charlie back safe and sound, alright?"

"But what if you need another person?" she asks again. "Take Anthony too. Here, I have a gun, you can take the bullets, just in case."

"Thanks Becky," Phil says, taking the bullets from her earnest hands. When Anthony approaches him, however, he waves him off. "No, stay here, Ant. We'll be right back."

"See you in a few," Blake calls out as he slips through the exit. Phil immediately follows, but not before Bella hands him off some bandages. He shoots Becky a reassuring smile, but I notice it slip into a troubled frown as he exits the camp. Despite his words of reassurance, he doesn't know what to expect. As they leave, Bella gathers the plates they left behind and walks off from dinner.

"I'll be right back," I mutter to Jack before following her.

"Bella!" I call out, jogging up to her side as she nears the small pond that serves as our cleaning station. "Oh my goodness, it smells awful over here."

"It's the urine. The ammonia is good for cleaning the blood and dirt off clothes and weapons," she responds, absentmindedly. "If you need something to be washed, you come here."

She kneels down beside the pool and dips a bucket into the flowing water. When it's full, she dumps a rag into it to scrub the plates.

"I clean when I'm nervous," she says, her head staying low while her eyes glance up at me.

"This is a pretty impressive setup you guys have here," I say.

"It is. I don't know who started it all," she says. "Probably a group of people from years and years ago. All the knowledge has just been passed on ever since. You should see the infirmary. The list of herbal recipes is insane."

I notice the pile of bloody clothes, bones, and weapons on the side of the small pond.

"Blake just collected those undead bones," I say, indicating the pile. "I was with him in the forest."

"Ah, yes, from decayed undeads," she mutters in response. "The one thing they are useful for."

"Do you know why they act the way they do?" I ask curiously, still staring at the bones. "From a doctor perspective, I mean."

"Ha! I'm not a real doctor," she scoffs. "But, we assume it's some sort of infection because it can spread. Actually… the prior camp doctor did pass down some stories to me."

"Stories?" I ask in a hesitant voice.

"Yeah, someone in the camp *years* ago collected undead bodies and cut them open to examine them," she explains, grimacing as she continues to scrub the plates. "Pretty messed up, I know. But essentially, they saw that the undead brains look consistently deformed in certain areas. These areas then get smaller and more decayed as the undead is around longer. The hypothesis is that the virus is keeping some parts of the brain alive, while killing other parts and using the 'unneeded' brain material to help fuel it when it's lacking food. Essentially, it's eating itself. Eventually, however, the whole thing decays with time along with the rest of the undead's body."

"That's so interesting," I mutter, nodding. "To think that the prisons are fueling this..."

"Do you have something you wanted cleaned?" she asks suddenly, glancing briefly over to inspect if I was carrying anything. "Or did you just come over to chat about the undead?"

"I wanted to talk to you about something else, actually," I mutter, anxious to meet her eye.

"About what?" she asks again, raising an eyebrow.

"Well," I begin quietly. "Do you know… Dana?"

"What did you say?" She stops cleaning.

"Dana," I repeat, more confidently. "One of Headmaster's agents?"

"What about her?" she asks, refusing to turn toward me again.

"She gave me these before I left." I pull out the pills from my pocket, showing them to her.

"What are they?" she asks as she places the dirty plates on the ground and stands up next to me, partially relieved by the shift in conversation.

"They're nutrition pills," I say quietly, humbly. "I'm…I'm pregnant."

"Oh," she responds in utter shock, blinking hard. "You're…pregnant?"

"Yeah," I confirm, rubbing the back of my neck with my hand as I feel my cheeks redden.

"I'm sorry, I just…I thought you were sixteen," she says, clarifying.

"I am," I say again, lowering my flushed face.

"Riley," she scolds briefly. She then glances down at the pills sorrowfully, and I see her slide her hand into her pocket.

"Dana asked me to make sure you were alright," I say after a moment, and I watch as a small smile gradually blooms on her face—the type of smile reclaimed from a memory. "Are you alright?"

"I am now," she says softly.

"How do you know her?"

The question hangs in the air for a while and it seems like time has frozen. Her stare remains on the pills and her slight smirk remains etched into her lips like it's been made permanent. She hasn't worn this smile in a while I can tell. The resurfaced memories that flood her mind seem like they've been repressed for too long. Still, she wears the smile like clothes perfectly broken-in to comfort over the years.

She moves her eyes up to meet mine and I see her tears begin to gloss over. She shuts her eyes in a blissful pain and opens her mouth to let out a breath. When her eyelashes flutter open again, they let a tear drop out from between them. She studies me, looking to find something: not necessarily friendship, but…comradery. She trusts that I'll understand whatever pain she yearns to talk about.

"She's the reason that I'm here," she says finally, her voice lower, slower. "I was in my last year of Level 3. We were in love. She'd sneak me out at night, and we'd hide out together in the woods on the complex. But…well, you can be so secretive about something and the BAA will still catch you. They always do."

Suddenly, she pulls her hand out of her pocket, light reflecting off the glimmering diamond ring she carries in her fingers.

"She gave me this not long before I was expelled," she explains, slipping it on and holding it out to show me. "I always keep it in my pocket so that it's safe."

"It's beautiful," I say, aghast as the jewelry shimmers and shines with seemingly its own exceptional radiance.

"Thank you," she responds gently. "You know, Headmaster didn't even care that Dana was involved with a cadet. Like water on a duck's back, he just brushed it off. The drill sergeants, the teachers, the agents can really do whatever they want. It's a messed-up system."

I take her hand in mine and she breathes in deeply.

"Thank you for passing on her words," she says. "I've been here for something like...three years or so with no word from her. It means a lot that she still thinks of me. She remembers me."

"Of course."

Then her focus shifts to me. "You're here because of your pregnancy?"

"Yeah."

"And Jack…"

"He's the father."

"Do you love each other?" she asks again, the question catching me off guard.

"Yes," I respond without even having to think and she just lowers her eyes back to her ring. Her stare lingers for a long moment before she slips it off and slides it back into her pocket. She then looks back up at me.

"I don't want you to worry about your baby," she reassures. "I'll deliver it when the time comes. It'll all work out."

"Thank you," I say, and I can't help but wrap my arms around her and pull her into a hug, which she graciously accepts.

Another gunshot rings through the forest, its echo barely audible like the first ones. She tenses up and we remain hugging not for sentimental reasons, but because we're both too frozen in fear, too scared to move. We wait for the sound to occur again. Only a few seconds, another shot rings and she separates from me. On our way back to the campfire, a final shot rings out.

"Probably something really big happening over there," Andrew says as I find my place beside Jack again. "Maybe one of them's bit."

"Would you just shut up, she's already freaking out," Anthony exclaims from beside Andrew. "Becky, everything is probably fine."

"Why does everyone keep saying that?" she yells.

I look around at the rest of the campers who all sit in a circle around the fire. Andrew and Lie are across from each other. I catch them sharing a few glances at each other. Andrew's hand rests on his gun. Lie does the same. Nobody else at the fire is carrying a gun. Everyone usually keeps their guns and weapons in their tents during dinner.

"Because worrying about it isn't going to do anything," Kris remarks from where she sits between Corinne and Lie on another log. "I don't trust Jenn and Xander, but I do trust Blake and Phil."

"Should we send more people?" Becky asks. "I'll go this time. I want to. Anthony, me and you should go."

I nudge Jack, but before I can tell him about Andrew and Lie's weapons, Andrew strikes out at Anthony, with the butt of his gun. In the same instant, Lie mimics Andrew and knocks Corinne out cold. The two bodies fall over, spilling their food onto the ground. I hear gasps as everyone stands up. A shot rings out and Jack leaps to the side, pulling me down to the floor.

"Everyone freeze and get on the floor!" Andrew barks, aiming his gun around at the others.

Kyle, sitting not far from Lie, suddenly lashes out, throwing the smaller woman to the floor. However, before he can wrestle the gun from her hands, she swings her legs and knocks him swiftly off his feet. Lying in the dirt with Lie's gun pointed straight at his head, he freezes in surrender.

In the commotion, Becky desperately pulls out one of the burning logs from the fire and, raising it above her head, hauls it at Andrew. He dodges it and the flaming log falls against a tent behind him, lighting it up. He aims to shoot her with his gun, but he stops.

Instead, with a swing of his heavy arm, he punches her across the face and she collapses to the floor. She begins to crawl toward a tent in search of a weapon, but he grabs another stick from the bonfire and tosses it. The stick lands at the base of the tent, causing it to ignite and stopping Becky's motives.

Dwayne bravely makes an attempt to tackle Andrew from behind, but Lie shouts out a warning too quickly. Andrew instantly whips around with his gun raised. Instinctively, he fires off a shot straight into the martyr. The bullet lodges into Dwayne's neck and the stout man staggers back, choking on the blood that cascades and sputters from the fatal wound. His eyes dart around to the other campers, desperate for help as his hands hover helplessly in front of his neck. Before anyone can overcome their shock to do anything, he trips over his own feet, falling backwards into the large raging fire. I tear my eyes away and cower my face in my hands.

Frozen in place, we listen to the roar of the growing fire as he drowns in his own blood while burning alive. Quickly, however, the struggle stops and Dwayne's burning body stops moving. The threat of Andrew and Lie's guns coupled with the horror of witnessing Dwayne's horrid death finally force us to lower ourselves to the floor. Andrew can kill. And there's nothing stopping him from doing what he did to Dwayne to any one of us.

***

Andrew and Lie rile the entire camp into a straight line, each of us on our knees by the eastern entrance. Andrew figured the others would return from the north entrance. He was hoping that the fire, now settling down as the afflicted tents crumble into ash, would catch their attention first and lure them into the middle of the east farming field. There, they'd be without cover and vulnerable to Andrew's gunfire.

Corinne has regained consciousness and now joins us as a hostage. Anthony, on the other hand, still lies motionless before us as we await for him to come to his senses as well. Jack had tried resisting, so Andrew made an example out of him by binding his wrists and dragging him from our line. He then throws himself into a heavy punch straight into my boyfriend's face. Blood flies from his nose and he writhes to try to free himself.

"No, stop! He's had enough!" I yell frantically, springing up from my place in line. Instantly, Lie's gun shoots up to point at me.

I freeze. Between my screams and Jack's fruitless attempts to escape, Andrew is only fueled and throws another forceful kick straight into Jack's gut. Jack gasps for air as he weakly tries to recover.

"Andrew, what the hell?" Becky shouts, standing up as well. Lie's aim shifts to her instead and Becky's glare turns cold and threatening. "Put that gun down."

"What?" Andrew asks through his smirk. "I'm just showing this little prick I'm not one to mess with. These outsiders are only problems for us. They can't be trusted. Just look at what happened when we trusted Jenn. "

"Is that what this is all this about?" Kyle demands, though he remains on the ground.

"Please! Stop it!" I plead, attempting to take advantage of Lie's focus on Becky to rush over to Jack. Lie's too quick. Before I can make it past her, the stout woman grabs me and holds me back. She throws me back toward the line and then whips her gun across my face, bruising my cheek and exposing a shallow slash in my skin. I fall to the floor, silent as I look up at her in horror.

"Lie!" Becky shouts in disbelief, but Lie already has her gun aimed at her again.

"Sit down," Lie responds stoically.

"Not so tough are you, now?" Andrew mocks as he throws another punch into Jack's bruised face.

"Go to hell." The words shutter out from my shaking lips as a tear slides down my cheek, mixing with the trail of blood.

"What did you say to me?" Andrew says, stopping mid-punch and glancing over at me with an eyebrow raised in amusement. I fall silent again, and a smirk reappears on his face. "Get up."

When he strides over to me, I hesitantly rise to my feet. Although I lock my jaw, hold my chin high, and keep eye contact like Jenn would do, I know that he can see the fear in my eyes. We stay silent for a moment just staring at each other when suddenly he pulls out his gun and presses it to my forehead. I let out a little gasp at the cold metal on my skin.

"What did you say to me?" he repeats, his expression suddenly flat and serious. I remain speechless, scared that if I talk my voice will shake. "C'mon, just say it. It may your last words."

"Leave her alone," Becky warns from her place in line. I try to feign stubborn confidence as my heart hastily shoots the blood throughout my body, my pulse throbbing in my head and pounding against the weapon pressing deeper now into my forehead.

"Shut up," he barks at her, suddenly releasing the gun from me to point at her instead. "Or you're next."

"Andrew—" Becky begins to say but is cut off by the blasting sound of Andrew's gun firing. Dirt sprays as the bullet shoots into the dirt at her feet.

"What did I say?" he remarks, and she looks down. I feel the cold end of the gun against my forehead again. "Now, what did *you* say?"

I bite my teeth together tighter to prevent my lip from quivering, and I try to slow my rapid breathing. *Just a little braver,* I urge myself.

"Alright, your choice," he says, a devilish smirk on his lip as he takes in my fear like its oxygen and he's a flame. "You know, I'm actually doing you a favor by killing you. You wouldn't last one day on this island alone before you'd be gutted out there. This camp was just delaying the inevitable. A bullet to the brain is a lot less painful anyway."

"Riley?" Jack calls out, finally regaining his breath and shaking off his daze. His eyes are nearly swollen shut, but he tries to search for me. My eyes begin to water again as I look at him. "Riley? I swear Andrew if you touch her, I will kill you!"

"It'll be easier on him too, you know? Then again," he contemplates, a sinister darkness filling his eyes as he leans in, his cold breath brushing against my ear. He takes the barrel away from my head and shoves it back into its holster. "Why should it be that easy?"

With his face close to mine, he lets a hand rest on my waist, and I feel my lip begin to quiver.

In a single quick motion, I slip my hand past him onto the handle of the gun on his side and pull it from its restraints. I hold it as a barrier between us, the barrel pressed up against his abdomen now.

"Go to hell," I snarl at last.

"Freeze or you die," Lie orders, her gun pointed at my head. My heart is beating a million times a minute by now as adrenaline pumps through my blood and the realization of death sets in again. For a long moment, we all stay exactly as we are, before finally Andrew begins to step away from me. Flashing me a sinister smirk, he holds up his hands.

"I could kill you right now," I threaten under my shaky breath, my eyes wide with shock. I grip the gun tighter in my grasp to hold it steadier.

"Could you?" he taunts cynically. "Being smart only gets you so far, hun."

My finger hovers over the trigger, and I can feel a breath escape past my lips. I had never held a gun before, and its burden weighs down my hands. Thousands of thoughts flood my brain. The way his muscles flex around his right shoulder, the slight twitch of the arm. In the second before he strikes, I'm already way ahead of him. I know what will happen and could evade him. I don't. I don't know why.

Andrew's strike comes, shoving his entire body mass at me and swiftly tearing the weapon from my hands. A shot is fired aimlessly at the ground as I fall backwards. I see Kyle and Becky charge toward Andrew and Lie in my defense. But Lie doesn't hesitate to fire her gun, and Kyle drops to his knees. Deep red blood oozes over his fingers as he clutches the spot where the bullet skimmed his arm.

Becky attempts a spinning hook kick, but Andrew dodges, grabbing her foot midair and throwing her to the floor. She tries to scramble back to her feet, but he thrusts out a follow up punch and her head flies back. Dazed, she scoots backwards as Andrew storms off back to Jack. He roughly grabs Jack up from the floor and drags him back over to the line. His hands are still bound behind his back, but he curls up in pain beside me. I take the risk to put my hand out to touch his shoulder and drag my hands along his warm skin, trying to help him feel anything but his pain.

"What is all this for, Andrew? *Why*?" Becky demands.

"This is to make things right. Finally," Andrew begins, trying to cool his temper as he walks up and down our line. "This camp needs order and safety again."

"And how is violence the way to go about that?" Becky sneers.

"I don't want anyone to get hurt. I don't want anyone to die," he says firmly, running a hand through his coarse hair as he composes himself. "A 10 year old girl was just murdered by undeads within our fence borders. At Becky's order, our most vulnerable camper was isolated at the lake with no weapons. Her only chaperone was not even one of us: an outsider, who shouldn't have been trusted."

"There was no way of knowing—" Becky exclaims, aghast.

"Last month, Evan, Patricia, and Jasper all died, while Becky walked away unharmed. I've said it before, and I'll say it again: Becky does not care about any one of you or the safety of this group."

"Andrew," Becky pleads. "I did everything I could. Don't you realize I had to watch those people die? That I had to live with that?"

"I don't buy it," Andrew remarks, disregarding her and addressing the group again. "She'd let you die before harm comes her way; how else do you think she's made it so long on this island?"

"This is crazy—" Becky begins to say.

"Now we do things my way," Andrew states. "Building up the fences around the hunting safe zone, walls instead of hedges around the camp, larger groups for hunting."

"We don't have the resources, the tools, the manpower," Becky says. "Our farm should be our focus, if you neglect it now—"

"We'll do weekly outings in the forest to clear the undeads," Andrew continues, ignoring her. "We'll thin their numbers week by week."

"You'll thin *our* numbers!" Becky pleads. "It's a fruitless fight to try to clear the herd. It's a setup for onslaught."

"This is a military camp, it's about damn time we start acting like one—"

"No, it's *not*! We were kicked *out* of the military! We're not at war—"

"Three people died last month! People are *dying*—"

"You just killed Dwayne!" Becky screams out, her voice aghast and wavering in defeat.

"Safety of the *group* comes above everything else," he barks, ignoring her. "I will not let us continue to live unsafely. How long until the undeads come knocking down the little bush we depend on for safety? One swarm and we are dead. There's no need to take a risk when there's something to do about it."

He continues to walk up and down the line, and I am constantly switching my gaze between him and the main entrance. Jenn will come back. They all will. They'll help.

"Now each of you has a choice to make. Do you want to join me? Or do you want to resist?" Andrew continues, waving his gun dramatically through the air. "Speak up if you're with me. If you're not, you will pay the price."

Kyle stands after a moment. His expression is drawn tight and stoic as he bites back the pain from his bleeding arm.

"Kyle…" Becky mutters.

"I was close with Jasper...Patricia. They were good people. Could happen to any of us again," he says quietly, but he won't look at her.

"I'm with you." Everyone in the line's heads turn simultaneously to look at Corinne. She stands with her head high and struts over to Andrew as well. "I'm not dying today."

"Perfect," Andrew murmurs sinisterly as his eyes follow Corinne. His gaze then shifts to the rest of us who remain quiet.

"You're sick," Becky mutters, spitting. "What about the people at the graveyard?"

"They're probably already dead by now," Andrew confirms. "Jenn and Blake are violent, and I'm not letting them risk our safety. If the others come back, they will have the same choice to join as you did."

"We're with you," Jack announces just then.

"Wh—Jack?" I mutter in a panic, my wide eyes glued to him. "What are you doing?"

"We have to," he says quietly to me. His expression is drawn tight like Kyle's, but I know it's not the pain. It's anguish. I know I'm to blame; he'll protect our baby at all costs.

Andrew motions for us to come over, and we both stand. I feel the heat of the others' stares as we join the rival group, choosing life over dignity. I refuse to meet anyone's eye.

Kris stands up next and silently walks over to Andrew, who sports a devilish grin as his ranks grow.

"Anyone else?" Andrew demands. Only Becky and Bella are left on the ground, and he pauses to allow them a final chance to give up their pride. Bella reaches out to the side and grasps Becky's hand. They aren't moving.

"You'll lead us to worse deaths," Bella says, daring to look up at Andrew's towering figure. "Starving from resource depletion and being torn apart while hunting undeads is not how I plan to go."

"Fine," Andrew says. "Have it your way. You die tonight."

Becky spits, and the saliva lands on Andrew's shoe. His face turns red with hatred as he bends down so that they're face to face.

"I'm sorry, did you want to say something?" he asks sarcastically. Becky just raises her eyes to his, glaring. "Speak up, sweetie. These may be your last words."

Still Becky remains quiet, her eyes holding the tension between them. Andrew takes this in like its fuel and he's a fire.

"You think you're just so tough, don't you?" Andrew taunts, lost in his sadistic thoughts.

When Becky refuses to answer, Andrew lashes out in anger, striking her across the face with his gun.

"Answer me when I talk to you!" he screams in her face.

"You're going to pay for what you're doing," Becky continues, her voice low and menacing.

"By the entrance!" Lie suddenly calls out just as a bullet zips through the air.

Andrew reacts just in time to miss the shot and falls flat to the ground. Instantly, a barrage of gunfire shoots back at the hedge from Lie. Blake leaps out of the eastern entrance, dodging bullets, and dives behind a large pile of logs lining the hedge right beside the entrance. We keep the pile there because it's a convenient unloading spot for the trees we chop down for firewood and building material; though, right now it serves a more dire role.

CHAPTER 21

Jenn

Sparks fly off the edge of the wood pile as the battle of bullets rages on the other side of the hedge. From my hidden spot peering between the branches of the hedge, I survey the camp. I grip the gun in my hand tightly and place my finger on the trigger.

The campers all scatter in the chaos, running for cover. However, without a second thought, Lie spins around and fires her gun at the dispersing crowd. Most of the bullets miss amongst the scattered campers, but one lodges in Kris's shoulder, and she falls to the floor. Kyle charges at Lie in an attempt to take her down. Though before he can reach her, she instinctively pulls the trigger on her gun, sending a bullet straight into his abdomen. He collapses onto her, and she fires off two more shots, each spraying streams of blood out of his back, until finally his limp body slides off of her and onto the dirt.

Becky, horrified at the sight of Kyle's limp body on the floor, appears at Lie's side, surprising her with a punch straight into the side of her face. Blood flings from Lie's nose, and she staggers off balance. Becky strikes out again with an uppercut before grabbing Lie by her hair and yanking her down to thrust her knee into the smaller girl's eye. She falls to the floor, sending off a few accidental shots into the dirt around them. Becky leaps on top of her, throwing her elbow right into Lie's forehead. The two wrestle for a bit until Becky manages to ply the gun from Lie's grip.

"Corinne, cover me while I help the others!" Becky screams, sliding the gun across the dirt over to Corinne's feet.

Corinne swoops up the weapon but then freezes, letting her eyes dart between Becky and Lie. Becky just watches her earnestly as she scrambles to her feet again, fear in her eyes at her realization. *Corinne's not on her side.*

Andrew aims at Becky, but before he can shoot, I let myself fully emerge from the hedge and pull the trigger that my finger has been hovering over. The sound explodes from the gun as the first shot is fired, and the weapon, compelled with its own force, flings from my grasp. I flinch, but I know I only have seconds to make my next move. Andrew is looking right at me, a mixture of shock and anger displayed vividly on his face. I leap forward, rolling behind the pile of logs just before a line of bullets zip above me.

"I gotta reload! Get low!" Blake calls out to me as I lie myself flat beside him.

The sound of splitting wood smacks my ears. Panic fills my body. *Where's my gun?*

Just then, the bombardment stops.

Taking a risk, I peer my head up carefully. It's Anthony. He's wrestling with Andrew for his gun, until it flies from both of their grasps.

After only a few seconds, Andrew finally frees himself from Anthony and leaps toward the fallen weapon. Once it's in his possession, he turns over and aims it up at Anthony, who stands above him. However, with a fluid kick, Anthony knocks the gun from Andrew's hands, just barely evading a bullet. He then swoops down and delivers a solid punch directly at Andrew's nose. Blood flies from the tip of Andrew's nose as his head whips to the side, but when Anthony tries to punch again, Andrew blocks and pushes Anthony to the ground.

In the meantime, I dash out from my cover to retrieve my gun. Before I can even scramble back, Blake shoots a bullet in between the fighting men to separate them. Andrew falls back closer to the unclaimed gun.

"Anthony!" I scream out.

Without a second thought, Anthony sprints toward me at full speed. Bullets fly between Andrew and Blake again just as Anthony dives over my cover, pulling me down with him. Above our heads, deafening balls of lead soar like airplanes.

"Stay down!" Anthony shouts at me over the noise, his arm around me to hold me down.

Regardless, I risk my head around the corner of our cover. Most of the campers are missing now, but Lie rejoins the fight with a new gun and sprays our cover with more bullets. Taking aim, I return the favor. From behind a tent, Becky fires a newly retrieved gun as well. Though my shots fly carelessly into the air, they couple with Blake's and Becky's to send Andrew and Lie scrambling for better cover.

I look back at Anthony, and he's staring back at me. I feel like saying something, but my mind can't process a sentence in the chaos. Instead, we just look at each other, his eyes jumping around my face. Strands of hair, fallen out of my ponytail, lay sloppily in front of my face, both of which are splattered with dirt and mud.

"They're making a run for it!" Blake yells as Andrew bolts to the nearby entranceway with Lie in tow. They continue to fire off bullets as they run, and within seconds, they disappear into the hedge.

"Save your bullets!" Becky orders. "They belong to the undead now."

A hush falls over the entire camp. The only sound that still resonates is the buzz of the phantom gunfire in my ears. From among the tents, I see Bella's figure dash across the campfire.

"How many hurt?" Becky calls over to her, refusing to move from her position behind cover. She refuses to drop her aim at the exit where Andrew and Lie escaped.

"Kyle's dead. Jack and Kris are injured," Bella calls back. "Riley and I have it under control."

"Any blood needed?" Becky calls again.

"Riley's donating!" Bella's voice rings back.

In the following silence, I begin to hear the growling of undeads from outside the camp walls behind me. Their hungry moans become louder and I hear the sound of branches snapping as they try to tear through the hedge.

"Noah..." I mutter under my breath. My words catch Blake's attention, and he nods. "Noah's still out there. Come grab him with me."

"Grab your axe, you're terrible with a gun," he says back as he approaches me. When he does, he quickly switches our guns. "I'll need the ammo."

"I'll grab your axe," Anthony offers before dashing off.

"What's happening?" Becky calls out quickly, still stubbornly keeping her eye on the hedge.

"Noah's in critical condition. We left him outside the walls for his own safety," Blake explains as he strides over to her, making sure to keep his voice just loud enough so she can hear him. I jog after him. "Gunfire's attracting the undeads and now with those goons out there too, it's just not safe for him. I'm heading out with Jenn to go grab him."

"Damnit," Becky curses, frustrated. "Make it quick. And quiet. Get him and get back immediately. I'll help Bella with the injured. Anthony watches the entrances."

"When we come back, we have to go back to the cemetery too," I explain, finally reaching the two of them. "Xander, Charlie, and Phil are waiting there. Xander's injured."

"If I left the camp, that's where I'd go for protection. It has walls. Andrew is probably headed in that direction now too," Becky says under her breath and then shakes her head. "They're not safe there."

"Here!" Anthony calls out, running at full speed toward me with my axe in hand.

"C'mon, let's hurry," Blake orders as soon as I have the axe.

We head out of the exit and when we're on the other side of the wall, I immediately look over to where I had heard the undeads clawing at the hedge. There's only a few and so we avoid them.

My eyes dart quickly between the trees, scanning for Noah in the direction where I last saw him disappear. He's nowhere to be found. We continue to trek through the forest, staying low to avoid attracting attention, and I search earnestly as we move, swiftly dodging encounters with the straggling undeads that wander toward camp. More are bound to be on their way after the amount of noise the gunfire caused—it's just a matter of *when* they'll get here.

"Jenn! Blake!" I hear the frantic voice and turn around to see Noah's thin, weakened figure stumble between the trees.

"Noah!" I exclaim.

"We have to go, Jenn," he stammers, staggering a few more steps closer to us before collapsing out of exhaustion. "I heard the gunfire and tried to find a better hiding spot when I saw the undeads starting to gather by the camp. But now, th-they're coming. They're everywhere."

"Jenn, you got him?" Blake asks, glancing over his shoulder at me.

"Yeah, I got him," I say, leaning down and helping Noah to his feet. I let him lay an arm around my shoulder, and with his other, free arm, he presses onto his wounded shoulder.

A low moan catches me off guard, and I turn around to come instantly face to face with a grisly undead. A shot rings out as I instinctively pull the trigger, blood splattering back onto my face as the undead drops. I see a few more undeads emerge from the trees, their mouths hanging open in hunger for human flesh, and I fire off a few more half-aimed bullets in their direction.

"So much for being quiet. We gotta go," Blake commands, turning back around for only a brief moment to fire off a few shots at the growing crowd.

He slides a dagger quickly out from his waist before charging forward to a nearing undead, digging the blade up from the chin into the brain. When he yanks the knife out, the undead drops to the floor, motionless.

"Follow me," Blake calls back, stabbing his blade into another one's eye, killing it.

"No," I state. "You follow me. Guard my back."

"You know the way back?" I hear him call out.

"What don't I know?"

I hear him jog up behind me, fending off undeads that get too close while I steer Noah away from the large group through narrower trees, leaving the bulk of the undeads behind us.

"Thank god you came back," Noah remarks as he leans his weight on me. Struggling to stay conscious, he lets his voice slip out in sharp breaths and quivers. "I…I can recover quickly. I'll bounce back from this quicker than you'd think. I can do more around camp. I'll —ah!— I'll be...I'll be useful."

"I know, Noah."

Looking around, I see more undeads beginning to crowd me. I raise my gun again and fire off some more shots before finally, to my horror, the gun clicks and the bullets cease.

"Stupid weapon," I mumble, shoving the gun in the back of my pants, and I unlatch my axe from my waist. I swing at a nearby undead, chopping its head cleanly off.

Under Noah's weight, I stagger. My grip on him loosens, and he slips from my grasp, falling against a nearby tree.

"It's alright," he stammers with a smile, holding himself up with his good arm leaning outstretched on the tree. I wrap my arm back around his waist for additional support as he catches his breath. "I got it."

Winding back, I swing my axe at another undead, lodging it into the undead's skull. The undead falls to the floor, while my axe, still stuck in its face, slips from my hand to follow it.

An undead appears from the other side of the tree, but before I can even open my mouth, it has both hands firmly gripping Noah's outstretched arm. Blood pulses out as the undead's teeth tear through his arteries, and Noah screams out in agony. I fumble to pull my axe out of the dead undead's skull while supporting the entire weight of Noah's falling body.

The undead lifts its head up, tearing out a large portion of flesh. My axe finally free, I bring the blade down in one swing, splitting the skull of Noah's attacker in two.

I catch Noah's limp body as he falls into me. His arm is bleeding profusely as he struggles to comprehend what just happened. I lift the bottom of his shirt and press the fabric hard against the exposed wound. Keeping the pressure on it, I try to drag his body quickly out of the way as I see more undeads appearing, hoping to catch their next meal. One steps out first, coming dangerously close as I struggle with moving the weight of Noah's body. In the nick of time, however, Blake appears, grabbing the menacing monster by the shoulders and throwing it against a tree. He digs his dagger straight through its decayed gray forehead. Without acknowledging me, he then swoops up Noah's limp, unconscious body into his arms and takes off, yelling at me to follow.

CHAPTER 22

Riley

"Where's Bella? Get Bella!" Blake yells frantically as he charges through the east entrance to the camp.

"W-what happened?" I stutter, looking on in horror at the limp body in his arms: Noah. Blood pulses steadily out of a wound on Noah's lower arm, dripping down into his hand and onto the floor to leave behind a trail. Frozen in shock, I stand still, and Blake shoves past me roughly. Soon after, Jenn bursts in from the hedge as well, splattered with blood.

"Where's Bella?" Blake yells again, lying Noah's body down in the grass.

"The infirmary tent," I say absentmindedly, mesmerized by the sight of the exposed and grotesque bite wound. A large chunk of his flesh is missing, opening his arm into a crimson chasm.

"Jack was skimmed during the battle, and Kris was shot," Anthony explains, jogging over. "Bella's patching them up now. Becky's with her."

"What about the others?" Blake repeats, extending Noah's arm to fully examine the wound.

"What others?" I stammer nervously. "That's everyone."

"The infirmary tent's too far, it'll just be easier to get Bella than to move Noah. I'll go," Jenn immediately offers.

"Give me the axe," Blake orders before she leaves.

She hesitates, shifting her eyes between Blake and Noah.

"We can't wait any longer; the toxin is already in his system. We have to stop it before it spreads any further," Blake barks impatiently, looking over at Anthony. "We have to cut it off."

"Let me clean it first," Jenn says immediately, taking back her weapon. Ducking quickly into a nearby tent that hadn't burned down, she returns with a cloth and a bucket of water that had been used by the tent's prior occupant for drinking. Hastily dropping the supplies along with her axe, she motions over to me. "Riley: clean."

Jenn darts off after that, and I drop to my knees to begin scrubbing the blade.

Noah's body suddenly begins to move. His eyes slowly open and dart around the room frantically. When they land on his arm, still leaking significant amounts of blood, they immediately go wide.

"Hold him down, we'll need to do this quick," Blake says sternly. He roughly grabs Noah's arm and extends it, but Noah begins struggling, pulling away in fear.

"Get-g-get away! No! Stop it! Get away!" Noah screams out desperately, writhing in the dirt as Blake tries to control him.

"Hold him down!" Blake yells again over the kid's crying.

Anthony immediately grabs both of his shoulders and pushes them into the dirt. He then readjusts his grip on the boy, placing one hand on the elbow of the boy's free arm and the other on the boy's opposite shoulder. Anthony digs Noah's torso into the dirt and sits on his abdomen, effectively restricting his movement.

"Come grab his arm!" Blake yells at me, and I drop the axe and cloth. "Keep it flat."

"Please, no, please," Noah cries out again desperately, squeezing his eyes shut to wish away the world. Willing my nerves to steady, I gently place them on Noah's blood-splattered arm only inches away from the gaping hole that threatens his life now. When he shakes me off, I grab his wrist harder and hold it down using all of my weight and muscle power to maintain control. Above us, the full moon shines brightly overhead as our only light source and its glare shimmers in the slimy layer of sweat lining Noah's skin.

Blake snatches the freshly cleaned blade.

We all watch as he brings down the first strike on Noah's arm above the elbow. The boy screams out in pain, struggling to pull free from our restraints. Blood spills out from the new wound and over onto the dirt. Blake then swings the axe again. Harder. The heavy blade slashes straight through the bone, and blood sprays up to splatter across my face and clothes. I just look on in horror, my eyes glued to the gruesome scene before me. Noah's struggling dies down as he passes out and falls limp again on the floor. Blake swings the axe down a third time, cutting through the remaining muscle and skin and completely severing Noah's arm from the rest of his body. Suddenly, I'm not holding down Noah's arm anymore. No, my hands now only clasp a dead limb that just used to be his.

As soon as it's done, Anthony grabs the amputated arm from me to move it out of the way, and Blake tears off his shirt to wrap it around Noah's bleeding stub of an arm. Blood quickly begins to soak through, and Anthony offers up his shirt as well. Stumbling over my own shaky hands, I slide off my belt and hold it out to Blake. When he takes notice, he quickly grabs it from my hand and wraps it over the bandage, tightening it until the bleeding begins to slow.

"I'm here, did you cut it off?" Bella calls as she jogs over, her arms full of a myriad of medical supplies. "This is too much of a crowd; I need everyone who doesn't need to be here to step away."

I jump to my feet, making room for Bella to settle in with her equipment. My head spinning, I trip over my feet a little as I walk away. Suddenly, a feeling a nausea washes over me, and I am unable to stop myself from bending over and vomiting all over the dirt.

***

Looking for an escape to collect myself, I've been waiting at the east post. In my solitude, I'm on watch for any threats to our camp's main entrance.

Though I stare out into the forest underneath the night sky, the stark images of Noah's writhing body are all I can see. I didn't watch Dwayne burn, but his screams blend in with Noah's in my mind. Their agony leached into their desperate voices, yearning for a help that they know they won't get. The pain in their screams seeps into the bones beneath my skin, gripping me from the inside and holding me in place to listen to them on repeat. Kyle didn't get to scream, but I watched the bullets tear through his body in an instant. I watched the light leave his eyes as he lay there on the ground. I felt breathless in that moment as he took his last breath. I don't think I've taken a true full breath since.

What were their last thoughts before losing consciousness? I ask myself as if to seer the pain into my brain further. *Were they scared? Did Dwayne and Kyle know that it would be the last time they were awake?*

None of them signed for this when they joined the BAA. None of us signed up for this. I didn't sign up for this. Their parents don't even know what they signed up for. My breathing begins to speed up as I imagine a mother and father hearing of their son's condition. What would that phone call be like? What were they doing today in the moments before they would get that phone call…in the moments before their life changes forever from the news?

Dismissive of my duty on watch, I let my gaze drift to the night sky above me where dozens of stars shine above me through the break in the canopy that our camp creates.

"Why?"

The whisper comes from my lips in a voice just loud enough to be audible to myself. I'm hoping they can hear it in the sky. I'm hoping I can hear them back from down here.

Anthony had been collecting the bodies of Kyle and Dwayne when Blake and Jenn came back. Now the bodies lie side by side, dead and bloody. Dwayne's body is deeply charred from the fire, which had eaten down to the bone at some parts. Luckily, the other casualties of tonight, Jack and Kris, were not as severe. After Kris was shot, Bella had dragged her body to safety.

Corinne is missing. We all saw her look of indignant self-preservation when she broke our lineup to join Andrew's side. We all saw her then betray Becky by refusing to shoot at Lie and Andrew, letting us confirm where her new loyalties were. But I think back to Corinne's face as she fired at me and Jack: she was terrified. The bullet knocked Jack to his knees, and she could've finished us off right then and there, but she didn't. She dropped the gun and ran — I'm not sure where, but no one saw her after the chaos settled.

I am jolted from my thoughts when I begin hearing voices coming from camp. I look down and watch as people start exiting the tent that they had transferred Noah into. Before I climb down the ladder, I gather the small collection of blue flowers I had assembled.

"How is he?" I ask as I slow down my jog in front of Becky.

"It's hard to tell," Becky says with a sigh, stopping in my path to meet me in conversation. Her shoulders slump from the weight of stress and exhaustion. "His body's been through a lot of trauma. With the stabbing, the bite, and now the amputation...he's lost a lot of blood. We're not even sure if we were able to stop the toxin from spreading in time."

"Is there good news?" I ask hopefully.

"Well, he's alive right now; you guys gave him a chance," she says, pushing her lips into a forced half-smile before relaxing them again. It's the same smile a mother would smile at a child when they don't know how to break bad news.

However, in Becky's case, she's not worried about me; her shifty eyes and rushed expression are just another indicator that her mind is on so many other things than me. Behind those eyes, she's running playbacks on all the events that occurred. She's strategizing, calculating, and planning next steps. With her energy preoccupied, her lame smile was all the positivity she could offer me at the moment. I wonder if she watches my brain run the same Olympics on a daily basis. Same mind, just used differently. Just then, her eyes flick down to the tiny bouquet in my hands.

"Are those for Jack?" she asks.

"Noah," I correct meekly, unsure of how much more to elaborate without taking up too much of her time. I pause for a beat before continuing. "I noticed he would decorate his tent with these blue flowers that grow in the corner between the east and north hedges. I wanted to bring him some for his stay in the infirmary tent. He'll like it."

"That's…sweet," she says, nodding slowly as if the word was an unfamiliar taste she was trying to pinpoint. Though, the flowers also seemed to be an unfamiliar sight, and I understand that she probably never even knew Noah fancied them. She tears her eyes away from them and begins to walk away when suddenly, she stops and turns her focus back to me. "I'm sorry what Andrew did to you back there."

I am caught off guard, but after a hesitation I slowly give a response. "It was definitely not the highlight of my night."

"I should've done something," she scorns herself. It's a firm scolding in a matter-of-fact tone rather than an emotional one. "I apologize."

"Don't," I say softly, shaking my head quickly. "There wasn't anything you could've done."

"I'm going to kill him," she declares, placing her hands on her hips. "I don't know when or how but…I will."

"You would?" I ask, much to her surprise.

"You wouldn't? After what he did? Everything he planned? What he almost did to you?" she asks.

"No…I couldn't," I answer honestly, thinking over my words. "I could never *kill* someone. The undeads are one thing because they're not people anymore. A person..."

"He wouldn't hesitate at the opportunity—he didn't with Dwayne. Why should you?" she asks sternly, her eyebrows furrowed.

"Because he wouldn't. If I kill him…then won't I be just as bad as him?" I respond. "In a place like this, it's easy to lose yourself. I won't let this island make me into just another monster."

"Sometimes it's inevitable," she says softly, her troubled eyes still studying me. "Everything changes."

At that, she takes in a deep breath, straightening her back. Then, she begins to head off.

"Aren't you going to look after Noah?" I ask, stepping toward her as she continues to distance herself.

"The world doesn't stop for one casualty," she states.

"I do," I mutter. "His parents would want us too."

"We can't afford that. Xander, Charlie, and Phil are still at the graveyard," she explains quickly, her words running almost as quickly as her mind. She had turned around briefly to face me and walk backwards as she spoke. However, the moment she's finished, she turns back around. "A few of us are going to head over and help them back."

She continues to walk off, and I head over to the tent where Noah lies.

"Oh, sorry, I didn't know you were in here," I say once I duck into the tent. Sitting cross-legged and slouched beside Noah's bloody, unconscious body is Blake. "I can leave."

"Nah, I just donated blood for the kid, so I figured I'd chill here for a bit, make sure he doesn't die or anything," he says, shrugging.

"That's nice of you," I say softly, still hesitating at the doorway.

"I'm O negative, I'm always a go-to for donations," he says and then rubs his eyes roughly with his fists.

"I gave blood too earlier…for Kris," I say, unsure of how else to fill the silence. "We're both B positive. She didn't need too much thankfully, though."

"Why are you here?" he asks tiredly.

"I figured I'd keep Noah company," I say quietly as I sit down next to the young boy, my eyes examining the bandages wrapped tightly around his shortened arm. I lay the flowers at his side. "Someone needs to be there for him...to pray for him."

"Ha! Pray? What are you, the Virgin Mary or something?" he remarks hostilely. "I bet he's a goner."

"C'mon, don't say that," I say, my eyebrows drawn together.

"I've been through this many times," Blake explains, his eyes slightly narrowing at what he interprets to be my naiveté. "There's a reason that there are so many undead around his age."

"What's that supposed to mean?" I ask.

"Level 1 and 2 expel the worst at the end of each year, not the best," he explains with a demeaning tone, receiving enjoyment as his words break my heart. "Noah was expelled for being unskilled. People like him never survive long. I'm being realistic."

"Then do so quietly," I declare, and he blinks in surprise.

"You're not at the BAA anymore, blondie," he states. "You're here now. On an island full of man-eating beasts. Bad things are gonna happening. We're just surviving out here. And you just gotta realize that or else you'll let down your guard and one of those bad things will happen to you next. Go through a few more of these and you'll learn not to get your hopes up."

"That's a terrible mindset," I protest. "Without faith, without hope…well, that's not living. Maybe your life is just about survival, but mine is about much more than that."

"How do you know?" he teases.

"Because I know. I have something more to live for," I respond. My thoughts travel to my baby, still growing within me. "Because I still have faith that not everything is and will be bad."

"You gotta toughen up, blondie," he spits, shaking his head. "Faith won't do it for you. And it's not gonna do anything for Noah either. Just ask Ana—oh wait, you can't. Faith didn't work there, did it?"

His comments catch me off guard, and my head snaps up. But then I see him. He's not digging into me with the same sadistic tone as before. He's withdrawn, his gaze aimlessly staring at nothing in particular.

There's a moment of silence before I speak. "Becky told me about what happened last month…with the 3 hunters…"

I see a small rage instantly arise within him, but when he notices my unthreatening motive, he calms down, locking his jaw. "What about it?"

"It wasn't your fault, you know that, right? You couldn't have known what would happen. Same with Noah," I reassure, to which he just shrugs.

"Were you there?" he brushes the subject off. "Doesn't matter anyway, they're dead."

"Still—"

"I said it doesn't matter," Blake repeats. "What are you trying to do?"

"I—"

"Just shut up," he lashes out defensively. "Just like I said before, you've been here on this island for how long? You don't know anything about this place."

"Maybe. But I just thought that if I went through that, then I would want the reassurance," I admit, shaking my hanging head.

I expect him to curse me out with another comeback. He doesn't.

"You did good today," he says in a low voice, averting his eyes. "With Noah. Honestly, I would've taken you to drop like a fly the moment blood is spilt. Proved me wrong."

I don't respond, but the compliment gives rise to a slight smile on my lips.

Suddenly, there's a shout from outside. It's Becky yelling at the others to get behind cover. Blake jumps to his feet, pulling out his knife and rushing outside. I follow cautiously behind, peeking my head out of the door. Outside, everyone is behind some sort of cover, guns aimed at the east entrance of the camp. With everyone's focus gathered on one spot, I quickly scan the other entrances around the camp, observing them for any movement just in case.

We all watch impatiently as the first steps appear through the hedge. Pine needles rustle and shake off as someone guides their way through the path. We wait in anticipation as the shuddering of the bushes continues until we hear a voice.

"Don't shoot!"

Phil's face pokes through, and I have to catch my breath. He helps an injured Xander through the opening, and I see Becky rush over to greet Charlie trailing behind them. Xander's pale and hobbling, leaning his weight on both a makeshift cane and Phil for support.

"What happened?" Becky asks, draping Xander's other arm over her shoulder. They begin heading for the infirmary tent.

"I'm gonna go keep watch," Blake mutters to me before heading off. I follow the others to the infirmary.

"Stab wound to the middle thigh, maybe a couple hours old," Phil explains. "There was a good amount of bleeding, but it definitely missed the femoral artery. Tourniquet is loose, and sensation of the toes is intact."

"We'll have to clean the wound immediately before an infection settles in," Bella says, examining Xander's bandaged leg as he enters.

"Guys I'm fine, the knife barely broke the skin," Xander insists, but Phil shakes his head at Bella to disregard his words.

"What *happened* at that graveyard?" Kris groans from where she lies in the infirmary tent. I can't see her too well from my position, but I can tell she has several bandages wrapped around her shoulder. "Noah was stabbed in the chest and you in the leg. Jenn came back looking like crap…"

"Ditto," Jenn says, suddenly appearing out of nowhere. She pushes past us and approaches Xander, instantly wrapping her arms around his shoulders in a large embrace. "We told you to wait until we returned."

"We made it, didn't we?" Xander says with a proud voice.

"Yeah, you did," Jenn responds with a relieved breath.

"No, seriously, what happened at that graveyard?" Becky repeats Kris' unanswered question. "Are Vincent and Patrick still there?"

"There was a fight," Jenn begins, stealing a glance at Charlie. "Patrick and Vincent were working with Andrew. Attacked Xander and me. Charlie was not involved. He was out of harm's way."

Her eyes lower as she talks, and she pauses in between her sentences to tighten her lips and collect her words. Her voice doesn't waver but still doesn't command the same attention that it usually does. She's lying.

"How did Noah get stabbed?" Kris calls out again, daring her to answer.

"He heard me scream so he came to help. He risked his life for me," she says. "Vincent got to him, though."

"How is Noah doing?" Xander asks as Phil helps him lie down in the tent.

"He's not good," Bella says in a grave voice. "He got bit. Blake had to perform an emergency amputation of his arm."

"Oh man," Xander mutters.

"What happened to Patrick and Vincent?" I ask. No one answers, and I begin to regret asking despite my curiosity. "Sorry, I shouldn't have asked…"

"No…everyone should know." Jenn takes in a long breath and exhales slowly before continuing. "Patrick and Vincent are dead."

"How'd they die?" Anthony asks.

"I mean they attacked Xander and I so…" she continues. "Xander killed Vincent, and I killed Patrick. He was the one that killed Ana. They all planned it together, but he was the one that sabotaged the lake's fences while we were fishing. The undeads got in."

"I'm just going to say it," Kris starts again, her tone brash and loud. "She and her gang of goons have been here how long? And look, already five of our own are dead, two got stabbed, one got bit and lost his arm, three are missing, and look, Jack and I were shot!"

"Kris, you should stay still," Bella says, placing a hand over Kris' bandages.

"How are you?" Jenn mutters the question to me, placing a hand on my shoulder. The abrupt action catches me off guard, but I nod. She returns my nod and removes her touch.

"What are you implying, Kris?" Xander asks, taken aback by her accusations as he lies besides her among the injured.

"If it wasn't for them, we'd have a lot more casualties," Becky interjects. "If you want to place blame, it should be on Andrew, Lie, Vincent, Patrick, and Corinne. They're the ones that tried to kill us."

"Corinne?" Phil asks in disbelief.

"Guys, I need everyone to get out," Bella commands and we oblige, except for Becky who stays inside by the entrance to help Bella. "There's not that much room in here. I need you guys to be on standby for blood donations, though."

"Take as much as you need from me," Phil offers.

Through the opening in the tent, I spot Jack's limp body passed out on the floor. I have to take in a deep breath when I see his bloody bandages.

"He's fine," Becky reassures, noticing my staring. "Honestly, there's nothing to worry about. You saw what he's been through today; he's just resting."

"Oh my god…" Phil says under his breath when he notices Kyle and Dwayne's covered bodies lying in the grass.

"Kyle and Dwayne. Murdered by Andrew and Lie," Anthony says instantly. "They would've killed us if Blake and Jenn hadn't shown up. Then they took off like cowards."

"Corinne left with them too?" Phil clarifies.

"She slipped out during the battle," Anthony explains. "She was the one that shot Jack, so she probably figured we wouldn't take her back. Honestly, she was probably right."

"She's probably with Andrew and Lie right now," Jenn mumbles.

"We should block the entrances," Phil states. "It'll give us a barrier. Andrew knows the path through the hedge—he's smarter than undeads. Right now, he can get in whenever he wants."

"We can use the logs we have to reinforce it with a fence. If we run out, we'll chop some more trees down," Anthony suggests to which Phil nods. "We start immediately."

"I'm going to go check on Noah," I say.

I head back to Noah's tent, following the trail of blood right up to the entrance. When I arrive, I find Charlie already there, sitting beside Noah's body.

"Hey," I say. "Keeping an eye on Noah?"

When he doesn't answer, I sit down beside him.

"How is he?" I ask.

"I saw him get stabbed," he answers in a low voice. "Patrick stabbed him."

"I'm sorry you had to see that," I say softly.

"I killed him," he blurts out, cutting me short. "I heard Patrick admit to killing Ana. It was his fault that my sister's dead. He was going to hurt the rest of us. I shot him."

"Charlie…" I begin, unsure of what to say, my eyes still searching for a sign of remaining innocence in his heavy eyes.

"Twice. I shot him twice. I wanted to make sure he died," he says again, still staring at the floor in front of him. "I did what I had to do."

"It's ok," I say suddenly. Confused, he brings his eyes up to mine.

"You don't…think I'm a bad person?" he begins hesitantly, his voice still low.

"What you did...wasn't the correct thing to do," I say slowly. "Patrick was a bad person and he would've continued to kill people if he wasn't punished. But killing should not be that punishment if it doesn't have to be."

"I don't regret it."

"You're not a bad person, Charlie," I reaffirm. I am gradually becoming more aware of my heartbeat. My vigilant eyes watch him as to determine his next movement, to read his emotions. He's ten years old. Yet, when he flinches at the hand I place on his forearm, I see much more than just a child. He's darkened inside.

"I feel like I am," he admits quietly, letting his head drop.

"That's a good thing," I say again, my eyes softening as his eyes lighten back up a bit, and I begin to allow the tentative tone in my voice to fall. "It shouldn't feel good to kill someone."

"Is Andrew a bad person?" he asks.

"Yes," I answer, putting a hand on his back to comfort him. "A very bad person."

"Why didn't Blake kill him?"

"Well…like I said, you don't always have to kill bad people. You shouldn't," I answer, thinking it over. "It's better to punish them in other ways. The less blood spilled the better, right?"

"No," Charlie speaks again to my astonishment. He takes in a deep breath and returns his gaze to Noah's still body. "I liked watching Patrick die. I want Andrew to die like that."

"Don't say that...it's okay to be sad about Ana," I say, carefully watching him.

"I just wish it would've been me that got bit," he says firmly, his voice cracking as he tries to hold back a sob.

"No, don't say that," I say immediately. I wrap my arm around his shoulder and pull him closer, but he quickly shrugs me off.

"It should've been me," his voice cracks, and a tear hits the dirt. "If only I can switch our places right now. Look at me and tell me you wouldn't want to see Ana again. Alive."

Suddenly, his head shoots up to face mine, unveiling his wide eyes that stare expectantly into mine.

"I could never trade her for you. No one would," I reassure, horrified at his assumption. "You can't believe that."

"But you'd like to see her again?" Charlie asks, his face scrunching up. "Everyone would."

"We all would love to see you both. But what's done is done," I say softly, putting my arm around him again. This time he doesn't reject it. "We love you. We need you here with us Charlie."

"I just feel like there's this…hole now that she's gone," he says quietly. "I feel empty."

"Yeah, I know that feeling," I say after a short pause, and my gaze drifts off to nowhere in particular. "I lost my parents."

"How did you get over it?"

"You don't really get over it. It's like losing a leg, you don't really get over it. You live with it," I answer honestly. "For my parents, it helps to know that they're together in heaven, though."

"Why?" he asks again, looking up at me with big damp eyes, hopeful for some inspiration yet skeptical to believe.

"Because, I know that although it's sad without them here," I answer, sighing, "it's nice to know that they still exist somewhere. They didn't disappear, they're just waiting somewhere else."

He looks back down at the floor, thinking about my words. I can't tell how he's taking it though. There's a part of me that knows that we don't see eye to eye on this. I can't make him. Instead, I pull him closer again, and we sit there in silence, the words of our conversation still hanging in the air. I watch Noah's chest go up and down as he breathes, finding its mesmerizing motion sort of calming.

Then the motion stops. My trance ends.

I freeze in shock at first, unsure of what to do as I watch the body in front of me, waiting for it to start inhaling again. I peel away from Charlie, scrambling right up to Noah's body.

"Help! Somebody help!" I yell frantically, hovering helplessly over the body. "Charlie, go get help!"

Charlie dashes out of the tent and I position my hands on the center of Noah's chest. I press down as hard as I can, pumping his chest in desperation for him to start breathing again.

"Help!" I cry out again, my adrenaline kicking in.

Suddenly, Blake dashes into the tent and immediately takes over the CPR. I fall back, panting hard. Anthony scurries into the tent a few moments later and right behind him follows Phil. Anthony assists Blake with the CPR, providing breaths to Noah's lifeless body as Blake pumps his chest. After a while, Phil takes over Blake's job. The snap of his ribs shoots through the air, sending a jolt down my spine and slamming my eyelids shut.

"Get the kid out of here," Blake orders, motioning at Charlie, who still sits beside me.

"Charlie, let's go," I say, taking his hand and guiding him out of the tent. He follows my instructions docilely. He's not panicking. His hands don't shake like mine. His voice probably doesn't either. "Go back to your tent. I'll come back to you later."

He nods, and I immediately rush back into the tent, much to Blake's surprise.

"Get out of here!"

"I'm not leaving," I insist, dropping to my knees beside the group. "I helped you cut off his arm, I can help with this."

"Someone switch with me," Phil says through her pants.

"I got it," Anthony offers instantly, and without missing a beat, they switch roles.

The CPR goes on for a while. My mind is too cluttered to comprehend the time. We rotate positions and for a brief period, I assumed the role of administering chest compressions, and later, I gave the breaths. Noah's body lies before us through it all, shifting submissively with each compression. I wonder if he knows what's happening and is waiting impatiently for us to return him to his body. Or maybe it's just too late.

"It's not working," Phil says finally. He's sitting at Noah's head, currently in charge of providing the breaths.

"Breath!" Blake orders impatiently, halting his compressions temporarily. "Administer a breath!"

"Blake…look at him," Phil says again quietly. Noah's skin has become even paler than it used to be. Death has already settled itself in and gotten comfortable. In a couple hours, his body will stiffen as it progresses into rigor mortis.

"We gotta keep trying," Blake protests roughly, leaning down to supply air to Noah's mouth before quickly resuming pumping his chest.

"Blake!" Anthony shouts now, putting a hand on his shoulder to stop him, but Blake shoves him off. A few moments later, exhausted, he begins to ease the strength of his compressions. "Blake…he's gone. We tried."

Blake shakes his head in protest, staring down at Noah's lifeless body.

"No," he anguishes in a gruff voice before resuming CPR with full force.

He continues on for a few more minutes, hoping the kid will start breathing again. Finally, he falls back off the body and sits down on the floor in defeat. Looking at Noah's lifeless body, tears well up in my eyes. As my gaze drinks in the view of his body, I become more aware of the air he can't breathe and the heartbeat he won't feel. Suddenly, it's hard for me to breathe too, and I open my mouth to welcome in as much air as possible. By some spur of willpower, I am finally to peel my eyes away and push myself to my feet. Without a word to anyone, I leave the tent.

"Charlie…" The name stumbles from my lips as I come face to face with the child right outside the tent. I hastily wipe my cheeks. "I told you to go back to your tent."

"Noah's dead," Charlie responds, his flat voice lacking any inflection.

"He's…" I stutter, too wrapped up in my own emotions to talk.

"In heaven now?" Charlie finishes my sentence, and I feel a shiver run over my body. It's not just the monotone way that he said it; it's also his pursed lips tightened together. It's his blank stare that he focuses on me. "At least there's that."

CHAPTER 23

Jenn

"So, we're really not going to talk about what happened at the graveyard?" Xander asks, chucking a heap of dirt to the side.

"Nope," I reply easily, digging my shovel into the ground again. Fashioned years ago at the camp from old rusted axes, the shovels are surprisingly holding their strength against the workload we have been putting them through this week.

No one slept last night. Almost immediately after Noah died, we were faced with a large group of undeads, who had finally found the source of the gunfire. Blake had told me that there were three specific sites that he had set up for scenarios like this: three large campfires that when set ablaze would attract the undead away from camp without starting a forest fire. Blake, Phil, and Anthony ventured out into the night with torches to lure them away, splitting up to light the sites. The smoke from the fires was visible all the way from camp, blocking out the stars and filling our noses with the stench of burning wood. Ultimately, the undead were drawn to the fires, clearing us of their immediate threat.

Throughout the rest of the night, everyone remained anxious and terrified that Andrew, Lie, and Corinne would slip back into camp in a surprise attack. With fresh water and a well-established farm, it's undeniable that the camp is the most prized territory on the island. Even if they retreated to the graveyard, they would need to do a lot of work to make a new camp within those walls. We know that they'd be back to kick us out. We just don't know when.

The morning after, we decide to bury our dead: Noah, Kyle, and Dwayne. Xander and I volunteered for the task, burying them just outside the camp walls. A funeral was then going to be held inside the camp walls to commemorate their losses.

Above us, Blake keeps watch on his post like a hawk protecting the eggs in its nest.

"Maybe it is best to wait some time," Xander agrees, regarding my response to his question. "It's too soon."

"What happened, happened. That's all there is to it," I state.

My eyes drift behind Xander to a figure approaching us. Charlie.

"Charlie, get back inside," I demand, trying to keep my voice as quiet as possible. "It's not safe, you're not supposed to be out here."

"And the story about Charlie?" Xander asks me in a hushed voice, and I freeze.

"There's no story," I correct, glaring over at him. "Charlie was out of harm's way."

"Does he know that?" he asks with a raised eyebrow.

"Aren't you supposed to be with Becky?" I ask Charlie when he's finally upon us.

"I spent all night with her clinging onto me," he moans. "I don't need to be coddled."

"You need to be safe. You can't sneak out like this. Ok?" I remark. He rolls his eyes, but when he turns to head back the way he came, I stop him. "Charlie, actually, can I talk to you about something?"

"What?" he remarks, walking closer. I step away from Noah's grave in order to reach him.

"At the graveyard, I told the others that you weren't a part of the fight," I say, leaning down on my knee. "I told them I killed Patrick."

"Why would you say that?" he asks, furrowing his eyebrows. "I killed Patrick. He killed my sister; I wanted him dead."

"I know," I say, nodding. "But you can't tell people that. They wouldn't understand. Becky would never forgive me. Promise me you'll say that I killed Patrick. You were not a part of the fight at all."

"I promise," Charlie says begrudgingly.

"And one more thing," I say again, thinking over my words as I stare into his dark eyes, searching for the boy that I went fishing with. "Thank you for saving me, Charlie."

"By killing Patrick," he finishes my sentence stoically. "It was the right thing to do."

"It shouldn't have been," I say, and then let myself pause. "But yes."

"Jenn." Xander's scorn is apparent in his tone.

"But," I start again, carefully, still looking at Charlie. "It's still not something you should do. It's a powerful and permanent thing to end someone's life. To put them in the ground like Andrew and Lie did to Kyle and Dwayne. Killing is horrible, Charlie, you have to understand that."

"Patrick killed my sister," Charlie repeats, clenching his jaw as if I've offended him.

"He did. And Andrew and Lie helped," I continue, and I feel Xander's stare boring into me in my peripheral sight. "You can't just kill anyone that does a bad thing. It's too permanent of a solution and it does carry consequences. But that said…you were right to fight back. If you know someone does a lot of really bad things and are threatening to hurt or kill you or me or someone you care about…you fight back."

"I want to fight," he repeats, his face still cold and expressionless, scarred from the weight of murder.

"Only in self-defense," I correct.

"I want to kill all the undead," he states next, catching me off guard.

"Ok," I say hesitantly, standing up and dusting off the dirt from my knees. When he doesn't walk away, I sigh. "They only die if you damage their head."

"Jenn, we shouldn't be doing this," Xander says, stepping over to stand beside me. He places a hand on my forearm, but I shake it off. "Charlie should be inside. Becky will be worried sick."

I pick up the small backup dagger that I took with me out here, and I lean down beside Charlie again.

"Like this," I say before thrusting the dagger into the dirt in front of us. "Into the undead's head. Aim for an eye or under the chin like this and into the back of the brain."

I motion around the underside of my jaw. Then, I hand him the blade, feeling my heart rate spike a bit as he wraps his fingers around the hilt. Abandoning the thought of guiding his hand, I'm instead compelled to back away. He digs the blade weakly into the dirt the first time. Then, gradually, he begins to jab the blade into the ground with more force. Although chaotic, and often mimicking slicing rather than discrete stabs, he gains more comfort with the motion.

"Good, now put the blade down," I instruct, and he obliges, allowing me to quickly swoop it up. "Now look at me, Charlie."

He's enthralled by the holes in the ground, and I have to grab his shoulders to point his face toward mine.

"Only do that to an undead if you are defending yourself or saving someone's life," I say strictly. "Do not put yourself or anyone else in harm's way just to kill or hurt an undead. It's not worth it. In a fight with an undead, you have a high chance of dying. Understood?"

"Understood," Charlie repeats, and I study his eyes, unsure if I believe him. But, I have no choice but to trust him.

"Now go back to Becky," I instruct, standing up again.

"Thank you, Jenn," he says before turning around and scurrying off back toward the hidden entrance of the camp.

"Jenn, what was that?" Xander scolds again harshly. "Do you have any idea—"

"Do you?" I interrupt swiftly. "We are burying three bodies right now, Xander. It's a blessing it isn't more. And the murderers are still out there and are likely coming back for more."

"And you think Charlie is our secret weapon that will save us all if he learns how to use a knife?" Xander retorts. "You just gave him permission to give up whatever ounce of innocence he has left. You gave a 10 year old permission to hurt and kill people."

"I watched his sister die, Xander," I state. "Torn apart, bled to death. The undeads aren't going away. He should know how to kill them if he needs to, so that he doesn't end up like Ana. And if

Andrew, Lie, and Corinne come back with guns raised again while we are weakened, tired, and injured…yes, Xander, I gave him permission to kill and defend us. He's not a secret weapon, but we have only 11 of us left. We should all be on our game to defend ourselves before it's too late. He's part of that now."

I walk back over to Noah's grave and reclaim my dropped shovel. The ditch is almost deep enough now. I steal a glance up at Blake, still perched high above us. Similar to Xander, his stare bores into me. However, he doesn't raise objection. And when he returns his gaze calmly to the forest again, I know that he agrees with me.

"It's about to get a whole lot worse," Xander mutters in resigned agreement.

"This is just the beginning," I say.

CHAPTER 24

Riley

Agony. The screams pierce my ears, interrupted only briefly by the hungry snares of the undead feasting. Blood pours over torn flesh as it's ripped away by greedy teeth.

I had tried to hold on to the sleeve of Annemarie, but she is pulled down too roughly. Her jacket slips from my grasp. Her strained eyes bore into mine, and I know that it is only a matter of seconds before she loses consciousness, and I will be the last sight that she ever sees. The fear, flaming out of her mouth like a forest fire, will be the last emotion that she feels. Or maybe betrayal.

I hurl one of my throwing knives, and the blade soars through the air briefly before sticking its landing into one of the beasts fighting for her body. One of the undead in the crowd latches onto me just then, and I use another small blade to stab it from underneath its chin.

Two arrows whisk past me, and two more undead drop. The hole that they leave in the crowd reveals Enrique's body on the floor. Much of the part of his face in my view is indistinguishable. He had died first.

"Phil!" Blake calls out, suddenly appearing at my side. He swings his bow across his body and unsheathes his short sword again. Both his and Phil's guns had run out of ammo. "Retreat back!"

He charges forward toward Annemarie's body, stabbing the undead above her straight through in the temple. I let loose another knife to knock down an undead by his side. Blake's leaning down now, and every ounce of my being yearns for him to swoop Annemarie up from the floor. But an undead, whose meal we interrupted, grabs his shoulder.

When kills his attacker, he's doesn't pick up the young girl. And when he runs back past me, I know that her body no longer belongs to us. And like for Enrique, I hope I never have to see their bodies again.

Blake leads the charge back to camp. I follow close behind, and behind me is Jack. Trailing behind and covering our tail is Phil, who thankfully escaped from the bloodbath as well. It's the four-person group we left camp with. But, it's not the 6-person group we hoped we would return with.

Almost a week after Andrew and Lie led their uprising, Blake became motivated to search the island for stragglers to join the camp. Overnight, our camp's population had fallen from 19 to 11 people. Among the dead were Noah, Kyle, Dwayne, Vincent, and Patrick. Andrew, Lie, and Corinne were missing and considered traitors of the camp. Blake, and ultimately the rest of us, agreed that we could use more manpower to keep the camp's chores running if we wanted to also take on the additional project of fortifying the camp. We also knew that if Andrew, Lie, and Corinne, did decide to attack the camp again in some form, there is safety in numbers.

I didn't want to join the search crew, but Blake and Phil agreed that I may help them appear less threatening to strangers. A small blonde girl doesn't tend to scare anyone. Ignoring any possible insult in their comments, I chose to focus on the implication that I am a welcoming presence to strangers. Jack wouldn't let me leave without him, and so our group became four.

After scavenging the forest again and again for a few days, we finally found a pair of survivors: Annemarie and Enrique. We didn't get to talk much besides exchanging names and information about our camp. They looked young, maybe a bit younger than me, but I don't know their age or the Level they were in at the BAA. I didn't get to ask how long they've been here, but by their looks, it appeared that they weren't that new. Their skin was hardened by dirt and the sun, their clothes torn from previous fights, and their cheeks gaunt from surviving off the bare minimum for far too long. When I mentioned the camp's farms, their eyes lit up with hope. They had so much hope. We were ambushed by a group of undeads on our trek back to camp. Blake suspected it was an outcropping from the herd that walks along the shore. When we couldn't shake them, Phil was the first to fire his gun, but the noise only brought a bigger crowd. That's when the bloodbath ensued.

As soon as Blake bursts through the hedge into camp, he aimlessly slams his bow into the dirt to his side, sending it skidding a few yards. His heavy stomps yield power as he bounds through the camp.

I stumble in after him, and Jack soon appears behind me next.

"Come here," he mutters, halting my steps and pulling me into an embrace from behind. "We're safe."

"Don't touch me," I mumble, absentmindedly, my eyesight still spinning before me. My body slows down despite the rapid movements around me, and I'm too frozen to shake off Jack, who ignores my request.

"Who is bit?" The voice belongs to Becky as she jogs over. I will myself to look up at her, and she's scanning Jack, Phil, and I, who all still stand by the entrance of the camp. Jenn appears beside her.

"I'm fine," Phil states quickly.

"We're ok too," Jack announces, indicating me. I want to scream out. I'm not bit, but I'm not ok.

"We found others, a girl and a boy, both Level 1," Phil explains. "Neither made it back past the undeads."

"They're all dead!" Blake barks, suddenly stomping back to us. I feel a shiver run down my spine at his imposing presence approaching. "Lives lost and ours risked! God damnit, Becky, what was this for? They were better off before we tried to move them."

"It was your idea, Blake, I agreed," Becky states firmly, swallowing hard. She maintains eye contact. "I'm sorry they're gone. How can we improve for next time?"

"There's no goddamn next time, these chumps are useless!" he yells again, motioning at Jack and I. "I've had it! I've seen enough. From now on, any new arrivals to the island can go die without me needing to watch."

Wretched screams still echo in my ears, beginning to overpower Blake's and Becky's argument.

"Are you with us, Riley?" Jenn asks, but I barely register the question. When her hand touches my forearm, it feels like spikes shooting are through it. No…teeth tearing through it. Teeth tearing through and ripping the fair skin off the children I spoke to only moments ago. With a squeal of pain, I flail my body away from her and clutch the spot where she touched as if to stop the bleeding of a wound that I know exists on another's body but not my own.

"Riley, you're safe, I got you," Jack says softly, encouraging me to relax by wrapping his arms tighter around me from behind. Suddenly, I can't breathe, and when his breathe whisps across my neck, I recoil and try to keep breaking out of my frozen state long enough to escape his body.

"They trusted us," I mutter. "They trusted us to help them."

"She's having a breakdown," Phil states. "She was there for everything."

"Everything," I repeat, and Jack finally lets me break away from him.

"You're shaking, Riley," Jack says, but I hadn't noticed. "Let me help you. What do you need?"

"Give me a break," Blake scoffs, motioning me to go away, but his voice fades in my ears as he gets louder.

"Stay present, Riley," Jenn says while grabbing my wrist tightly.

Though I initially squirm, Blake's continued muffled yelling has convinced my thawing muscles to freeze up again, and I have no choice but to oblige. Jenn roughly pulls me away from the others across the field until we reach an isolated corner of the camp's hedge. Once there, standing in front of the hedge, she lets go and steps back.

"You're stuck in that moment, Riley, you need to get out," she states firmly.

"You don't get it, you didn't see them," I say, clutching both of my arms with my hands. "You didn't see them get ripped apart like that. They…were brutalized. They were so scared."

"Like Billy," she says again, and I inhale sharply. "Like Noah. Shot dead like Kyle, and burned alive like Dwayne. They were murdered in front of you in the most brutal way."

"Their parents don't even know," I say quietly, the tears welling in my eyes for the first time. "They don't even know their child is dead."

"It's horrible. And you're stuck on it, Riley. The deaths are piling on you, and you are letting them."

"I'm not…letting them," I try to explain. "But I saw her eyes as she died. What were her last thoughts? She woke up this morning, not knowing it was her last. What would she have done differently? What did she like and dislike in the world? What are her parents' plans for the night, not even knowing what happened today?"

"You can't even breathe properly," she says, and I notice my jagged breaths.

"I just…feel…everything. I feel it all from everyone."

"I know," she says softer this time, and I can't meet her eye like she wants me to. "You feel everything, and you feel it hard."

Then, with a brisk movement, she slaps me across the face. The pain seers into my skin, and my eyes jolt alert.

"So, did you feel that?"

Then, while my mind still spins around my reddened cheek, she steps back closer to the hedge and dips down swiftly to grab a clump of grass.

"Feel everything, Riley," she demands, before tossing the grass up into the air and letting it rain down on me. "Feel this."

Within a second, speckles of dirt brush my skin. The gently sharp spikes of grass fall onto my shoulders with barely a sensation through my clothes, but their earthy scent floats past my nose in the process.

"Listen to me," she continues, stepping closer, then claps her hands briskly in front of my face. I wince as the sound reverberates in my hands. She then lets her hands rest on my shoulders. I let her. In an instant, she spins me around so that I'm no longer facing the hedge. A blast of sunlight sears into my eyes, and I wince away. "See that."

"It hurts," I mumble.

"Not as much anymore," she replies, letting her gruff voice dampen tiredly.

I open my eyes slowly again and admire the blue sky above me, embracing the sun shining in the middle. Its golden white rays dance in my close peripheral view as I watch a cloud just so gradually drift by. I follow the shaded curves of the floating mass, the beauty in its blended colors ornately crafted as if painted. I let my gaze fall down to the camp before me, dressed entirely in the green of the hedge and the grass. In the distance, the darker forest trees rise up above the camp's border, stretching toward the sky with wonderous elegance.

"Feel this," Jenn says, grabbing my attention by holding a stark yellow dandelion in front of me.

As I stare at the flower, which grows like weeds in this area of the camp, I marvel at the many delicate folds in the pedals that perfectly emanate from a central core. I take the flower from Jenn and caress its pedals with my thumb, letting their softness tick off the gentle sensors in my skin.

"Feel the wind around you and as it enters your lungs," Jenn continues, her voice strict, and I let her instructions guide me into a deep breath. My chest expands as the air floods my lungs, and I imagine the turmoil of the air particles swirling around each other within me. "Your heart beat. Your clothes. The unbearable heat of the island. Take off your shoes and let your feet feel the grass. You've seen horrible things, Riley. I didn't give you that credit before, but I will now. You have a big brain, Riley. A busy brain, busier than mine at least. It's a gift. But if you find yourself feeling everything, then make sure you feel everything. Be here and stay here in the moment, not the past. You won't survive otherwise."

I let the words sink into me, as I take another deep breath and focus on the world around me. After a moment, I turn to look at Jenn.

"Why did you help me?" I ask.

"You needed someone to snap you out of yourself," she says with a shrug, then smiles. "Becky was about to try sedating you, so I figured we would try something else first."

"Yeah, the slap was a bit much, though," I mutter through a breath, letting my shoulders relax.

"I enjoyed it." She smirks.

"I'm sure you did."

"We came here together, Riley," she adds. She stops short, unsure of what to say after. We're both unsure why it matters that we arrived at the island together, but it does matter. "We stick together."

"We stick together," I repeat. I let myself focus on the air circulating in and out of me, before turning my attention back to the painting in the sky.

CHAPTER 25

Jenn

"Ugh, that bird poop over there reminds me of Andrew," I sneer, to which Xander lets out a hearty laugh.

"That's what you said about the slug you stepped on yesterday," he says.

"Yeah, well, gross things remind me of Andrew," I spit out quickly.

It's been two months since Andrew, Lie, and Corinne left. In response to our new human threats, new defenses were installed. New winding entrances were carved out in the hedges, and overgrowth and seeds were stuffed into the old ones to clog them up. In addition, wooden boards now block off the inside openings of old entrances, while sliding doors were built at each new entrance. Now, rather than just being able to slip in and out of the hedge, the door would have to be moved aside from the inside of the camp. Lastly, a fence was built along the entire inside border of the hedge in order to reinforce its strength.

A stricter schedule has also been instituted. No one made any more search parties for lone scavengers on the island, but hunting for prey was started again. Blake and Phil decided to only go hunting on certain days and always returned well before sundown. However, overall, we relied mostly on the food provided by the fields. There were set meal times, and everyone knew where everyone was at all times. The three posts were always occupied—they had to be, or else Becky would have a panic attack.

"Are you alright?" Xander asks after a moment of hesitation, raising an eyebrow. His leg injury suffered from recurrent infections during its healing course, and after the gore of Bella having to carve out the infected dead tissue, it still hasn't fully healed right. We've been gradually letting him take on more labor work around camp as he recovers, but on his rest days, he occupies the posts to keep watch. I had decided to stop by today and keep him company for a bit.

"I just can't stop thinking about the whole thing," I say, cross-legged and spinning my axe on the wooden floor. "We just let them leave without any punishment."

"Making them leave is a punishment," he clarifies. He sits against the short wooden fence that borders the elevated platform, and he lazily peers through its large slits. "I'm just happy they're gone."

"Happy?" I scoff, but then my tone lowers as I let out my next words. "I didn't know that was possible on this island."

"I just mean that after what they've done, it's better they're not around," he explains.

"After what they did, they deserve something harsher," I say. "We should've gone with my suggestion."

"Which was?"

"That we tie up the band of good-for-nothing lunatics and dump their pathetic asses in the middle of the forest with a sign that reads 'Free Meal, Enjoy,'" I explain with a smirk.

"Including Corinne?" he asks again, and my smile instantly dissipates.

"She chose her path," I affirm, looking down. "And she hurt Jack."

"From what I heard, Jack and Riley joined Andrew too," he counters. "Maybe Corinne didn't know they switched back over? Maybe she was trying to help us?"

"They were unarmed and running for cover. They didn't even try to hurt anyone once the battle broke out. You also didn't see the way Corinne refused to help Becky when Becky called on her during the fight. She ran away with Andrew and Lie because she's guilty," I say flatly, disregarding his point. "Besides, Jack and Riley would never seriously join the other side. They were doing what they had to in order to survive in the moment. Riley's pregnant after all."

"Wait, really?" he inquires, looking back at me.

"I overheard Jack mention it to Bella the other night," I say with a shrug.

"Does he know you know?"

"Does he know anything ever? He's oblivious," I say. "I've been giving him half of my dinner since, and he just hands it over to her. He thinks it's just 'cause I'm too stressed to eat."

"That's…nice of you," Xander says again, his eyebrows furrowed.

"Oh, shut up. I'm only doing it because it's not safe to hunt as much anymore, and I don't want that baby anemic or something," I say. Then, after a moment, I pound my fist into the floor. "Damn, Andrew really screwed everything up. You're not at all bothered by the fact that they're still out there?"

"Of course I'm bothered. They were cruel and terrible…"

"Don't say 'but,'" I say, shutting my eyes.

"We're reprimanding them for killing," he explains. "If we just do the same back to them, don't you think that is sort of hypocritical?"

"No, not really," I continue bluntly, shrugging off his argument. "You're starting to sound like Riley, you know that?"

"Is that a bad thing?" he says, letting out another laugh.

"Don't get soft on me!" I exclaim, and though I say it with a smile, I know I'm serious. "If there's one thing the BAA taught us how to do, it's how to kill."

"When needed," he specifies, holding up a finger. "Besides, according to my book, the BAA doesn't always have a good track record of teaching the right things."

"Valid point," I say, nodding.

"I…killed Vincent that night," he says, and suddenly, the lighthearted tone of the conversation ends, and his expression darkens.

"You had to," I say, shifting in my seated position.

"I know I did," he says, his voice lower now. "But I didn't like how it felt. To end a life. I'd do it again if I'm in that situation again. If it's not needed, though, I wouldn't."

"And what if Andrew, Lie, and Corinne aren't done with us?" I say, posing the hypothetical as a threat. "They'll come back for their revenge and we have to be ready for it."

"I know," he says, but he averts his gaze back to the forest. "You ever think about if our parents went through this type of stuff during deployments?"

"Yeah...yeah, they probably did," I mutter, biting my lip. "All deployed personnel probably do."

"Like the ones now rebelling against the war?" Xander poses the question.

"Especially them," I say, looking down.

"I guess you never understand the toll of it unless you go through it yourself," he says again softly. "I wonder how they get through it."

"My parents never talked about their deployments," I say. "But I don't think they had emotions—at least they never showed them. If there was help, they wouldn't have accepted it anyway."

"That's terrible..." Xander murmurs again.

"It was still always the source of their pride and purpose, though," I say, joining Xander in staring off between the trees ahead of us. "The military, I mean. Despite the sacrifices. They were so dedicated to it. And yet now they're in the rebellion."

"Makes you wonder who's on the right side after all, don't you think?" Xander poses, much to my surprise. "I mean, the government is turning prisoners into undead. Officials at the BAA are ordering kids to their death on this island. Leaders aren't always right. Am I crazy to think that the rebels aren't crazy after all?"

"If you think the BAA is so corrupt, do you still want to rejoin?" I ask, hesitantly.

"I don't know..." he mutters. "Do you?"

I don't answer. I finally let my gaze drift to the gun in his hand.

"Give me that," I say. He gives me a confused look for a moment, before handing it over. "Did they teach you how to use it?"

"Briefly, yeah."

"What are you doing?" he asks hesitantly as I stand up.

"I had never shot one before that night," I say, adjusting my grip so that it fits comfortably in both of my hands. I hold it out in front of me, aiming it into the abyss of the forest. "I sucked."

"Wow, I thought a Bellator never sucked at anything," he responds jokingly, pushing himself to his feet as well.

"Exactly. And guns are a big part of being a soldier, so I can't suck, especially now with the others out there," I respond. "So, show me how."

"Alright," he says with a chuckle. He leans back against the fence of the platform to alleviate the pressure off his leg. "First rule of shooting is safety. Some of these guns are very sensitive so the safety is always kept on until needed."

"This?" I ask, turning the gun over and pointing out a little lever on the side. He nods.

"Close one eye and line up the sights so they point toward your target. Aim for the stump over there," he coaches. "And then when you're ready you can—"

He is cut off when I pull the trigger. The shot fires and the gun lurches up. The sound makes my stomach turn. I hadn't heard it so close since that night.

"You have to keep it steady," he says. "Here, give it."

He steps up beside me, slides the gun into his hand, and holds it out toward the stump. I watch as he carefully breathes a few times and takes the time to adjust the way he lines up his shot. When he fires, specks of dirt fly off the wood as the bullet collides with it.

"Are you done showing off now?" I say, grabbing the gun back.

"I'm just trying to help you. It might save your life one day, you know, no biggie," he says again with a smug smile on his face.

"Yeah, yeah, watch it with the gloating, especially when I'm the one carrying the gun now," I say again, and he just laughs me off.

"Stop wasting bullets!" Blake's call shoots through the air like a bullet in its own right. He's standing at the base of the post, staring up at us. "You want to alert all the undeads in the area to swing by? Keep firing and I'll let you make do with a knife instead from now on."

"Roger that, sorry," Xander calls back down.

"I should go," I say to Xander. "I'm supposed to help prepare dinner tonight."

"Is it almost dinner time already?" he says, stretching his arms. "Wow, time flies when you sit up here all day doing absolutely nothing."

"Shut up," I say, exaggerating an eye roll before dropping onto the ladder leading down from the post. "See you later."

I climb down to the bottom and head over to the campfire where Phil and Riley have just carried over baskets of vegetables from the field.

"Oh, my favorite...salad," I say loudly as I approach them.

"Does that joke ever get old to you?" Riley mutters, and I smile. "Besides, we're actually out of salad, so we're going with your second favorite meal: raw vegetables and grain."

"Wow, you just read my soul," I say again. She eyes me carefully.

"Why do you seem in a good mood?" she asks, a small grin appearing on her lips in response to mine.

"I just fired a gun while envisioning murdering Andrew. It was a good time," I say, throwing my hands up.

"You were with Xander," she states, her smile pushing into her eyes.

"Are you 10?" I reply quickly, waving her off.

"Oh shoot, we forgot the utensils," Phil says, examining the materials they brought over. "Jenn, could you run back to the storage cabin and grab some?"

"Fine," I reply, drawing out the word. "But you owe me an extra portion then."

"If I could, I would." I hear him reply, but I'm already headed off.

"Love you too, Phil," I call back dramatically.

The storage cabin is right next to the field. It's a sorry sight to behold, honestly. Though four times the size of one of the tents that we sleep in, upon entering it, the cabin holds nothing but empty promises. Our decreased manpower coupled with recent dry spells has decreased crop production and increased the spoiling rate of whatever surplus we do maintain. The cabin is far from full, with its contents mainly localized to the corners. None of it is meat.

I gather the makeshift plates in my arms along with some of the knives. As I'm leaving, I spy Anthony walking nearby. I catch his eye, and he diverts his path over to me.

"Let me grab those," he offers.

"I got it," I insist, but he approaches, nonetheless. He takes the majority of the stack and throws it under his arm. "Fine. If they get too heavy for you, you can hand them back over."

"Ouch," he responds. "Way to bruise my masculinity."

"Someone had to," I say, smirking l. I glance back down at the plates in my hands and notice that the vines have snapped on the top one. "Great, this one's broken."

"What do you mean?" he asks, and we slow to a stop. He comes in front of me and peers down at the plate. "Oh, that's an easy fix. I'll see if I can grab another vine from one of the trees around camp.

"Ok, I'll just leave it at the campfire then.".

"Hey, actually don't move, you got a little something…" he says just as I'm about to begin walking again. I pause as he brings his hand up to my face.

"I should warn you, back at the BAA, I once broke a guy's wrist for putting his hand on my shoulder," I say, flinching as his thumb brushes my cheek.

"I don't doubt it," he says, letting out a melodic laugh. It's the type of laugh not necessarily genuine, but trained enough to sound like it is. "We're not at the BAA anymore, though."

I raise my eyes up to him, and it's then that I notice our faces are only inches from each other, close enough for me to make out each individual hair in his short beard. His keen eyes look back straight into mine and their dark irises add to an effect of continuous darkness arising from his pupil. There's a mesmerizing effect about them. I feel his thumb trail from my cheek back toward my ear and the rest of his hand comes to join it. He leans in slightly.

"What?" I say abruptly pulling away. "What are you doing?"

"It's called a kiss, Jenn. You're supposed to lean in too," he says with a seductive smile. "Don't tell me you don't want to."

"What happened to your little plaything, *Kris*?" I ask, narrowing my eyes.

"Forget about her." He shrugs nonchalantly.

"Why?"

"Am I married to her?" His voice is low as he leans back in close to me. Although I back away in response, his deep stare continues to lure me in. "C'mon, I see the way you look at me. Let's try something."

My instinct immediately compels me to reject him and lash out with a myriad of sharp comments. It's repulsing the way he curls his lips into a smug smile. Yet, it's alluring.

"I don't need you," I say, my voice and face remaining stern. I keep my gaze on him for a moment longer, though my mind has blanked. "But...I would agree to that."

"Sweet, so…what are you doing after dinner?" he asks with a proud smile. As for me, I remain still, trying to will myself to relax as he steps closer.

CHAPTER 26

Riley

"I know she hasn't always been the nicest person on the outside, but she's a good person underneath, and she deserves Xander. You know?"

"Are we talking about the same Jenn?" Jack asks. It's almost sundown now and we decided to go on a stroll around the perimeter of the campus, just the two of us. I've been doing most of the speaking though, rambling off everything that's been on my mind while Jack feigns interest and attention. "Back at the BAA, she once broke a dude's thumb for smiling at her. I don't know about you, but she doesn't strike me as the romantic type."

"We're not the same people we were at the BAA," I reply, to which he shrugs.

"As fun as talking about Jenn and Xander's non-existent love life has been," Jack says. "I was going to meet up with Bella sometime tonight. She's probably waiting for me back at the infirmary tent."

"Oh," I say, my voice quiet. "This late?"

"Yeah, I told her earlier I'd head over. I don't want to leave her hanging," he says again with a shrug.

"What are you two going to do?" I ask, letting the words trail off.

"Just hang. She's really chill," he affirms. I stop walking. "Is everything ok?"

"Yeah," I say, but when he furrows his eyebrows, I push my lips into a grin and wave my hand briefly. "It's nothing."

"What is it?" he asks again. "You can tell me."

"It's just that…with everything that's happened at the camp, we've both been so busy with our chores that I don't really get to see you anymore," I explain. "Only at night. And half the time, you spend it with Bella."

"That's not true—"

"Do you enjoy her company more than mine?" I ask abruptly.

"What? Of course not," Jack reassures, the wheels in his brains turning as he tries to understand my point of view.

"I'm…It's just with the baby and all…I can't do this alone. I need you," I begin to say.

"Riley…I'm still yours," Jack says earnestly. "I'm not leaving you."

"It just felt like you were pulling away from me," I mutter, enduring the pain of speaking my thoughts so directly.

"Riley…" Jack explains looking away. "Bella came up to me a while ago, not long after Andrew and the others left. She told me that she knows what love looks like and she sees it with us. She gave me a ring, Riley. She's been helping me memorize a certain speech too."

I give him a confused look but then catch my breath when he gets down on one knee.

"Oh my…" I say under my breath, bringing a hand up to my mouth when he pulls out a ring from his pocket.

"Love…" he begins, staring up at me. He's silent after that for a few seconds before a smile blooms across his face and he releases a nervous chuckle. "Wow, now that I'm actually doing this, I don't remember what I was supposed to say. This is why I needed the practice!"

"Jack!" I squeal, joining in his excited laughter. If I hadn't been caught speechless, I would have caressed his cheek and told him that he didn't even need to say anything. I would have told him immediately that I'm all his. Instead, I stand frozen.

"Riley, you mean the world to me," he says, his laughter dying down to a sigh. He is still holding out the small band, and its shimmering diamond matches the sparkles of light in his blue eyes. "I want to marry you and spend the rest of my life with you. I *love* you, Riley. There's no better way to say it. And this ring will symbolize that. And with our baby…we'll be a family. I promise I will be the *best* father any baby could ever ask for. And I will work to my last breath trying to provide the best life for you and our baby and making sure you're both happy."

He stops to shake his head, unsure of what to do with the excited energy still radiating out of him. He inhales a deep breath, allowing himself to calm down for a moment.

"Riley, will you marry me?"

"Jack…this is crazy!" I exclaim, the words coming out in another squeal.

"Then let's be crazy!" he exclaims back. "What do you say?"

"Yes!" I blurt out, my eyes filling with tears. The smile on his face could put the beauty of a field of roses, a sky of stars, and the most colorful sunset all to shame, and its largeness would embarrass even the grandest ocean.

I hold out my hand, and he slips the ring on. The cool metal against my skin instantly sends sparks through my body. When he stands back up, he wraps his arms around me and pulls me close. I touch his face with my hand and bring his lips down to mine while wrapping the other arm around his neck. He then tilts me back, dipping me and leaning down into the kiss. In this moment, the rest of the world doesn't exist. The moment lasts forever, but even that's not long enough.

CHAPTER 27

Jenn

"Alright everybody, listen up. We have some announcements to make," Jack speaks up the next morning at breakfast.

He and Riley both rise to their feet, and Riley fumbles with her hands, picking at the tips of her fingernails. I figure that they would be announcing Riley's pregnancy, but nonetheless, I still raise my head to feign interest while finishing my meal.

"First, I'd like to tell you guys something that I've kind of kept mostly to myself for a while," Riley says slowly, inhaling in a deep breath and keeping it there. She waits a moment. "I'm pregnant. I've actually been for a while now."

Silence. Some raise their eyebrows while others furrow theirs. Riley's fair cheeks redden, her skin all but painting itself the color of a ripe tomato.

"A baby?" Becky asks, her stern face drawn seriously. "You have to be joking."

"We're not, actually," Jack says slowly, the nerves in his gut straining the expression on his face. "But, we've been handling it well so far. Riley's strong and healthy, and the baby will be too."

"Do you understand how difficult and dangerous childbirth will be out here?" Becky states strictly again, her eyebrows pulled tightly together in thought.

"I know the risks," Riley mutters, and the lightness of her words shows that even she knows that she's not convincing.

"You could die, Riley," Becky repeats. "We're not doctors here. We don't have the medical equipment for this. If there's a complication…"

"How far along are you, Riley?" Phil asks.

"About five and a half months," she answers instantly.

"Ha! How the hell do you think you would even raise a baby here?" Blake scoffs, shaking his head with a smile as he returns to his food.

"Riley and I will be their parents, we'll do whatever it takes," Jack answers.

"Even when it cries and wails and alerts every undead within miles from here?" Blake asks again, but when he looks up at them, his face lacks any of the amusement it held just moments before. His words are cautionary.

"That baby would kill us all," Kris remarks.

"Guys, she's already months into her pregnancy," I say, letting my loud voice draw the others' attention. "You might not like it, but it's going to happen. The birth, the baby. It's happening, so we might as well just start planning for it. That way at least when it does happen, we'll be prepared."

"We could transition to living in huts instead of tents to help insulate the noise," Riley offers after a moment, letting her eyes travel between Becky, Phil, and Blake. "If we start building now, we could be ready by the time I give birth."

"I'm sure we can make some sort of binkie too," Anthony says, shrugging. "We'll brainstorm a few ways to get that ready too in the coming months."

"I'll make sure to store up more herbal remedies for the birth," Bella states, giving Riley a soft smile.

"Tell me what to look for," Blake says suddenly, his focus on Bella. "I'll search for what you need during trips outside the walls."

"We could also try to gather more spare cloth from the undeads while we're out there," Phil adds, tilting his head in contemplation.

"These are good ideas," Becky says, nodding. She takes in a deep breath before letting it go with a breath of a chuckle. "Definitely some interesting news, but I agree, we'll figure it out and try to prepare ahead of time. Amenities for the birth should be high priority so that we can do our best to make it safe for both Riley and the baby. Does anyone have anything else to add?"

"Actually…we do have one more thing to announce," Jack says with a hesitant smile, and I see the fear strike across Becky's face.

"Dude, it better be good news," Blake says, standing up.

"It is!" Jack says quickly. "Riley and I are also getting married."

I have to shut my eyes briefly before reopening them, and when I do, Riley's beaming red again. Jack, on the other hand, is smiling gaily as if trying to convince the others to mimic his enthusiasm.

"He asked me yesterday and I said yes," Riley continues, locking eyes with Jack and then ultimately slipping her hand in his. "We weren't thinking of anything crazy, but I mean…if we could do a little ceremony or something and have everyone attend, that would be nice."

"A baby…and a wedding," Becky repeats. The rest of the camp is silent again.

"Not a formal wedding, but something small maybe," Riley suggests.

"Well, we've definitely never had one of those here before," Anthony says.

"There's always a first for everything, right?" I say the moment I notice Riley's smile falling. When she looks at me, relief washes across her face. "Congratulations, you guys."

By some compelling force, I stand up and walk into her eager open arms. She lets out an exhilarated laugh as I embrace her small body into a tight hug. It's a strange feeling, and I wince at the level of intimacy. Yet, at the same time, with the beat of her pounding heart breaching our contact, and her thin arms wrapping over my shoulders...her hug feels warm.

"Alright, that's long enough," I comment, pulling away, her grasp so tensed up with enthusiasm that I nearly have to pry her arms off.

"Congratulations, sweetie," Becky says, wrapping her arms around Riley next. "This is a lot of news, but we'll work with it."

"Thank you so much," Riley responds genuinely, squeezing the older woman. Beside them, I find Xander congratulating Jack.

"Where on earth did the ring come from?," Becky asks with an amused smile, and the blond eagerly extends her hand.

"Isn't it beautiful?" Riley exclaims, and then I follow her gaze to Bella.

Bella lays a hand on Jack's shoulder as she walks past him, before meeting up with Riley. The two embrace tightly, and when they separate, Riley wipes her eyes with the palm of her hand.

"Well, Virgin Mary, should we expect Jesus to pop outta there?" Blake appears by Riley's side, a sarcastic smile drawn devilishly across his face. "I want to know if I should start getting on your good side."

She rolls her eyes before reaching up and pulling him into a comfortable hug. When they separate, he gives a quick nod of congratulations to Jack from across the group.

"Now, I don't mean to destroy the moment, but you can have your little wedding ceremony later," Blake continues. "There's a lot to be done around the camp."

"Right," agrees Becky. "There's a bunch of undeads messing with the fence surrounding the safe zone. Blake is going to take Phil and Anthony, and you guys can walk the perimeter to find and fix any breaks. If you could also start gathering some logs for huts as well, that would be helpful. Jack and Jenn will do a short hunting trip and also start gathering more firewood. Riley's north post, Kris is east post, Xander's south post. I'll work with Charlie on east field; Bella, you can work on west field."

"Why can't Xander and I switch jobs?" Jack asks again.

"He's still got a busted leg," Blake says, walking off. "Besides, what would he do out there anyway? Throw his sword? Wrestle the birds?"

"You're the best with the bow. Jenn will help you carry stuff and protect you if you run into any of the undeads," Becky explains further.

"C'mon, you heard the woman. Get your bow. I'll be your bodyguard," I say, walking past Jack toward my tent to grab my axe. "I'll be waiting by the hedge when you're ready to go."

***

I run my fingers over a smooth grey rock, pinpointing an unseen area in the canopy above us. Sunlight sparks down in flashes as the wind brushes past the leaves that cover it, and I bring up the back of my hand to wipe away a bead of sweat on my forehead. It's a lot cooler under the protective canopy of the dense forest, but a thick humidity still hangs in the air and the ever-present heat seeps into my skin.

"Ready?" I ask Jack through my breath. He stands motionless by my side while raising his bow up to the canopy.

"Yeah," he responds, and I wait another moment before hurling the small stone through the air. It flies past the thick collection of branches above us and ricochets off the side of a trunk, alerting a mass of birds that had been resting on an adjacent branch. The group takes flight, and with the snap of a string, Jack propels an arrow like a bullet into the soft belly of one of the larger birds. Before they disappear from sight, he quickly draws and releases another arrow, which catches another heavy bird.

I let out a burst of impressed laughter as the last of the birds escape.

"Who would've guessed you were so good with a bow," I joke, and he rolls his eyes.

"Who would've guessed we'd make such a good team," he says back, starting forward toward where an arrow sticks up from the ground.

"Blake, apparently," I answer. "He's got a good eye for that sort of stuff."

"Riley too," he responds, and after another minute, we reach the first bird. He retrieves his arrow, wiping the tip off with the rag hooked onto his belt. "You know, the two of you aren't as different as you think."

"You sure about that?" I scoff, holding open the large sack I have been carrying. So far, it contains two squirrels.

"You don't see it?" He throws the bird into the sack.

"We're about as opposite as the North and South poles."

"Maybe," he says with a shrug. "But, if you think about it, they may be on opposite sides of the globe, but in the end, they're both just cold and covered in ice."

"What are you saying?" I say, doubtfully raising an eyebrow. I have a hard time taking Jack seriously.

"You're both really smart and amazing at your own things. You're both fighters for what you believe in. And you're both here, aren't you?" He steals a glance at me, but I just listen silently to him as we walk over to gather the next bird. After all, I find his bluntness and honesty refreshing. "You guys *are* different from each other. But not *that* different."

"Is that so?" I ask again, this time with my smirk faded.

"Yup," he responds, retrieving his other arrow.

"When did you become so philosophical?" I ask, forcing a laugh.

"I'm just really happy, I guess. It makes you see things clearer," he says with an exaggerated shrug, his grin extending from ear to ear.

"Speaking of…where'd you get the ring?" I ask after he places the second bird into the bag.

"Bella gave it to me. She received it from someone she used to love at the BAA, but she said it was time to pass it on," he answers as we continue our trek through the trees, our eyes bouncing attentively in hopes of spotting another animal. "I didn't think I had the guts to finally ask Riley, but once I did…man, I just love her so much."

"She loves you too," I say. Though he looks at the ground, biting his lip gently, I can tell that all he's seeing is Riley. The corners of my lips push themselves into a smile. "I'm really happy for you two. Besides, it's just nice to see something good happen after all the crap we've been through."

"Thanks, Jenn. Really," he says. I nod. "I just want the best for her, you know? I mean after what happened to her family, and then the expulsion and the island…I just want her life to go uphill from here on out."

"That's…sweet," I say. Yet, there's a pit in my stomach as my smile fades quickly, and I'm not sure why. I can't help but want the conversation to end.

"When we get back to the BAA, we can get her to a hospital and she can have her baby," he continues, looking off into the trees as he plans his future. His smile widens, but I tighten my own lips, bare and chapped from the heat. "We can have a second wedding. And another baby. If Headmaster lets me, I'll rejoin the BAA. I don't think she'd want to, though. Maybe she could just stay home with the kids—she's so good with kids."

"That's what the nannies are for," I mutter, correcting him. In reality, since the military is Riley's assigned career, she would be forced to rejoin the BAA if they decide to have us back. If that's the case, a career nanny would care for her child. That is, of course, assuming we do not become Rejects upon returning, in which case Riley would then get to be the primary caregiver for her baby…in absolute poverty. I decide to not bring this up to Jack.

"We'd have to work out the details when we're back home," he finishes, his faraway gaze staring off into nowhere— or at least no place that exists yet. Finally, the silence in the absence of his voice pulls him back to reality, and he watches me stare at the grass covered floor. "Did I say something wrong?"

"No, you're fine," I say, suddenly snapping out of my own thoughts. I force a small chuckle. "It's just that…you have a plan. You have Riley and a family after this no matter what."

"Nah, I'll leave the official planning for Riley, she's much better at that—"

"My point is that you guys have each other. *That's* a future. What do I have?" I ask, and he tilts his head.

"Are you kidding? Headmaster would have to be an idiot to not take you back at the BAA. You're, like, the best there is," he says, shrugging like it's obvious.

"I've never counted on anything besides the BAA," I say again, staring at the ground. Then, my voice lowers even more, to a point when it's barely even audible to myself, like a simple breath going unnoticed. "But now I don't know if I even want to rejoin."

A flash catches my eye, and as I look closer, I realize it's the reflection of the sun off something a few yards ahead.

"Wait, follow me," I say, crouching down a little and motioning with my hand.

"I love surprises," he mutters.

When we get there, I find what I was looking for. A glimmer of sunlight shines off the crimson blood coating the sharp edges of the broken wooden fence that surrounds the safe zone.

"The undeads must've torn it down here too," Jack says, reaching up to retrieve his bow from his shoulder. "Do you think Andrew did it again?"

"No," I say, examining the mess. "It looks like it was broken inward from a few undeads pushing into it while walking this way. They must've torn their way through and cut themselves up on the way in. Andrew would've just smashed it, it would've been a cleaner wreckage."

"Should we go back? Tell Blake?"

"What's the point? We'll lose precious daylight by the time we find him, and then he'll just send us back here anyway. We'll just have to be more careful," I say, drawing my axe. "Besides, it's probably only a few that sneaked in anyway."

"I don't know, I've got a bad feeling about this," he murmurs.

"Don't be a wimp. Just keep an eye peeled," I command in a hushed voice, glancing around cautiously.

Wary now of not making too much noise, I creep through the dense overgrowth surrounding the fence. Minutes pass as we continue on. Holding back a rather flimsy branch, the slippery surface catches me off guard; .turning my hand over reveals a palm stained red.

"It's fresh," I announce quietly to Jack. I take another hesitant step forward, my ears sensitized to the twitches in the forest.

A low rustling grabs my gaze to a distant area just beyond a thick tree, and my fingers subconsciously close around the hilt of my axe tighter. My keen ears are suddenly aware of the leaves crunching under the heel of my boot as I slowly walk over to the origin of the noise. Behind me, I hear the click of an arrow clipping into a bowstring.

I glance back at Jack and hold up my hand, signaling for him to stay put while I approach. Step by step, I get closer. When at last I reach the tree, I slow down my pace to nearly a stop, cautiously moving around the trunk to get a better view.

Before my eyes, squat two undeads hunched eerily over a mess of blood. Only when one of them turns its gruesomely disfigured and decayed face toward me, my view is fully exposed to the hole burrowed into the grass between the two of them. Surrounding the small defenseless den and strewn across the grass are the bloody carcasses of roughly five infant bunnies.

As the closer undead attempts to get up, I swing my axe horizontally. The undead's head is instantly chopped off upon impact and, not wasting a second, I slice the blade across again, this time across the throat of the second undead. He staggers for a moment, blood rushing from his neck, and I bring my axe down a third time to split his skull into two completely separate parts.

"Ha!" I scoff, stepping away from the deceased bodies and back into Jack's view. I glance up at him arrogantly. "I thought these things were supposed to be scary. All they can do is pick on something smaller than them like rabbits."

He reproduces my smirk, rolling his eyes at my boasting. At the sound of leaves ruffling, my head spins back toward the fallen undeads to catch a third stepping out of the underbrush.

I easily swing my axe in an uppercut, and the force knocks the undead's smashed head backwards, spraying bone shrapnel and blood as it collapses to the ground. As I watch the trail of blood carve its way through the dirt, images of Ana flash into my mind. In my head, I see her body lying dead as the blood spreads across the sand, pooling in the divots of the uneven terrain.

"Jenn, look out!" Jack exclaims. His back straightens as he pulls the string of his bow back, and, when he releases, I catch my breath as the sharp wind shoots past me. A subsequent thud follows, and a new undead collapses to the ground only a few feet to my left—an arrow sticking out of one of its eyes.

Gaps in the trees up ahead reveal another two undeads, and I step toward them.

"Jenn! Where are you going?" Jack calls out again. I quickly glance back at him to see him fire another arrow into the skull of an undead coming from another direction. "The group is larger than we thought, we have to turn back!"

"We got this!" I yell stubbornly back at him, continuing forward. When I reach the pair of undeads I had spotted, I'm reminded of the one that peered around the tree to bite Noah. He was injured and defenseless, but he would've survived if not for the bite. I swing the curved blade of my axe through their heads.

"Jenn!" Jack yells again as I step further out of his view. Behind me, I hear another snap of his bowstring followed by the pounding of his shoes against the dirt.

"The less alive, the better," I call back. Another undead rounds a tree up ahead, and I let my dark eyes watch it approach. I spin my axe in his grasp. "I asked you what I have, right? This. This is what I have. This is what I can do."

I dash forward toward the nearing undead, driven by a vengeful fury, and leap toward the woman. Throwing my foot out before me, I slam into the beast's chest and push off causing its weak body to fall back. Then, after bringing my axe briefly above my head, I slam the blade down. Blood sprays all over the grass as its head is split.

"Jenn, we should really turn back!" I hear Jack yell desperately, his voice sounding more far off than before. Stepping past the bodies of my previous victims, he raises his bow again and lets the string loose. The arrow finds itself in the skull of an undead the moment that it steps toward me past a low hanging mass of branches. The monster's head flies back as it falls to the floor.

"I can't Jack," I respond, my eyes lifting to find the figures of a few more undeads walking through the trees. We left Billy behind. He was torn apart by these monsters, and we couldn't protect him. These undead were people who lost their life to other undeads. I have to end the cycle.

One steps toward me, and I immediately swing my axe at it—with more force than the weightless weapon needs—and the blade cuts straight through the creature's deformed head. I push past a low hanging branch and instantly come face to face with the startlingly horrid face of another undead. It snarls at me, and with an instinctive movement, my axe takes its head clean off. Yet another appears at my side, and I bring my axe down on its head. Blood spurts out from the large crevasse I make in its skull, and when I try to remove my axe, it won't budge. I have to let the body fall to the ground, placing one foot on the beast's face, I yank the weapon free at last.

Suddenly, I hear a yell, and I immediately spin back around to Jack. In his hesitation for a shot, an undead had stepped out of the shadows from beside him. It latches onto his arm.

"Jack!" I call out, rushing toward him as he struggles to free himself from the inescapable grasp of a starving undead.

I catch a glimpse of him attempting to grab an arrow from his quiver before he collapses under the forceful weight of his assailant and falls out of my line of sight. I continued my dash through the trees, whipping my axe back and forth to knock away the branches and leaves.

Rounding a tree, I stumble upon Jack at last. He's regained his stance with the body of his attacker lying at his feet. Another still grasps onto his shirt, reaching for his neck. With a desperate grunt, he charges sideways and smashes its body against the trunk of a thick tree. Taking advantage of the undead's daze, he lashes out with the arrow still clutched in his hand and jabs it through its eye.

"That was a close one," I say as he retrieves his arrow. The action sprays beads of blood across his face, and he lets the limp body of the undead fall to his feet beside the other one.

He's panting heavily and looks up at me through low eyes. "We have to get out of here."

Together we sprint through the forest, running from the undeads following distantly behind. Finally, when we're certain we've outrun the group, we slow down to a stop. Out of breath, I drop my axe and lean on my knees, breathing heavily.

"I swear, Jack, when I heard you scream, you scared the crap out of me," I say, in between breaths and letting a chuckle slip through. "You were right to turn back, though. There was definitely more than I thought."

We lock eyes momentarily. His usually bright eyes take on a gloomy presence and stare blankly ahead of him…straight through me. He tries to take a step backward and, losing his balance, suddenly collapses to the floor.

"Jack!" I exclaim, rushing over beside his body, which now lies in the dried up leaves and dead grass of the forest floor. "Wait, Jack what's wrong? Jack, stay with me! Jack!"

His eyes spin a little, and I can tell he's trying to focus his eyes on me and struggling to find words. I shake him a little and pull him up against the trunk of a nearby tree. I shake my head in confusion and he reaches over to his left arm to pull up the sleeve.

My body freezes in place as though every inch of my body has suddenly become coated in ice. Flutters shoot through my chest in a wave of nauseating anxiety. Though, despite this, my breathing slows down, and my widened eyes follow the trails of blood up to a grizzly wound in Jack's skin. Blood pulses out and pushes past the flaps of skin still hanging off the fresh bite. Suddenly, a wave of heat rushes throughout my skin and I feel the shivers go down my spine as my frozen body thaws.

"It's ok. It's going to…be ok," is all I am able to say as I instantly strip from my sweatshirt and lay it out on the ground. I grab my axe and chop off the sleeve. "I'm going to put this around it. It'll stop the bleeding. When we get back, Bella will be able to treat it."

"Is it…is it bad?" He asks, still dazed with his eyes half closed. "What if…what if we cut it off?"

"We can…try," I say, taking his injured arm and wrapping the cloth around it.

"Noah." The name escapes from his lips in a shallow breath, and I feel my cheeks burn red.

"Bella will fix this," I state, tightening the knot on the makeshift bandage to create an effective tourniquet. "For now, this is what we do. Maybe we can slow the spread of the poison."

"I don't want anyone to know," he says, swallowing hard to grasp his consciousness, and I give him a double take.

"What? No, we have to tell the others. This is serious."

"Jenn, this is my wound," he stutters, wincing in pain. He grunts, and I place a hand on his cold, pale cheek to steady his head.

"Jack—"

"Do this for me. This is just between me, you, and—ah!—Bella," he yelps out in pain as he sits up further against the tree. His eyelids begin to open again and lock onto mine.

"Everyone will have to eventually find out."

"After my wedding," he says again, his face strained. "I'm getting married."

"Yeah," I force a smile, trying to stay positive. "Yeah, you are."

CHAPTER 28

Riley

I wasn't even aware when Jack came back from the hunting trip. Jenn said she had tripped and gotten a nasty abrasion on her side, so she went straight to the infirmary tent. Jack went with her to make sure she was alright, but he eventually passed out from exhaustion once he got there. We decided to let him sleep.

"Who here wants to leave this island?" Jenn suddenly asks at dinner that night.

"Why are you asking this?" Becky raises an eyebrow.

"I was thinking about it yesterday. Headmaster sends us here on boats," Jenn explains. "Which means that if we can get our hands on one of the next incoming boats, then we got a free ticket away from…all *this*."

"We've tried that," Blake speaks up. "We used to camp out in the forest at the shore whenever we were expecting a boat. We were never able to catch a boat in time before it crashed, though. And with the herd, it got too risky."

"But what if we built a raft and paddled it up to the rocks," Xander suggests, and Jenn nods along. "We'd go in advance and just wait on the water until a boat comes. We'd be safe from the undeads."

"We sucked at building a raft last time…" I start to say.

“We have help now. Besides, it just needs to be good enough to get us to the boat before it crashes,” Xander says.

“You tried sailing home on a raft?” Anthony asks. “It would never survive the high seas that we’d have to pass through. The ride back to the BAA is supposed to be a week, right? That’s a pretty good stretch of water. We don’t know what’s out there.”

“If we could catch a boat, that would work,” Becky says quietly, thinking it over. “Our group is now actually the smallest it has ever been. We could make a raft that would fit us all, and then we can wait for a boat. We’d have to start making the raft now though and start saving up food.”

“I have a pretty good idea where most boats come through," Blake chips in.

“And since we’d be on a raft, we can always just paddle along the shore looking,” Phil offers. “But I mean, what happens to us when we go back to the BAA anyway? I doubt Headmaster will actually give us our spots back in the BAA.”

“He will if he doesn’t want word of the island getting out,” Kris says. “He can’t risk us becoming Rejects and leaking his secret to the rebels. That would have to be probably some of the worst press there is.”

“Maybe we’re better off as Rejects,” Phil counters. “Better than supporting an institution that sends its students to an island for torture and murder.”

“Don’t forget the prisoners,” I say, and some of the others furrow their eyebrows at my comment. “The prisons are killing their prisoners, making them into undeads, and the BAA is clearly supporting that.”

“They’re prisoners, Riley,” Kris says, scrunching up her face in disregard.

“They’re people too and they don’t deserve that. If we go back and become Rejects, there’s a good chance we will become prisoners, too,” I insist, raising my eyebrows. “If that happens, we’ll just be sent back here as undeads.”

“We’re getting ahead of ourselves. Headmaster will shoot us dead the second we arrive,” Blake scoffs.

“It’s worth it to try. Whatever happens to us will be better than staying on this island,” Xander says, and a few of the others nod in agreement. "We could die here or we could die trying to reclaim our lives back there."

"Wait, am I missing something? How do we know when the next boat will come?" Kris asks. From where she sits, she rolls her shoulder back, wincing through the pain as she stretches through her gunshot wound that never healed right.

"We know a boat will definitely come in December because that's when the lowest ranked of Level 1 and 2 are booted," Phil explains. "We'll just aim for that one."

"But when the heck is December, though? Has anyone been keeping track of time?" Anthony asks.

"Riley has. It was May 1st when we were expelled," Jenn says, recalling the month. "Riley, how pregnant are you?"

My cheeks immediately flush with embarrassment. "About five and a half months. We've been on this island for about three and a half. The next boat should come in a little over 4 months."

"It's almost December?" Charlie asks Becky quietly to which she nods. "Is there gonna be snow?"

"No, the temperature on the island doesn't get cold enough," Becky quietly says.

I zone out of the conversation after that. Jack isn't here.

***

"Riley!" Bella exclaims at the first sight of me as I open the flaps to the infirmary tent.

"Bella!" I exclaim back jokingly, and then my eyes gravitate to Jack, who lies down on the sheets usually reserved for patients. Blood stains it. "I figured I'd deliver you guys some dinner."

"Wow, this is some top-quality dining service. I see the chef sent his prettiest waitress," Jack says, greeting me with a bright smile and pushing himself to his feet. He takes the plates from me and places them on a tree stump that had been made into a side table. The plates push a threaded needle off the edge of the table, and the wound up string crumples into a messy pile. With the food now gone from between us, Jack wraps his arms around me, embracing me in a warm hug, and plants a small kiss on my lips. "Thanks, love. I've missed you all day."

"You're hurt," I state, my face relaxing into a solemn frown. Cloths stained red from blood lay strewn across the floor along with rolls of bandages with hastily cut lines. "Show me. How bad is it?"

"No, no, I'm fine," Jack says earnestly, his wide eyes locking with mine. "I know it looks bad, but the mess is from Jenn."

"Yeah, she wasn't very cooperative when I tried to stitch her up," Bella says from the back, but she doesn't look up at me. Instead, she's busy shuffling through an array of herbs in baskets, seemingly re-sorting the variety.

"Bella…" I say softly, pursing my lips. Her movements slow until she stops to steal a gaze at me, and her wide eyes lock with mine for only a moment before Jack puts his hands on both of my shoulders.

"I was just helping her clean the place," he says, raising his eyebrows. "Please believe me. I'm fine. I'd tell you if I was hurt."

I let my tired eyes finally close, and though I've erased Jack's pleading face from my view, he's still all I see. After a breath, I open them again.

"Fine. You just had me worried," I say, offering a small smile. "Warn me or something beforehand, you know?"

"Warn you? You don't like when I surprise you?" he asks, and his face softens into his usual glowing grin, brightening up the room as it brightens his face.

"I only like *good* surprises," I say back, and though I shake my head, my smile remains.

"Then how about a good surprise then," Jack says next, and I raise an eyebrow. "Let's get married tomorrow."

"Tomorrow?"

"What's the point in waiting? I love you and I want to be married to you already," he says passionately, kissing me on the lips again.

I don't even have a reason for objecting. Hearing his suggestion has me ready to perform the ceremony right then and there. As he stands there, his eyes are sparkling blue as always, and I'm already lost in them as always.

"I mean, I guess I can fit it in my schedule tomorrow." I shrug my shoulders and exaggerate an eye roll.

"Thanks for the accommodation in your busy schedule," he says, bowing down a bit.

"You're welcome," I say, and hold out my hand for him to shake it. "Glad doing business with you."

Ignoring my gesture, he leans down quickly to give me a peck on the lips; however, I inadvertently turn my head slightly, letting the kiss touch the corner of my mouth. By the time I turn my head back, the kiss is over.

"Oh, I see how it is." This time, he pulls away, turning his head to feign anger rather than amusement. "I just asked to get married, and you don't even want to kiss me."

"I'm sorry," I manage to say in between my laughs. He goes back in for another try, but I'm still unable to contain my laughter in time, and he plants his kiss on my front teeth.

"Oh, c'mon!" he exclaims again playfully, pulling away further this time. "Alright, I'm done. We tried. No more kisses for me apparently."

"One more," I insist after a heavy bout of laughter, grabbing his hands and pulling his retreating body back to mine. Getting closer again, my laughter calms, and I raise my lips to connect briefly with his. When we separate, we take a moment before sharing another small, sweet kiss.

CHAPTER 29

Jenn

"Jack, can I talk to you for a second?" I ask, approaching him while he speaks to Blake later that evening.

"Hey Jenn, what's up?" he says as I take him by his uninjured arm and drag him away from Blake.

"Why did I just find out that tomorrow morning you're going back out there with Blake and Phil?" I ask once we are out of earshot from Blake.

"I'm taking Blake to where we saw the broken fence. It wouldn't be right to leave it broken like that. Better sooner than later that we fix it up," he explains quietly. "And while we're out, Blake said if we have extra daylight, we could hunt a little."

"But you're...handicapped," I persist. "You're also precious cargo. Riley just told everyone that you're getting married tomorrow afternoon. If something happens and you get hurt or the stitches break—"

"I think you're freaking out more than me," he jokes. "I got this, Jenn. I'm coming back in one piece."

"I'll go," I insist. "I remember the way there probably better than you do anyway."

"We'll probably go hunting after and I'm a better archer—" he begins to say, but I cut him short.

"Not if you can't even pull the string back. And when you can't, then what?"

"I want to go, Jenn," he insists. "It's a nice distraction, and maybe we can get some meat for the ceremony dinner. Besides, isn't it bad luck to see the bride before the wedding anyway? I don't know if I can resist the temptation if I'm here—"

"When are you going to tell everyone?" I bite my lip.

"After my honeymoon. I'll tell everyone in the camp," he states decisively.

"Honeymoon?" I ask, furrowing my eyebrows.

"Becky said we could spend a day or two at the lake by ourselves after the wedding," he says, smiling.

"Are you sure—" I begin, but before I could comment on the safety of the decision, he switches the topic back to the point.

"Besides, it's not like telling anyone will change anything, they can't help me. The only one that can help me is Bella. Actually, I'm starting to think she's part witch or something with all of her herbal potions," Jack says, and at first, I think he's joking, but the puzzled look on his face tells me otherwise.

"Jack, I'm…" I stammer, feeling my breath getting thicker.

"Jenn," he says almost inaudibly as he places a hand on my shoulder. I just shake my head at the act and shrug it off as my heartbeat begins to rise.

"Back in the forest…I didn't mean for things to get so out of hand…" I take in a gasp of air and blink away a veil of hazy vision as my eyes begin to water.

"Jenn," he says again, this time stepping forward and pulling me close.

"Oh, no, what am I doing? I'm fine, I should be comforting you," I say, pulling away and taking in a deep breath to recompose myself. After a second, I bring my eyes back up to his, and we just stay still for a while. I shake my head regretfully. "I'm just…just sorry, Jack. I just wanted to tell you that."

"I'm not mad at you," he mutters quietly.

"Why not?"

"You're not the one that bit me, right?" he answers, offering a small smile.

"No, I mean that would've been really weird if I was," I stammer back. The sarcasm is a nice relief from the seriousness of the situation, and he lets out a chuckle.

"This isn't your fault," he says. "It's not mine either. I just got dealt a bad card and have to make do with what time I have left."

"Don't say that," I say quietly, straining to purse my lips together.

"We both know what comes next, Jenn," he says, heaving in a big sigh.

Though he offers another simple smile, I can see that behind his facade of nonchalance, he understands exactly what this bite means. In my entire time of knowing him, I have never perceived him as so self-aware as I see him now.

"I see my clock, Jenn, and I know midnight is coming now. Sooner than I thought," he says, then lets out a chuckle. "But it's a little different than midnight on New Year's Day."

Just then, fading out of his laughter, Jack lets out a cough. I don't say anything, but I watch him carefully. He pauses, then continues with another cough. Another follows that one, this time pushing through phlegm.

"Jack, are you alright?" I lay a hand on his back.

He doubles over, heaving in a deep breath before abruptly letting out an aggressive procession of coughs. This time blood flings from his mouth to splash onto his hands. He looks at me with grave eyes.

"I'm bringing you to the bath area, and you can get some water," I command, helping him walk. As we make our way over, his arm starts to twitch in spasms. I just hold my jaw locked. I hold my heart steady. This is a man down. My body can react later.

We move through the barrier of trees blocking off the bath area from the rest of the camp, and I lie Jack down next to the pool. He is shaking more now and hovers over an empty bucket.

"Jack, what do you feel?"

"I feel it," he says, through his teeth. "The poison. My blood is boiling."

"It's going to be alright. You'll get through this," I say as I help him take off his sweatshirt.

He lets out a wail, throwing his head back as he spazzes, and I see each and every distinguished vein bulging from his infected arm. His fresh bandage, which Bella had gingerly wrapped around his sewn-up wound, begins to oversaturate with the blood that's leaking out now. He flinches, and his arm, as if possessed, flies from my grasp.

"Is it happening? Is this me g-going?" he stutters quickly in between coughs, curling up to cradle his dying limb. He squeezes his eyes shut, overcome with the pain that burns through his body.

"No, this is not. You're going to get through this—"

"You d-don't know that."

"Jack, I need you to calm down," I say, trying my best to control my own voice. "Can you focus on that? The poison in the bite is trying to take over, but you have to fight it. You're not going tonight."

His face turns red as he holds his breath, squirming to dig himself deeper into the dirt below him. I scoop up his sweatshirt and fit it underneath his bobbing head, and then I fill up one of the nearby buckets with some water from the bath. Since the stream is constantly pushing the water through, I take relief in knowing that it's relatively clean.

The seizure ends, but he continues to breathe heavily as he tries to repress the monster he knows is trying to claim his body. I pour some water onto a towel and bring it up to his burning forehead. I wipe down his face, constantly dampening the towel to keep it wet and cold.

"Jenn, I want another baby with Riley," he sputters. "I want a real wedding, and I want our child to have siblings. I want to introduce her to my parents."

"I know, Jack, I know," I say softly, squeezing my lips tightly after the words just nearly escape my mouth. "She should be here for you right now, Jack. She would want to be."

"No," he says, heaving in a deep breath. "I don't want her to see me like this."

I brush the soaked locks of hair from his forehead and hand over the rest of the water. "Drink this. I don't want her to worry."

He forces himself on his side and grips the bucket with all his might as small fidgets reoccur.

"Keep drinking. I don't know what else will help right now," I say, upturning the inner corners of my eyebrows as I look upon him with worry.

"Bella knows," Jack musters the words to say.

"I'll be right back. Do you think you can manage without me until then?" I ask, and he nods quickly.

Taking a moment to compose myself, I bolt through the trees over to the infirmary tent and burst in to find Bella grinding an herb for one of her concoctions. Out of breath and my head spinning, I tell her about the situation with Jack.

"Alright, alright, let me think," Bella says quickly, dashing to the back of the tent. She opens a chest of some sort to reveal a bunch of large pieces of bark.

"What are those?" I ask.

"Recipes."

"You made them?"

"Oh, no, definitely not. This is the cumulative knowledge from all the 'camp doctors' before me. I just add," she explains, her eyes still scanning the different recipes.

After a minute or so, she begins rushing around the tent, gathering pre-made pastes and creating what is not already available. I offer my help, but she dismisses it.

"Thank you, Bella, for everything you're doing for him," I say. She only gives me a half-smile before looking away.

"I can ease his pain. But nothing will change. It never does," she says somberly as though she's done this before.

I help her carry some materials, more than we need just in case, as we return to Jack. When we reach the pond, we see him lying on his back, staring at us through slit eyes. The sight of his weak, collapsed body is sickening, and I fall to his side.

"Jack, are you with me?" I exclaim, holding his face and lightly slapping his cheek. He lies deceivingly calm, yet his breathing remains rapid and his heart still races.

"Jack, it's me, Bella. I have some stuff that can help," Bella declares. She mixes some powder into his bucket of water and for the next couple minutes, she helps him drink while I clutch his hand.

"How are you feeling, Jack?" I ask softly.

"I won, Jenn." The words come out with his breaths, yet are filled with a confidence that sends chills through me. He's strong. I can't help but feel proud of his perseverance. He shuts his eyes and allows a smile to bloom on his lips.

"You got this," I say softly, sitting down beside him and running my fingers through his grown-out hair. "I'll take Blake to the fence tomorrow. You stay here and regain your strength."

His face is devoid of all color except for his ever-bright blue eyes, which are now surrounded by bleeding vessels that redden the whites of his eyes. He's so weak in this state—so vulnerable. But he's a fighter.

Eventually, Jack drifts off into a peaceful sleep. Bella cleans his wound again, wraps it in bandages, and hides it under his sweatshirt. She finally leaves to go to bed, but I remain by his side, keeping a watchful vigil over him. I watch his chest rise and drop with each breath. I don't know how many hours pass before I finally lie down beside Jack and surrender to my exhaustion, falling asleep.

CHAPTER 30

Riley

My ear is tuned to the delicate silence, and the millions of excited thoughts that normally run through my head are gone, leaving my mind blank and stunned still.

I'm standing at one end of a walkway, which, although only a steps in length, is outlined by glittering pebbles and small stones. Jack stands on the other side. His eyes flick up to meet mine, and he holds me captive and frozen with his stare. We set up the walkway perpendicular to the hedge so that I could decorate the backdrop with a mosaic of whatever flowers I could find growing locally.

The familiar tune of 'Here Comes the Bride' jolts me back to reality. Everyone looks at me with bright smiles as they sing the corny melody, their unharmonious singing in a discordant mismatch of vocals. It's terrible, but it's perfect. Laughing, I walk over to Jack, clutching a small bouquet of the best picks of my accumulated flower collection.

"You look beautiful," Jack says softly when I reach him, making me blush. I absentmindedly hand my bouquet off to Jenn beside me, and Jack takes my hands in his, intertwining our fingers. I catch my ring in the periphery of my gaze as it shimmers with the reflection of the sunlight bouncing off its curve.

"Alright, let's do this," Phil announces suddenly from beside us. "Jack Anderson, do you take this woman to be your wife?"

"I do," Jack says endearingly, refusing to tear his stare from me. He then clears his throat a little and raises his voice. "I *so* do."

"Riley Amore," Phil says again, turning toward me and instigating an uncontainable smile to spread across my lips. "Do you take this man to be your husband?"

"I do."

"Jack, please repeat after me," Phil speaks again, "I, Jack Anderson, take you, Riley Amore, to be my wife, for better, for worse, in sickness and in health."

"I, Jack Anderson, take you, Riley Amore, to be my wife…"

I stop listening. He called me his wife, and I'm mesmerized by his lips as he says the word. I'm his *wife*. Though he's talking, his eyes squint in the smile he's waiting to express.

"Riley?" The voice that pulls me out of my thoughts belongs to Phil, and I soon realize he's already asked me once to repeat him.

"I, Riley Amore," I begin immediately, "take you, Jack Anderson, to be my husband, for better, for worse, in sickness and in health."

"Riley, Jack, by the power I pretend to have vested in me, I now pronounce you husband and wife. You may now kiss the bride!" Phil proclaims ecstatically and the second he finishes, Jack swoops in.

He wraps his arms around my waist and pulls me in close before tilting me back a little as we kiss. The campers all applaud but the noise is deafened in my ears. When Jack and I separate, and I open my eyes, I see the same Jack I'd always known. But now I also see my husband.

***

"Words can't even describe how much I love you right now," Jack whispers in my ear from where he lies down beside me. Beginning at my hairline by my ear, he trails his fingers back, letting them drag along my scalp through my long locks.

Grabbing a few baskets of food, we ditched the camp as soon as the ceremony was over to celebrate our 'honeymoon' at the lake. Tonight will be our second night here.

"I feel the same way," I say back and give him a peck on the lips.

We recline on the grassy edge of a cliff that overlooks the expanse of the calm lake. I search the sky and find the moon, its glowing figure full and bigger than usual behind the few transparent clouds that drift in front of it. Below us, like crystals in the light, the steady ripples in the water sparkle as they reflect sparks of moonlight.

"What's that one?" Jack asks, pointing a finger up at the sky.

"The North Star, maybe?"

"Nope."

"Oh yeah?" I ask sarcastically.

"It's Jack's Star," he says bluntly.

"Douchebag," I comment with a laugh.

"C'mon, don't you even want to know the reason?" he says again, grinning.

"Fine, amuse me as to why you're naming a star after yourself." I roll my eyes, but when they land back on him, I see that, despite the small grin stretching his lips, his expression is rather serious.

"For you," he says, his voice quieter than before. "For whenever you feel sad or angry or lonely or anything at all…you can look up in the sky, and I'll be right there. I'll feel it with you."

"Jack…" I say, leaning in and kissing him. "You're always going to be with me."

He stares at me for a while and then changes the subject. "How's the baby?"

"It's hard to tell without a calendar, but I think I'm in my sixth month," I say.

"Only a few more months then," he says with a wink. "Exciting."

"Do you think it's a boy or a girl?" I ask, curiously.

"I have no clue," he says with a simple shrug.

"Which do you want?"

"Both," he says. "I want multiple kids with you."

"Maybe we can try for more when we're safer and ready to have another on purpose," I say and then furrow my eyebrows when he bites his lip. "Jack, what's wrong?"

"We should think of names," he suggests abruptly.

"Alright…" I say. "If it's a boy…"

"Easy! Jack," he answers, and when I look at him, I see him grinning proudly.

"And for our daughter?"

"Jackie," he offers again, shrugging as if it's obvious. I just let out a laugh.

"C'mon, seriously," I say, nudging him.

"Alright," he says through his chuckle. "Okay, so if it's a boy…"

"Connor," I state, thinking about the name.

"Nice. If it's a girl, I think we should name her June," he says.

"That's your birthday month!" I exclaim with a laugh. After another moment, I add, "I love that name."

"I love you," he says, and we share another kiss. When we pull away, I see him fidget a little. He coughs.

"Jack, are you alright?" I ask, sitting up.

"Yeah, yeah," he stutters, sitting up as well. He shakes his head a couple times with his eyes shut and jaw clenched.

"Are you going to barf?" I ask, inching out of range of his mouth.

"No, I-I'm fine," he says, the color returning to his face. He reaches back into the picnic basket and pulls out a bottle filled with a brown liquid.

"What is that?"

"Bella made me a tea yesterday," he says.

"You like tea?" I ask.

"Love it," he says again in between sips.

I nod while he puts the tea back. Then, when he turns back to me, he places a hand on my stomach. I see a bead of sweat falling down the side of his face.

"You're sweating," I say while wiping the layer of water coating his skin with the sleeve of my sweatshirt. He shakes my hand off but I'm able to feel his forehead first. "Holy crap, Jack, you're burning up!"

"Are you calling me hot?" he teases, temporarily composing himself enough to smirk at me.

"You have a fever. Where did this come from? How long have you had this?" I retrieve a towel from another basket and place it in the nearby pale of water. "Here, let me."

I bring the damp towel up to his forehead and let the water cool him.

"Please Riley, I'm fine," he insists, taking some more tea.

A tear gathers in his eyelashes, and I bite my lip when it falls, sliding down his cheek. At the same moment and in the same fashion, a line of blood runs down the palm of his hand from underneath his sweatshirt. When it reaches his fingers, I watch as it drips onto the grass below.

"Jack!" I exclaim, my hands trembling as I hurriedly help him peel off his sweatshirt. Frayed at the edges and browned in color from the dried blood that used to soak it, a bandage wraps around his forearm. Around the area, his skin has turned a pale purple, thinned to the point of revealing the details of the anatomy underneath. The decay extends from just above his elbow to all the way to his wrist before the skin fades back into a healthy color. "Oh my god."

"Riley—"

"Jack what the hell is this?" I yell again, falling back away from him, one hand strapped over my mouth.

"Riley," he says, opening his eyes and bringing his uninjured hand up to my face. He takes a moment to admire me before continuing. "You can't even begin to understand how much I love you. And you don't understand how hard this is for me to tell you this."

"Jack, cut the crap, what's going on?" I stammer as the adrenaline begins pumping through my blood, and I feel my cheeks get hot.

"Riley, that day I was hunting with Jenn… the undeads came out of nowhere," he begins, holding my shoulders to still my body as I begin to shift around in my spot on the ground.

"The undeads? This is just a hunting wound, right? An…accident with an arrow?" I ask quickly, and his eyes search mine. He's not answering. My voice lowers to a whisper. "Jack, please don't tell me what I think you will."

"I'm bit, my love," he states solemnly and my heart drops.

"J-Ja…Jack…hold on," I stutter, trying to comprehend his words resounding through my head. "No."

"I'm sorry," he says, and I feel a tear fall down my own cheek.

"This isn't happening." I shake my head, looking back down at his arm which continues to leak blood through the bandage, forming a shallow pool above the fabric. "No, no, no, no, this *can't* be happening! How could you not tell me, you *asshole*! We just got *married*, Jack! You're going to have a child, how could you do this?"

"I didn't plan for this to happen!" he exclaims. "There is nothing I would rather do than stay here with you forever. I want nothing more than to be with you and to be a father and to love you and make you happy!"

"I want that too!" I yell back, turning away from him and gasping for air to breathe. "I-I need... I need you."

"Riley, listen to me," he says, softening his tone and placing a hand on my arm from behind. "I *love* you. I do! And the only reason I didn't tell you sooner was because I wanted you to have the perfect wedding ceremony without worrying."

"Screw the ceremony," I say quietly after another moment. "Having you there was what made it perfect."

"Please, Riley," he says earnestly. "I'm sorry I didn't tell you earlier. Please be here with me now."

He coughs, and I flinch as though it was a gunshot. My breath escapes in shaky bits, and I struggle to grasp control of it in order to ease the lightheadedness that is causing my vision to spin. After a minute, I turn around to face him again and throw my arms around him in a huge embrace.

"Can't we do something? Can't we stop it? What have you tried?" I ask, my voice muffled as I speak directly into his shoulder.

"It's the curse of this island, Riley. There's nothing anyone can do," he says softly, wrapping his uninjured arm around my back.

Flashbacks of Noah's amputation flood into my mind, and I squeeze my eyes to try to shut them out. I see Noah's chest stop rising. I feel the cloth on his chest from when I helped with CPR compressions. He died, and he died without even knowing what was going on around him.

"Did I make you happy?" I ask quietly, tears still running from my eyes.

"Riley," he says, slightly shocked, and he pulls us apart so that he can speak to me more directly. "You made me the happiest man in the world. And that's saying a lot, considering we're on Expulsion Island."

"I love you so much," I choke under my sobs. "M-maybe you can still beat the infection. Maybe it's not too late."

"Riley…" Jack begins, when suddenly he's hit with another wave of pain originating from his arm and he yells out.

"Jack…"

"I—I'm dying," he says, swallowing back the pain. "I can feel it. It's different now. I'm not surviving this, Riley. But you will."

"I can't live without you," I insist through heavy gasps for air, putting a hand on his cheek. "I can't…breathe without you. You have to live, Jack. I can't do this without you."

"I need you to. I *need* you to survive. You're going to give birth to our baby and live the rest of your life. Don't rejoin the BAA, I know you don't want to. Move in with my family. They…they'll really love you, Riley. Just like I do," he says, forcing a small smile past his damp eyes. "You are going to have a future."

"I don't want a future without you," I object.

"Yes, you do, Riley," he says, dismissing my protest. "And you're going to make our child happy."

I try to compose myself. Looking down, I see the tear stains I left on his shirt. It's still the shirt that he had worn on the day we got married. Soon everything will be in the past tense.

"I believe in you," he says quietly.

"This is too soon, Jack," I say through my croaking voice. "We have so much left to do."

"Hey, we got this far, right?" he says, forcing a small smile, and his lips curl easily into the creases of his cheeks as though his face was made to grin. "We escaped the BAA. We lived our dream. We made it. Don't ever think we didn't make it."

Then his expression darkens, and he tightens his jaw. His heavy eyelids shut a few times as the nauseating pain swirls through his body like a parasite draining him from within.

"I'm going to turn when I go, Riley."

"I don't want to think about that—"

"You have to," he insists, letting another stream of tears drip from his eyes. "It'll be quick after I die. I feel it readily itself inside me, waiting for me to let it free. I need you to leave me once I pass. I don't want you to see me that way. Go back to camp, get help. Have someone put me down so that I can't ever hurt anyone."

"I can't leave you," I say, shaking my head.

"You have to," he demands, and I nod quickly. "You can't let me hurt you when I turn. I would never want that. You can't let me hurt anyone."

"Jack, I just…I-I want you to know that I am so lucky to call you my husband," I manage to say through my sobs. The words are rushed, but I force them out. I don't know the time limit we have, but I can't waste it processing the moment.

"And I'm even luckier to get to call you my wife," he says with a smile, which begins to quiver when tears come from his eyes.

"I'll always love you," I say, wiping my face clear. "You're my soulmate."

"You're my soulmate too," he says, and a smile breaks out on my lips. He brings his hand up to my face and caresses my cheek with his fingers, wiping away my tears again. "I want to see you smile forever."

I see him try to swallow back the pain from the venom that's running through his body.

"Is it happening right now?" I take a moment to blink slowly. I wish he wouldn't answer.

He presses his knuckles into the ground in front of him and lets his head hang down forward on his exhausted neck.

"Is this goodbye?" I ask. I wish he wouldn't answer.

Letting my delicate fingers touch his cheek, I raise his head back up. His blue eyes, exhausted and straining to stay open, meet mine again.

"Please stay," I say. But yet, I still wish he wouldn't answer. I know I won't like the answer.

"I think it's happening," he says softly, and then points up at Jack's Star. "But it's not goodbye. I'll always be with you."

"It's not the same." My face scrunches up as I feel more tears coming, and he strokes my cheek.

"It will be okay," he says in a shaky voice, trying to stay strong. "I know it's scary but…it will be okay. You'll be okay."

He takes both of my hands in his just as we had done at the wedding. We just stare into each other for a while before at last, I lean in and we share a long kiss. When we separate, I look up at him and it reminds me of when we looked at each other after our wedding.

Suddenly, I feel his grasp on me weaken, and his body begins to slip from mine.

"Jack?" I ask cautiously, clutching his body tighter to mine. My eyes are forced open with fear as he finally releases his grasp on me. His weight is too much for me to support, and he collapses to the floor with a pained grunt. "Jack!"

Hyperventilating, I hover over him, only relieved by the sound of his panting and the sight of his eyes squeezing shut: signs of life.

"I'm…I'm fine," he moans exhaustedly. "I think I should lie down for a bit, though."

Frozen in place, I watch him alter his position slightly for comfort. A strained expression remains on his face, though, and I gently place a hand onto his shoulder.

"Lay down with me," he says, his voice mixed with another grunt. Carefully, I oblige, lying down on the ground beside him. He wraps his arms around me, cuddling me from behind and places both of his hands on my stomach. I put both of my hands on top of his.

The minutes pass as we lie like that. I keep my eyes shut, focusing on the synchronized rhythm of our chests rising with our breaths. Shrouded in the darkness of my eyelids, I could be anywhere. In this moment, with Jack's warm body behind me, we could be back at the tent in camp. We could be on the boat on shore, listening to the waves outside. We could be at the BAA, sharing another stolen moment together. In this moment right now, we could be safe and we could be healthy. Tonight could be just another boring night on the island as long as I just don't open my eyes…as long as I continue to feel his breath against my neck.

So, I don't open my eyes, and I don't break the fantasy. I let the moment last in its purity as I appreciate every sensation of having Jack at my side. He's here, and I'm here with him, and I choose to let that be the only thing that matters right now.

"Jack?" I ask, barely audible.

"I'm still here," he breathes in my ear, and I feel the chills go down my spine.

"I love you," I mutter softly.

"I love you," he says and as soon as I turn my head, he plants a soft, delicate kiss on my lips.

"You feel that?" he says in a hushed voice, his energy drained and his eyelids threatening to close.

"What?" I respond, turning around fully to face him, our faces now a mere inch apart. "Jack?"

"June," he mutters again, the words coming out in a wispy breath. "I felt her kick."

"How do you know she's a girl?" I ask. I try to mask the concern in my voice when he doesn't respond quickly enough, and my eyes finally flick open. "Jack?"

"It's a girl," he murmurs again, his eyes staring straight ahead. Suddenly he drags his slow gaze up to meet my eyes. "I'm sorry...that I won't be there to help you raise her."

"J-Jack…" I stutter, and I interlock my hands with his, clutching them tightly. "Jack, please don't go. Jack, I love you."

"Goodbye, love," he whispers, his glossy eyes still locked on mine before softening into a neutral position.

"Jack," I say, my voice cracking from a small whisper as my eyes run over his motionless body. "No, no, no, no, no, no, *no.*"

I begin to shake his shoulder, gently at first, but then increasingly vigorously, sitting up to move him with the full strength of both of my hands. His body flops limply along with my pushing, and he rolls onto his back. Pressing a hand against his neck, I feel desperately for a pulse. None. My nails dig deeper into his skin as I press more firmly, trying to feel something. Nothing. My hands, shaking, drop to his wrist and I press my fingers there. None.

Off instinct, I immediately begin CPR compressions on his chest, interrupting it only to provide breaths to his mouth. I feel my breathing begin speeding up in the absence of his. I'm releasing all of my air without absorbing any to replace it fast enough. I might be dying too. The way my heart bursts through both my chest and ears, it feels that way. After only a couple minutes, my vision is shaking as my brain begins to starve from the lack of oxygen.

"*Jack!*" I shriek, releasing whatever air I have left, and I let my arms fall helplessly to my sides at last. "*No!*"

Just then, his eyes move. No, though still blue, they're not *his* eyes. They're the eyes of a stranger. Staring blankly, they shift to find mine. His lips part slightly. Jack warned me about this stranger I would have to face. Yet, as I gaze upon his face, I can't help but look for the man I once knew.

His mouth opens wider, and his neck lifts slightly. I raise my gentle touch back to his chest and feel his body push against it now. With my other hand, I reach behind me, brushing it against the basket of food that we had brought. I continue feeling beside it until my fingertips touch the cold metal handle of a gun.

The weapon weighs heavily in my hand as I bring it over. We had brought it for protection; I never thought I would have to use it like this. Without ever breaking my gaze on Jack, I press the barrel of the gun against his temple.

He continues to gradually stretch toward me, his reanimated body sluggish, but I use my hand to hold back his movements.

I squeeze my eyes shut, but his words ring fresh in my mind. *Goodbye, love.*

It would be so easy to let him at me right now. He could tear at my throat, sever the vital blood vessels, and let my blood join his on the ground around us. I would die quickly.

The sound of the shot explodes through the air, shattering the dull silence with its intensity. The resistance I felt against my hand stops as the body relaxes back into the ground.

I just wait there as the ringing from the shot reverberates in my ears. When I do reopen my eyes, I'm faced with his bright blue eyes again. Dots of blood speckle both sides of his skull. A fresh pool of blood is already growing below his head, spreading over the grass and staining my knees. The gun falls from my hand as I lose the ability to grasp it, and it clatters to the ground on the other side of him.

Tears now pouring out of my flooded eyes, I collapse onto Jack's lifeless body. I bury my head deep in between his jaw and shoulder and clutch onto his lifeless body. As my exhaustion overwhelms my adrenaline, I caress his hair, unwilling to let go as I lie there with him.

"My baby."

CHAPTER 31

Jenn

Xander had been on night watch at the time that he heard the single shot fired. He immediately roused the camp and went with Blake to check on Riley and Jack at the lake. When they return, everyone's waiting beside the entrance. Walking beside him is an exhausted Riley. Her blond hair is streaked with dark crimson blood, which has dried to clump strands of hair together so that they hang stiffly on her shoulders. More blood dots her face and neck. A single bloody handprint marks the spot where her shirt slightly bulges around her stomach.

Jack's not with them.

"Riley!" Becky exclaims, ditching my side and jogging up to her. I walk timidly behind the rest of the group now crowding around Riley. "What happened? Are you hurt? Where's Jack?"

Becky lays a hand on her shoulder, but Riley doesn't even notice nor care. With eyes glazed over and eyelids low and struck by exhaustion, her stare is unwavering. She's staring at me. She's staring *only* at me. A few people move out of the way as she takes a few steps closer. The questions cease as a grave silence engulfs the camp so thickly that it seems to have command over the entire island. I take in a breath and tighten my jaw as I brace myself for her approach. She steps right up to me.

"This is your fault." The hushed words come out croaking but piercing as it shatters the silence. She's not a towering figure. She's not a fury of rage. She doesn't raise her voice or narrow her eyes. Yet, I feel smaller than I have in a while as her stare conveys a hatred that can only come from betrayal and a crushed heart. The way she looks at me, so defeated and broken, conveys an utter indifference to me and lack of any care for anything that I am. She lacks care for anything at all. And I'm the source in her eyes.

"Riley, I am so sorry," I say slowly.

"You let it happen," she says again. Her eyes are red and swollen from crying. Among the red splattered specks on her sickly pale cheeks, I notice the tear stains that smear paths in the blood. She barely looks like she has enough energy to be standing here right now. She's furious, she's heartbroken, she's hurt. She's experiencing every negative emotion at once.

"Riley, it's not what you think," I try to clarify.

"Just stop it," she says, cutting me short. "Jack is *dead*."

Her voice cracks at the last word and the weight of the sentence pierces my eardrums to ingrain directly into my memory. Jack is dead. I cower my head.

"You let him get bit out there. And you helped him hide it from me so that I had to find out when he was already taking his last breaths in my arms. There are no excuses you could come up with to make that okay," she says again, her voice lowered again to just above a whisper. "This isn't the BAA; this isn't a simulation or training. And this isn't another 'favor' like Billy."

"I know that—"

"He was with you when he was bit," she promptly cuts me off again, but I have to let her. "You let the single most important person in my life die. And I had to kill his body."

I avert my eyes as she scorns me, and my cheeks burn red.

"You're a murderer, Jenn." The words come out as less than a breath and as simply put as it could've been. She was stating it as a fact, not an accusation.

"Alright, that's enough," Xander suddenly speaks up, stepping up to my side. "Riley, I am so sorry for what happened. Jack was special to us all. And I know this very hard for you, but it's not fair to take it out on Jenn. This is the undeads' fault. This is Headma—"

"Fair?" Riley speaks softly, her grave voice cracking briefly again, but her tone is almost threatening now. "Nothing's fair."

"I'm just saying that—" Xander starts.

"Well maybe you shouldn't," Blake barks, glaring at Xander. "This isn't about you. Keep your mouth shut."

"I don't care what happens to you," Riley adds softly to me, and my eyes spring up to be met with her cold gaze.

At that, Riley turns away, walking off to her tent. I feel like I can't breathe, and I must force myself to refrain from hyperventilating. I take in deeper breaths to keep myself from breaking down. My eyes dart around the faces of the other campers, their judging faces looking still back at me. My eyes finally land on Xander, who, although had defended me, still looks at me with disappointment and a deeply rooted sadness for the loss of his friend. He's torn between falling into the same grief-induced rage as Riley and trusting my innocence. Honestly, I don't even know which he should choose.

***

The next day, Jack's body is buried right outside the camp walls alongside Dwayne, Kyle, and Noah. It's still not a perfect area, but we are still under the assumption that the graveyard belongs to Andrew, Lie, and Corinne.

Everyone gathers for the funeral as per usual. Though this time, it feels worse. Jack was special. He was a light in our circle. But our circle keeps dwindling, and I feel more detached from the others as ever. I haven't even stolen a glance at Xander or Riley.

As had been done with Ana, the blood had been washed from Jack's body the best that it could be. We couldn't risk sacrificing a sweatshirt or bandages, though, so he still wears the old grimy bandages he had at the time of death. Any color that used to paint his skin is stripped away, allowing a pale, sallow hue to infect his features. His radiant blue eyes— the pinnacle of his appearance with their awe-inspiring brilliance— are forever hidden, trapped under the veil of his eyelids. It hadn't felt entirely real until this moment. Yet now, looking down upon his still body, there's no escaping the truth.

The time drags on as we wait in silence. I don't even know how long, nor do I care. I do know that I must speak, though. The scorching sun above us instills its burning heat into my flesh, trying to persuade me to begin a eulogy.

"I would like to say a few words," I nervously say, attracting everyone's gaze. I'm surprised my voice even works. I have to pause before continuing. As painful as it is, I can't find the strength to tear my eyes from Jack's motionless, dead body. That's all we see right now. But that's not all he is. I have to keep that alive.

"Jack is…too much for words. But I can try. He deserves it. He was a great friend—the kind of friend that would stand by you when you need somebody to be there," I say. The words were pouring out of mouth without my control. "He saved my life when we first got to this island. I was attacked by an undead, and he *immediately* came to the rescue. He risked his own life to save mine and I will be eternally grateful to him for his outstanding courage. He also had a great sense of humor…even if he didn't realize it. He always just wanted to make people happy. Just his smile alone could light up a room…and he was always smiling."

My eyes slowly rise to land on Riley, who stands across from me with her hands clasped in front of her. Her eyes are fixed on Jack and her face is as still as his.

"The attack was so sudden," I say again. "We got surrounded. But he didn't want to worry anyone when he got bit. He wanted everyone to be happy on his wedding day. He loved with the biggest heart I'd ever seen in anyone. He knew what was happening to him, and all he could think about was getting married to the girl of his dreams. That was his one wish before he died, and he got it."

Riley shuts her eyes, squeezing them together in silent agony. She brings her hand up to mouth, ultimately breaking her stoic manner as she becomes overwhelmed with the sight of her husband lying in his grave. I hear her let out a sob.

"He loved you so much, Riley," I say finally, my own eyes watering as I watch her break down. "He was so proud of it, too. He only wanted the best for you. You are the only person that mattered to him—forever his top priority."

She continues to cry into her hands, louder this time. Suddenly, Blake reaches out from beside her and pulls her close to him for support. I halt my speech and try to focus on my breathing to prevent breaking down. We all just wait in another moment of silence.

"We won't ever forget Jack," I begin again. "We should all be thankful that we were given the chance to have known him. And although he may not be here physically…I know he's still here. He'll always be here with us."

***

"Hey," Xander says to me after the funeral has ended. "Your speech was nice."

"Thanks," I say, briefly glancing around us to see everyone one by one disappearing into the hedge.

"No one blames you for Jack's death," he says.

"Except the one it matters to most," I finish.

"I just can't believe he's actually gone," he says again.

"I know," I agree quietly, and he eyes me. At first, I think there's something on my face and touch my cheek to wipe it off, but then he speaks again.

"Jenn, I think I love you," he blurts out, taking me by surprise. His eyes widen and he stutters, almost more surprised than I am. "I'm sorry, that's not how I planned to start."

"Xander," I begin to say, blushing and looking around us again. By now, the last of the campers are clearing out, and after another few seconds, we're all alone.

"No, it's true. I care about you, Jenn," he says, his tone full of fire and passion. "And what happened with Jack…it made me realize that life is too short to live with regrets. And I don't want to die knowing that if only I had the courage to tell you…"

"I can't do this right now," I say, not knowing what to say but as soon as the words come out, I regret it. I don't know why.

"I'm sorry, I didn't mean to do this at Jack's funeral. I just...everything sucks. And I want something to not suck right now," he says again, shaking his head. "Please say something."

"I'm sorry," I stammer, trying to retain the strength in my voice. "I have to go."

CHAPTER 32

Riley

It's been a couple weeks since the funeral. I haven't left my tent since. Sometimes the other campers crawl into my tent to console me. Bella often comes by to force my nutrition pills down my throat and check on how my pregnancy is coming along. She'll rub a salve over my growing stomach, elevate my legs, and massage my swollen feet to aid my circulation. Even my fingers had swelled during my pregnancy. However, only after Bella threatened to cut off my finger if it lost circulation, I let her tear my engagement ring from my bruised purple skin. Despite the kind treatment and the alleviation of my discomfort, I still haven't figured out how to smile again. After a short thank you, my silence would eventually beat her down and she'd leave. I haven't spoken much at all since the funeral. Bella gave up trying to talk to me. Most people did.

As I stare at the dirt in our tent, I can make out the indents that his body made when he'd sleep. I hadn't dared to cross over into his side of the 'bed' we had shared. I still hear his voice, though. In my mind, his words are always interrupted by the loud blast of the gun I had used to put his body down. I still feel him with me and remember the feeling of his warm hug growing cold as we waited for him to die. I lived in heaven with him; now everything's hell.

Some days, I feel as angry as I had been at Jenn immediately following his death. I want to scream at Jenn for not protecting Jack; I want to scold Jack for not being more careful and not telling me about his injury sooner; I yell at God for seemingly abandoning me. Other days, especially at the beginning, all I want to do is cry until my body runs out of water. The pain I feel is almost physical, and I cry in agony as it burns, stings, and scorches me from my core.

But most days, everything just feels…numb. It's as if my soul had been so entwined with Jack's, that it had ascended to heaven along with his and left behind the shell of a girl. Alone. Just existing. My body hangs onto the earth, trapped by its own longevity and waiting for the required causes of physical death.

Jarring me from my daze, rays of daylight flood my tent. I look up to see Jenn opening the flap that covers the entrance, and I cower my gaze, returning it to the floor as she steps in cautiously.

"How are you doing in here?" she asks hesitantly, but I keep my stare fixed. We wait in the silence before she finally speaks again. "The crops are doing good. I brought you some."

She takes a few steps closer to me and sits down in front of me, placing the plate of food between us. I'll eat some of it when she leaves just to feed my instinctual hunger, enhanced by the parasite of a child living within me. For the moment, though, I don't stir.

"Charlie made it," she says to fill the silence—the same thing she's been doing routinely for the past couple weeks. "He says it's salad, but to me it just looks like a bunch of scraps thrown together as usual. But it tastes good. We also caught a squirrel wandering through the hedge and thought you should have some...for your baby."

I remain motionless, too lethargic to move.

"C'mon, Riley, you can't be silent forever," she suddenly says, and my eyes rise slowly to look at her. "Talk to me, Riley. I can't do this anymore."

"*You* can't do this anymore?" I croak. My voice is rusty and when it cracks, I cough to clear it. Still, the whisper catches her off guard and I see her sit up a little straighter. "Can't do what? The four minutes at breakfast, two minutes at lunch, and five minutes at dinner?"

"You…count my visiting times?" she asks slowly. She's struck by the resurgence of my voice, though she won't acknowledge it.

"It's the only thing I can do," I mutter, staring at the floor again.

"Riley, I couldn't have saved Jack," she begins to say.

"You could've done…more. You could have prevented it," I say under my breath again, shaking my head a little with my words. "Death follows you. Ana, Patrick, Vincent, Noah. Now Jack. You're never at fault?"

"I did not just *let* all those people die," she says, aghast.

"You let Jack die. You were the only one with Jack when he was bit. You didn't tell me. You didn't let me help. You didn't give me the chance to be there for him while he was hurting," I sneer. A rage rebuilds inside of me, providing the vigor to release my suppressed words. "I've seen the way you treat death. You don't care about anyone's life but your own."

"I do care," she asserts. "I'm so sorry for your loss, Riley, but I…"

"No, you're not," I say quietly, humbling Jenn with my sharply projected words. "You didn't give a crap when Billy died, and he was murdered right in front of you. You don't give a crap now."

"I *do* care!" she says again, this time stronger and louder. "Jack was my friend, too. His death affected everyone in this camp."

"Jack was your friend?" I say, my voice cracking at her statement. "You don't know the meaning of the word. You have no respect for anyone but yourself. Even Xander was just 'King of the Losers' to you because we were all lower ranked than you. You weren't Jack's friend. You didn't care enough about his life to protect him. And he didn't care about you either."

"I do care about Jack. And I care about you," she says, raising her eyebrows. "I do. I tried to help Jack the best that I could. I got Bella involved and made sure he felt comfortable. I didn't tell you about his bite because he wanted you to have a fairytale on your wedding day. It was *his* wish, not mine. He didn't want to ruin your spirit and I respected that. He wanted things to be perfect for you for just one day before…"

"He died?" I finish her sentence, and I can see that my plain voice gives her shivers.

She pushes the plate of food closer to me. "You should eat. And get out of this tent. And be with everyone. We all want to help you through this."

I just shake my head lazily, and I hear her sigh.

"You can't just stay in this tent forever," she says again, catching my gaze. "It won't bring him back. Nothing will. You're going to have to accept that."

"Accept it?" I reply in shock, my voice still low as the anger still boils beneath my skin. "Accept the fact that the love of my life just died in my arms and that I'm widowed and pregnant at the age of sixteen? Accept the fact that there is a ninety-nine percent chance that the undead will kill me and my child like they did to Jack and everyone before him? I've accepted it, all right. I can't escape it."

"I didn't mean it like that," she mutters quietly, but before she can finish, I interrupt her with a loud slap across her left cheek.

Her head flies to the side and she clutches it, glancing back at me with only a mild level of shock as though she had partly expected it. I am caught off guard by her lack of defensiveness in this moment, though I keep my glare steady.

"You should eat," she commands gently before promptly lifting herself up off the floor. "I promised Blake I'd go with him into the woods and survey the fence again."

She ducks out of the tent, but before she disappears, I call out to her. "Try not to get him killed too!"

She disappears outside, leaving me alone in the tent once again, and my rage fades back into an all too familiar feeling of hollow emptiness. It's easy to shoo people off. Because even if you do let them in, I know they wouldn't understand the numbness and debilitation that I actually feel. It's pointless.

I stare at the plate of food for a few minutes. There's a small mess of "Charlie's salad" on one side, and on the other side is the squirrel meat. I look past it, though. Peeking through the cracks in my tent, the sunlight sheds a shimmer of light down the length of the small knife on the plate intermixed with the food. A shiver shoots down my spine as I stare at the blade's sharpened edge.

Stealing a glance back up at the tent's entrance, I can hear the others going about their daily business, unaware of the dark thoughts running through my mind.

CHAPTER 33

Jenn

By the time I leave Riley, the rest of the campers are cleaning up from lunch and dispersing to resume their activities for the day. When I join them, Becky immediately approaches me while carrying the collection of used plates from the mealtime.

"She talked," I report quietly to her and we begin walking over to the cleaning station to drop off the dishes.

"That's great," Becky breathes out, relieved. When she takes notice of my expression, though, her smile fades. "What did she say?"

"She still blames me," I respond, biting my lip.

"That explains the red mark on your cheek," she remarks, acknowledging the area where Riley slapped me.

"I don't know what else I can say to convince her to trust me. To let me in and let me be there for her."

"Jenn, she just lost the love of her life," Becky explains softly, placing a hand on my shoulder. "You're not supposed to convince her to trust you again. You have to prove it. And that means being there for her despite what she thinks of you. She needs you. She just doesn't know it."

"I don't know," I mutter, shaking my head. "I've been spending time each day with her since his death. She only reacted today, and it was basically to tell me how much she hates me. I just…I'm not feeling good about this."

"It's not hopeless, Jenn" Becky says.

"No," I respond after a moment. "It never is. That's what Riley would say."

"She would, wouldn't she?" Becky says, letting a soft smile infiltrate her stoic expression and loosening the ever-present crease between her usual furrowed brows.

"When I first got to camp, people were blaming you for the deaths of Evan and some others," I say suddenly, and Becky immediately sucks in air sharply. "You were your only witness, and so people believed their own story. I get how that feels now. First Ana…then Jack. You think watching a person you care about die is the most painful thing you can experience. But then someone blames you for it. I'm sorry I ever doubted you…thank you for believing me anyway."

She keeps her gaze level with mine for another moment, before giving me a slight nod. "We stick together."

Just then, I spot Xander walking across the camp carrying part of a broken log on his shoulder. Yesterday, a branch had fallen off one of the trees that comprise the hedge. The branch itself wasn't that large, but from the hole it left, we could see that other branches within the hedge had also fallen, leaving several empty patches in the hedge. Of the branches still attached to the tree, many of the leaves in that area had also already freed themselves to take refuge on the floor. Though none of the holes were enough to completely pierce the thick hedge, Blake had concluded that one of the trees there was dying, which could risk the functional use of the hedge as a wall, especially if more trees were in the same condition unbeknownst to us. Dry, dying trees are also more susceptible to forest fires.

Xander had been watching me as he passes, but as soon as our eyes meet, his dart away. He awkwardly tries to walk faster and ends up colliding with Anthony. Xander quickly apologizes, but Anthony shrugs it off, slapping Xander's shoulder with a smile before walking away.

Whenever I see him, all I hear is his voice telling me that he loves me. He still hasn't spoken to me since. In all honesty, I've been avoiding him too. With Jack's death, Riley's pain, and Xander's confession on top of the everyday chores and worries of maintaining the camp, it's all just too much to deal with. It's lonely.

"'Sup babe," Anthony says, coming up from behind me. I jump out of my skin at his sudden appearance and the touch of his hands on my waist.

"Don't touch me like that," I state, not even feigning a smile as I grab his wrists and pluck his meaty hands off me.

"I'm going to go find Charlie," Becky says to me, taking a quick look at Anthony before walking off.

Anthony turns me toward him and leans in for a kiss. I try to resist, but his lips lock with mine anyway. I look past him and see Xander now talking with Phil. Anthony is about to pull away from the kiss, but I pull him back closer. I want to enjoy this. I really do. I want him to pull me from my exhaustion.

"Gross," Kris sneers, shoving herself against me as she walks past.

"Are you jealous?" Anthony teases. Kris stops in her tracks and turns back to face us again.

"Nope," she remarks casually. "You just want me to be."

"Oh really?" Anthony asks again, and I narrow my eyes at him this time as he smiles at Kris playfully. "How are you so sure that's true?"

"Because," she purrs, "you can't tell me it's not."

"I can't?"

"Try," she tempts.

He bites his lip through a smirk, and she winks at him.

"Enjoy him while you can, Jenn," she says tauntingly, a satisfied smile on her lips. "But thanks for babysitting him for me for the time being."

I glare at Anthony as he watches her walk away. Then, suddenly, he turns toward me and tries to pull me into another kiss.

"Ok, that's not happening," I say, pulling away this time. When he looks at me with confusion, I raise my eyebrows.

"What?" he asks, dumbly.

"Alright," I roll my eyes. "I know you prefer her. I don't need to be a part of your love story, so don't drag me into it."

"What are you talking about? I never even said anything like that—"

"Am I right?"

"I thought we were just having fun," he says, playfully placing his hands back on my waist.

"You know what, Anthony," I say slowly, irritated by his lighthearted tone. I pull his hands off my waist again. *Is he blind to everything happening around us in this camp?* I ask myself. I don't know what I want to say or what I even have the energy to say right now. My mind is on everything but him. "I'm not having fun."

Free from his hold, I begin to head off.

"Oh c'mon, what's the big deal? Why are you being such a priss?" he calls out after me, and I stop in my tracks, slowly tilting my head to the side.

"Are you serious?" I say warningly, turning back around. I take a step closer, preparing myself to unleash a stream of vile words, but he cuts me short before I can even start.

"Don't act like this is only about Kris," he scoffs, rolling his eyes.

"What are you talking about?" I ask, giving him a look that mixes disgust with boredom.

"I see the way you look at Xander," he says, "and I see the way he looks at you."

"I don't want to hear it, Anthony. Go have fun somewhere else, Anthony," I command, ending the conversation effectively. Though the truth is it's me without anything more to say.

At first, I'm just walking away aimlessly, replaying the conversation over in my head. I spot Becky by the campfire again with Charlie.

"Hey Jenn," Charlie greets as I approach.

"Hey Charlie." A small smile blooms on my lips when I see his bright face.

"How's Riley?" he asks. "Did she like the food I made?"

"Yeah, she said it was great, Charlie," I say, forcing myself to keep my smile. At the same time, though, Charlie's smile begins to fade.

"She didn't say that," he says disappointedly, and I let my fake grin fade away too. "I just hope she likes what I made."

"I'm sure she does." I take in a deep breath, wondering how much she's even going to eat of it. Charlie begins to walk away but turns back suddenly.

"When she's done, can I use the knife? I asked Blake to teach me more about how to stab undeads," Charlie says, biting his lip with excitement.

"You are going to learn what?" Becky immediately asks with wide eyes. "Let me talk to Blake about that first. Just, with everything that happened, I don't know if I'm okay with that."

"Wait, what are you talking about?" I ask Charlie. "What knife?"

"The knife we gave her to cut the meat," Charlie clarifies as if it's obvious. "How else do you expect her to eat it?"

"She has a knife," I repeat under my breath. As if something clicks inside of me, I turn to Becky with a rather frightened expression. "She has a knife."

"It's ok." I almost miss the small comment from Charlie. If I didn't know any better, I would have figured him to be just an ordinary innocent kid, confused by my concern. But I've seen him shoot Patrick twice to make sure he was dead. He understands the situation entirely.

"Maybe she'll be happier," he says again. I can't tell what fills me with more horror: the danger that Riley is in right now, or the fact that Charlie facilitated it.

Just then, an eerie scream shoots through the air, and my head swings over to its origin: Riley's tent. In that moment, I'm brought back to the same panic I'd felt with Ana. In that moment, as her shriek reverberates in my head, nothing else in the world matters as I sprint over to the tent. Adrenaline pumping through my blood and my head spinning, I fly straight through the flaps of the tent's opening. Only when I'm standing inside the tent do I pause for a moment, overwhelmed with shock.

Riley hunches over where she still sits on the floor. Blood pours out of the vertical slice on her left wrist, spilling over and dripping ceaselessly onto the floor around her. With her elbow pulled in tight to her side, she extends her forearm out in a helpless manner. The accumulating puddle of crimson blood collides with the small, piercing blade that had been dropped hastily in the dirt. Tears stain her cheeks and she sobs haphazardly, overcome with utter pain. She's helpless from paralyzing shock as she gazes upon the most harm that she's ever caused— harm she would've never imagined having the capacity to inflict. And she's done it to herself.

I rush forward, pressing down on her wrist while putting my other arm around her shoulders. My hand slides around her wrist as the blood continues to pulse out, and I feel it slip in between my fingers, spilling over and dripping down my own wrist. I swoop up Riley's sweatshirt from the floor, using it to apply pressure in place of my bare grasp. Becky darts in after me and supports Riley from the other side.

We're not even out of the tent before Riley's legs give out. Her skin is pale and clammy and her eyes spin, rolling to the back of her head.

Becky calls out for help, but Anthony is already joining us. We lift her up, with Anthony at her feet and Becky supporting her shoulders.

"Get her in, get her in." Bella ushers us into the infirmary tent, bandages already in her hands.

"What happened?" I hear Blake shout from outside as he bolts toward the tent.

"She's losing too much blood!" Bella yells, wrapping bandages around Riley's bloody wrist.

"What the *hell* happened?" Blake yells again, this time appearing at the tent's entrance, but we are too preoccupied to answer.

"We need a donor: B+ or O," Becky orders, ruffling through her supplies.

"C'mon, Riley, stay with us," I plead, scrambling to her side as she lies there limp, almost lifeless.

I slap her cheeks gently and place a cold rag on her head. Eventually, I find myself shaking her frantically, trying to revitalize a girl so close to fading for good…trying to return life to the girl who should have never had it slip away.

"Riley!"

CHAPTER 34

Riley

Light shines brightly overhead, breaking through my eyelids and forcing them to flitter open. Above me the beige tent leaks in warm sunlight, which spills onto my cold cheeks. I lie there, motionless in the tent, feeling the sun on my skin. In that moment, it has never felt more comforting.

"You're awake," someone says suddenly, making me jolt a little. The voice is a low one, speaking with a rough sarcasm. I raise myself up so that I'm sitting, and I see that near the entrance of the tent sits Blake. "What? Not excited to see me?"

"I thought I was alone. You scared me," I mutter in a soft voice, barely audible. His eyes slowly move up from the floor to glare at me.

"I scared…you?" he mumbles through his teeth. His hair has grown much longer with time and he ties back his wild, dark curls into a small ponytail. A few strands by his hairline, too short to reach the hair tie, fall freely at the outer sides of his eyes and frame his face. "God forbid, right? It's not like you just scared the hell out of everybody in this camp, right? No, but *I'm* sorry for scaring *you*."

My eyes lower to my wrist. Bandages wrap it tightly, concealing the mess that I know is underneath. The blade had been so sharp, drawing like a pencil. I watched it as my skin unzipped, allowing the blood to spill out. It all happened so fast.

"Is she okay?" I ask after a moment. "Jenn."

"She'll be fine. The rest of us too. You're not the first suicide attempt we had," he spits out. "Not the first time I had to help sew up someone's wrist. And for what? To save someone who didn't wanna live?"

"Then why'd you save me?"

"You've got a baby," he barks back. "I'm not letting a kid die for your stupid decision."

"It wasn't stupid," I shake my head, shutting him up. "You should've just let me bleed out."

"What about having some hope?" he spits back. "Faith? What happened to that? You said that without it, we're no better than the undeads."

"There is no hope, Blake," I state, letting the words escape as a tired breath. "Not here. You knew it. I know it now."

"Shut up, Riley. You almost *died,* don't you get that?" he barks again, springing to his feet.

"I'm already dead," I say back under my breath, my eyes locked on his.

"Blake," Jenn says just then, appearing at the tent entrance.

"She's all yours. I'm done," Blake says, looking back at me once to shoot me a glare before leaving.

Jenn watches him go and waits until his footsteps die out before coming over to kneel down next to me.

"Suicide?" she asks quietly. Her face has been drained of its tan color except for the darkened pigment hanging under her heavy eyes. "What were you thinking?"

"It's the only way out of this," I state, but the way I say those words almost surprises me. It sounds…weak. I felt it the moment I cut myself that I didn't want it to be the way out. But suicide makes sense. I need it to.

"How can you just give up?" she blurts out.

"Look at where we are, Jenn!" I exclaim. "Everything here is *terrible.* I can't handle any more of this."

"Look at what you *did* to yourself..." she says, her voice weaker this time. She's...pleading.

"I did do this to myself," I repeat, staring ahead. "This whole thing. Headmaster gave me the option to abort. I was expelled for refusing. I was so desperate to escape my life that I chose this life instead with Jack and our future family. A *stupid,* stupid fantasy from a *stupid* girl."

"You couldn't have known, Riley," she says slowly, but her eyes are wide with shock. "You couldn't have expected the horror of this island."

"But I still suffered the consequences," I say, and I have to look away and take a moment of silence to hold back the tears resurfacing in my eyes. "I just didn't want to live with them. I didn't want this island, I just wanted *him.* But now all I have is this terrible island, and it's nothing but a nightmare without him."

I look down at the dirt and bite my lip as tears begin to swell in my eyes.

"He used to snore when we shared a tent," I continue. "Sometimes I'd get lonely when he'd spend time with you or Xander or Bella. He was stupidly clumsy and had a terrible singing voice—and not even ironically. He wasn't perfect, but I don't remember that when I think of him. I'm just left with the good stuff, Jenn, like his laugh, his humor, his smile, and when he'd make me feel *loved.* I can't get it out of my head."

"So, you were just going to opt out and kill yourself?" she asks again, her voice tired and defeated.

"The moment he stopped breathing," I say quietly, "I knew I wanted to stop breathing, too. I died with him that night. I was just waiting for my heart to finally give out to let me be with him."

"I can't believe this." She shakes her head a little in disbelief. "You're stronger than this, Riley."

"I don't feel everything, anymore," I say, to which she inhales sharply. "I feel nothing. I lost my everything, Jenn."

"You have your child," she says, furrowing her brows, trying to understand.

"And bring her into a world like this?" I counter. "She shouldn't be punished like that."

"You can't just give up, Riley," she states, her voice suddenly hardened into a demand. "The knife isn't meant for you, and it isn't meant for your baby. You want to use it, use it to fight. Use it on the undead."

"What good would that—"

"Just fight this, Riley," she demands again, and her order sends a shudder through the back of my neck. Earnestly, she clasps the hand of my uninjured side. "You've been through hell, and you have every right to be hurt and angry and broken. But it's poisoning you. In all honesty, I have not been in your place or felt what you've felt. But I am right here for you. We are *all* right here to help you get through this. We love you, Riley, and we are not going to let you die. Fight for Jack and fight for your child with him. That's what you did when you refused the abortion. You took control of your life. Take control again and fight these feelings. Stay alive now. It's the harder option…but do it anyway."

She stares at me for a while after that, her eyebrows upturned and her lips pressed together. When she lets go of my hand, I'm caught off guard by the longing I feel as the warmth slips away. I drop my gaze to it, but instead, my eyes land on my bandaged wrist. Flashes of the event fly through my mind again. The gliding knife. The searing pain as my skin opened. For the first time, as my heart begins to speed up and a pit forms in my chest, I see its horror. I see the desperate mutilation on an arm that I don't want to be mine.

"Fight this, Riley," she repeats.

CHAPTER 35

Jenn

"I'm going to check up on her later. Don't let Blake back in there for now," I tell Becky. After leaving Riley, I had to take a few moments to myself before seeking out Becky for a status report. She just nods and puts a hand on my shoulder. I hear footsteps and look up to see Xander approaching us.

"I should probably go check up on Charlie. I know he was pretty shaken up when he saw all the blood," Becky says, though I know it's not true. Nevertheless, she walks off.

"Is she awake?" Xander asks when he finally reaches me.

"She's awake," I say, letting the tired smile break through my exhaustion. However, I only let it hang in the moment long enough to watch Xander's tense face fall with relief. "Though, you might want to give her some time alone before you go see her."

"Of course," he says. "How was she when you talked to her?"

"Vulnerable," I respond, looking down. "I think I may have gotten through to her a bit, though. I told her to fight through this."

"Good," he says. "She wants to live. She probably felt it the moment she woke up that suicide wasn't the solution she was looking for. She needs time to figure things out."

"We have to be there for her as she does," I add. My eyes shut momentarily as if to shield myself from an ugly truth. "She still hates me, though."

"Jack didn't blame you. You didn't know that anything would happen in the forest. You're a soldier, not a psychic." He pauses before continuing. "How have you been doing?"

"Me? Riley's the one who tried to kill herself," I murmur, glancing back over at her tent. When he doesn't respond, I give him an inquisitive look. "What?"

"Are *you* ok?" he asks again, still staring at me.

"No." I sigh after a moment. "I mean…I have been *utterly* powerless ever since we got to this island. It feels like everyone just…falls through my grasp. And I can't stop it. And I don't know how to help."

"You always try, Jenn. You do what you can, and that's all that anyone can do. Horrible things happened, but they're beyond your control," he consoles, wrapping an arm around my shoulder, but I shrug it off. "You did what you could."

"It's just never enough," I mumble. Then, firmly, I say, ""I'm no soldier. I never was."

"What do you mean?" he asks, and I furrow my eyebrows as I think about my words.

"Billy, Ana, Noah, and Jack got bit, all right in front of me and I couldn't do anything about it. I'd never even seen death before, and especially not like this. I picked a fight and got my ass kicked by Andrew the moment I got here because I was both arrogant and *scared* of who he reminded me of, and I let myself get carried away," I continue sternly. "I treasured my ego and had no discipline; I know that. I was a product of the BAA, but I was no soldier. Not a good one, at least."

"And what about now?" he asks hesitantly, and I nod slowly.

"I'm ready to learn," I respond.

The conversation ends after that, but I know there's more to be said between us…about us. He wants to say something, and I wait for him to come to it on his own.

"Jenn, I wanted to talk to you about what I said after the funeral."

"Was it true?"

"It was."

"I wish it wasn't," I say quietly. I glance over at the campfire where the rest for the campers are setting up for lunch. "I never expected anything..."

"I know," he says abruptly, catching me off guard. "And I get it."

"I don't need a relationship, that's not a part of life that I need," I state quickly as though trying to rush the conversation.

"I know you don't *need* it. But what about what you want?" he poses. "I know your guard is up when it comes to this sort of stuff, mine is too. But I wanted to let mine down to tell you this correctly this time."

"Xander…" I say under my breath, shrinking away at what I know he's going to say next.

"I love you, Jenn," he states, but I avoid his gaze. "When I said it last time, it didn't come across the way I wanted it too. I've known you for a while now. You're strong, Jenn. And self-assured. And when something needs to get done, I've watched you spring to action and you get it done. You *are* powerful, Jenn, even if you don't feel that way. I see it. And I didn't want to tell you this and make you feel like you have to say something back. You don't. I just wanted you to know how I feel. And if you don't feel the same, I understand. I'll still be right here for you as a friend. I wanted you to know that too."

He takes a moment to pause and take a deep breath.

"But if you feel something too. If you want to try letting your guard down. If you want me to tell you that I love you again. Let me know. When you're ready."

I keep my focus on the dirt in front of me. We stand there for a few minutes in silence, and I bite the inside of my cheek. I wish to disappear, or for him to disappear— either would work. I open my mouth to speak but then shut it.

"It's ok," he says, offering a warm smile. "I'm going to head back to keep watch again."

I watch him walk away and before I know it, he's already a good distance away. Yet, my mind's blank. It's as though I've lost the ability to think.

"Wait," I shout suddenly.

His walk slows to a stop in his path, and he turns around. I take a few steps forward and he does the same. At last, I'm in front of him. His mouth opens slightly yearning to speak, but he waits for me. But he's right there. And I'm right here. And it's easier to shout when you're far away.

"I'm sorry, Xander," I say, rather quietly. "I can't."

I'm not even sure what I mean by the words, but his expression falls nevertheless. And after he walks off again, and I still stand there in place, I don't call after him. And I don't know if I regret it.

***

"Get up!" I awake to the sound of Blake yelling into my tent. My eyes flicker open, and as I sit up, a wave of heat smashes into my face. Outside my tent, I can hear campers scrambling around, yelling at each other. "Get up! Get out here!"

Blake grabs my arm and yanks me roughly to my feet, dragging me out of the tent. I stop in horror at the treacherous sight before me, and Blake runs off without me. The camp's protective hedge is ablaze, burning down by the second and spreading the flames to everything near it.

It has been over two and a half months since Riley's suicide attempt, and the camp was finally healing from the tragedies we endured. We'd even built a secure raft, complete with ample room for everyone, that we were going to bring to the shore in December.

Xander and I never reopened the conversation about furthering our relationship, and he didn't press it. We settled back into our friendship, and it was enough. Sometimes, though, when his gaze lingers on me a bit longer than typical, or when I find that he's the only one I want to talk to after a long day, my thoughts bring me back to the day that I shut down his offer. But I move on. It's easier this way, and we're happy. It's enough.

Riley, with her bandaged wrist, had been re-integrating into the camp. Though mostly keeping to herself and speaking very sparsely, she still sits down for every meal and pulls her weight around the camp. She has avoided social contact with mostly everyone except Bella, who checks in on her baby and is the only one that can still make her smile. Riley's alive. And healing.

Life was coming together.

Now, campers run frantically out of their tents, grabbing buckets and filling them up with water from the stream. Though, the water, small in volume and fruitlessly hurled at the intimidating fire, has no effect. The inferno continues to destroy everything that had kept this camp safe for so long. Beneath the burning trees, the new fences smolder as well. Against the black sky, the fires rage brightly, daring the undeads to come. Ash hangs thick in the air, and I begin coughing, desperately trying to rid myself of the poisonous substance clogging my lungs.

"Jenn!" Becky yells over the roar of the fire and when I take notice of her, she tosses an empty bucket over to me. I catch it in my hands, and jog over to the stream. Becky meets me there.

"What happened?" I ask, frantically looking around. Smoke limiting my vision, I can't make out the faces of the scrambling campers.

"It was Andrew," she quickly responds, filling up her bucket. "He, Lie, and Corinne. They kept Blake busy with undeads while they threw torches throughout the hedge. It broke through to the compost center, which ignited, and everything went downhill from there. They have the outside forest burning as well."

During these past few weeks, there were a few sightings of people darting between the trees beyond the hedge at nighttime. Andrew, Lie, and Corinne were the prime suspects, which got the camp nervous of a revenge strike. But, nothing was ever confirmed and nothing ever came of it. It was too risky to play offensive, so we just reminded each other to keep a watchful vigil at night in case of an attack. No one expected something of this caliber.

"Where's Xander?" I ask again. Before she can answer, a disheveled Kris collapses beside us at the stream. Coughing hysterically, she helplessly holds her hands out in front of her, catching the blood and ash that shoots out of her mouth. When Becky kneels down beside her, Kris just grabs the bucket of water from her and begins desperately chugging it, only to choke it back up and continue coughing.

"We all have to get out of here!" I exclaim as I watch Kris struggle. "Trying to stop it is pointless by now."

"We're *trying*," Becky enunciates. "There's fire in each of the exits. Andrew knows the layout of this camp…we're trapped."

"Then we wait it out," I state hurriedly, my thoughts racing. "Let the hedge burn until it's gone, and then we leave. We can hide in the tents for cover from the smoke until then."

"The undead will come sooner or later," Becky warns.

"Where's Riley?" I demand.

"No one can find her," Becky answers grimly.

I hear a scream from the other side of the camp and turn around to see the south post collapse under the weight of the fire. The fire had eaten through the tall logs holding up the immense structure, and without its roots, the rest of the wooden post falls. Its deteriorated pieces feed the surrounding fires with fresh fuel, and the vitalized flames spread rapidly to the nearby trees that surround the bathing area. Finally, much of the southern hedge caves in as the rage of the fire engulfs it entirely. Its leaves burnt up and its scorched branches cracking, the naked trees collapse on top of each other.

I spot Xander running from the falling wall. His leg still healing, he runs with a small limp. Suddenly, one of the burning trees from the bathing area cracks and the top part, blackened from the fire, collapses to the floor. The fire continues to devour it as it lays on the ground, and the wild flames spray with the wind, catching on Xander's shirt. Frantic in fear, he trips and falls onto the floor, screaming as fire licks his skin.

Without a second thought, I fill up one of the buckets with water and lug it over to Xander's thrashing body. My adrenaline helps me run as panic floods in. He rolls desperately in the dirt, trying to extinguish the flames. Fighting my way through the heavy smoke, thicker over here, I manage to reach him and empty my entire bucket. The flames extinguish, and I drop to my knees by his side.

Then, the nightmare worsens before my eyes. As they emerge from the clouding ash and blinding flames, silhouettes become bodies of undead hobbling through the huge gap in the burning hedge. Fire trails from their ragtag clothing like flaming wings, and their skin chars black, exposing sections of bone. Monsters from hell.

Scrambling to his feet, Xander hangs onto me for support, and we trek across the camp, away from the growing crowd of undeads behind us. Though at this rate, we're not much faster than them.

"Meet at the center! Campers to the center by the tents!" I call out, though it's fruitless in the chaos. I see Bella running over to us, but behind her, Blake and Phil are running opposite directions.

When Bella finally reaches us, she stops and raises her gun to shoot a couple of the undeads behind us, the bullets blasting straight through their softened skulls.

"We need to get out of here," I command.

"Blake, Phil, and I are rounding up the campers," Bella explains quickly. "I need to find Riley. She went to the bathing area last night, I'm going to check if she's still there."

As more parts of the hedge crumbles, masses of undeads invade the camp. In a matter of minutes, the camp will be overrun. At the same time, the fog of smoke thickens, and my visibility decreases further.

"Over there!" Xander yells through a choking cough. My eyes follow his outstretched arm to an emerging hole in part of the nearby hedge, the fire continuing to eat away at its edges.

Suddenly, there's a scream, and I look over to see Charlie nearly 50 yards away desperately trying to run away from a few straggling undeads chasing him.

"Bella, you find Riley, I'll get Charlie," I state firmly and she nods earnestly.

"You have to go," I say to Xander, to which he gives me a questioning look. "I don't know how many undeads are still coming, but if you leave now, you might still have a headstart before they arrive. I have to help gather the others. Go, I'll be right behind you."

"What? No, I won't leave you," he objects, but I separate from him.

"You have to," I say again, unhooking my axe from my belt. "Stay low to the ground. I'll meet you outside."

"And what if you don't?" he asks again.

I don't respond. I don't have an answer.

I turn away from him, only to face an approaching undead, its skin burnt away to the bone like many of the others. I swing my axe, chopping its head clean off as I sprint past it and leave its severed body to fall to the ground. I look around, trying to find the spot where I had last seen Charlie. He's not there.

More and more undeads swarm into the camp as the fire incinerates everything that had once been our home. The fire had even spread to the crops in the fields by now and to the raft that we had built for our escape. We had just finished the final touch-ups on its build yesterday. Ashes from our crumbling civilization continue to soar up through the air in a thick black smoke, darkening the sky even further and blocking out sunlight.

A sharp burning tears in my throat as I run through the camp, panting heavily. Gunshots ring in the distance. Suffocating smoke fills my lungs, and I fall to my knees, exhausted. My head spins. All around me, the gray fog veils most of the camp from my view now. I try to just breathe, but I can't find much oxygen—just the hot, dry air that pulses out of the flames and hangs in the area. The burning air singes my skin, sending a stinging sensation radiating throughout my body. My tongue is parched, and I try again to breathe, but the air rubs up against my dehydrated throat. I feel as though all the water in my body has left me to shrivel up. The fires around me laugh, mocking me.

Bella's on the ground now as well only about ten feet from me. She seems to be in the same position I am. She throws her backpack off and gets up off the ground, wearily.

It happens so fast that I don't remember if I yell out a warning or not—or if I was even physically able to with my cracked throat. When Bella finally regains her stance, an undead strikes from behind, clenching onto her shoulders and sinking its teeth into her neck.

I fall back on my butt, slowly crawling away in horror as Bella's neck is ripped apart by a pair of yellowed teeth. Blood spews out and I see an artery fling out from the side of her neck, raining down blood as if it were a hose. A shot rings off from her gun, and the undead's head is jerked up as the bullet tears through its brain from its chin to the top of its head. With blood still pouring out of her neck, she loses hold of the gun and it slips from her fingers, clattering across the grass. Another undead catches her as she falls and tears a messy bite from her arm. Her scream seems far off in my daze, and though my vision is hazy, I see her finally hit the floor. A growing group of undeads surround her.

I crawl over to where the dropped gun had skid across the dirt, and my hands grip onto the cold metal handle. Ultimately, determination overcomes my pain, and I push myself off the floor.

I fire off a few bullets at the group of undeads huddling over Bella. Some of them fall to the floor and, through the holes in their huddle, I see an undead lean down and wrap its jaw around Bella's face. Her screams have died out by now, and her limp body is helpless in the hands of the monsters around her. After peeling away flesh from her cheek, the same undead goes back for more and crunches down on her eye. Blood spurts out as I see an eyeball get slowly dragged out from its socket with the connected blood vessels and nerves trailing behind. The undead clamps its jaw shut, and the eyeball bursts.

I run off as fast as I can, my throat burning from the smoke, and I empty my gun into the endless hoard. Undeads fall as the bullets fly. I see another group of huddled undeads moving in the direction opposite me as if following something on the floor. I shoot into the hoard, and as the bodies fall, I spot Phil crawling backwards as his group of undeads step closer. He scrambles to his feet and unsheathes his sword. With one swing, he slices straight through the head of a nearby undead.

"Phil!" I call out. Just then, I feel the rotten, bony hands of an undead on my shoulder. Before I can jerk away, the undead knocks me down, pinning me with the weight of its body. I look over to where I had seen Phil, but he's already gone, and the area swarms with more undeads.

I hold back the undead on me with my elbow as I fit my gun against its grit teeth. The bullet smashes through its bridge, and the limp head flings back before crashing back onto me so that our foreheads touch.

I hide underneath the dead body, evading the passing undeads, and as I devise a plan for my escape through an opening in the hedge. Finally, when there's a window of opportunity, I bolt out from underneath the body and sprint along my planned path.

I continue to shoot nearby undeads who wander way too close until the clip empties. Frustrated, I shove the empty weapon into the waistband of my pants and deliver a high kick to a nearby beast's face. There's a loud crack, and when the undead recovers, its mouth hangs open with its jaw broken and drooping greatly on the left side.

I reach at my belt and unlatch my axe as more undeads begin to gather. With one swing, I swiftly chop off a head on my left. With another, the blade wedges down in the center of another skull. A final swing slashes a deep vertical slash through an undead's face. I watch as a mangled brain slowly slips forward out of the face, and the force pulls the skull apart.

I continue running until I reach where the burnt down hedge lies in ashes in a gaping doorway to freedom. I take one last look at the demolished camp that now belongs to the flames and undead.

CHAPTER 36

Riley

Fire rages around me. My eyes blur momentarily and my balance wavers as I raise myself to my feet, clutching my bulging stomach. The intense heat of the nearby flames smothers my delicate skin.

After I woke up last night screaming from nightmares, Bella gave me some sleeping herbs. My nightmares vary widely, but this time, it was Ana's body lying in her grave at the funeral. In my dream, she wakes up as an undead and tears my baby out of my stomach, exclaiming that kids are not allowed to survive. After taking Bella's medication, I went to take a bath to escape my thoughts but ended up passing out at the side of the small pool.

Now, the dangerously thinning air forces me awake. The bathing area, built to be shielded off from the rest of camp by a circle of dense trees, now engulfs me in a ring of fire. Trapped. Suffocated. Isolated from the others and lost in the chaos. Though my vision is limited by the thick veil of smoke, dozens of silhouettes walk toward me with the distinctive hobble of the undead. The rancid smell of burning flesh singes my nose, and I recoil, gagging silently.

I must assess quickly. If the undead are here, the camp's walls are compromised. The fire must be camp-wide. With the camp burning down and undeads swarming, the others are likely planning an escape. For all I know, not all of them are even still alive. The camp is lost. I have to leave.

Just then, a thought dawns on me. A few days after my suicide attempt, I contemplated slipping out of the camp and making it on my own in the forest. I created a stowaway bag of food and water and buried it near the bath. As my mind and body healed, my plan for escape dissipated and so did the memory of having a hidden stockpile. Now, when I need it most, I'm grateful to know exactly where to look.

My hands shaking and my eyes bulging from their sockets, I scope out the familiar location and drop to my knees. Desperately, I claw at the dirt. Every few seconds, my head whips to my sides to watch the encroaching flames and scope out for undead. I spot an opening in the fire, likely caused by the collapse of charred trees. Smoke smothers my vision and lungs. I don't have any more time.

Just then, the fabric of the bag reveals itself in the ground. I rip the bag out of the dirt and instantly take off. Though I'm free from the bathing area, the rest of the camp is ablaze as I feared. My visibility is still hindered heavily by the thick ashy cloud I dart through, but I can tell that the fires are everywhere. Everything we called home is burning. Our safety. Our remnant of civilization. Our family. All dissipated.

My throat burns as I struggle to sprint, and as I dash through a large gap in the destroyed hedge, I narrowly avoid the swinging arms of more swarming undeads arriving to raid the camp. I spot a gun on the floor, clearly dropped by its owner, and I swoop it up.

Finally, by the time the flames of the camp fall just out of sight, it feels like an eternity has passed. Though the smoke around me is considerably thinner in the forest, remnants of the massive forest fire still cloud the area. I'm panting heavily and can feel my heartbeat in my ears, but I force myself to continue through the trees nonetheless. I'm heading nowhere in particular, but I know I have to keep going.

An undead appears in front me, and I nearly collide with it. I raise my gun, the tip of the barrel nearly touching its forehead. I pull the trigger, and the shot explodes from the gun, sending the undead's head backwards. The sound reverberates off the nearby trees, being thrown in a million different directions and echoing back to ring in my ears as if to taunt me with the danger of the weapon I'm wielding. My knuckles are white from the strength of my grip as I squeeze the gun firmly in my hand. The cool metal warms as the body heat from my sweaty hands transfers to it, seemingly fueling it for its next bullet. I've held a gun before, but not like this— not in a situation like this.

A few more undeads begin appearing through the trees, and I raise my gun to point it at them. Shot after shot, the undeads fall, dead with blood oozing out from the holes in their skulls.

Just then, the gun clicks empty as one of the undeads steps right in front of me. I back up, terrified, as more undeads crowd around. Their group must've been headed toward the fire. Now, with an injured wrist, bulging stomach, and no weapon, I'm in a losing battle.

No, I tell myself. *I'm not going to lose.*

Briskly, I use the butt of the gun to smack the undead in the face. It staggers back a little, giving me room to strike out with my heel, knocking it back and buying myself time. I spot a fallen branch at the base of a tree and snatch it. A sharp pain sears through my injured wrist as I swing the thick branch across the face of the undead, knocking it to the floor. I pause when I raise my new weapon above my head. Then, a loud crack resounds in the air as I smash the undead's head. Trails of blood flow down from its split skull into its face and mouth. Just as the beast is about to get up again, I bludgeon its head again and then a third time, finally splintering the branch. Blood and pieces of brain splash up at me, flicking my legs and shorts.

I take off running again. Alone. *Just a little braver,* I repeat to myself again and again. *You have to just be a little braver now.*

I guide myself through the forest by following the stream that had run through camp. Sticking close to its bank, I follow it until it empties into the lake. But after deciding that the lake is still too close to the herd and wildfire at the camp, I continue on into the abyss. I can't risk getting caught in the fray. All I know is that the farther I run, the clearer the air gets, the quieter the sound of the undeads' moaning becomes, and the greater my chance of survival is.

***

A group of undeads walk past the thick trunk of the tree that I hide behind. I wait patiently, scoping them out. I let my gaze bounce between them, watching for any slight changes in their movements that would indicate that I'd been exposed. At the anchor of the group is a gruesome-looking female carrying a large blue backpack on her back. Despite its empty appearance, I can tell there is something in there by the soft patter of materials bouncing against each other as she walks. For once, I no longer feel like the victim—I'm the predator. In my hands, I clasp the hilt of a rusted dagger that I had swiped from an undead. I wait until the majority of the group disappears into the trees before I let out a soft whistle.

My target slowly turns around, its grotesque face looking at the trees near me. I whistle again and, hearing the noise, the undead hobbles away from the group to approach the thicket that shields me. Once it's practically upon me, I lash out, grabbing it and holding it against a tree. Then systematically, I dig my blade straight through its soft skull and immediately drag its body into the bushes. As long as I minimize my noise and stay out of sight, this undead's group members won't get suspicious of anything.

Up close, I let my eyes examine the undead's face once again, looking for cues of someone that I may recognize. The height is about the same as Jen, and the long strands of dark hair resemble hers. Black eyes stare blankly back at me, surrounded by masses of popped veins that spill out crusts of blood. Jenn has brown eyes.

I flip the body on its stomach and crouch to rummage through its backpack. Though mostly empty, it contains three cans of soup, which I instantly slip into my backpack.

It's been only 8 days since I fled the camp, but it feels like forever. The food I had taken only lasted a few days, as expected. Since then, the days seem longer as I travel alone, scavenging for food. The nights, too, drag on as I lie awake, terrified of my surroundings and nightmares alike. Yet each night, while my ears tune to the dangers of the world around me, I let my eyes lock on the brightest star in the sky and my fingers run over the smooth ring that I carry in my pocket. I long for Jack's touch, but I feel his protection. Though the radiant light of his star can't warm my skin, it fuels me inside. He keeps me going because I know that I'm never truly in this fight alone. As long as I feel the glow of his star, I will fight for him, for our baby, and for myself.

"Think I could have one of those?"

The hushed voice catches me off guard, and I spring to my feet, holding my blade out. My eyes quickly scan the forest behind me until I spot the source. A wave of relief washes over me at the sight of a friend I thought I would never see again. Only a few feet away and hidden behind the overgrowth of the forest, Blake is squatting.

"Blake!" I exclaim louder than I should have.

A familiar groaning comes from behind me now, and I turn around to see the rest of the group of undeads now approaching. They must've heard the commotion.

Suddenly, an arrow pierces through the head of the nearest undead, and its head flings back before it collapses. It's Jack's arrow: gleaming silver with a fletch of white feathers streaked with green. Blake, silver bow in hand, flies past me toward the undeads. Hanging on his back is a quiver filled with the familiar silver arrows. He darts around the nearest undead, grabbing it from behind to restrain it and stab the back of its skull with a dagger.

I reach down and rip the arrow out from the fallen undead's head. Striding over to where the last undead hobbles, I use the arrow to stab it through the eye. As I yank out the makeshift knife, blood sprays back at me and splatters my face with dots of blood.

"Riley," Blake says softly as he grabs me by the arm. Instinctively, I pull him into a tight hug. When he returns the embrace, I revel at the feeling of safety and compassion in his arms. It's been too long since I've felt something like that.

"How long were you hiding there?" I ask as I separate from him.

"I saw that blond head of yours from back there," he says, indicating further into the forest. "You looked busy, so I didn't want to interrupt until you were done."

"Have you seen anyone else since…" I start to ask slowly.

"You're the first," he says simply. "Not the answer you were hoping for?"

"I guess I was just hoping that everyone evacuated together and were still out there," I say. Thoughts run through my mind, and I have to sit down to prevent the wave of nausea that I feel coming.

"You're not with Bella?" he asks, though by his tone, he already knows the answer. "She doesn't happen to be just around the corner or something, right?"

"No, I escaped on my own. Why?" I ask, hesitantly. "What happened at the camp?"

"Andrew set fire to the walls," he explains, and I furrow my eyebrows at the news. "The place burned to the ground fast."

"And everyone scattered?" I ask in disbelief.

"We were trapped inside at first. By the time we had the chance to get out, everything had already become chaos," he says. "Bella went to find you."

"She never did," I say, pursing my lips.

"We all had no choice but to leave, especially with the undeads swarming," he continues. "Phil, Bella, and I were all together at first, but we decided to split up and try to round up the others and then regroup at a checkpoint. I went looking for Becky and Charlie, but I couldn't find them. When the place was overrun, I realized I just had to get out of there. I waited at the checkpoint for days…no one ever came."

"Have you seen their…"

"Bodies?" he says, finishing my question, and I nod, still unable to raise my gaze from the floor. "No, I haven't."

"I don't know if that makes me feel better or not," I mutter mainly to myself.

"Doesn't matter," he says, shaking his head.

"What about the graveyard? I've been on the fence about heading there. Maybe Andrew will let us stay if we play by his rules?" I ask hopefully, wiping some sweat from my forehead.

"I already scoped it out. Nothing's there," he replies.

"What do you mean?" I ask again. The graveyard was my last hope at a sanctuary. "Did the fires and herd reach it?"

"I guess so. It's just a bunch of old ashes now. It's completely abandoned," he explains, shrugging. "Get up. The sun's starting to set, and we don't want to be caught out here when it's dark."

***

Another week passes as Blake and I roam the wilderness, endlessly trekking through the forest in search of food and the others. He walks in front of me, crouching as we near the spot he claims to have spotted a squirrel.

As I follow him, I can't take my eyes off the arrows hanging off his back. He told me he picked up the weapon last minute as he was fleeing the camp and his gun ran out of ammo. As the widow of the bow's past user and the better archer between the two of us, I had been yearning to claim Jack's bow. However, since the string's tension was set to Jack's strength, I wasn't able to pull it back to use it. It was initially unnerving to see someone else wield Jack's customized weapon. Yet at the same time, as I admire the silver of the bow, dulled with dirt and frayed along the bowstring, I couldn't help but see Jack in it. He is the bow, and he found me.

"We've been searching in this direction for an hour," I finally grumble from behind my teeth. "Whatever you saw is gone now."

He blatantly ignores me, continuing to step forward in search of his imaginary prey.

"Blake, we've been on our feet all day since dawn. I need to sit down for a bit," I say again, louder this time. When he still doesn't acknowledge me, I stand up from my crouched position.

"You trying to get us killed?" he spits out, standing up as well. "Make yourself known and you scare off any animals nearby and alert the undead."

"I need to take a break," I state sternly, but he quickly waves me off. "*You* try being pregnant!"

Still not taking any of my comments into consideration, he turns around to head off again, and I force my tired legs to follow. I hear a small splash and find my mud-caked shoe stepping in a shallow puddle of dark crimson atop the saturated dirt.

"Blake," I call out softly, and he turns around sharply, his brows furrowed in annoyance. Without saying anything, I point to the red trail on the ground that stretches from my foot into the nearby overgrowth of the forest. He follows it, and I stay close behind. When he stops, I move around him to see a mangled body sprawled out on the ground.

Among the blood-stained mess, coated smudges from handprints can be made out in the dirt. The left arm is completely missing, torn off wrought with shreds of remnant tissue hanging off. The corpse's abdomen also caves in, missing all of its organs and muscles that had been greedily ripped out. Several exposed ribs are cracked and broken in. The lower half of the body is devastated too, eaten away nearly to the bone. Horrified, I dare to look at the face of the poor victim, whose skin and facial features had also been torn off. Only one eye remains, shifting quickly between Blake and I. As its jaw slowly opens and closes, I can't tell if the reanimated body is longing for a meal or for mercy. Despite its desires, with most of the rest of the body eaten away, it lies on the floor motionless.

Petrified with fear at the gruesome sight, I am barely able to rip my gaze away. I step back with horror and hear a crunch under my foot. A small handmade wooden cross.

"This is Phil's necklace," I say quietly. As I speak, I cover my mouth with my hand as if trying to keep the words that acknowledge the reality.

"And that's his body," Blake adds. He doesn't move, though.

Unable to contain my grief, I feel a tear cascade down my cheek, carving a road in the grime that smears my face. Blake unsheathes his dagger and plunges the blade deep into Phil's skull, silencing his twitching eye and stretching jaw.

"The only thing worse than being eaten like this," he says, standing back up and wiping his bloody dagger off on his pants, "is having to become the monster that murdered you. Phil was a good guy; he doesn't deserve that."

He leans back down and picks up Phil's dagger. Staining the once pristine BAA-quality blade, dried dark crimson remnants of blood radiate out from the blunted tip and along the length of the knife.

"Trash blade, but we can keep it as a backup," he assesses.

"Any ammo?" I ask, slipping the cross necklace into my pocket. In my backpack, I have been holding onto the gun I had from camp, hoping that we would stumble upon more ammo. We've had no such luck.

"Nope," Blake retorts after ransacking Phil's clothes. He steps away from the body with two cans of soup and hands one off to me. "Bon appetit, courtesy of an old friend."

"I spent that first week alone just wondering what had happened that day at camp when everything burned down," I mutter, still looking at Phil's disfigured body. "This is what I feared most. Finding everyone like this."

"So far, Phil and probably Bella," Blake says simply, heading off through the trees again. "Should we keep a checklist?"

"That's morbid," I say, narrowing my eyes at the back of his head as he walks away. I take a look at Phil's destroyed body one last time. "And who said Bella is dead?"

"She was supposed to rouse you from your beauty sleep. You said she never did. She probably died," Blake explains, pointing to a different spot in the air with each sentence to obnoxiously emphasize his reasoning.

"It wasn't a beauty sleep, I had a sleep medication. Bella said it would help my wrist heal and stop my nightmares," I say again, catching up to walk beside him. He's already opened his can of soup and slurps down the contents. Looking at my own, I notice that the pull tab is broken off. "I can't get mine to open."

"So?" He mumbles through a mouthful of food.

"Can you help me?" I ask, struggling to grasp onto the tiny piece left on the tab.

"Your wrist is healing," he grudgingly says, chugging the rest of his meal before throwing the empty container aside. "Help yourself."

"Please, Blake," I say humbly.

I furrow my eyebrows in frustration as I clean off one of my knives and try to use it to pry the can open. Suddenly, he reaches over and rips the can and knife from my hands. Immediately jamming in the knife, he slides the blade around the edges to lift the lid in a matter of seconds. Still avoiding eye contact, he hands me back both the can and knife.

"Thanks," I say quietly before drinking up the soup.

"We should keep hunting," he says. "We got lucky with the soup."

"We should go to the shore," I propose, watching cautiously for his reaction.

"Too dangerous," he says, instantly dismissing me.

"But that was the original plan, wasn't it?" I counter. "Back at camp, we said that we'd go to the shore after we built the raft. It must be close to December now, so the boats should be coming soon. You know the way there. We could camp out near the shore until—"

"We had a team back then. Alone, you won't stand a chance against the herd," he corrects, his expression filled with distaste. A few strands have fallen from his ponytail and the curls are strewn messily across his eyes. "And don't say 'we.' You weren't part of any of the planning. If I remember correctly, you were too busy trying to kill yourself in your tent."

The comment catches me off guard. We hadn't spoken about the suicide attempt since our very first confrontation immediately after it happened. When he glances up at me, I humbly look away.

"Why'd you cut your wrist, anyway?" he sneers again aggressively, raising his voice slightly in frustration. "What were you—"

"That's my own business," I interrupt.

"No, it's not," he spits back at me abruptly before I can even finish my statement. He stops walking, and I do the same. "You almost died die. That was everyone's business. You *chose* to die. You didn't even want to live, yet here you are. And look at what happened to Phil and the others. They wish they had the choice you had."

"It was a mistake, I know that now," I respond, raising my voice in defense. "And I'm trying to get past it."

"A mistake?" he exclaims, mockingly grinning. "All that hope you used to talk about. Means nothing."

"Fine," I say, tightening my jaw. "Think what you want. But regardless, I'm going to go to the shore and get my baby off this island. Are you coming with me?"

"Yeah right," he quips. "You don't even know where the Graveyard of Boats is."

It's true. Of those of us that potentially made it out of the fire, Blake and Becky are the only ones that would really be able to navigate to the Graveyard of Boats with certainty. It's such a specific location on the eastern shore of the island; with some exceptions, like the boat I arrived on, most boats solely arrive at this location.

"I'll figure it out," I state.

"You know, you're getting creative with these suicide attempts," he says.

"I'm not going to kill myself!" I yell back, my voice louder than I had intended as my passion builds, and I try to calm myself slightly. "I was naïve when I first got here, I know that. I chased a paradise that only ever existed in my head. When Jack died, I wasn't prepared—the thought of the most important person in my life dying hadn't seemed possible. So, I lost myself. But I am *trying* to find myself again. Because having hope doesn't mean that nothing bad will happen; It's knowing that when something bad does happen, you'll be able to get back up. Because you can still see the good."

For a moment, we just stare at each other, silent. My eyes examine his, trying to see through the impenetrable darkness that fills them.

"I'm 9 months pregnant. I have a *child.* I see that as 'the good'. And I'll be damned if I force her or him to grow up here and die like Jack did," I affirm. "There were times when I first got here that I'd stare across the water, waiting for someone to come and rescue me. It's almost December, and someone's *coming.* I'm taking my baby, and I'm leaving this island with or without you."

"With me," he says. He still stares at me with his sharp beady eyes; however, it's different now. "We go together."

CHAPTER 37

Jenn

Blood sprays as the head of an undead is swiftly separated from its neck with one swing of my axe. The head lands on the floor, but its mouth continues to chomp at me. Furiously, I kick the head, sending it flying into a tree, where it leaves a red splatter of blood as it crashes into the bark.

With undeads hobbling around me, I swing my axe again, splitting the nearest one's skull into two. At the sound of another undead's moan coming from behind, I whirl around and launch my axe through the air, the weapon jamming itself in the beast's face.

At last, two final undeads come my way. I wait until they come closer before I strike the first one's knee with my heel, breaking their leg. As it crashes to the floor, I grip the second undead's shoulders with both hands and slam it against the tree. Its neck reaches out and its jaw snaps at me, splashing me with waves of rotten breath and flinging strings of spit.

I briefly loosen my grip, and the undead lurches forward. But as soon as it does, I push it back again, knocking its skull against the trunk multiple times, widening the maroon stain left on the bark. When I hear the crackling splatter of the skull caving in, I let the creature fall to the ground.

Full of raging energy, I walk back over to the undead whose leg I had broken and jam the heel of my boot into its forehead, breaking through the frontal bone. Then, retrieving a large nearby rock, I smash its face in.

I haven't been able to find Xander— or anyone— since I left the camp. It's been weeks. Maybe even more than a month, I'm not sure. I commend Riley for always keeping the days straight in her mind.

The entire landscape of the island, I've learned, is relatively uniform. With slight variations in elevation and terrain, the forest is continuous and homogenous, bringing the same trees each mile after mile. Undeads are also a guarantee no matter where you venture. I've been trying to stay close to the shore, though. I figure if I were to find the others, they might be headed to the shore to wait for an incoming ship. Though, I'm not exactly sure where the Graveyard of Boats is, and it's risky to check the shore directly too frequently because of the herd. At least it gives me a sense of direction.

The images of Bella's death replay over and over again in my mind, and I picture Xander having the same fate. Until I find a dead body, I will continue to believe he's alive. I just have to keep looking.

After retrieving my axe, I continue to trek onwards, trying to find anything that would lead me to *anyone.* Soldiers aren't lone wolves; you only realize that when you're forced to be one. It's like Xander had said so long ago: the campers are my unit, my team. But it's more than that. They're my family.

Suddenly, my eyes catch something on the ground: a series of footprints in the dirt. For a moment, my heart stops. But then, I realize the steps are too messy and uneven. An undead.

"Dammit!" I yell in frustration, kicking at the dirt.

I feel tears begin to well up in my eyes as I drop to the floor again, falling back against a tree trunk. Breathing in deeply to contain my sob, I look up at the sky. Somewhere out there, Xander is waiting for me to find him. Somewhere out there, he's trying to find me too.

The moaning of an undead startles me, and I look over to my right to see one approaching me. I stand up swiftly and swing my axe into the side of its skull. Once it's on the floor, I flip it over onto its stomach, unzip its backpack, and ruffle through the contents: two empty bottles and broken medical supplies. I toss the empty bottles in my bag along with whatever medical supplies I could salvage.

After several hours of roaming around the forest, I find a small stream of water carving a path in the dirt. I follow it for a bit until it opens up more. Baking under the bright daytime sun, I wipe drops of sweat off my forehead and splash some of the river water onto my face. Settling down, I fill up one of my bottles with the river water and cover it with a strip of cloth. Carefully, I pour the water into the other bottle, using the strip of cloth as a rudimentary filter. Too impatient and parched to properly purify the water through boiling, I greedily chug the bottle. My aching stomach yells at me, pleading to be satisfied as well.

The crunching of twigs from the forest catches my attention and I freeze in place. The steps are quiet, careful, and coordinated. I shoot to my feet and whip out my gun from my bag.

"Show yourself!" I demand, aiming my gun at the trees where I heard the noise.

"Don't shoot!" a man calls out, and I watch as Anthony steps out from behind the trees. His hands are up, but after he notices it's me, his face softens. "Jenn?"

"Anthony," I say to myself. He looks different than the last time I saw him. Dirt and blood smear his face and his ripped clothing, which now hangs looser on his thinner body. Exhaustion hangs onto the skin below his eyes, dragging it down into folds cradled by the cheekbones that define his hollowed cheeks. It's hard to see how someone who used to look so strong now look so vulnerable. "Why were you sneaking up on me?"

"I didn't know it was you. I thought you were an undead at first. I just assume everything is an undead out here," he answers, his hands still up. "Are you going to lower the gun now?"

"Oh, yeah, sorry," I stammer, immediately lowering my gun and shoving it in my pants. "It's empty anyway."

Anthony just looks at me for a moment, his lips curled in a small smile. He treks across the shallow river until he meets up with me. I'm about to say something but before I can, he wraps his arms around me, pulling me into a large hug.

"It's so good to see you again, Jenn," he says. "I knew you would make it."

"It's good to see you too," I say back, hugging him. The sensation of his contact is striking. It's been so long since I've had company. "I was…starting to think that no one else was alive out here."

"Me too," he says, finally pulling away from the hug. "After the fire…I was just wandering out here with Kris. I guess I've gotten so used to life in the camp. It's really different being out here on your own, you know?"

"Kris made it too?" I ask quickly.

"Not just Kris," he says, smiling again. "Becky and Charlie, too. Kris and I found them together one day as we were wandering in the woods."

I feel the wave of relief flow throughout my body. My eyes shut, and for a moment, as the tension releases from my muscles, I feel as though I could pass out and collapse right there.

"They're alive," are the only words that I'm able to say. They made it.

"We have a little setup not far from here. I'll show you," he says.

Regaining my bearings, I gather up my materials and shove them into my backpack before hauling it over my shoulder.

"It's not much. It's just temporary, but it was a nice place to stay for a night or two," he says as he leads me through the forest. "It's on a hill and kind of secluded. It would be a great place to set up an actual camp. You know, if we weren't constantly on the move for food. You mind sharing your water, by the way?"

"Not a problem," I say, handing over the bottle.

"Kris is at the campsite right now holding down the fort. Becky and Charlie took off earlier this morning in the opposite direction as I did. We usually travel as a group, but today we decided to split up to look for supplies. We're out of everything, so we're sort of desperate to cover as much ground as possible," he explains. "But we agreed to meet back at the campsite by sundown, so we still have quite some time before they'll be back. I'm sure they'll be happy to see you, though."

"You don't even know what it means to me to hear that you guys all made it," I say. As we walk, I look around for roaming undeads—a habit I've honed since being out here. "It will also be pretty nice to just settle down and feel safe for a night."

"Safe?" he repeats. "I said it was a temporary setup. Jenn, nowhere is safe anymore."

I nod at the brutal truth of his words, and we walk in silence for a bit before he speaks again.

"Have you seen anyone else out here?" he asks quietly.

"No," I say. "It's just been me out here this whole time. I've been trying to find some of the others but…nothing."

"No…bodies?"

"Bella," I confirm, her dying figure branded into my memory. "Back at camp, while it was being overrun, she was surrounded by the undeads. There wasn't anything I could do."

"Oh," he says solemnly.

"Have you seen any…bodies?"

"Nope," he responds. "Becky and Charlie didn't either. I guess that's a good sign."

"Do any of the others know what happened to Xander or Riley?" I ask, glancing nervously at him.

"No," he answers apologetically. "But hey, who knows who else is out there, right? We ran into each other after all this time. Maybe in a few days we'll run into them too."

"They have to be out there," I agree under his breath.

"You know, I thought that with Andrew gone things would actually get better at camp. This island is just one long, never ending nightmare," he says.

"This island isn't forever," I say. "It doesn't have to be. We could leave. It must be almost December by now. I'm not sure where the Graveyard of Boats is, but the shore is just that way. I've been nervous of getting too close to the herd, but a group has a greater chance. You could walk along the treeline until you find the correct spot."

I point, and he nods his head slowly.

"Becky had the same idea. Her, Blake, and Phil are really the only ones that would know the way. That's why we ultimately made our way out here," he says, still staring of through the trees.

"The boat should be coming one of these days," I say.

"Life's just been about finding food ever since the fire. It's crazy to think of leaving," he comments, thinking to himself.

"Crazy," I repeat. "But good. You should head there in the morning."

"You're...not coming?" he asks slowly.

"Not yet," I say. "I need to find Xander and Riley. I'll just keep wandering the forest until I do."

"What if you miss the boat?"

"I don't know," I say. "I'll figure it out. I guess when you get on the boat, don't be in too much of a rush to turn it around. Maybe I'll hop on."

"I'll hang around a bit," he says. I hear him chuckle and find him staring at the floor in front of him. When he notices my staring, he meets my eyes. Like a soft glow, the warmth of his smile pierces through his dreary, mud-splattered exterior. "What if we actually do this? Leave the island."

"Then we'd...have left the island," I respond, returning his smile. There's nothing else to say. We have no idea what the future holds after that and whether it's good or bad. But it needs to happen. "Where's your campsite?"

"Just a little ahead," he answers. "We'll sleep there for the night and then head for the shore in the morning. Blake said it was on the eastern side of the island, right?"

"I think so," I say, looking up at the sun. We'll have to mark where it sets tonight.

"Well, look who finally decided to show up."

The words instantly send shivers down my spine. I know that voice.

Standing not even 30 feet before us is Andrew. Nearly unrecognizable, he has withered to a fourth of his size since the last time I saw him, and his clothes, torn and ripped, hang in grimy shreds off of his body. His eyes bulge out of his face with the intensity of a rabid dog, and two of the teeth in his wicked grin are missing. In his hand, he grips a long machete placed roughly over Kris's pale throat.

"Pleasure to see you again," Andrew says, his smile crazed. "How's the family? Girlfriend? Oh wait, she's right here, two seconds away from spilling the entire volume of her blood on my shoes."

"Get away from her," Anthony demands, his teeth gritting together in anger as he unsheathes his sword. I raise my gun and aim it at Andrew's head. Even though it's empty, it still provides a threat. In Andrew's grasp, Kris weakly struggles for freedom. I hear her whimper Anthony's name as her captor's blade threatens to take her life.

"Drop the weapons," Andrew demands. Behind him, I notice Corinne and Lie, each disheveled miserably and armed with knives of their own.

CHAPTER 38

Riley

I watch patiently from my crouched position in the bushes as a pair of undead hobbles through the forest. Still hiding under the overgrowth, I slowly make my way forward to a tree and stand up, leaning my back against it. Listening to the soft moaning of the closest undead, I track its movements as it passes by my tree, oblivious to my presence. I unsheathe my dagger and stalk it from behind, quickening my speed until I near it. Then, in one swift movement, I thrust my dagger up through the occipital part of the brain with the tip of the blade emerging between the eyes. I pull out the blade smoothly, letting the undead's body fall to the floor.

Hearing the subsequent noise, a second undead looks over, but I'm already behind a new tree. My back following the curve of the trunk, I glide around the tree carefully. As I move, I slide Jack's bow off the quiver on my back along with a clean silver arrow. Then, dragging the string back, I line up the arrow with the undead's head. It wanders mindlessly, unknowingly in my sights, now made the victim by its own prey. I hold my breath to steady my aim and then release the string. With a *twack*, the arrow digs into the brain of the undead.

"You're really enjoying the bow, aren't you?" I hear Blake comment from behind me.

Incidentally, not long after the commencement of our journey to the shore, we had stumbled upon an undead carrying a bow across its body. Blake cut part of the string off, and we tied it to the existing string on Jack's bow, lengthening it and decreasing the tension to fit my strength. It's been three weeks since then, and I've been using it ever since.

"Of course, it's less painful than watching you try to use it," I tease, smiling proudly to myself as I retrieve my arrow and wipe the tip off.

"Ok, I may be mediocre with bows, but you full on suck with guns," he mocks back.

"Mediocre is a strong word," I say, my narrowed eyes complementing the smirk on my lips.

"Anyway," he says, drawing out the word in an over-exaggeration. "I couldn't find any food."

"I found a few berries but that's it," I say, pulling the fruit wrapped in a cloth out of my pocket.

"How's the baby?" he asks, dropping to his knees and shuffling through the dirt.

"Hungry," I say, holding my massive abdomen with both hands. "I should be almost nine and a half months by now."

"That means…"

"I know," I respond quickly.

"Here," he says, pulling a long worm out from the earth and holding it out for me. "Eat this to tide you over."

"If I have any more of those, I'll barf," I say, backing away from the squirming creature.

"You sure?" he asks, watching the insect struggle to free itself from his grasp.

"Yeah, I'm positive," I repeat, popping some berries into my mouth. "I think I still have one or two nutrition pills left."

"Fine, more for me," he says, shrugging before shoving the insect into his mouth.

"We should focus on getting to the shore," I say before placing some of the berries into my mouth. "We wouldn't want to be late. Becky's waiting."

Blake and I have been talking as if we're meeting Becky there. We don't know if she's still alive, or even headed to the shore, but it's a nice thought. It was his idea.

"True," he says, eating another insect and standing back up. He glances up at the sky before pointing up ahead through the trees. "That way. But be careful."

He points off in between the trees, and following his finger, spot a small group of undeads. There's a lot more of these small groups of undeads by the shore. Blake had explained that they're off-shoots from the main herd on shore. It's yet another risk we've been evading.

"Here, this way," he says. Lowering down a little, he leads me a little farther away from the group. "Alright, this should be good. We should be at the Graveyard by the end of the day."

Just then, Blake grabs my shoulder and yanks me a step back.

"Watch it," he mutters, and I follow his gaze to a figure lying not far from my feet. It's another mutilated body.

Its missing most of its abdomen, like Phil, and nearly all the meat has been stripped from the bones of its arms and legs, inhibiting it from getting up and walking. Only one arm is strong enough to weakly stretch out toward me, reaching hungrily with a mutilated hand partially wrapped in dirty bandages.

Most of its skin elsewhere on its body is missing too and what does remain is gray and hangs off in shreds. The man must've been already old with wrinkled skin already weak. Through its torn and trashed clothes, I notice that the lungs are missing, and the heart seems to have been torn out as well, leaving the chest cavity empty behind a collapsed rib cage. Its throat seems to have been gauged out as well. The soft skull is dented and bleeding as if had been trampled. With the strands of muscle still tying the mandible to the rest of the skull, the undead slowly snaps its mouth at me, yearning for one more meal. The rest of the face is thinned out and patchy, allowing its eyeballs to poke out from their sockets so that I could see most of the grayed sphere. With a starving yet desperate look, its gaze shifts quickly back and forth to examine me and Blake.

Blake takes a step forward, but I stop him.

"Wait!" I exclaim, holding up a hand to block his path.

"What?" Blake asks as I drop to my knees, barely out of reach from the undead's grasp.

"I know him," I whisper, still in shock.

"You do?"

"Billy," I respond, still staring at the destroyed body in front of me. "He was the captain that sailed my ship here. He died right in front of me."

"C'mon," Blake says after a moment, extending his hand down to me. "You shouldn't have to see him like this."

"No," I say softly, refusing his hand. I feel a tear well up in my eye, but I immediately lock my jaw to prevent any more. The way this man's death affected me—changed me—is inexplicable. "I can't leave him like this. The only thing worse than being eaten is turning into the monster that ate you, right?"

He nods, unsheathing his dagger.

"I should do it," I say.

"You sure?" he asks, not fully believing me.

"Yeah," I answer hesitantly. I glance back down at Billy's struggling body again and take in a deep breath before jamming my blade in his soft skull. As I slowly pull the knife out, his arm drops limply into the soft dirt and his eyes cease their rapid movements. "There. He's released. Now he can rest properly."

Blake slips his sweatshirt off his waist and lays it down over Billy's small figure, covering his head.

"What are you doing?" I ask in confusion. "You should keep it."

"Nah," he says, shrugging. "I was gonna toss it anyway. In this heat, another layer's the last thing I need. Besides, now it's like he's buried."

He holds out his hand again and this time I grab it, rising to my feet.

"You okay?" he asks.

"I actually feel a little better now," I say, looking down at the body. "At least he's not out there still, wandering around."

He doesn't say anything more. Sometimes, the best thing to say is nothing at all. Blake understands that.

CHAPTER 39

Jenn

"Let her go," Anthony demands again, stepping a little closer to Andrew.

"I wouldn't do that if I were you," Andrew warns, letting out a little chuckle. He stands up straighter and presses his blade deeper into Kris's throat. His forearm inadvertently presses into her bad shoulder, and she winces from the chronic pain of her old wound. "Don't think I won't kill her. Drop the weapons."

"How about I just kill you instead," I threaten.

"With what? An empty gun?" he retorts. His eyes, bulging, jump between Anthony and I with a deranged ferocity. "Yeah, I know what an empty gun looks like. We had them too after we left camp."

"Maybe if you hadn't tried to take over the camp, you wouldn't have had that issue," I reply. This isn't the same Andrew from back at camp. With his smaller, hunched appearance and rapid movements, his presence doesn't hold the same threatening yet controlled dominance that it used to. Rather, his demeanor matches that of a rabid animal, and I'm cautious of the drastic yet impulsive actions he may take. Still, as I look at him after all this time, my resentment floods back.

"The camp was doomed to fail the way it was going. What is a community without a leader?" he says.

"A team," I answer sternly.

"I could've made the place so much better," he says in a low voice.

"You killed people. You *burned* everything down!" I yell, raising my voice inadvertently in my fury, and I feel my fist autonomically clench.

"*I'm* the killer?" he says again, grinning. "Tell that to Patrick and Vincent."

"And Dwayne, Kyle, Noah, Ana...Bella. Just let us go, and we can each go our separate ways," I say, breathing in deep to control my words. "We'll never bother each other again."

"There's only one thing wrong with that idea. It's that I just don't want to. It all became clear when the cemetery caught fire," he begins, and I furrow my brows.

"What are you talking about?" I demand.

"Oh, you don't know?" he taunts, but now he's not smiling anymore. Even in his craze, he can't find humor. He shifts his focus from me to stare down Anthony at my side. "When your little friend over here tore down our sanctuary."

"Anthony, please tell me you didn't…" I begin to mutter, letting my quiet voice trail off. I don't want to have to finish that sentence.

"He set us ablaze first," Lie sneers. "We gave you guys a taste of your own medicine back."

"They were stalking our camp, Jenn, almost every night like a cat waiting to pounce," Anthony exclaims hurriedly, glancing at me quickly before looking back at Andrew. "We weren't doing anything, and I knew it was only a matter of time before these freaks decided to attack."

"Anthony, what did you *do*?" I repeat, fear beginning to settle in.

"I left my post that night and set one of the hedges of the graveyard on fire," he states, and I feel my breathing quicken. He won't look at me. "It was just supposed to threaten them to stand down—"

"You burned down the graveyard? Anthony!" I exclaim, unable to believe my ears.

"They had killed our own people, they shot Kris, and they were coming back for more!" he yells back.

"Oh, and we did," Lie taunts. "As the graveyard burned, we brought the fire to you that same night."

"That's how this started?" I mutter, and I have to run my hand over my face as I process the news.

"When the graveyard burned to the ground," Andrew continues, "and the undead stormed through, they trampled those poor graves. What was that little girl's name? Ana, was it? The dirt was so fresh that when the undead walked over it, it just broke right through—"

"Shut up!" I shout, but he disregards me.

"Last thing I saw, the dirt had already brushed off her little arm," he continues regardless, and his smile returns as his voice gets lower. "I didn't see the rest, but I wouldn't be surprised if the undead…finished what they started."

"Shut up!" I scream again, louder this time as I take a step forward. He quickly responds, and Kris whimpers as he presses his blade deeper into her neck, letting a small trail of blood trickle out.

"Whoops," he quips, greedily watching the blood drip. "I almost got too excited and slashed her neck too soon."

"You don't have to do this," I say. Kris just strains her neck up, and I can see her try to slow her breathing so that her skin stops pressing into the knife.

"You had your revenge. Let Kris go," Anthony says, the muscles in his hands straining as he grips his sword tightly. His eyes lock with Kris'.

"Oh, no. Because I've been waiting you. Even after I destroyed your camp like you destroyed the graveyard, I knew that…I wasn't done. I don't need to kill you for revenge. I *want* to kill you," he shrieks the last part suddenly in a brief fit of instability as his anger boils just beneath the skin and his haunting smile fades.

"Then take me, already. Let the girls go," Anthony pleads, trying to maintain his voice. "This is between you and me."

"It's not," Andrew responds softly, and his face becomes still after the words slip from his lips.

Then, in one strong sweep of his arm, Andrew slices his blade sharply across Kris's neck. The blade drags across its entire length, splitting right through her throat and scraping the bones of her cervical spine. Blood spews out, flooding her neck and pouring onto her shirt. She doesn't even get to scream or even choke on her own blood; she bleeds out almost instantly. Andrew throws her dying body to the floor, and her head, nearly disconnected, flails backward as she falls, spraying blood across the ground.

Anthony yells with rage, charging toward Andrew with his sword outstretched. However, flicking her wrist, Lie hurls a knife through the air. With a thud, it jams into Anthony's chest. Momentum still propelling him ahead, he trips over his feet and collapses forward onto the floor.

Instinctively, I drop to his side. My vision shakes as I help turn his body over onto his back, and when I do, his limp head flops back against the floor. The force of the fall had jabbed the blade deeper than it landed originally. The blood seeps out of his wound, drenching his shirt already. His eyes are squeezed shut, and a vein presses against the thin skin of his forehead, straining to pop out.

"What have you done?" I shout at Andrew.

"What I should've done a while ago," he says, and when I look up at him, he spins his machete in his hand, spraying out drops of Kris' blood. "Anthony burnt the graveyard. But you killed Vincent and Patrick."

He steps closer, and Corinne and Lie tail close behind. I spring to my feet, my heart racing as I unclip my axe.

"I did." My eyes dart between the three of them. As they step closer, I step back. I know I'm outnumbered. I know I can't take them. But Anthony's blood is still wet on my hands and dampens the grip of my axe. "I wonder if you'll cry like they did in their final moments."

"I got Kris, Lie got Anthony, that means...Corinne, you know what you have to do," Andrew taunts, glancing over expectantly at the young girl at his side. She stares up at him, her lips drawn tightly, emotionless. "Time to prove yourself. If not...three is still my lucky number. I would hate to leave today's death count at only a mere two. It just wouldn't feel right."

I continue to inch backwards, maintaining our distance apart, and now Andrew stands above Anthony. Anthony squirms on the dirt, and Andrew leans down above him, taking the moment to bask in the glory of his pain.

I can't spar with Andrew, but if I throw my axe, I can take him out, I plan silently. *Lie will throw a knife. If I can dodge her projectiles, I can take her down. Then, I'll convince Corinne to help me help Anthony. He can still make it. He can still...*

Blood squirts out as Andrew's blade quickly slices across Anthony's throat. His scream shrieks through the air— one of the most vulnerable sounds I've ever heard from one of the strongest men I've ever known. The sound dissipates as soon as it appears and is replaced by stifled gurgles as blood pours through his windpipe and into his lungs.

My eyes are frozen open as I watch the murder that had occurred in such a brief second. Before I have time to process, I raise my axe, gearing up to throw it. Then, from the corner of my eye, I see Lie swing her arm back as well, and I instantly know my plan would fail. Instead, I hurl myself to the side, barely dodging the knife as she throws it. I'm scrambling myself to my feet when I feel the blunt force of a body thrown against me.

The world spins as I tumble down what I imagine must be a hill. Blurs of trees and leaves fly by around me as I fall. Then, I feel a bump and my body flies into the air. With a hard thud, I land on the ground at last.

My whole body aching, I attempt to focus my eyes on the spinning treetops above me, and I moan in pain as I lift myself off the floor. In my clearing vision, I make out Corinne's figure recovering from the fall as well. Having regained my stance first, I charge her, tackling her back down to the ground.

My fist clenched tightly, I swing down on her face, punching her repeatedly as blood flies from her nose and mouth. She manages to block me and rolls me off of her. When I try to get a hold on her again, she quickly unsheathes a short sword. I fly off of her as she swings the blade between us, but she still manages to draw a shallow gash across my collarbone.

"Corinne, I don't want to fight you," I stammer as I scramble to my feet again. "Come *with* me, let's leave Andrew and Lie behind."

With a scream, she lunges at me again. We collide, and I fall back on one knee, holding back her arms that try to complete the swing at the side of my neck. We struggle for dominance as she pushes forward. *I will not die today,* I tell myself, knocking her back with a surge of energy.

She stumbles back but recovers quickly, charging me once again with her weapon raised. When she reaches me, I slide my body sideways, avoiding her attack. Reaching out from behind her now, I take a hold of the guard on the hilt of the sword. Then, modifying a technique that I had learned from the BAA, I snap Corinne's index finger in one swift motion by simultaneously pushing down on her wrist and pulling up on the sword. I push the blade straight for the ground and her broken grip disintegrates, leaving the weapon to easily slip into my own hand.

Still standing behind her, I pull the blade out of her reach before bringing the hilt of it back against the rear of her skull, and she knocks into a nearby tree. When she turns around, there's a trail of blood trickling down from her forehead. I charge toward her and push her back, holding her against the tree. That's when I notice that her arm is now raised up, clutching the hilt of a new dagger and prepared to stab into my neck. Before I can even comprehend my action, I pull back the sword and stab it deep into her abdomen.

Her mouth and eyes wide open, she looks down at only the hilt sticking out from her clothed stomach. Only when her gaze meets mine again does my hand drop from the weapon. Her stance wavers, and I catch her in arms as her strength wanes, bringing her down to lean her back against the tree trunk.

"I was just...surviving," she says painfully, and I stare as her shirt is damped by her own blood. "He would've killed me. I'm…I'm sorry."

"Corinne, I…" I struggle to find the right words but stop when she coughs. Thick blood, having mixed with saliva, drips out of her mouth. I just stare, wide-eyed and frozen in horror at my own actions.

"I would have k-killed you," she struggles to say, wheezing with her words and squeezing her eyes in pain.

"I'm so sorry, Corinne, you didn't deserve this," I say, and suddenly I see the same girl I spoke with while cooking dinner at the camp. I remember her stubborn yearning for free will and her sacrifice for Bharat Kaur, who got to stay at the BAA because of her. She stood up to Andrew for me. She's only 14 years old. "I know that."

“I d-did,” she says, spitting up some more blood. Her voice is calmer now. She doesn’t look like she’s in pain anymore. “Jenn?”

“Corinne…” I begin to say, overcome with sorrow.

“Survive,” she says, struggling to get the word out. Her pleading eyes look up at me, and I nod.

“I’ll try—”

“Kill,” she continues, much to my surprise, “Headmaster.”

Corinne’s eyes become blank as they stare fixated on a point straight ahead.

She’s dead. I killed her.

Suddenly the air thickens around me; I can’t breathe anymore. Riley’s words in ring in my head. *You’re a murderer,* she had said. I choke, unable to move, unable to think as blood continues to leak out of Corinne’s abdomen.

In the silence, I hear the pounding of feet against grass from behind me.

I immediately dodge to the side, and just as I do, a knife flies from behind me and lands in Corinne’s chest where I had been standing. I glance up and see Lie quickly jogging down the steep hill.

Spotting my axe on the grass only a few feet away, I dart over and snatch it up. The full force of another wave of adrenaline fuels my body as I sprint away. Leaves and branches swipe past me, hitting my face and scratching the surface of my skin.

Bloody images of Anthony, Kris, and Corinne flash through my mind; the lives of friends all taken within the last few minutes. As if on a switch, my anger soon returns, replacing any grief. I have to face their killers. They deserve that.

I jolt to a halt and throw myself against a tree. I try to control my panting and swallow my breaths while listening to the sound of rustling leaves approaching. Lie’s running footsteps become louder until finally, I hear her approach my tree. I kick my foot out into her path, and almost immediately as I do so, I feel a stinging pain hit my ankle at full force. Lie trips over, sliding face down in the thin layer of dirt that covers the rocky ground. I leap onto her small body and throw her face back into the ground. Her hand swings around lmk I’m and reaches for my face, latching onto my neck to dig her nails in. In my attempts to shake her, my grip loosens slightly, and she turns her body around to face me, revealing her now sliced up skin from the sharp edges of the rocks below her.

She releases her grip on my neck and I deliver a punch straight into her nose, causing her head to fly back again into the ground again. A trail of blood flings from her nose when I punch her a second time. When I raise my fist for a third rage-filled punch, her hand strikes out right into my neck. As I gasp for air, she hoists her legs up from behind, wrapping them around my torso. Lurching her body to the side, she drags me to the ground off of her and quickly slides the rest of her body on top of me now to pin me down.

Before she can throw her first punch, I knock away her fist and strike at her instead. Both of her hands shoot up to her face, and, taking advantage of her moment of weakness, I shove her off me. She staggers to her feet and backs away a little. I get on my feet as well and unlatch my axe from my belt again.

Her expression beams with loathing, and I raise a coy eyebrow in return. She whips out a short dagger from her belt.

She charges forward toward me, but before she reaches me, she hurls herself into a spinning kick towards my head. Evading the strike, I grab her ankle mid-air and throw it to the ground, and the rest of her body follows, collapsing in front of me. However, she instantly springs back up, slicing her dagger at me in a series of vicious strikes. I dodge her quick movements and, calculating a brief break in her movements, take a swing with my axe. When she dodges, I swing the axe back up in an uppercut. She just barely manages to maneuver her body out of the way, with the very edge of the blade nicking a cut through her shoulder. She disregards it, though, taking advantage of my now undefended abdomen with another kick that lands its target this time.

I attempt to take her out again with my axe, but she avoids it again, and this time, she pounds the back of my wrist. Her hit strikes a nerve and my grip weakens, causing her second hit, this time with the hilt of her knife, to free the weapon from my grasp. My axe clatters to the ground by our feet. I swing with my other hand, which snags her eye and makes her head whip to the side. Sequentially, I knee her in the stomach, and she staggers back a little, hunching over. Using the increased distance between us, I jump slightly, snapping my leg up into a high kick to her face.

Lie falls to the ground, but before I can make a follow up attack, she sweeps her leg and knocks me to the floor as well. My back hits the ground with a hard thud just a foot or two below where my axe still lies on the rocks. I'm about to reach up for it, but she leaps onto me, pinning me down. I try to move my hands, but my right hand is trapped underneath her knee and my left one is being held down by her right hand. Larger and heavier, her weight along with her strong hold defeats my resistance. I try to lift my legs, but she sits on my hips so that my limited range of motion is useless.

The world seems to go in slow motion as she raises her knife and stabs it into my abdomen. A searing pain shoots through me and, though I know my eyelids explode wide open and my gaze swings overhead into the canopy above me, I don't seem to be looking at anything at all. It's as if I shut off an active interpretation of my sight. After a moment, however, it returns, and I'm looking out through glossy eyes, watching her smirk in satisfaction. I'm not breathing either, my entire body having instantly and subconsciously locked up as to resist grinding my entrails against the sharp edges of the blade piercing them.

Time seems all but frozen until she suddenly yanks the knife out again. This time, I let out a whimper of agony, nearly lurching up off the ground in rhythm with the movement. She stabbed me, and now I'm on a timer. I don't want to look down and see the wound. I know what it should look like, but I just can't imagine it on myself.

Lie just sits on top of me, continuing to restrain me. She wants to wait for me to bleed out. I writhe underneath her body, thrusting my torso upwards toward her, trying to escape but she pushes my weakened body down. At last, I give in to temptation and crane my neck to look down where blood pools over my stomach and stains my shirt crimson.

Suddenly, a gunshot blasts through the forest. Lie's head whips to the side in the direction that the sound came from. Her eyes scan the trees, searching for an enemy.

I don't think. I don't have time. With her distracted, I swipe my hand from beneath her grasp and bring it immediately up above my head to grip onto the cool and familiar rubber-padded handle of my axe. By the time she returns her focus to me, it's too late.

Lurching my torso off the ground with my swing, I bring the axe through the air over me. With a cry, I slam the axe down at an angle into the crease between her shoulder and neck. The sharpened blade slices through flesh and muscle and snaps through her clavicle. Her body collapses to the side in the motion of my swing, and her scream, like Anthony's, lasts only a brief moment as the blood spilled from her chopped vessels releases everywhere, clogging her lungs.

Lie's lifeless body now lies to my right. From her drenched torso to the splashes that reached her forehead, she is covered in her own bright blood that continues to cascade out of her wound and pool around us both. The woman that had yielded so much power over my life just a moment ago is now just a crumpled heap of a person. Her eyes, open, stare blankly ahead of her.

I feel the sweat bead down my forehead. Through shaky eyes, I watch as rich red blood leaks out quickly from the wound on my stomach. A surge of agonizing pain engulfs my body, holding me hostage. I want it to stop so badly, to give up, to die.

I hear the sharp firing of bullets dampen as they get further and further away until the sound stops altogether. I know the undeads would be lured in by the gunshots. Thoughts spin rapidly through my head. I need to get out of here. I need to patch up my wound. I will die if I don't.

Swallowing back the piercing pain stemming from my abdomen, I begin dragging my body backwards out of the rocky clearing and into the crowded overgrowth of the forest nearby. Smears of blood, a mix of my own and Lie's, lingers along the ground as my dampened clothes tug across the jagged rocks beneath me. My outstretched hand wavers in the air as I reach to touch the trunk of a nearby tree. I attach my axe back to my waist and haul myself to my feet. Behind me, the blood around Lie continues to grow, running in streams between the rocks in the ground. Her body remains motionless...mutilated.

"Help!" I try to call out but my voice cracks before I can finish the word. Andrew didn't have a gun, which means whoever is shooting must be someone else. Becky was supposed to be back by sundown. If she heard the screams and came back with Charlie early, they could have encountered Andrew.

I stumble further into the forest, one hand clutching my wound as I try to make my feet move as quick as my darting eyes.

Just then, I drop exhaustedly to my knees. I bite my lip as I look down at my dampened shirt, the thick blood molten and sticky as it runs over my hands. Trying not to stretch my wound too much, I slowly pull off my shirt. I examine my stomach briefly, using my shirt to smear away the mess of blood. I can see the clear slit in my skin where the knife had penetrated my body. The cut is only visible for a second before blood begins to pulsate out of it again. I blink back the water in my eyes, trying to clear my vision. Then, I fold my shirt up along the long end to create a long cloth and tie it around my stomach as a bandage.

"Jenn! Jenn!" The voice sounds far off, but a face immediately appears in my line of sight, partially blocking the sunlight sneaking in between the trees. It's Xander. I didn't realize I'd lied down. "Jenn, you have to stay with me. Just stay awake. I'm going to help you."

"X-Xander," I stammer exhaustedly.

"What happened?" he asks quickly, and his hands press down on my abdomen, applying pressure to my wound. I cry out as the pain sears through me.

"Lie stabbed me," I respond, taking a moment to swallow hard and blink open my eyes again. "Removed it at...an angle. It's not that bad, though."

"It's ok, I got it," Xander reassures as he begins working at the knot I'd made in my impromptu bandage.

"It didn't hit my abdominal…aorta or the vena cava o-or anything important or else I would be..." I continue through a few rapid breaths, "…be dead."

"Jenn, you're ok, stay with me," he pleads, tearing himself away from my abdomen to look into my drifting eyes. He places a hand to my cheek.

"Anthony…Kris. They d-didn't make it," I stammer.

"We're going to make it," he says quietly. He reaches over to his bag and hands me off a canteen of water. The cool sensation reaches my lips, and I try to refrain from guzzling the entire bottle. He yanks out a sweatshirt from his bag as well.

"Changing the bandage?" I ask, straining my neck up to watch him.

"Yours is too bloody and thin. My jacket will work better," he responds. He brings a hand to my shoulders and presses me gently back to the ground. "Don't move."

"Just make sure you tie it better than how you used to at the BAA," I tease. This catches him off guard, and he involuntarily lets out a chuckle.

"C'mon, I crushed you during the trauma unit," he teases back as his hands untangle his sweatshirt and fold it into a bandage.

"You wish," I scoff back.

"This will hurt," he mutters, and I take in a deep breath. He removes my bandage to expose my wound again. The release of pressure allows my skin to expand and the edges of the wound separate again, sending a wave of pain through me.

"Felt worse," I say, grinding my teeth in efforts to absorb the pain without moving.

He tilts his canteen, pouring water over my throbbing abdomen. The sting of the water causes me to cry out, and I squeeze my eyes shut only to throw my eyelids open again.

With one hand holding my balled-up shirt against my wound, he fumbles with his bag.

"It's honey," he explains briefly, pulling out a small sac made from a large leaf tied closed by a small vine. "Mixed with some herbal anesthetic Bella made. It will help prevent infection. Bella gave it to me when my leg was injured, but I never used it."

He pours more water on my stomach and washes away blood with the rag of my shirt once more. I squeeze my eyes shut again as he opens the delicate confines of the sac and drips some of the thick golden liquid into my wound. It's then that I notice that the searing pain is fading.

"Hey," he says suddenly. Reluctantly, I flick my eyes open again. "Anyone ever tell you that you look great without a shirt?"

When he says it, he cracks a smile, and it forces me to let out the breath of an exhausted chuckle. As quick as his smile came, though, it disappears. His hands work fast on bandaging my abdomen; that's his focus.

"Oh, shut up, King Loser," I mutter, and though he looks away from me, I still stare, mesmerized by the presence of the man I had been searching for in the forest all this time. The sunlight breaks haphazardly through the canopy behind him. He has dirt smeared on his jaw and small cuts on his neck presumably from passing overgrowth, and I wonder how the past month has been for him after the fire. I've never been happier to see him.

"I was looking for you," I say softly, staring up at him.

"I was looking for you, too," he responds, and for a moment, we share a gaze. I don't think I've ever noticed that his eyes aren't completely black, but now I make out the thin brown ring lining his pupil. Has it always been like that? "I wanted to start searching for the spot on the shore with the boats, and so I started heading here. I came across Becky and Charlie a few hours ago. When we heard yelling this way, we came as quick as we could."

"What are the odds," I mutter, shaking my head a little and my vision wobbles as I do so.

"I wish I found you sooner," he says back, biting his lip.

I let my eyes wander up to the sky above me. As I stare through the leaves to the blue sky beyond, my smile fades away again.

"I killed Lie and Corinne."

He doesn't respond immediately, and my eyes are drawn back down to him. He's biting his lip again.

"I killed Vincent."

He doesn't console me. He doesn't tell me that it's what needed to be done. He doesn't tell me that it won't still haunt me, either. Yet, with just that one phrase, he is telling me that and more; he understands what it feels like to take a life.

"I wanted to say yes…when you asked me if I felt something for you," I say, and he freezes. "I still do."

I return my stare to the sky. All of my muscles feel numb now. The clouds peaking through the canopy begin to mold together into blobs as I blink through blurry eyes. The leaves enlarge and fall out of focus.

"Jenn, stay with me!" Xander yells, startled, and I suddenly notice that he's leaning directly over my face again.

In my delirium, I see his dark eyes flick worriedly over my face. He's mouthing something, but the forest is too loud as it buzzes loudly in my head. I want to say something back, but I'm so tired; I can't muster the energy. As I look up at him, his head becomes three in my vision. Behind him, the light of the sun overhead shines brighter, and shapes become harder to distinguish. I don't even remember closing my eyes.

CHAPTER 40

Riley

There's a shot in the distance, quiet but still audible to a vigilant ear. Freezing, I look over at Blake, and we both wait in silence, listening.

"There was only one," I remark. As if on cue, there's another shot, this time a little farther away. I look toward the new direction, and a few more shots echo in the forest, one after the other. "It's only one gun. Who do you think it is?"

Ignoring me, he keeps his ears peeled to the forest. "It stopped."

All of a sudden, a dull pain sears in my lower back and I lurch backwards slightly.

"Are you ok?" Blake asks, though he already knows the answer. I've been having these pains every now and then recently, and he asks me if I'm alright every time.

"I think the gunshot startled my uterus," I joke, cringing as the pain gradually subsides.

"This one seems worse," Blake says again.

"It's fine. We have to go," I state, nodding my head in the direction of the gunfire. "They're in trouble."

He nods, and we immediately begin heading off. After some jogging, I hear a shout and come to a halt, causing Blake to run into me. It's a call for help.

"That way!" I exclaim, pointing in the direction I heard the cry. In preparation, I whip an arrow out of my quiver and notch it in the bow.

Undeads begin appearing, attracted to the noise as well. I thrust my small dagger forward and stab one of the undeads in front of me straight through its eye. Blood splashes back at me as I whip my dagger out, and I continue running, stabbing another one on my way. Blake does the same, knocking down an undead as he follows on my heels. Finally, we stumble upon a group of undeads tightening a huddle around…

"Xander!" I exclaim reflexively.

He lashes out with his sword, slicing the head off one of the undeads and then swings it around again to slay another. When he looks over at me, his face goes white— the look of someone who has just seen a ghost. My gaze, however, shifts to fixate on Jenn's limp body, which lies at his feet. Taking advantage of Xander's stupor, an undead comes up from behind him, latching onto his arm.

Blake is already charging forward, and in an instant, he's over there. Grabbing the undead's shoulders from behind, he hauls it off Xander and drives his blade straight through the back of its skull. The bloody tip pierces out of the monster's gruesome mouth, and its body freezes, dead at last.

My path is blocked by an undead, and I strike out with a kick to its stomach. With its frail legs stripped nearly clean of muscle, the undead doubles over and stumbles backward, unable to muster up the strength or coordination to maintain balance. I smash the butt of my knife against the side of the undead's head, and its weak body finally tumbles over. Only hesitating to take in a deep breath, I raise my foot and bring it back down on its soft, decaying skull. Blood spews out, gushing onto the floor from where its face caves into its head.

Xander stabs his sword through the abdomen of another nearby undead. Then, in one swift movement, he yanks the sword out and swings it back to chop off its head. Another one comes up from behind him, and I quickly pull back the string of my bow. Just as the undead is about to reach Xander, I release an arrow and the streak of silver soars through the air, spearing the undead through the temple.

"What happened?" Blake asks hastily, indicating Jenn's body.

Bright red blood heavily stains the skin around where a sweatshirt is tied over her abdomen. Her crumpled body lies without the strength and vigor with which she always stood. Her axe now hangs off Xander's waist. I keep waiting for her to open her eyes and spring to her feet to fight with us. *Just open your eyes, Jenn,* I command silently.

"She was stabbed," Xander quickly explains, glancing around at the nearing undeads. His mind is spinning. "I fixed up the wound and carried her as far as I could before—"

Xander's cut off by an undead reaching for him. He strikes the beast with his elbow and then steps back to swing his sword, chopping its head clean off.

"Undeads," he finishes his thought. "We have to get out of here…"

I drop to my knees beside Jenn. Then, with a shaky hand, I reach out to touch her pale neck. Her skin is so cold. This is what I must've looked like when I tried to commit suicide. This is what I put them through: uncertainty. "She has a pulse."

"The Graveyard of Boats is right up ahead," Blake states hurriedly, turning around to keep an eye on the undeads beginning to close in around us. One steps toward him and Blake strikes forward, stabbing his blade into the beast's eye.

"Becky and Charlie are out here, too," Xander says, a pained expression on his face as he stares down at Jenn, who's barely clinging on to life. "I lost them when we ran into Andrew back at their campsite."

"Becky and Charlie?" I repeat, perking up.

"Becky, Charlie, go to the shore!" Blake calls out. Then, he scoops Jenn into his arms. "We have to go. Riley, gotta guard my back, ok?"

"Y-yeah," I stutter, shaking as I watch Jenn's unmoving body. I try to swallow, but my mouth feels as if it's been drained and filled with cotton.

"Don't worry about her," he orders. He's already beginning to jog away. "Just guard my back, got it?"

"Got it," I respond, sharing a glance with Xander before following after Blake.

The three of us begin heading away from the growing crowd of undeads. Xander runs to the front, striking down stragglers that appear in front of us and clearing any overgrowth for us to maneuver through. I stay close to Blake, slaying undeads that near too close. With Blake carrying Jenn and me managing my pregnant belly, our pace is not much faster than a light jog.

"Riley!" I hear Blake call out my name. I swing around and find him attempting to fend off an undead that had jumped out of the trees from his side. It grabs him by the shoulders, attempting to bite him as he pulls in the opposite direction.

I aim my arrow at the scene, trying to steady my hands as Blake struggles against the undead's grasp. I know the arrow could hit either one of them, maybe even Jenn. There's no time to think.

Just shoot.

I take in a deep breath before releasing the string. The undead's head whips to the side as the arrow tears through its brain.

"Thanks," he murmurs, staring at me in surprise. After a moment of hesitation, he begins wiping the blood splatter off his face with his shoulder and readjusting his hold on Jenn. "You could've shot me."

"But I didn't," I remark, to which he just smirks. "That's why you gave *me* the bow, remember?"

"I think we're getting close," Xander announces from only a few paces in front of us.

Blake and I follow him as fast as we can, desperate for our destination. My throat burns as I run, and I'm panting, but I make sure not to fall behind.

"I sm—smell it," I say in between heavy breaths, clutching my bulging belly. The strong stench of the beach fills my nose, and I'm reminded of the day that Billy died. Jenn, Xander, Jack, and I were running with him through the forest back to the shore. We were terrified, disorganized, and naive of how truly horrifying things would become here. We're different now. And though Jenn is now the injured one that we are shuttling through the trees, I think she would be proud of how far we've come.

As the beachy stench grows stronger, we finally burst out onto the sand. The sun's bright rays strike my eyes, and I recoil a little. However, despite the searing brightness and the reeking smell of the seaweed, the warmth of the shore greets us, inviting a sense of accomplishment. The air opens up too, allowing my lungs to breathe without the clutter of the forest smothering me.

I drop to my knees out of exhaustion. The others stop as well, allowing a moment for me to recuperate. The pain in my lower abdomen and lower back burns, and I squeeze my eyes to get through it.

"Riley, is something wrong?" Xander asks worriedly.

"Cramping pretty bad, but I'll be fine," I explain quickly through my labored breaths.

When my eyes adjust to the bright sunlight, I realize the length of the sand between the forest and the rocks is much greater than where our boat had wound up all those months ago. But despite the distance, footsteps from the herd of undeads still make depressions in it all over. Like the shore our boat had washed up on, blending into the edge of the plain of sand are dark rocks. They're small at first but gradually increase in size and number until the sand ends and all that's left are the rocks protecting the shoreline from the sea. The scattered rocks fade into still water, which extends out nearly 300 feet before ending in a second jagged stretch of rocks that make up a second layer of barrier rocks.

"The Graveyard of Boats. It's like a lagoon," I mutter, finally regaining my breath, and I stand back up. Looking down the shoreline, I can tell that the two rows of rocks continue in parallel lines until being bookended by cliffs that jet out from the mainland and hang over the water.

"Where are the wrecked boats?" I ask as we continue to walk down the sand.

"Sunk. They hit the far rocks and can't get past. The water over there is deep so they plummet out of sight," he explains. When we reach the first conglomeration of large rocks at the end of the sand, we stop. Blake climbs onto a formation of rocks that form an even bed and lies Jenn's body down. "We have to keep moving. We're just sitting ducks if we stay on the beach. We bought time by running ahead, but we're not in the clear. The undeads are gonna keep wandering in the direction they last saw their food. They're coming."

"A boat should be coming any day now," I say.

"We could camp out on a cliff," Xander offers. "We would have a great vantage point to watch for boats, and we'd be close enough to come back to shore."

"We could get cornered by the undead too easily if the herd notices us," Blake counters.

"If we stay near the treeline, we could keep an eye out for a boat and duck deeper into the forest for food or when the herd floats by," I propose.

"She's waking up," Xander suddenly exclaims. I rush to his side and sure enough, while she lies on her back with limbs spread out on the rocks, Jenn's eyes begin to flutter back open. I instantly clasp her hand with both of mine, but Blake roughly pushes me away.

"Hold on," he warns.

"She wasn't bit," Xander insists, appearing on the other side of Blake, but he blatantly ignores him. I steal a hesitant glance at him.

"You did a full body check? Examined her head to toe? No," Blake grumbles at Xander.

After checking Jenn for a pulse, Blake steps back and nods at me. I throw myself forward again, clasping Jenn's hand and bringing it close to my chest.

"Oh, Jenn," Xander breathes through his lips, throwing the back of his hand against his forehead.

"You did good, kid," Blake remarks, hitting a heavy hand against Xander's back.

Jenn's eyes sluggishly move from Blake's face to mine before finally landing on Xander's. Her lips separate, and we all watch anxiously, waiting for her to say something. Then, her lips close again and, to our relief, curl into a small smile.

"Jenn," Xander mutters through his breath again, letting out another sigh. One hand holding her cheek and the other touching her shoulder, he leans close and lets his eyes take in the view of Jenn's smile.

"Not to ruin the mood, but we ain't got all day," Blake says. "The undeads are gonna catch up soon."

"W-where's Becky? And Charlie?" Jenn croaks, glancing around. Her voice is soft and groggy.

"Jenn…I lost them when I came for you," Xander says, struggling to find the right words.

"They had to have made it," she states, her weary face looking desperate. "Lie and Corinne are both dead. They can handle Andrew. Does anyone know what happened to Phil?"

"He didn't make it," Blake answers, anxiously glancing into the forest of darkness behind him.

"Anthony and Kris didn't make it either," she replies, rubbing her eyes as she awakens from delirium. "Or Bella."

"We could split up," Xander says. "Half of us go back into the forest to look for Becky and Charlie. The other half stays here to look out for a boat. If one arrives, we secure it and wait for the others."

"It's risky," Blake says. "Jenn's in no shape for a fight, so it's just us three. We can't send someone back into the forest alone because we don't know what we're up against with the undeads in there or Andrew. Especially if Becky isn't alive to help."

"I could stay and protect Jenn on the shore. You and Riley could go back for Becky," Xander says.

"Riley's 9.5 months pregnant," Blake states firmly. "It's too risky out there for her with all the undead, especially if we run into Andrew. And if she goes into labor, then she's down for the count and will need help and protection. We can't risk that in the middle of a battle in the woods."

"You're due soon?" Jenn asks me, and I nod stiffly.

"Besides, the shore is a hive for undeads, we can't leave someone here alone to defend themselves and Jenn, especially if she needs help walking in an escape," Blake continues.

"There's no way to split us up that keeps us all safe for all the possibilities that could happen," I say, finishing his point. "We're only strong when we all stick together."

"Look!" Xander suddenly shouts, pointing out to the sea.

We all turn our heads on command and there...there it is. Along the horizon a tiny sail juts out of the water.

"The boat," I mumble quietly, disregarding the might of the sun's bright rays as I stare in disbelief at the approaching ship. I breathe out a laugh. Silence among the others prompts me to turn to them. Everyone's just staring, dumbfounded by the actual impending reality of escape.

"We could…leave," Xander murmurs mostly to himself, cupping his hand over his eyes to get a better view and make sure it's not a mirage.

"C'mon, let's go," Blake grunts, taking the first strides across the rocks.

"Wait!" Jenn protests, weakly. "What about the others?"

"There's no time. If we don't reach that boat soon, then it's gonna crash. We'll be stuck here," Blake explains as he quickens his pace to a jog. The rest of us help Jenn onto her feet. Xander slips off his shirt and helps Jenn climb into it so that she can cover up.

"Becky and Charlie are our team," Jenn says, wrapping an arm around Xander for support. "We can't go without them. I know there's risks, but I like the idea of Xander's plan. We should split up now. There must be a way to divide us that makes sense."

Blake spins around but the momentum of his run keeps his body going as he backpedals away from us.

"Charlie's just a kid. He could still be alive," I call up to him. Blake takes one quick glance back at the distant boat before jogging back toward us. When he gets closer, I continue. "What if I was the one back there left behind?"

"You think I don't know that? You don't think it's killing me?" he responds quickly. "The boat is right there. I don't even believe it, but it's *right* there. You said you were going to get your baby off this island. I'm not letting you risk that. Jenn's injured, too. You both need the food and medical supplies on that boat."

"I'm no more important than Becky and Charlie," Jenn states.

"We catch the boat," Blake insists. "But once we catch it, we put down the anchor. We wait for the others. We'll be out at sea, so we'll be safe if the herd comes by."

"They may not come. Becky may not want to risk running into more undead while she's alone with Charlie. Especially if she's injured from Andrew," I say. "Some of us will go back to look for them. We'll recruit the cadets on board for help."

"That's a good idea," Jenn agrees, but we both know that I'm not offering a suggestion; I'm laying out the plan.

"Let's hope the newbies are cooperative," Blake remarks.

"I'm on board," Xander says.

"Me too," Blake says with a nod. "But if we don't actually *get* on board now, then we're all stuck here."

With that, we all begin our trek across the rocks, hopping from stone to stone. As the rocks become sparse, we enter the shallow water. The current has pushed most of the sand toward us, fortunately creating a rather large sandbar for us to walk on. At some points the water comes up past our shoulders, but most of the time it only reaches our waists. Xander carries Jenn for the majority of the distance, trying his best to keep her wound above the water; though, eventually Blake has to take over. I lag behind, gradually losing the ability to pull my body through the water. It feels as if the liquid around us had morphed into gelatin. My only refuge is that under the hot sun, the cool water washing against my reddened skin feels refreshing.

It's Blake that first notices the undeads behind us. Breaking through the treeline, a swarm begins spilling out onto the shore. They're following the food they saw in the forest.

My eyes trained on the nearing boat on the horizon, I power through. Finally, I lay my hand onto the slick surface of a rock jutting out of the water: the second barrier of rocks.

"We beat the boat," Xander announces proudly as we climb onto the lined up piles of rocks.

Made of imperfect wood and with its off-white sails flapping sloppily in the wind, the boat rises out of the water much less than majestically. It's nearly 20 yards in front of us.

"So, this is…this is it," I say, astonished. Once on a stable portion of the platform, I drop to my knees in exhaustion. The distinctive pain in my back returns, and I wince as it travels around my waist. Watching the boat sail in front of us, I could almost feel the cabin's muggy atmosphere. I've never been more excited to lie down on the scratchy mattress.

"Hey!" Blake calls out, waving his arms in the air. "Hey asshole, over here!"

Everyone begins calling out to the boat, waving their arms in hopes of catching the captain's attention. Amide their yells, however, I turn around to glance back at the approaching undeads still making their way through the water. It's worse than I expected. The full force of the herd has now descended on the beach, either pouring out of the forest or appearing from down the shore to my left.

"Wait guys, there's someone in the water," I exclaim, my small voice overpowered by their excited screaming. I have to cup my hands over my eyes to get a better view of the small figure in the distance. "I think it…it could be Becky!"

The others all turn around at this. Visible as a mere dot at the head of the swarming herd, Becky is running through the shallow water. Another hulking human figure runs behind her: Andrew. They must've emerged from the empty trees to my right and cut in front of the undeads.

"Where's Charlie?" Jenn says, the panic becoming clear in her voice as she scans the frontline of the approaching horde.

The undeads' prison jumpsuits make them combine visually into a sea of orange that covers the shore and melts into the water. Piles of bodies gather as the undeads fall off the rocks and into the shallow water. Their bodies create a ramp that eases the transition of elevation for the rest of the swarming undeads to use.

"I'm going back," Jenn announces, pulling away from Xander, who just grabs her shoulders and helps guide her to the floor.

"No, you're in no condition to do that. I'll go," he says, unsheathing his long sword. He detaches Jenn's axe from his belt and hands it over to her before walking over to where the rocks meet the shallow water.

"Riley, Jenn, hold up the boat," Blake instructs.

"You're going back too?" I ask.

"They're alive. I'm gonna make sure it stays that way," he responds quickly, and I nod. "Have the cadets on the boat help you and Jenn. Don't shy from giving out orders, I know you can. And if something happens or it gets too risky—"

"Don't say that—"

"Take the boat and get off the island. Save yourself and your baby—"

"Nothing's going to happen, Blake—"

"You heard me," Blake barks louder this time, beginning to step toward the edge of the rocks. He's taking in a deep breath. I'm releasing one.

"You heard *me*," I respond earnestly, my sweet voice forced into a bark like his. He hesitates for a second before hopping into the water with Xander. "Stay alive. And come back with Becky. We'll be here when you do."

I force myself to turn back around to the small ship as the boys run off.

"They have to put down the anchor," I tell Jenn, while watching the ship dangerously near the jagged rocks straggling out at sea. I call out to it. "The anchor! Put down the anchor!"

"Put down the anchor!" Jenn yells, standing up to join me.

No response. The boat continues to head toward the rocks.

"He can't move from the steering wheel if he's attached to it like Billy," I say. "Steer left! Towards our voice!"

"He won't make it," Jenn says, and I hear her breath becoming more rapid. "He's too close."

"Steer towards our voice! You're going to hit the rocks!" I call out again.

"Can't he see the rocks? He could've avoided this," Jenn remarks, frustrated. "That boat is the one chance we have, and the captain can't steer properly."

I place a hand on her shoulder, but she smacks it away. She's too riled up.

"Don't you want to live! Come here, goddammit!" Jenn yells frantically out to the captain, and I have to hold her back as she nears the edge of the rocks.

"Jenn, hold on," I warn, stepping in front of her to block her path.

"We won't just lose our boat, it'll be another captain dead if it sinks!" she exclaims, gesturing wildly out to sea. "Just like Billy. Dead without a chance to live."

Holding her mouth just slightly ajar, she shifts her gaze from the boat to me. She brushed his death off when it happened. Yet, as we share a look now, I see a girl who has never truly gotten over it.

"Maybe he's blind," I state, abruptly turning my attention back to the boat. "Look, he's got bandages all wrapped around his head. Must've been a part of his torture. The fabric muffles his ears, and the wind and the flapping sails drown out our screams. To him, it's like we're not here."

"Then how the *heck* did he sail here?" she says in exasperation.

"I don't know…if you don't need vision to sail here, the route must be an easy straight line…which means the boat never goes through the winds and waves of deep waters," I comment, expressing the thoughts as they come to mind. "Jenn, I think Headmaster has been exaggerating the distance between here and the BAA."

"So, we don't try to swim back or build a raft when our boat inevitably crashes," she says, finishing my thought.

The ship continues to sail, veering to its right and giving us a view of its side. I watch anxiously as it narrowly glides past some of the scattered rocks.

CHAPTER 41

Jenn

I hear the sound of a clip and turn to Riley just in time to see her raise up her bow, pulling the string back. Her eyes narrow in focus as she follows the boat, keeping it in her sights.

"What are you doing?" I ask in a haste.

My eyes dart between her and the boat, now nearing closer to another large rock emerging from the surface of the water. As I watch the boat, though, blackness begins to close in on the outskirts of my vision. I know this feeling of lightheadedness, but adrenaline continues to surge through my veins, making my senses jittery and keeping me on my feet.

Riley holds her aim for a good twenty seconds, trying to perfect her shot before she lets go. She sends the arrow soaring, and I follow it with my eyes as it flies narrowly past the back of the ship. Nearby, I spot the anchor tied to the rear of the ship by a rope.

"Dammit," Riley mumbles to herself. Without wasting any more time, she pulls out another arrow and notches it into place. "If we could cut the rope, we could let the anchor loose and stop the boat."

"You do your thing, Riley," I say, trying to soften her hastened voice while taking a glance over at the boat. She doesn't move at first until I return her gaze and nod. "You got this."

She slides out another arrow from her quiver. Then, adjusting her stance slightly, she takes in a few breaths to steady her arm and aim at the boat again. She lets go of the string, and with a snap, the arrow flies and the anchor instantly drops from the ship into the water. We both watch anxiously as the ship continues on until finally the anchor's chain tightens, and the ship halts to a stop.

"You did it," I say, smiling with relief.

"I…did," Riley mutters back.

Andrew has already caught up with Becky, their figures closer and much more visible now. It's then that I notice that she carries something in her arms: Charlie. Andrew launches himself at her, and she staggers under his weight, dropping Charlie's small body as she collapses into the water. Andrew raises himself up a little before falling back down on top of her with a punch. Her head is thrown downwards under water, and he scrambles to his feet. Then, a realization hits me.

"He's not trying to kill her, he wants to slow her down. He's going to use her as bait for the undead," I say out loud to Riley. "He wants the boat."

I see Becky grab onto his pants, but he just kicks her off and begins running toward us, but by now, Blake and Xander have reached them.

Blake, charging, collides with him. In the thigh-high water, Blake holds Andrew's head down for a few seconds before letting him go and running back to help Becky. Andrew lifts his head out of the water, gasping for air, but as soon as he does, he is met with an uppercut punch from Xander. He then instantly thrusts the butt of his sword into the side of Andrew's face, knocking the man's weakened body back into the water.

Blake pulls Charlie out of the water and cradles the young boy in his arms. Xander runs toward them, swinging his sword at some approaching undeads and reddening the water as he slices their heads off. With Becky and Charlie weak, their speed is hindered and on par with the undeads hot on their tail.

"We're going to have to swim," I tell Riley, turning my attention back to the boat. "We have to secure the boat and get help for them."

"Are you sure you can swim?" she asks, biting her lip, and I nod hastily. "Alright, let's go."

I hop into the water first, sinking down beneath the surface briefly. Immediately, a sharp sting sears through my abdomen as the saltwater rushes into my wound. I cry out, but my words are swept away in bubbles that rise to the surface without me. I open my eyes briefly to gather my surroundings, and I see all of the underwater mounds that make up the rock formations that we stand on. Unlike the sand bar on the other side of the rock barrier, the water on this side is much deeper. From underneath the water, the rock barrier appears as a steep cliff that overlooks the ruins of dozens of ships at its base. Scattered wood and torn sails drift amongst the larger ships, covered in the flora of the ocean.

Riley follows me into the water and together, both with great difficulty, we paddle through the sea, keeping our heads above the water. I help support her, nervous that the extra weight on her stomach will tire her out and that I'll lose her to the deepening water. At the same time, though, I bite down on my lip as I try to hide the pain of my wound and the feeling of it shearing against my sweatshirt-bandage with each movement I make.

When at last we reach the anchored ship, I help Riley onto the adjacent rock formation that it had nearly collided with.

"Hey! Someone!" I yell upwards to the deck. The ledge isn't too high above our heads. If I were to climb on Riley's shoulders, I could reach it and pull myself up— but I don't think either of us are in the proper physical condition for that right now. "Let down the rope ladder!"

"We're not here to hurt you!" Riley calls out from beside me. "We need help!"

"Let down the rope ladder!" I yell again, clutching my abdomen as I exert myself.

Suddenly, the face of a young girl peers over the ledge.

"Cadet Bellator?" she asks, astonished and her eyes wide open. She has fire-bright red curls pulled back into a tight bun and wears a Level 1 shirt. Her soft features give away her youth; she must only be about 13 years old. Her eyes trail down to my stomach where dried blood stains my makeshift bandage. "What happened? What's going on?"

"Help us up!" I command again, startling her. She fumbles with the rope ladder for a bit before dropping it down in front of us. I let Riley climb aboard first and follow closely behind. Finally on the deck, I am swamped with the eerie memories of our own ship that brought us here.

"What's happening over there in the water? Who are all of those people?" the girl asks frantically.

"Look, we'll need to turn this ship around and head straight back to the—" Riley starts to say.

"Oh my god, you're pregnant!" the girl exclaims.

"Listen, this island isn't safe, we're all in danger and need to head back—"

"Are you hijacking our ship? Is this a test? Harrison!" she calls down to the lower deck. "Are we going to have to fight? Because we're all from Level 1, so I don't think this is fair—"

"Alright, shut up and listen to me!" I raise my voice, and she looks at me with wide eyes again. "There is a…*big* herd of flesh eating monsters on this island, and if we don't get out of here, they will kill us all. And this boat is the only way to get out of here, so *yes*, we are hijacking it. And if you really believe that you are going to stand in my way, then I am going to go over there and rip out those red—"

"Jenn," Riley says rather quietly, her pained voice interrupting my rant.

"What?" I snap, turning back around. With one hand, she holds her stomach, and with the other she grabs my shoulder. She raises her dreary eyes up at me, and I furrow my eyebrows in confusion.

"I…I think my water just broke," she says, and for a moment I stand there speechless.

"Wh—no. No, it can't. You need a hospital. Your water couldn't have broken because I don't…I can't deliver a baby, Riley—" I stutter in denial.

"Please don't start panicking"

"I'm not! I mean you're just wet from the water we swam in. That's not *your* water, that's just *water*," I open my mouth to say more, but she just looks at me, her doe-eyes sparkling with both fear and worry. "Are you…Are you sure?"

"I'm sure, Jenn."

"What's going on up here?" I look over and see a dark-skinned boy emerge from below deck. He must be the one named

Harrison that the girl had called for before. Like her, he wears a Level 1 shirt.

"Are you two morons just going to stand there or are you going to help me deliver a baby?" I shout at them, and they rush over.

"Is this a test?" the boy mutters quietly to the girl, and she just shrugs timidly.

"Give me your sweatshirt!" I demand.

"We have a medical bag downstairs, I'll go get it," Harrison offers after handing over his sweatshirt.

"It hurts," Riley suddenly whimpers, clutching her distended stomach.

"Here, lay on this," I tell Riley, laying down the sweatshirt like a blanket. I turn to the redheaded girl. "Do you know how to do this?"

"I..."

"Good."

"What?"

"Where's that boy?" I ask, and as if to answer my question, he comes running back onto the deck. He hands over a canteen of water and a rag. Beside him now stands two other girls, both much younger. One of them slips off a backpack and places it down beside me.

"Riley, have you ever given birth before?" the redheaded girl awkwardly says.

"No!" Riley exclaims. "What's your name again?"

"I'm Quinn," she says.

"I think I have a little time. Are you going to be able to help me when it *is* time to deliver?" Riley asks her sternly.

"I'll do the best I can," Quinn reassures, to which Riley nervously nods.

I'm in the middle of dampening the rag when I hear an abrupt scream from above me. I spin around to glare at one of the new girls with short cropped brown hair. She is staring out into the water at the approaching herd.

"W-what is that? Oh my god, what are those things?" she stutters, her panic increasing with each word. "There's so many. They're getting closer!"

"Hey," I shout, forcefully grabbing the helm of her yellow shirt. I look between her and the other young girl beside her. "What are your names?"

"Lucy," the first girl says, quivering in my grasp and I release her.

"Rebecca," the other girl answers.

"Alright, cadets, I need you to get on the other side of Riley, sit down, and stay quiet," I say, blinking away the pain lingering in my stomach. "Ignore everything else. Got it?"

"Ahhh!" Riley screams, her torso lurching up off the floor.

"It's ok, Riley. Just lie back down—" Quinn begins to say.

"Shut up!" Riley yells, her anger overpowering her usually gentle voice. She squeezes her eyes shut and tries to force herself off the floor. "I want Jack. Get Jack."

"Riley—"

"No! He should be here. I'm not having this baby without him," she says breathlessly as I try to sit her back down.

"Riley!" I yell and with a last push, I force her back to the floor. She looks up at me, her expression pained as she realizes her mistake. When she's quiet, I continue, though I know I don't need to. "Jack's dead."

She just closes her eyes and takes in a deep breath.

"I'm alone," she mumbles, releasing her blink to look up into the sky. "He should be here."

"I know," I say, dabbing her sweaty forehead with the rag. I slip my other hand into hers. "But you're not alone."

"Alright, Riley, do you think you're ready to push? Or not yet?" Quinn asks, and Riley nods, preparing herself. "Ok, we'll try it out. Here goes nothing. On the count of three: one...two...three."

"Arghhh!" Riley moans, clenching her teeth together.

Almost in sync, there's a yell from off in the water: Xander. I strain my neck to peer over the edge of the boat's railing to see him and the others now near the rock barrier. He's wrestling with Andrew, and as the two men struggle for power, Blake uses his dagger to fend off some undeads closing in on them. Becky paddles ahead with Charlie in her arm, but the boy seems barely conscious.

"Is anyone good at ranged weapons?" I ask, and Harrison raises his hand.

"I've got a bow. It was the only thing that I was half-decent at back at the—"

"I want you to get it and aim for the swarm of those ugly creatures," I command. "But I swear if you so much as scrape one of my friends, I *will* hurt you. And make sure to shoot those creatures in the head. The *head*, nothing else will work."

"You want me to kill those people? What's wrong with them?" he asks quickly.

"Look it's a long story," I say frankly. "But, they're not people anymore. They're beyond saving. They want to eat us, and they will try to. Kill them. And save our fellow cadets."

"Got it," he says nervously, quickly retrieving his bow from downstairs and then running over to the edge of the boat.

"Remember, aim for the head. It's—" I stop when Riley screams and squeezes my hand, seemingly crushing the bones together. I wince at the sensation but continue nonetheless. "It's the only way to kill them. You'll be wasting arrows otherwise."

I watch him pull back the string and impatiently wait for him to release it. When he does, however, I follow it and watch it land a few feet in front of Xander in the stretch of shallow water before the rock barrier. Luckily, the flight of the arrow draws Andrew's attention, giving Xander the opportunity to separate himself from him.

"Jenn!" It's Becky's voice weakly calling out from over the ledge of the boat.

"Rebecca, Lucy, I need you to look out into the water and help that lady and little boy onto the boat," I command, and with diligence, the girls dart to the railing.

"Get out of me, geez!" Riley screams at her unborn child, clenching my hand in hers again and pulverizing my bones with some newly discovered strength I never knew she had. I dab her forehead with the damp rag again.

"Becky!" I call out once I see her appear on the other side of the railing.

Soaking wet, her black hair is strewn messily across her face, adding to an overall unkempt appearance that makes her look similar to one of the undeads. The restless expression in her eyes lets me know that her mind isn't even present right now but rather exists in a state somewhere in the future; she's planning, organizing, preparing for and worrying about something that hasn't happened yet.

A moan escapes Charlie's lips almost involuntarily as Rebecca lies him down on the deck. His right leg is limply displayed about the floor in a crooked position. Though the sea drenches his clothes, crimson blood sloshes among the water surrounding his lower leg.

Becky gently places her hand on Charlie's forearm and purses her lips together so hard that I'd have sworn they had been sewn together. Her eyes flicker quickly about his body; her deep sorrow for the boy is masked by her hurried scanning and quick formulation of her next moves. Though she's panting, she spends only a few precious moments sitting beside him and then springs to her feet again. Her loud eyes steady again as the sparks catch flame in her mind.

"I'll need bandages and painkillers, I'll need wood from the railing for a splint. Something that we can use in place of a rope to tie it together," Becky calls out to no one in particular; however, her commanding exclamation attracts the attention of those all on board. She looks straight at Rebecca. "Give me your medical bag."

"G-go," Riley stutters to me as Rebecca scurries to Becky's side. "They need help. I'll be…I'm fine."

She slips her hand from my bruised one and looks up at the sky. I take one more glance at Lucy before joining Becky.

"What happened?" I ask. I momentarily glance over at the others on board. "Quinn, stay with Lucy, keep doing what you're doing to make sure that baby comes out alright."

I rummage through the medical bag for a bit before pulling out the bandages, some painkillers, and another canteen of water wrapped in a rag.

Becky has already cut away Charlie's right pant leg. A deep purple color stains the inflamed flesh on his lower leg, which bends at an odd angle. Surface wounds scatter the leg, and the layer of water still sticking to his skin mixes with the blood to create a red sheen. Meanwhile, Charlie remains frozen in place with his hands holding his face.

"Charlie, I have some painkillers for you," I say softly, falling to my knees beside him. He doesn't budge. "Charlie, they'll help, I swear."

He doesn't move; he knows that if he does, he'll hurt. And if he lets just one tear slide by, it'll open the floodgates. By holding his breath, his tears, and his position, he's trying to freeze this moment.

"Charlie, please," I implore once more, my voice low but desperate.

Finally, though slowly, he brings his hands down from his scrunched up face, keeping his eyes squeezed shut regardless. His face flinches as he tries to ignore the pain in his leg, but otherwise, he remains very still. I raise up his head a little and place a pill between his lips. With some water, he swallows it, and I give him another. They're pretty strong, but the pain won't be eliminated. When he finishes swallowing, I lie his head back down slowly.

"We're going to have to move it back into place. That's the only way for the splint and bandages to work," Becky mumbles to me hastily, only momentarily pausing to examine the exact placement of the exposed bone. "How long until the painkillers kick in?"

"Should be any minute. They're supposed to be fast acting," I explain. Becky maintains her stare on Charlie's leg, her nostrils flaring broadly as she tries to catch her breath without breaking her pursed lips.

"While Andrew was attacking us back in the forest, undeads started showing up…Charlie and I got separated in the chaos," Becky explains briefly. Exhaustion finally kicking aside her fierce, determination-laden energy, she allows her expression to fall somberly as she looks upon the young boy. "By the time I found him again, Andrew was beating on him with this branch. He just had this sadistic blood-thirsting look in his eyes unlike anything I've ever seen from him."

A glaze of tears returns to her eyes, and she stops speaking, stealing her lip with the clutches of her teeth. She pours some of the water onto his leg to flush the open wounds.

"Please," Charlie moans, his crinkled mouth shuddering. "Please, just don't touch it."

"Baby, I know it hurts, but I have to put it in place. Just stay still," Becky says earnestly.

"We'll do it quick…you ready?" I ask, raising an eyebrow to which she takes in a deep breath before nodding. We get into position, hovering our hands above key places along the wound. I sit on top of Charlie's good leg, and Rebecca presses down on his chest to restrain him.

Charlie's scream shoots through the air like a volley of bullets spraying directly at my ears. He writhes and arches his back, but as soon as it had started, it's over. With the leg in the correct position, Becky immediately begins to wrap the area with bandages. Charlie's erratic struggling movements become sluggish shifts, and his shrieks become moans and eventually just whimpers.

"It'll all be alright," I hear Rebecca say and look up at her, stunned. Pleasantries like Rebecca's have lost their reassurance a long time ago.

"I have to splint it," Becky says. "But the hard part is over. Thank you."

There's another yell from the rocks and when I peer over, I see that Blake, Xander, and Andrew are climbing up the piles of rocks while the undead follow closely behind them. One grabs Blake's arm, but he is able to shake the creature off and hold it back long enough to re-grip his blade and jam it straight into the undead's forehead. However, as the body slips underneath the water, Blake, beaten to the last strand of his energy, is unable to pull out his knife in time.

"I'll go help them," Harrison says. He lifts a short sword from the floor, still attached to a discarded belt. I assume one of the girls must have unclipped it from their waist upon helping Riley.

"Harrison, no, stay here. We need you as an archer," I insist, but he shakes his head.

"They're injured and tired out there. They'll need help getting to the boat," he says again. Before I can protest any longer, he unsheathes the sword and jumps over the railing.

I don't hold Becky's shoulder like Rebecca does. Becky's mission is complete, but mine isn't. Exhaustion and pain hiding behind battle-ready adrenaline, I stand back up.

"Check the pulse, sensation, and movement of the area below the fracture," I command back to Becky and Rebecca as I leave them and walk up to the railing of the deck.

Blake, Andrew, and Xander are now surrounded on the rocks. They're trying to fight their way to the sea, but the undeads won't stop coming. In the chaos, an undead surprises Andrew from behind and digs its teeth into his arm. He screams out in agony as his flesh is ripped from him, but he manages to use his elbow to shove the undead off of him.

I watch anxiously as Harrison joins and climbs onto the rocks just as Blake dives into the water in escape. Blake yells something back at him, but Harrison freezes, struck by fear as he is faced with the disturbing creatures swarming onto the rocks. Panic setting in, he back-steps as one nears him with its decayed face and rotting teeth snapping at him. He desperately thrusts his sword into the beast's abdomen, exclaiming with surprise and disgust as it remains unaffected. When he attempts to pull the blade out, it catches in the undead's leathery skin, and he tugs on it at an angle, causing the flesh on its abdomen to tear when the sword becomes free. He staggers back as decayed organs spill out. Before he can recuperate, the undead reaches for him, wrapping its jaw around his throat. He screams in agony and fear as the undead, holding both of his shoulders, sinks its teeth deep into his flesh. Blood pours out from his neck, and the undead tears out Harrison's voice box. His body becomes limp, and others flock to feast on his body. Taking advantage of the distraction, Andrew leaps into the water.

"Xander!" I scream out when Xander dives into the water at last. A few undeads fall in after him, and once the splashing seizes, the water is calm. "Xander!"

In blind hunger, countless undeads begin to pour off the rocks into the sea. While the first ones in the water attempt to flap their arms in a swimming motion, they ultimately sink. Then, as the full force of the herd follows suit, the falling bodies meld into an orange-clad waterfall. Flailing hands grasp pointlessly as the overflow of undeads tumble in on top of each other and get submerged upon impact with the water.

"Where's Xander?" Blake yells, having already reached the rock at the base of the ladder. As he climbs the rope ladder into the boat, he's looking over his shoulder to scan the area.

"I think the undeads are holding him down. They'll drown him," I say quickly, my eyes shifting as I search the water for his presence. "Blake, prepare to raise the anchor. You're the only one that has a chance of lifting it."

I don't think about my next action. Screw self-preservation. In this moment, all I can feel is passion. Unlatching my axe from my belt, I climb over the railing and hop down onto the rock platform below.

C'mon, Xander, I plead silently. As I'm mustering the strength to dive in, Xander's head suddenly resurfaces gasping desperately for air.

"Take my hand!" I yell, extending out my hand for him to grab. He latches onto it, and I help pull him to the rock.

Around him, the undead begin to resurface as well, splashing spastically in a failed attempt to swim. I look over at the endless flow of beasts still pouring off the rock barrier into the stretch of sea between us. Their sheer numbers are now beginning piling onto each other in a stack that breaches the surface of the water directly adjacent to the rock barrier. They won't stop.

As I help drag Xander's body from the water, an undead surfaces as well, clenched onto Xander's ankle. With a swing of my axe, I slice straight through the undead's arm, and the monster instantly slides back into the depths from which it emerged.

"If they keep piling up, they'll reach the boat. We have to go now," I say quickly to Xander and shuttle him up the ladder. "I'm right behind you."

Suddenly, an undead flops onto the side of the stone I am standing on, reaching for my feet. I throw myself up against the hull of the ship, narrowly evading the undead's grasp. Without wasting any more time, I strap my axe back to my waist, grab onto the ladder, and begin climbing up behind Xander.

However, just as I begin nearing the railing, my footing on the ladder fails as a strong force attempts to pull me back into the sea. My knuckles turn white as I desperately try to keep my hold. The stretching of my abdomen strains my wound open, and I cry out.

"Jenn!" Xander yells, peering back over the edge of the boat. One of my hands loses its grip on the rung of the ladder, but Xander reaches down with a hand outstretched for me. I grasp it tightly, digging in my nails, and I thrash my free foot against my opponent's strong grasp.

With my grip on Xander getting weaker, and the splashing of the undeads increasing below me, flashes of blood and faces zip past my eyes. Billy, Ana, Vincent, Patrick, Dwayne, Kyle, Noah, Jack, Bella, Phil, Kris, Anthony, Corinne, Lie, Harrison.

I made it this far, I'm too close, I tell myself. *I can't go now. I won't.*

Suddenly, an agonizing shriek pierces through the air from beneath my feet. It's then that I risk taking a look at the vivid scene directly below me. Suspended in the air with only his lower legs in the water beside the rock, Andrew grips firmly onto my ankles. Hundreds of undeads swarm around the lower half of his body, occupying nearly every inch of the congested water. All of their combined hands grip onto various parts of his legs, and their sinking bodies and unhindered strength weigh our combined chain of bodies down. Blood sputters in all directions as the undead feast, painting their faces. Andrew screams and thrashes as flesh is torn off in large chunks from his thighs and muscle is stripped from bone. One of his hands falls free from my foot as his entire lower leg below his left knee is torn off to be licked to the bone by the unsatiated undeads below us.

I take one last look into his pleading eyes before raising up my one free foot and slamming it at full force straight into his face. With a loud snap, his head is whipped back, and a mix of water and blood sprays in a parabolic arch as he falls backwards. His remaining hand, which was already slipping, releases from my foot, causing my body to smack against the side of the boat. Regaining my hold on the ladder, I quickly scramble up to the deck.

"Jenn," Xander says, scooping my body into his arms.

Exhausted, I lean my head on Xander's shoulder. I'm shaking. My stomach burns, and I double over as I notice the blood soaking the sweatshirt bandage again.

"I got you. Hang in there." I hear his voice through deafened ears. He wraps his arm around me. Around us, the deck is alive with activity.

Charlie, now splinted, lies passed out on the ground. Still crouched beside him, Becky lunges her torso forward sharply, hunching over as she expels a throaty cough into her arm. Another follows immediately afterward, and she heaves in a deep breath before releasing it once more in another cough. When she's done, she doesn't rise up, letting her head rest on her arm as if it's a bowling ball far too heavy to lift. From the other side of the boat, Riley bellows, nearly blowing out her vocal cord as if trying to outperform Becky's coughs.

I turn my head slightly to look behind me at the island. Slowly the shore, still teeming with undeads, gets smaller. Blake must've pulled up the anchor.

"We did it," I mutter as the wind flutters in the sails above us and leads us away from the island. The splashing of the drowning undeads fades away.

CHAPTER 42

Riley

My eyes blur in so much pain that I'm no longer seeing the faces before me. They're calling to me, but I only hear myself. *Just a little braver now,* my words urge me. *You can do this.*

Through the hazy veil, I make out the ghost of my one true love. He smiles softly at me, and for a moment, it's like he's right here with me. The pain eases, and I blink away his face and return to reality. Instead, a few moments later, in his place is the head of a small newborn.

"It's a girl," Quinn's sweet voice tells me. My eyes clear up and focus on the soft features of my little girl wrapped up in a cloth. Quinn adjusts my arms and then fills them with the delicate baby. I breathe out a long sigh of joy as the little one stops crying and stares up at me, its disproportionately large eyes blinking bright blue with wonder and innocence.

"Hi there," I say softly, unable to contain my beaming smile. "Hi baby."

"She's got Jack's eyes," I hear Jenn say, and I look just in time to see her sit down beside me. Xander appears on my other side.

"Yeah, she does," I agree, sighing from the exhaustion hanging over me. "She's beautiful."

"Are you ok?" Xander asks, placing a hand on my shoulder.

"I just wish Jack was here. He would have wanted to meet her," I say, not taking my eyes off the beautiful newborn in my arms, and I let my hand glide against her delicate dusting of blond hair.

"Does she have a name?" Jenn asks.

"June," I say without even stopping to think about it. It's what Jack wanted. I shake my head and let out a squeal of pure and ultimate happiness. "I'm a mother."

***

It's nighttime now, and I am standing at the edge of the boat, still holding June. Everyone else—all the survivors— gathers in the center of the deck.

After Jenn got back on the boat, Xander and Blake helped re-clean and patch up her wound again. She now reclines beside Xander. Beside them, Charlie is fast asleep with his head in Becky's lap as she strokes his hair.

"Hey." I hear Blake's voice as he approaches me.

"Hey," I reply, greeting him with a smile.

"What are you doing over here?" he asks, leaning against the boat railing beside me.

"Thinking," I answer simply and take a glance back over at the rest of the group. Quinn divvies up some food, distributing the rations before sitting down beside Lucy and Rebecca. "The new cadets on this boat…they helped more than they could ever realize. Our new honorary camp members."

"Yeah, we're all pretty much in the same boat now," he says, and when I look at him, he's stifling a smile.

"Very funny," I say, chuckling. My smile softens as I stare back out at the water. "I heard Becky filled them in about this island. Still…I can't imagine the stories *quite* capture it."

"It's better that they don't know," Blake says.

"Oh, definitely, I envy them," I say. "It reminds me of how I was when I first came here. Innocent."

"The first time I met you, you stuck your face into the end of a gun. Nearly blew your head off right then and there," he comments, and I let out another laugh.

"I'm a lot more than what I used to be. I'm a survivor now. Maybe even a soldier," I say, finally confident in my ability to state those words. "And I don't mean the mindless, narrow-minded fighter the BAA wanted me to be. I'm not entirely sure what it takes to be a true soldier, but for the first time, I hope I'm getting there."

"Me too," he says quietly, nodding his head.

I look back over at the rest of the group, and my expression turns solemn when I find Charlie again.

"You think he's going to be ok?" I ask.

"I don't know. What he's seen can really mess up a person," he replies, knowing exactly who I was referring to.

"His parents don't even know what happened to him...and his sister," I continue.

"Are you gonna be ok?" Blake asks.

"I don't know," I say. "I mean, there will always be a scar on my mind from everything. But it's over now. The only thing I can do now is make peace with it, so that it remains a scar and not an open wound, you know?"

"Easier said than done," he says with a shrug.

"I have June now," I state, not really responding to him. "It's all…ok."

"You have so much of your life left. We all do, thanks to you catching this boat in time," he says.

"No...we all did this together," I clarify. After a pause, I return his question. "Are *you* ok?"

"Eight years here…never thought I would actually get to leave," he says, and the relief in his voice reflects the deep pain he feels inside. For a moment, we don't say anything else until he speaks again. "I'm gonna go see if I can catch up on sleep. It's been an interesting day. You should get some rest too. You went through a lot."

"In a bit," I respond. "I think I'm just going to stay here for a bit longer."

"I'm proud of you, Riley," he says, locking his gaze with mine. "I mean it."

A soft smile falls upon my face as he walks away. I wait until he's gone before turning around again to admire the long stretch of the glistening midnight sea. If I look closely, I can still faintly see a bump in the horizon where I know the island is. My eyes wander up to the night sky, and I instantly spot Jack's Star among the other seemingly lackluster stars.

"We have a baby, Jack," I whisper, too tired to let the words come out in a stronger breath. "Her name's June. You should see her. She's…she's the cutest baby you've ever seen. She has your eyes and it's the best part about her. We're all…we're all alright now."

My face scrunches up a little, and I feel a tear slide down my cheek. I have to take in a few breaths to regain my composure.

"I love you, Jack. I will always love you. It kills me when I'm not with you. Like I can't…*breathe* without you, that's how I feel. But…I keep breathing. And…I'm going to be ok. *We're* going to be ok."

Through my teary eyes, I swear I see the star twinkle—or at least that's what I'll believe. I don't move for several minutes, frozen, as if waiting for him to respond. He won't. I let my gaze lower to stare into the dark sea, vast and mysterious below me.

"Hey," Jenn says, appearing beside me.

"Hey," I say. She comes up next to me, leaning against the rail for support. "How's your…?"

"Hurts like hell, but I only punched Xander once when they were rebandaging it, so I managed," she explains, involuntarily placing a hand over her abdomen. "I'm just scared of infection."

"When we get to the BAA, we'll get you and Charlie proper medical attention," I say reassuringly.

"Becky too," she mutters worriedly. "I think she has a fever. Luckily the new kids have some antibiotics, though, so we should be good for a little bit. It all depends on how close we are to the BAA."

"Who knows what they're going to do once they see her," I remark, turning my attention down to June.

"We'll protect her," she states, though the words don't provide much reassurance. Her face softens as she watches my baby. "She really does look like you and Jack. She's beautiful."

"Every time I look at her, I can't help but smile," I say with a chuckle as the smile already spreads automatically across my lips.

"You chose to give her life," Jenn says. "You didn't have to, but you did. I see why."

"No regrets," I say quietly, still smiling.

"She's so peaceful," Jenn whispers, stepping closer to admire her.

"Do you want to hold her?" I offer.

"Oh, no, I can't. I'll probably make her cry," she says quickly. When I glance up at her, she takes a breath. "She should be with her mother anyway."

We just stand in silence for another minute or so, appreciating the life that I carry in my arms. June's small figure, wrapped in a cut portion of the sheet from the bed downstairs, lies fast asleep close to my chest.

"Jack's dead," I breathe out. "He's really gone."

"Yeah," she says solemnly, placing a hand on my shoulder.

"I'm ok," I say again.

"It's ok if you're not. It's nothing you can really ever get used to," Jenn comforts, rubbing my back.

"No, I am," I repeat, nodding to myself. "It's ok."

"She's really lucky to have you as a mother," Jenn whispers, talking about June. "You're going to do great, Riley."

"I hope so. I just want the best for her," I say. She's about to say something, but I cut her off. "Thank you for trying to help me after Jack died. I know I kind of lost it, too busy focusing on what I had lost rather than what I still have. You stuck with me, even when I wouldn't listen."

"I care about you, Riley. We all do," she says. "I would never abandon you."

"Without you or Blake—or anyone for that matter—I easily wouldn't be standing here right now," I say. "There were countless times where I could've lost my life and my baby's life on this island. And I would have if not for you guys."

"*You're* the reason you're still here, Riley," she says, shaking her head. "You're strong, Riley. I mean, hell, without your careful eye and quick thinking, we would've lost the boat and *none of us* would be here. I admire that, you know."

"Wow, the almighty Jenn Bellator admires me?" I joke, secretly glowing from the compliment.

"I'm serious," she says. "I'm lucky I have you."

"I'm not that bad after all, eh?" I tease, smirking sheepishly.

She lets out a breath of a chuckle before her expression falls away to a more serious arrangement: humbleness. I look past her at our new boat captain. Motionless, he rests his hands on the wheel in silent despondency.

"He made it, too," I say, and Jenn follows my gaze over to him.

"Billy didn't," she states, pursing her lips.

"But *he* did," I reaffirm.

We stand there, waiting for nothing in particular as we admire the expanse of the ocean and sky, which seems at this moment to protect us from everything that may cause us harm. Separated from the island and the BAA alike, we remain in a sort of limbo on the water—a blissful limbo that we know all too well is temporary. Suddenly, the buzz of conversation behind us on the deck ceases and is followed by a few confused mutterings.

"Did you feel that?" I hear someone say, their voice heightened in the silence.

On the deck, everyone remains the same as they did before, and nothing appears immediately out of place. However, rather than relaxing in the temperate nighttime weather, they stiffen up. Some draw closer together, and others clutch their arms and retreat into themselves.

I don't have a chance to inquire before I feel it too. It feels like a brief gust of controlled wind, rushing past us as the boat cuts through it. Once the wind passes, the warm comfort of the night that we had rightfully been enjoying is extracted from the air, leaving us in the cold of December.

"It's a barrier," I realize, spinning back to try to catch a glimpse at the invisible wall that we leave behind. "A synthetic barrier around the island. That's what causes the weather."

"By simulating a warm climate, Headmaster has us believing we are actually far away from the BAA," Jenn finishes, shaking her head. "That bastard."

Lucy and Quinn, who had each been sitting on their sweatshirts, hand the clothes over to Becky and Charlie, who begin to head below deck. Before disappearing downstairs with the others, Quinn grabs Harrison's sweatshirt from where we had laid it out for me on the deck. Jenn instantly jogs over to her, and after a very quick conversation, Quinn eagerly hands over the sweatshirt.

"Thank you," I say, taking the sweatshirt from Jenn when she returns to me. I wrap it around June. "Aren't you cold?"

"Been through worse," she replies easily with a shrug, and I let out a chuckle. "Besides, we've been trapped in that heated greenhouse of an island for most of the year. *This* is refreshing."

"Definitely," I agree. As the night's frosty chill nips at my body, I fill my lungs with the cool air. "What are we going to do when we get back to the BAA?"

"It's funny, the only thing I wanted to do when I came here was to go back: rejoin the BAA and get my status and rank back. For so long, I just wanted things to go back to how they used to be," she says, her eyes staring straight out into the water.

"And now?" I ask, and as I watch the gleam in her eyes, I see a completely different person than she used to be.

"I don't," she mutters as if talking to herself. "I can't."

"What do we have instead?" I say rather rhetorically. "There's no other place for us in society."

"We're the first ones back, Riley—the first to actually survive that place," she says earnestly. "That means something. They're killing prisoners and turning them into undeads. And Headmaster is supporting it and murdering cadets by sending them here. We can't let them get away with that."

"But how? What can *we* do?"

"I don't know," she says, deep in thought. Finally, she just shrugs again. "I guess we'll just have to figure things out once we get there."

Made in United States
North Haven, CT
06 December 2023